"Where did this second set of footprints come from?" Erin asked.

Dillon scanned the area around them until he finally pointed to some underbrush. "Based on the direction of the shoe print, I'd say the tracks came from that direction."

Erin followed his point to a rocky outcropping—the perfect place to hide out and wait for someone to pass.

"You think someone abducted Bella, don't you?"

Dillon's gaze said everything even though he didn't say a word. That was exactly what he thought, Erin realized.

She couldn't fall apart. Not now.

She'd have time for that later.

Right now, all her energy needed to be focused on finding Bella.

The group continued walking. They veered off the main trail and into the woods.

Danger seemed to hang in the air at every turn.

Just then, Scout stopped walking and sat at attention.

Erin sucked in a breath.

She knew what that meant.

It meant the K-9 had found something.

Christy Barritt's books have won a Daphne du Maurier Award for Excellence in Suspense and Mystery and have been twice nominated for an RT Reviewers' Choice Best Book Award. She's married to her Prince Charming, a man who thinks she's hilarious—but only when she's not trying to be. Christy is a self-proclaimed klutz, an avid music lover and a road-trip aficionado. For more information, visit her website at christybarritt.com.

Books by Christy Barritt

Love Inspired Suspense

Visit the Author Profile page at LoveInspired.com.

DANGEROUS MOUNTAIN RESCUE

CHRISTY BARRITT

LOVE INSPIRED SUSPENSE
INSPIRATIONAL ROMANCE

LOVE INSPIRED®SUSPENSE
INSPIRATIONAL ROMANCE

Recycling programs
for this product may
not exist in your area.

ISBN-13: 978-1-335-55485-7

Dangerous Mountain Rescue

Copyright © 2022 by Christy Barritt

This edition published by arrangement with Harlequin Books S.A.

For questions and comments about the quality of this book, please contact us at CustomerService@Harlequin.com.

Love Inspired
22 Adelaide St. West, 41st Floor
Toronto, Ontario M5H 4E3, Canada
www.LoveInspired.com

Printed in U.S.A.

Who hath delivered us from the power of darkness,
and hath translated us into the kingdom of his dear Son:
In whom we have redemption through his blood,
even the forgiveness of sins.
—*Colossians* 1:13–14

This book is dedicated to the "coffee lobby" gang at church. I'm so thankful for all the laughs, stories and talks!

ONE

"Bella! Can you hear me?"

Erin Lansing paused at the edge of the trail and surveyed the wintery mountain vista in front of her.

She knew her search efforts were most likely futile. She'd already explored this area twice with no luck.

There were still no signs of her daughter anywhere on this mountain.

As she stood at the overlook and caught her breath, investigators were gathering a team to search for Bella. But Erin couldn't wait for them. Their process was too slow. There was too much time to lose, time she couldn't afford to let slip away.

Would law enforcement drag their feet on purpose? Maybe to get revenge on Erin or to show their loyalty to her ex-husband, Liam?

Ever since Liam had disappeared a year ago, she'd been the number-one suspect in the eyes of his colleagues. Just because she and Liam had had a public fight right before he'd vanished didn't mean Erin was guilty.

Liam had been a cop. But instead of looking at people he'd arrested as potential suspects, investigators had focused all their attention on her.

Had the person responsible for her ex-husband's disappearance decided to come after Bella also?

A rock formed in Erin's gut at the thought. She didn't even want to think about it.

All she wanted was to find Bella.

A sixteen-year-old shouldn't be out in this wilderness alone. The vast Pisgah National Forest of North Carolina, with its deep valleys, steep cliffs and wild animals was no place for an amateur. To make matters worse, Bella hadn't taken her anxiety medication with her.

Erin knew how Bella got when she didn't take her medicine. She would be beside herself. Close to panic. Jittery.

Tears pressed at Erin's eyes as she glanced at the scenic view in front of her one more time.

But there was nothing to indicate Bella had been there. No clues as to what had happened after her daughter had left for school yesterday morning. All she knew was that Bella had never made it to school and that her car had been found at the parking lot near the trailhead.

Bella had never shown any interest in hiking the mountain before. She wouldn't have come out here on purpose, would she?

Erin heaved her backpack up higher and turned to continue down the trail. She'd keep searching until she found Bella. She was even prepared to sleep in this wilderness if that's what it came down to.

But the one thing she wouldn't do was sit back and wait. Not anymore.

The old Erin had been passive. People had walked all over her. But after adopting Bella six years ago, she'd become a new person. A stronger person.

As her phone buzzed, Erin glanced down, surprised to have any reception out here.

The message on her screen made her blood run cold.

You deserve this.

She sucked in a breath.
Who could have sent this?

Someone evil—that was who. Someone who wanted to put Erin in her place. To let her know she was a villain.

Could this person have taken Bella?

A surge of concern and anger tangled together inside her.

This was becoming even more of a nightmare than she'd thought possible.

Quickly, she typed back.

Where is she? What do you want from me?

She waited a few minutes, but there was no response.

Disappointment clutched her, but she pushed it aside. She needed to keep moving.

Erin continued down the narrow trail that cut along the side of the mountain. She sucked in a deep breath, inhaling the vague scent of pine and old leaves left over from the autumn purge.

The trees around her were fragile from the winter. Branches seemed to reach for her, their sharp edges grabbing her hair and jacket. And the air was so cold out here that every breath hurt her lungs.

Was Bella out here somewhere? Was she cold? What had she worn when she'd left for school yesterday? Erin had already left for work, so she didn't know. What about food? Was her daughter hungry?

The questions made Erin's temples pound, made worry swirl in her gut until she wanted to throw up.

She hadn't passed anyone in the two hours since she'd been out here, even though this trail was normally popular, even in the winter months. But today, clouds threatened freezing rain or snow and kept most of the hikers away. Precipitation, thirty-degree temperatures and slippery slopes didn't make for ideal hiking conditions.

Erin heard a stick crack nearby and paused.

The hair on her neck rose as she turned.

She scanned the wooded landscape around her but saw no one.

So what had caused that sound? Could it have been an animal?

That made the most sense.

She swallowed hard, trying to push down her fear.

But as she continued walking, her fears escalated, fueled by her imagination.

What if Bella had met somebody online and come here to talk face-to-face? Erin had heard stories about things like that happening. Even though she wanted to believe Bella would never take that risk, she couldn't say with one hundred percent certainty that her daughter wouldn't.

Erin rubbed her temples, wishing she could clear the fog from her head. She needed to be sharp if she was going to hike out here. Distraction could get her killed, especially with the craggy rocks, steep trails and slippery passes coming at her from every angle.

She glanced down, watching her steps as rocks rose and jutted out from the soil on the path. A small stream cut down the side of the mountain and trickled in front of her. The moisture and freezing conditions made every step treacherous.

Just last week, someone had died after slipping off a cliff on one of these trails. The man's death had been all over the news, a grim reminder of how dangerous nature could be.

At the thought, more images of Bella filled Erin's mind and she bit back a cry.

Please, Lord. Watch over her. Please! I'm begging You.

She prayed nothing had happened to her girl. Bella had problems—more than her fair share for someone her age, it seemed. But she didn't deserve this.

Another stick broke in the distance.

Erin's lungs froze as she stopped and turned around.

Somebody else was out here. She felt certain of it.

Glancing ahead, she tried to measure how safe the upcoming section of the trail was. When she'd come this way earlier, she'd turned around before continuing through this section. She'd been afraid to go any farther.

A narrow path stretched against the cliff face. If she continued, this part of the hike would be challenging. Maybe even life-threatening.

But if she turned around to head back, she could be confronted by whoever shadowed her.

As she heard another stick crack, closer this time, Erin knew she only had a few seconds to make a choice.

She let out a long breath. For Bella's sake, she had to persist.

Erin rolled her shoulders back before continuing down the trail. She would need to move quickly but carefully.

She hit the first part of the narrow pass without problems—and without hearing any other mysterious sounds behind her.

Just as she reached the end of the stretch, another noise filled the air.

The sound of heavy footsteps rushing toward her.

As she turned to see what was happening, hands rammed into her back.

Then she began falling down the steep rock face into the valley below.

"I'm going to need you to give this everything you've got, boy." Dillon Walker knelt in front of his dog, Scout, and rubbed his head.

The border collie/St. Bernard mix stared back at him, his soulful brown eyes giving every indication that the canine had understood each word Dillon said. The two of them had worked together uncountable hours in order to reach this level of bonding.

Dillon rose and gripped Scout's lead as they prepared

to head down the steep mountain trail stretching beside them. As a brisk winter wind swept around them, Dillon pulled his jacket closer. Scout also had on a thick orange vest with "Search and Rescue" on the side.

The temperature had dipped below freezing, which would make the trails both slippery and treacherous. Those conditions also made it more urgent to find Bella Lansing sooner rather than later.

"I appreciate you coming out here to do this." Park Ranger Rick Manning appeared beside him, his breath frosting as soon as it hit the frigid air. "I know it's been a while and that you gave up this line of work."

Dillon held back a frown. "I'm only doing this as a personal favor to you."

Dillon had been a state police officer for nearly a decade before making a career change two years ago. Now, he trained officers on how to be expert K-9 handlers. He taught others so they wouldn't make the mistakes he had. He lived with guilt every day because of those very oversights.

"I wouldn't have called you if it wasn't for the snowstorm headed this way." Rick nodded toward the gray sky above. "We don't have much time, and you are the best K-9 handler I know."

"Some people might argue that point." Dillon frowned as memories tried to pummel him. Accusations. *Truths.*

"You're the only one who's inclined to argue." Rick lowered his voice. "No one but Laura blames you for what happened to Masterson, you know."

Dillon didn't acknowledge his friend's words. Instead, he readjusted the straps of the backpack he'd filled with water, protein bars and dog treats. He wanted to be prepared for anything while they were out here.

A team of rangers would accompany Dillon and Scout in their search efforts.

A teen was missing. She was believed to be out here in

the vast wilderness of the Pisgah National Forest in western North Carolina, and they needed to find her.

This was what Dillon and Scout had trained to do. The two made a great team.

But whenever Dillon had to utilize his dog in this way, it was never good news.

Not only was the situation precarious because of the missing teenager, but forecasters were calling for snow tomorrow. If Bella was out there, they needed to find her now.

"We're just waiting for Benjamin to show up," Rick said. "I'd like you to take the lead."

Dillon shook his head. "I'm not law enforcement anymore."

"It doesn't matter. You know what you're doing. You know these trails—far better than the rest of us," Rick said.

Thankfully, Benjamin strode up just then, giving Dillon an easy out in the conversation.

Dillon didn't want to be in charge. However, he'd do whatever it took to find this girl.

He glanced behind him at the parking lot. An ambulance waited there. Paramedics needed to be on call in case the team found Bella in an injured state. Dillon hoped that wasn't the case. He hoped the teen was simply lost but unharmed.

Please Lord, give her a happy ending. I can't handle another replay of Masterson.

Masterson was another hiker Dillon had set out to find. Only there hadn't been a happy ending for that search and rescue mission.

Dillon swallowed hard as he focused on the trail ahead.

The woods surrounding him were part of the Blue Ridge Mountains, and people came from all over the East Coast to experience the rolling peaks of the national forest, which boasted several different waterfalls. The area was simply breathtaking, even now at winter's end when the branches were bare.

As Dillon prepared himself to start, a gloved ranger brought a bag over. He held it toward Scout and opened the seal at the top.

Bella's sweatshirt was inside.

Scout took a deep sniff then lifted his nose to the air, trying to find the girl's scent.

Her beat-up Honda Civic had been found in a lot not far from here. This trail seemed the most logical as to where she would be.

Scout tugged at the lead before pulling Dillon along the trailhead into the threadbare forest. As he did, Dillon mentally reviewed the case.

Bella Lansing had been missing for twenty-six hours. She'd left home for school yesterday morning but had never returned, nor had she shown up for classes. The rest of the day had been spent calling friends and searching hangouts.

There had been no leads.

Then a ranger had found her car in the lot near these woods this morning. That's when the rescue had been organized.

She wasn't an experienced hiker, nor was she familiar with this terrain. According to the report, Bella had never shown any interest in exploring these mountains. She had no survival training, but her winter coat had been missing from the house. Dillon hoped that meant she was wearing it. She'd need it out here in these elements.

Scout's actions indicated the girl had traveled this trail. What Dillon didn't know was if she'd been alone. As one of the more popular hikes in the area, any footprints would have been concealed at this point.

The rangers working the case would figure out the details. Dillon's only job, along with Scout's, was to find Bella.

"You know who Bella's mom is, don't you?" Rick asked quietly as they started down the trail.

Dillon shook his head. "No idea. Honestly, it doesn't matter if she's a criminal or a philanthropist, either way, her daughter deserves to be found."

"I should have expected that reaction from you." Rick shook his head and let out a light chuckle. "You're a good man, Dillon Walker."

He didn't know about that. He only hoped this search didn't end tragically.

These mountains were no place for the inexperienced. He'd seen too many tragedies happen here. Tragedies that had changed people's lives forever.

Just like they'd changed his.

Pushing those thoughts aside, he continued down the path. Scout was on the scent—and that was a good sign. With every minute that passed, Bella's trail could fade with time and the elements.

If Dillon had known the girl was missing earlier, he would have advised the team to start at sunrise. Instead, they'd already wasted a good three hours of daylight.

What had his friend meant when he'd asked if Dillon knew who Bella's mom was? It truly didn't matter to him, but he was curious. When Dillon had been a state cop, he'd been headquartered an hour and a half from this area. He knew little about the small towns dotting these mountains.

They continued down the trail, the miles passing by.

As he reached an area of the hike known as Traveler's Bend, he tugged Scout to a halt.

What was that sound?

"Dillon?" Rick looked at him.

He raised a finger in the air, indicating for everyone to be quiet.

That's when he heard it again.

"Please, help me!" A soft voice floated from below.

Was it Bella? Had they found the girl?

As if Scout sensed something was wrong, the canine began to bark at the edge of the path.

Dillon hurried toward the slippery, rocky cliff and peered down below.

A woman clung to a branch there, terror on her face.

It wasn't Bella. Dillon had seen the girl's picture.

But this woman clearly needed help.

"Stay right there!" he yelled. "We'll get you!"

The woman opened her mouth to speak. But as she did, the rocks beneath her crumbled and she began plummeting to the ground below.

TWO

As Erin felt herself falling, she clung to the branch she'd been hanging on to, praying her grip was tight enough to catch her, praying the branch was solid enough to remain rooted.

Her body jerked to a halt before cascading to the rocky ground below.

Thank you, Jesus.

Her heart pounded in her ears at the realization of how close she'd come to death—again.

She'd heard voices above her. Or had she imagined them?

Was someone really there who could help her? Had the search party caught up with her? Or was it just simply the person who'd pushed her?

She continued to grasp the tree branch, praying her fingers wouldn't slip. Her arm was so tired. She felt so weak.

She tried to look up, but the cliff face jutted out just enough to make it difficult.

"Help me!" she yelled again. Her voice sounded as desperate as she felt.

She tried to take a deep breath in order to yell louder. But her lungs felt frozen.

The position she hung in didn't help. Her body bent, making it hard to get enough air into her system. What air she did pull in was so cold, it nearly took her breath away.

The side of the cliff face was directly in the path of the wind. The icy breeze hit her full-force.

How long would it take for hypothermia to kick in?

Oh, dear Bella... I'm so sorry. It wasn't supposed to turn out this way.

"We're going to help you!" someone yelled above her.

Yes, someone was there!

Someone who sounded like he wanted to help.

Not the person who'd done this to her.

She drew in as deep of a breath as she could. "Help me!" she yelled again. "I'm down here!"

Erin waited, trying to hear a response. But it was no use. The wind muffled the sounds around her.

Had it muffled her voice also?

Despair tried to clutch her, but Erin pushed the emotion away. This was no time for hopelessness. She needed to stay positive.

Just as the thought rushed through her head, a rock crumpled beneath her.

She looked down and saw it tumbling, tumbling, tumbling.

How many feet was it to the bottom?

She couldn't bear to think about it.

She drew in another breath. "I don't know how much longer I can hold on!"

Did the person above her understand the urgency of the situation? What was he doing?

A new sound filled the air.

Was that a...bark?

Erin felt certain that it was.

Maybe help really was here. Maybe this mountain wouldn't be her death.

She'd never meant to draw attention away from Bella and onto herself. And she wouldn't forgive herself for that.

But she needed to be there for Bella once she was found.

She looked up again, straining her neck as she tried to get a glimpse of what was going on.

A man stared down at her. "We're here to help! Are you hurt?"

That was a good question. Was she hurt?

Maybe she'd cut her leg. She might have some bruises. But none of that mattered, not if she was alive.

"I'm fine!" she called. "But please hurry."

"We're going to send a rope down to you. I need you to grab it with both hands."

The thought of releasing her lifeline—a tree branch—caused a shot of terror to rush through her. "I… I can't let go."

"We're going to talk you through it, okay? You can do this."

The man's voice sounded so soothing that Erin wanted to believe him. Plus, he'd said "we." Were there more people up there, more than just the man and his dog?

Another surge of hope swelled in her.

Erin had no *choice* but to trust this man.

From what she'd seen, the man wore a black jacket and a stocking cap. Was he a hiker?

As if to answer her question, someone else also peered over the edge of the cliff. This man wore a National Park Service cap. He was a park ranger, she realized.

Relieved, Erin tried to suck in a few more breaths to calm herself. But the task felt impossible.

"I'm sending down the rope," the first man said. "What's your name?"

She almost didn't want to say. She didn't want the scrutiny in case any of these guys recognized her. But she had little choice right now. "I'm Erin."

"Erin, I'm Dillon. My dog, Scout, is here, too, along with four park rangers. We've already secured the end of this rope to one of our guys up here. It's not going anywhere."

As she waited for the rope to be lowered, her arm continued to lose feeling even as the pain grew. She could feel herself becoming weaker. Feel her grip slipping.

She was so afraid that some kind of natural reflex would kick in and she'd let go.

She couldn't let that happen.

As she tried to find better footing, another rock below her tumbled.

She found herself being pulled downward again.

She scrambled, using her hands and feet to find anything that might stop what was about to happen.

But there was nothing other than air to catch her.

Dillon saw the woman beginning to slip and knew he had to do something.

They hadn't come this far to lose her now.

He swung the rope down, watching as she began to slide along the rock face. Nothing was below to catch her, and that's what concerned him the most.

"Grab the rope!" he yelled.

Her feet continued to skim the surface of the rock. The movement slowed her, at least. But if she kept going like that, she'd end up with crushed bones and a head injury, at the very least. Most likely, she wouldn't survive the impact.

As the rope dangled in front of her, her arm flailed in the air as she tried to reach for it.

"Come on…" Dillon leaned over the ledge, on his chest, and watched. He held his breath, praying she'd grasp it in time.

Just as she began to slide faster, her fingers closed over the rope and she jerked to a stop.

A moan escaped from her, seeming to be partly filled with pain and partly with relief.

But at least she was okay…for now.

"You've got to hold on to that rope," he called. "Use both hands."

"I'm doing my best." Her voice cracked. "But my arm... it hurts."

"You can do this, Erin. I know you can."

Scout barked beside him, almost as if the dog wanted to encourage her also.

She stared up at him, and something seemed to change in her gaze. Finally, she nodded. "I won't let go." She released the branch and transferred her other hand to the rope.

"I have a second rope," Dillon called. "This one has a large loop on the end. I'm going to send it down quickly. As soon as you can, I want you to pull it over your shoulders like a harness. Can you do that?"

"I'll try." Her voice sounded strained, but at least she was trying.

A moment later, the rope reached her. She did as Dillon said and wrapped it over her head and around her shoulders, pulling her arms through one at a time.

"Good girl," Dillon murmured.

If she started to slip again, at least the rope should catch her.

"Help me pull her up," Dillon said to Rick.

"I think that's... Erin Lansing," Rick muttered beside him as he grabbed the rope.

Dillon wanted to glance at his friend, but he didn't dare take his eyes off this woman. "Is that the missing girl's mom?"

"I'm nearly certain that's her."

What was she doing out here? Had she ventured down the trail looking for her daughter herself?

Dillon wanted to shake his head in dismay. But if it had been his daughter out here—if he had a daughter—Dillon would have done the same thing. He couldn't blame the woman for that.

"Now that the rope is secure, we're going to pull you up," he called to her. "If you can, use your feet and help walk up the rock face. Grab hold of the first rope again to help you. Got it?"

"Got it." But her voice trembled as she said the words.

This would be a scary situation for any of them.

Dillon glanced at his team and nodded. They then began working together to pull her from the cliff face. Even Scout used his teeth to help pull the rope. Thankfully, the woman wasn't heavy, so the rescue should be fairly easy.

But Dillon knew this wasn't over until this woman was on solid ground.

Erin felt her body lifting as she was pulled upward. She reminded herself to keep taking deep breaths. To keep trusting these strangers.

She had no other choice at the moment.

Slowly, she rose higher and higher.

She tried to do what the man had said and use her feet to walk up the side of the cliff. She held on tightly to the rope just in case something happened.

She'd never been so terrified in her life.

Then again, that actually wasn't true.

Knowing her daughter had disappeared was entirely scarier.

Still, she was wasting valuable time here, time that the search and rescue team could be using to look for Bella.

Finally, her head rose above the side of the mountain. As it did, two men grabbed her arms and lifted her over the edge of the cliff.

The next instant, she was on her hands and knees on the path she'd been pushed off of.

On cold but solid ground. Her trembling limbs could hardly hold her up. Finally, she collapsed and rolled over.

The air rushed from her lungs as relief filled her.

She was still alive. She couldn't believe it.

The dog who'd peered over the edge of the mountain

nuzzled her. She looked up and rubbed his face, thankful for the friendly eyes. The dog was white with brown spots, had intelligent eyes, and almost looked like a small St. Bernard.

The man—Dillon—squatted beside her, concern in his brown eyes. "Are you okay?"

"I think so. Thank you. Thank you so much."

His intense expression remained focused on her. "Can you stand?"

"I think so."

He took her arm and helped her to her feet. Before he let go, Erin froze, trying to find her balance. Her head still spun from everything that had happened.

Dillon studied her face before matter-of-factly stating, "You're Bella's mom."

Erin felt her cheeks flush. "I am."

"What happened?"

"Someone pushed me."

Alarm straightened his back. "What?"

She nodded. "I was trying to cross the trail. I thought I heard someone behind me. The next thing I knew, someone shoved me and I fell. Thankfully, I was able to catch that branch."

Dillon glanced back at the rangers, making sure they were listening. Rick nodded his affirmation.

"Did you get a glimpse of this person?"

Erin shook her head. "I didn't. I wish I had. I have no idea who would do this."

Dillon glanced at Rick again. "We'll all need to keep our eyes open just in case the person is still nearby. In the meantime, what were you even doing out here?"

"I couldn't wait any longer to search for Bella. I had to come see if I could find her myself. There's a storm coming in…"

Dillon frowned. "We need to get you to the ranger station so you can be checked out. You may have hit your head or—"

She swung her head back and forth. "No. Please. I don't want to go back to the station. I want to keep looking for my daughter."

Dillon's eyes narrowed as he continued to study her, clearly trying to measure her physical well-being and state of mind. "You're in no state to continue hiking the trail."

Her gaze latched on to his. "Please. I can do it. I can. I won't hold you back. I promise."

The man pressed his lips together in a frown before glancing at the men around him.

They all seemed to be waiting for his decision.

Erin wondered who this guy was. He didn't wear a uniform, yet he seemed to be in charge.

"I just need to find my daughter." Her voice trembled as she presented one last plea. "Please. That's all I want."

Finally, he nodded. "You can come. But don't make me regret this."

THREE

To say Dillon had reservations about letting this woman come with them would be an understatement. But if they took her back to the ranger station now, they'd be wasting too much time. Besides, the weather was turning nastier by the moment.

If Bella was out here, they needed to find her. Now.

They walked down the trail, past the narrowest section and on a path that cut through the forest. Dillon took the lead. Actually, Scout did. As Dillon walked behind him, Erin kept up the pace and remained at his side despite her rapid breaths and shaky limbs.

Erin looked younger than he'd assumed she would be, especially considering the fact she had a sixteen-year-old daughter. The woman was trim and petite with wavy dark hair that came to her chin. Her brown eyes were both perceptive and afraid. A splatter of freckles crept across her nose and cheeks.

Since the woman was with them, Dillon decided this might be a good time to get more information about the missing girl. Every detail could help.

"I'm sorry to hear about your daughter," he started, his eyes on the winding trail in front of him.

Scout tugged the lead, his nose on the scent. That was good news. There was nothing worse than a trail going cold, especially when they'd come this far. Especially when the stakes were so high.

"I just can't believe she's missing." Erin's voice sounded dull with grief. "It still seems like a nightmare that I should wake up from. But I haven't."

"Tell me what your daughter is like."

Erin drew in a deep breath. "Bella is… Where do I start? She's funny. Really funny. She makes me laugh a lot. I always think she's one of those people who could make it on a television sketch comedy one day."

"Do you like those late-night shows?" He'd never cared for them himself.

"Not really. They're not for me. But I *do* think you have to be intelligent to be funny."

"So, your daughter is smart? Is she a good student?" He tried to form a better picture in his mind.

"Not always. Bella likes socializing and…"

Dillon heard her hesitation and waited for her to continue. What was she thinking twice about before sharing?

"Bella also has anxiety," Erin finally said. "She takes medication for it every day. That's another reason why we need to find her."

He stored that information away. "What happens if she doesn't take her meds?"

Erin slowed as she climbed over an outcropping of small rocks. "Different things. Sometimes she's so anxious, she's beside herself. She can't focus or even function. Other times, she wants to avoid social situations and just be alone."

"Has she ever wandered away before?"

"No, never. That's why this is so strange to me. Plus, I got a text message."

"What did it say?"

"That I deserved this."

Dillon let that update sink in. "So you think Bella was abducted and the person who took her is mocking you?"

Tension stretched across Erin's face. "I'm not sure what to think at this point."

His mind continued to race. "Does she have a boyfriend?"

Dillon glanced at Erin as he waited for her answer. As he did, he saw her expression darken. There was another story there. He knew it.

"She likes a boy, but I told her she couldn't date yet."

"Did she give you his name?"

"No. She wouldn't tell me. But she's not mature enough to date. It was a bad idea."

"Did you tell the police that?"

"Of course. But I don't think they'll listen to anything I have to say." Her voice cracked.

Her words caught him off guard. "What do you mean?"

Erin glanced behind her at the rangers there. "It's a long story. But my ex-husband used to be a cop."

"Is that right?" Dillon was definitely curious now. Her words alluded to a deep history—a bad history—that she'd rather put behind her.

"It wasn't a good situation," Erin continued. "And it didn't end well…to say the least."

Maybe Dillon would ask around later to find out more information. Or maybe he wouldn't. What he really wanted to concentrate on right now was finding Bella.

Scout still continued to be hot on the trail.

Dillon glanced at the sky in the distance, worried about being out here if the storm hit them. He knew just how dangerous these mountains could be. They were hard enough to hike on a good day. But add rain, wind and snow? That could be a deadly combination.

He'd give this search another hour. Then they'd need to turn back. They couldn't take the risk.

Dillon knew Erin wouldn't handle that news well.

And he couldn't blame her.

* * *

Erin fell into step behind Dillon, incredibly grateful he'd allowed her to come.

The thought of simply waiting to hear if Bella had been located made her feel like her insides were being ripped apart. Bella needed her right now—and Erin needed Bella just as much.

But Dillon's legs were long, and his dog was fast. Erin had to scramble to keep up with him and the team of rangers accompanying him. The last thing she wanted was to hold them back.

She just wanted to find her daughter. To hold her in her arms. To never let her go.

If only she could do that.

As Scout's steps slowed, Erin wedged her way closer to Dillon. He'd pointed out a set of footprints on the ground, ones that seemed to match Bella's shoe size. Based on Scout's body language, the prints followed Bella's scent.

Maybe they were onto something.

Dillon and his dog seemed competent and exuded a sense of confidence that brought her a wave of comfort.

The man seemed like the quiet type. He had broad shoulders and serious eyes. He'd briefly taken his hat off earlier, and Erin had seen light brown hair cut close to his head. But he also seemed experienced and focused, two qualities Erin could be grateful for, especially in this situation.

His casual clothing—cargo pants, hiking boots, and a thick jacket—indicated he was a volunteer. But his command of the situation and confident actions indicated there was more to his story.

Erin needed to connect with the man. She needed him to understand how desperate she felt. She needed a team of people who wouldn't give up on finding Bella—not until she was safe at home.

However, this could all backfire if the man knew who

Liam was—and if he turned out to be on Liam's side. Erin would like to think those facts wouldn't change anything, that everyone would still be helpful.

But she knew from experience that wasn't always the case.

"Beautiful dog," she murmured, glancing at the dog again. "Are you a park ranger?"

"I'm a former cop and a current search and rescue volunteer."

A former cop? Erin sucked in a breath.

It was bad enough when she thought he might simply know who Liam was. But what if he had been friends with Liam?

Even worse, what if this man was just like her abusive ex? What if he was dangerous? Or what if he was like all her ex's friends and thought Erin was guilty in Liam's disappearance?

Erin's head swam at the thoughts.

Park rangers, she could handle. Some of them might have known Liam, but that didn't necessarily mean they were on his side.

Cops? Especially local cops?

They *always* took Liam's side—even when she'd had a black eye and a bruised rib.

Erin rubbed her temples, wishing she could clear the fog from her head. She needed to be sharp if she was going to hike out here. Distraction could get her killed.

Bella's image slammed into her mind again.

She didn't want to admit it, but she wouldn't put it past Bella to run. The girl had certainly threatened to do so enough times. She'd had a rough upbringing, and the urge to run seemed to be ingrained in her.

Erin had adopted Bella from out of a bad situation six years ago. Since then, she'd showered the girl with affection, had set clear boundaries, and had even taken her to therapy multiple times a week.

But some issues were hard to fix, no matter how much love and attention someone poured onto the person in need. Still, Erin hadn't given up hope.

And she never would.

"Right here, you can see another set of footprints joins the first set." Dillon paused and pointed to an area in the dirt.

One of the rangers stepped forward to snap pictures and document the prints.

"Where did this second set come from?" Erin asked.

Dillon scanned the area around them until finally pointing to some underbrush. "Based on the direction of the shoe print, I'd say the tracks came from that direction."

Erin followed his hand as it pointed to a rocky outcropping—the perfect place for somebody to hide out and wait for someone to pass.

Dread filled Erin.

No, it was something worse than dread.

It was terror—terror at the unknown.

"What does all this mean?" Erin couldn't stop herself from asking the question, even though she already knew the answer.

Dillon offered another side-glance at her, his face remaining placid and unemotional. "That's not something I can answer. Maybe one of the rangers can tell you more."

She looked around her, noting how the other rangers seemed distracted with documenting the prints.

More memories pummeled her.

Her ex had been a good cop but a terrible husband.

A man who took his stress and anger out on Erin.

No one had believed her when she'd cried out for help. Liam had been too charming. Too convincing. Too twisted.

Now she had to live with that aftermath.

"What do *you* think it means?" She nodded down at the ground before looking back up at Dillon.

His jaw tightened as he stared at the prints. "I think it means that Bella met someone here."

"Willingly?"

"I can't answer that." He softened his voice, as if he wanted to let her know he understood but had boundaries.

Erin knew he was trying to be professional. But she needed answers, even if those answers terrified her. The truth wasn't something she could be afraid of—otherwise, she'd live her whole life in fear.

She'd done too much of that already.

She stared up at Dillon as they stood there. She wanted to keep moving. But she had to respect the rules of their investigation. She'd promised to do so before she'd headed out with them.

"You think someone abducted her, don't you?" she whispered so just Dillon could hear.

Dillon's gaze said everything even though he didn't say a word. That was *exactly* what he thought, she realized.

She buried her face in her hands—but only for a minute.

Erin couldn't fall apart. Not now.

She'd have time for that later.

Right now, all her energy needed to be focused on finding Bella. Everything else would fall in place when this was over.

Two rangers stayed behind. As they did, the rest of the group continued walking. They veered off the main trail and into the woods.

Danger seemed to hang in the air at every turn.

Just then, Scout stopped walking and sat at attention.

Erin sucked in a breath.

She knew what that meant.

It meant the K-9 had found something.

The park ranger—Rick, if Erin remembered correctly—

sprang into action. Using his gloved hands, he moved away some dead leaves.

When he looked up, his expression was grim.

"We have a dead body," he announced.

Dillon pushed Erin back.

She didn't need to see the body.

Instead, he let the ranger take over the scene, and he stayed with her.

She let out a cry and nearly collapsed right there on the trail. Quickly, he reached his arm out and caught her by the elbow.

She practically sank into him as if grief consumed her until she could no longer stand up straight.

"We don't know who it is," he murmured, trying to bring her whatever reasonable comfort he could.

"Looks to me like this person has been dead for a while." Ranger Rick's voice drifted over to them as he talked to the ranger beside him.

Dillon felt Erin straighten ever so slightly. "Is there anything else that you can tell based on what you saw?"

Dillon glanced back, trying to get a better look at the body himself.

"I would say, based on that shoe size, it's a man. Ranger Rick is right, whoever it is has been out here for a while. You can hardly make out any of his features."

"What do you mean by 'a while'?"

"It's hard to say because of the elements. The medical examiner will be better at determining that than me. But if I had to guess, I'd say maybe a year."

She let out a cry. He'd thought that would be good news, that it would bring her comfort.

"Is there something you're not telling me?" Dillon waited, more curious than ever.

She looked up at him, her eyes red-rimmed with unshed tears. "The body...is there any type of jewelry on him?"

There was *definitely* more to this.

Dillon left her for a moment and wandered toward the man for a better look. The rangers had already called backup to help them retrieve the body.

Unfortunately, this was taking time away from their search for Bella. Part of him wanted to continue on with Scout. But it was too soon to do that.

As he studied the man, Dillon's eyes narrowed. It was hard to tell much about the body as a lot of decomposition had already started. But a piece of gold glimmered near the man's neck. He *was* wearing a piece of jewelry.

He squinted. It almost appeared to be a necklace with an eagle and a rose on it.

The jewelry was definitely unique.

"Dillon?"

He turned back toward Erin and saw the questions in her eyes.

After a moment of hesitation, he nodded. "There's a necklace."

"Does it have an eagle and a rose on it?"

His back muscles tightened at her exacting description. "It does. How did you know to ask that question?"

She ran a hand over her face, the despair on her expression making her appear years older. "Because that's the necklace my ex-husband always wore. He disappeared a year ago."

A bad feeling swelled in Dillon.

What in the world was going on here?

FOUR

Erin's thoughts continued to reel.

Could that really be Liam? Could he have been dead all this time?

Her hand went to her throat as she thought through the implications. Before, people had only *suspected* her of doing something. But now, if they had a dead body, Erin could only imagine the accusations would grow even greater.

How much more could she handle? It was a marvel that people in town hadn't yet run her off. They would have if it hadn't been for Bella.

Bella wanted to stay in Boone's Hollow to finish out high school. After that, Erin planned on finding a new place to settle down—a place away from people's watchful and accusing gazes. Somewhere where people didn't know her history and she could begin again.

"What was your ex-husband's name?"

Dillon's voice snapped Erin out of her dazed state and she turned toward him, trying to ignore the way he studied her face.

She swallowed hard before announcing, "His name was Liam. Liam Lansing."

Recognition flooded his gaze.

At that moment, Erin knew he'd no longer be on her side. At first, the former cop had seemed oblivious to her identity. It was part of the reason she'd felt drawn to him. Maybe he hadn't already formed a judgment about her.

But now all of that would be different. He'd probably look at her with the same disdain that everyone else did.

Dillon stepped closer and lowered his voice. "We don't know for sure that's him. Authorities will have to do an autopsy and get a better identification on him."

Maybe that was true, but the necklace seemed like it sealed the deal.

"What about Bella?" Erin's throat constricted as she said the words.

Liam had already taken so much away from her. But even from the grave—if that was his body—Erin wouldn't let him take away the opportunity to search for her daughter.

Dillon glanced at his phone and then up at the sky. "The storm is coming fast. We really need to head back."

"Now?" Grief—and a touch of panic—clutched her heart.

Giving up was the last thing that Erin wanted. She wanted to stay on these trails until she found her daughter.

It was only fair.

If her daughter was suffering, then Erin deserved to suffer, too. It had been her job to take care of Bella, and she'd clearly failed. Otherwise, her daughter would be safe and sound at home right now.

"What we don't want is another casualty while we're out here searching." Dillon's voice remained low and calm as he said the words, and his expression matched.

Erin tried to hold back her tears but hot moisture pooled in her eyes. They were so close. She could feel it.

"But Scout is on the trail," she said. "We can't lose Bella's scent, and after the storm…"

Dillon pressed his lips together and Erin knew she'd made a valid point.

"We'll go a little farther," he finally said. "But it's probably going to be you, me and Scout. The rest of the team will probably want to stay here to investigate this body."

Erin nodded. She would take whatever she could get.

Dillon went and talked to Ranger Rick for several minutes before returning. A moment later, the ranger pulled out a plastic bag, opened it, and Scout sniffed the sweatshirt inside.

Bella's sweatshirt.

Scout barked before starting through the woods again.

As a brisk wind swept over the landscape, Erin shivered and was again reminded that she wasn't cut out to do this type of search and rescue mission.

But she'd do anything for her daughter.

Even if it meant getting hurt herself.

Dillon had to give Erin credit for keeping up with him. Even though she didn't look totally steady on her feet, she was making a valiant effort as they continued to traverse the rocky terrain.

But his thoughts continued to race as they moved forward.

Liam Lansing had been her husband? The fact still surprised him.

Dillon had run into the man a few times while working as a state police officer, and he'd never been impressed. Anger seemed to simmer beneath the man's gaze.

But Liam Lansing had also been the type who could be charming and attract people to him. He was the type of guy who could get people on his side.

Whether or not that body they'd found was Liam's, Dillon could only assume at this point that the man was dead. He'd been missing for at least a year. He would guess that someone Liam had put in jail had found him and exacted revenge.

Dillon paused as they came to an especially rocky section of the trail. He reached back and helped Erin down. The last thing they needed right now was for anyone to get hurt on this trail. Planning and preparation meant they could use their time wisely.

Yet they'd already had so many setbacks.

"Thank you," Erin muttered before quickly releasing his hand.

He nodded and continued moving, not wanting to waste any more time.

Dillon knew a lot of people had blamed Liam's ex-wife for his disappearance. Looking at the woman now, seeing the fear in her eyes, he found it hard to believe that someone like Erin would be capable of something like that.

He generally had good instincts about people, and those instincts told him that Erin didn't have it inside her to hurt someone.

Still, he needed to be on guard.

A sharp wind cut through the mountain path, invading the layers of his clothing to hit his skin.

The winter storm was getting closer. Too close for comfort.

He didn't want to turn around now. Not with Bella still missing out here and Scout still on the trail. But he was going to have to make some calls soon, calls that may not be popular with Erin.

Several minutes later, Scout reached an area where water had trickled over the trail and had now frozen.

Dillon paused.

"What's going on?" Erin asked. "What does this mean?"

"That means Scout is losing the scent," Dillon said.

"Wouldn't it make sense that the trail would continue following this path?"

"As you can see, the path goes two ways from here, one

down into the valley and the other up this mountain to an overlook."

She frowned. "Which way are we going to go?"

Dillon swallowed hard before launching into his decision. "Here's the thing. We're running out of time."

Erin's eyes widened with something close to desperation. "But we're right here. We can't turn back now."

Just as she said the words, a smattering of snowflakes floated down around them. The icy precipitation brought with it the promise that more was coming.

"The weather's going to turn bad quickly," Dillon explained. "We don't want to be stuck out here when it does."

"But Bella…" Erin's voice cracked.

Dillon frowned, understanding the dilemma all too well. Understanding why she wouldn't want to leave. Understanding how heartbreaking this must feel to her.

"Erin, the truth is, we're going to be no good to Bella if we're killed out here ourselves. How would we search for her then?"

"But…" She stared at the trail in the distance, agony flashing in her gaze.

More snow began falling, snow that was mixed with freezing rain.

"Scout's lost the trail," he reminded her. "I know it seems logical that Bella went either to the left or to the right. But there are a lot of possibilities here. When the storm lets up, we'll have the helicopters out. We can put search parties out. We can narrow it down to this area. But right now, we need to get back to where it's dry and warm."

Erin said nothing.

Dillon lightly touched her arm. "I'm sorry, Erin. I know this isn't what you want to hear. But it's my job to ensure the safety of my team. Right now, you and Scout are my team."

Her hand went over her lips, almost as if she wanted

to let out a cry. She didn't. Instead, she nodded resolutely. "Okay then."

Dillon studied her a moment. She seemed submissive now. But he wouldn't put it past Erin to head back out into this wilderness by herself. He needed to make sure that didn't happen.

These mountains were no place for inexperienced hikers, especially with the weather like this.

He nodded in the direction they'd just come from. "Let's get going before this turns worse. There are a few passes that will be nearly impossible if they freeze over. There's another path we can take as a shortcut to the parking lot. I think we should take that."

Erin's eyes widened as if she hadn't thought of that yet. She nodded. "Let's go. I just pray that Bella is somewhere warm and dry right now."

Erin couldn't stop thinking about everything that happened. It felt like Dillon and his team were so close to answers. With every step Scout took, his nose on the trail, she'd felt like finding Bella was within their grasp.

And then it wasn't. Just like that.

What happened to Bella's scent? How had it suddenly disappeared like that?

The whole thing didn't make any sense. Bella's scent couldn't have just disappeared out of the blue, right?

Erin's heart pounded harder, louder, into her ears as anxiety squeezed her again.

All she wanted was her daughter safe and in her arms.

Out of the unknown. Out of these harsh elements.

The wind was so, so cold, and turning cooler by the moment. What if Bella didn't have shelter?

At that thought, Erin decided she'd come back here herself if she had to—at the first chance she had.

Erin started forward when Dillon pointed to another trail cutting through the forest.

"This is going to be a shortcut back to the parking lot," he said. "I think we need to go this way."

Disappointment filled her. She'd hoped to again go past the scene where they'd found that body, before taking the shortcut. She'd hoped to hear if the rangers had any updates for her.

But it didn't look like that was an option right now.

Instead, she nodded and continued walking.

Several minutes later, Dillon nodded toward a rocky ledge they would have to cross ahead. "We're going to need to be very careful at this section."

Even from where Erin stood, she could already see that the trail was slick. There was no handrail. Just a sheer drop—one similar to the area where Erin had been pushed.

Her heart raced as she remembered her earlier fall. As she remembered the person who had done that to her.

"Can you tell me more about what happened before you felt someone push you off that cliff?" Dillon asked.

Erin shrugged, wishing she didn't have to replay the scene. But she knew it was necessary if they were going to find answers. "I thought I heard somebody in the woods behind me a couple of times. Then I thought maybe I was imagining things. I wasn't really sure. But the next thing I knew, I felt two hands on my back and I began falling."

"Who would have done that?" He glanced back at her.

"The person who grabbed Bella?"

"Why would the person who took her follow you and try to kill you?" Dillon's eyes looked just as intelligent as Scout's as the man observed her, his thoughts clearly racing as he tried to put the pieces together.

She shook her head. "I wish I knew."

Erin sucked in a breath as she began to walk along the rocky ledge. Panic wanted to seize her.

She'd wanted to argue with the decision to turn back, but Dillon had been right to make the call. If they had been trapped out in a snowstorm, all three of them would also be in danger. As much as she hated to leave, staying out here wasn't an option.

"Keep your steps steady and slow. You can do this."

Dillon's words sounded surprisingly comforting, and Erin was grateful he was there with her.

She did as he said and moved carefully. As she started to look down, she paused. She glimpsed the vast expanse below her and quickly averted her gaze.

She couldn't put herself in that mindset. She just needed to focus on where she was going, not where she *could* go if she slipped up.

That was what she always used to tell Bella also. *You have to focus on the road ahead while remembering the lessons behind you.*

Erin's heart panged with grief as she thought about her daughter again.

Often, she'd wished she could go back to the sweet times when Bella had only been ten or eleven. Times when they'd had fun going on road trips. When they'd cooked together. When Erin had braided Bella's hair and they'd painted each other's fingernails.

But something had happened as soon as the girl turned fifteen. It was almost like her daughter had transformed into a different person. Certainly, hormones had played a role in that. But so had Liam. That had been when Liam's anger problems had worsened. When he'd stopped trying to hide from Bella that he took his frustrations out on Erin.

That's when Erin had known she'd had to get out. Not only had the relationship become unhealthy for her, it had also become unhealthy for Bella.

Finally, Erin stepped onto solid ground again. She

breathed a sigh of relief once she was finished with the crossing.

As she did, she glanced back and saw Dillon and Scout carefully walking past the area. They did it with much more grace and ease than she had.

They continued walking. Erin wished she could carry on a conversation as they did so, but the air had turned colder and hurt her lungs. She pulled her coat higher and tried to breathe into the collar.

But as the snow came down harder, her discomfort grew. She had to watch every step. Concentrate every thought on getting out of this forest in one piece and without any broken bones.

Finally, they reached the clearing where the parking lot was.

When she walked over to her car, she pulled in a deep breath.

Her tires had been slashed.

Tears pressed her eyes as she soaked in the deep gashes in the rubber.

Who would have done this?

As Dillon stared at the slashed tires on Erin's car, a bad feeling began to grow inside him. Somebody was bent on making Erin suffer.

Why was that? And who would want to do something like this?

"I'm going to send a crew out to look at your tires," he told her. "But right now, we need to get out of the elements."

"Of course." Erin continued to stare at her vehicle as she said the words, but her eyes looked duller now than they had earlier.

"I'm parked over here." Dillon nodded to his Jeep. "How about I give you a ride? Would you be okay with that?"

She stared at him a moment as if contemplating her

answer before finally nodding. "I would appreciate that. Thank you."

"It's no problem."

They walked across the parking lot to his Jeep. He helped Erin into the front seat before lifting Scout into the back. Then Dillon climbed in and cranked the engine. As he waited for the vehicle to heat, he gave Scout some water. Then he reached into the back and grabbed a blanket.

He'd just washed it, and the scent of fabric softener still smelled fresh between the folds. He handed it to Erin. "This will help take the edge off until the heat kicks in."

"Thank you." Her teeth practically chattered as she said the words.

As the air slowly warmed and heat poured from the vents, it offered a welcome relief from the otherwise frigid temperatures outside.

"I'm going to go ahead and call about your tires now before we take off," Dillon explained. "I'd also like to see if there are any updates on our search mission, as well as the dead body."

"Of course." She pulled the blanket higher around her shoulders.

He dialed Rick's number and his friend answered on the first ring. Dillon explained that they'd come back from the hike and told Rick about Erin's tires being slashed.

"How about you?" Dillon asked. "Any updates?"

"We were able to retrieve the body before the snowstorm came. I'll take it back to the medical examiner's office to get some more answers. We also recorded the scene and tried to find any evidence that had been left behind there."

"Hopefully, you'll get some answers to that soon."

"I'm glad you called," Rick said. "Chief Blackstone called and wants to know if you can bring Erin in for some additional questions."

Chief Blackstone? Dillon didn't know the man well, but

he'd worked with the Boone's Hollow police chief on a couple of operations. He'd found the man to be overbearing and quick-tempered. In other words, he wasn't Dillon's favorite person.

Dillon glanced at Erin, aware that she had no idea what they were talking about. Instead, she reached back and rubbed Scout's head.

Dillon looked away, turning his attention back to the situation. "I'm sure I can do that. Do you know what it's pertaining to?"

"I think he has more questions for her concerning Bella's disappearance. That's all that they told me."

"Very well." Dillon ended the call and glanced at Erin again, wondering how she was going to take this update.

He cleared his throat before saying, "The chief would like to speak with you."

Her face seemed to go a little paler. "Why?"

"I'm sure it's just routine."

She squeezed her lips together before saying, "Nothing is routine when it comes to Chief Blackstone. The man hates me."

Dillon wanted to refute her statement. But he couldn't.

He didn't know what exactly she'd been through after Liam, and it wouldn't be fair to state an opinion based only on a guess.

"I can stay with you and give you a ride home afterward," he offered.

The breath seemed to leave her lungs for a moment and she stared at him as if trying to read his intention. "You would do that? I'm sure you need to get home and tend to your dog."

"I don't mind."

Maybe it was curiosity or maybe it was concern. But Dillon wanted to stay with Erin and find out exactly what was going on here. Plus, he sensed that this woman didn't really have anyone else to help her.

Giving her a ride was the least that he could do.

He put his Jeep into Reverse and backed out. "Let's get going. The storm isn't going to be letting up anytime soon, and these roads can get bad."

Erin nodded and crossed her arms over her chest.

She had to be living a nightmare right now.

Dillon just prayed that she would have a happy ending.

FIVE

Erin knew Dillon was trying to paint this visit to the police station in a positive light for her sake. But she knew the truth.

She knew how this would play out.

Just as when Liam had disappeared, Erin was most likely going to be the main suspect in Bella's disappearance as well.

Didn't Blackstone and his crew know that she would never hurt her daughter? These guys just needed a suspect and, for some reason, Erin seemed to fit the bill.

A sickly feeling began to grow in her stomach. She didn't want to go to the police station. But if she ran, she'd only look guilty. On the other hand, if she were arrested, how could she help find her daughter?

The questions collided inside her until Erin felt off-balance.

What was she going to do? What if Blackstone *did* try to arrest her?

And was Dillon just playing nice? Was he playing good cop trying to get information from her?

Erin wished she could trust men in uniform. Most of them were probably good guys. But the ones she knew weren't. Their loyalties were misplaced and their justice biased.

She stared at the road in front of her. To say the weather

had become blustery would be an understatement. It was downright nasty out here.

In fact, it was nearly impossible to even see the road as the snow created whiteout conditions.

She uncrossed her arms and grabbed the armrest, trying to remain calm.

She remembered the time in her life back before she'd met Liam. She'd been so carefree and happy. As an only child whose parents had been divorced, she'd been determined to make a different future for herself.

But everything had changed and she could hardly remember that idealistic person anymore. Her parents had both remarried and started new lives. She hardly ever spoke to them anymore.

"This could get slippery," Dillon muttered.

As far as she was concerned, slippery roads and mountains didn't mix. "Are you good at driving in snow?"

"I'd like to think so. This girl hasn't let me down yet." He patted the dash of his Jeep.

Erin glanced into the back seat and saw that Scout looked pretty laidback as well. Couldn't dogs sense danger? Maybe the fact that Scout looked relaxed was a good sign. Maybe the dog knew things Erin didn't.

The road turned with the bends in the mountain. Erin had come up this way a few times before, and she knew that at one point the road traveled alongside the path of a stream. Then it climbed back up the mountain. Eventually, it even became a gravel road.

The truth was that, even on a good day, the road was hard to manage. Throw in this kind of weather and the trip was even scarier.

Erin pressed her eyes shut.

Dear Lord, I know You haven't let me down yet. Please, be with me now. Everything is falling apart, and I feel help-

less. But I know I have You. I know You have a plan. I just need You now more than ever.

She'd prayed prayers like that before, especially when she'd been with Liam. It was so easy to think that things couldn't get worse.

But life had proven to her that they could, indeed, get worse.

Would that be the case now also?

Erin glanced outside again, trying to get a glimpse of where they were. Dillon was traveling slowly, which made her feel better, more secure.

But she sensed something shift in the air. It was Dillon's body language, she realized. He seemed more tense. More alert. Had something happened?

She glanced behind her, desperate for answers. "Dillon?"

He gripped the steering wheel and glanced into the rearview mirror again. "I think we're being followed."

"You mean somebody is just behind us?" Even as she said the words, she knew they didn't sound correct.

His jaw tightened. "I can't be sure. Most people in their right mind aren't out on the road right now."

The breath left her lungs.

Erin knew what he was getting at. There hadn't been anybody behind them in the parking lot when they'd left. The rescue crew and the remaining rangers had already left. Only Erin's car had remained behind. Not only that, but there were no other roads between that lot and where they were on the road now.

That meant somebody had parked on the side of the street.

Had that person waited for Dillon and Erin to go past and then pulled out behind them?

She remembered the person who'd pushed her down the cliff. What if that person was following them now? What if that person wanted to fix the mistake they'd made earlier when Erin hadn't died?

Dillon hadn't wanted to alarm Erin. But the woman was observant and had noticed the tension threading through him. It was only fair of him to tell her the truth.

Right now, the car behind him maintained a steady distance. Dillon could barely see the vehicle. Occasionally, he got a glimpse between the drifts of snow coming down.

The drive was already treacherous. The last thing he needed was somebody tailing them. Dillon just hoped that the person behind them would maintain a steady pace and not try to do anything foolish.

He quickly glanced at Erin and saw that she seemed to be getting paler and paler. If somebody was following them, was this person connected to Bella's disappearance? Could it be the same person who'd pushed Erin off the cliff?

If Erin were guilty in her daughter's disappearance, why would somebody be going through all this trouble?

Dillon knew the answer to that question.

They wouldn't.

So many questions collided in his head, but this wasn't the time to think about them. Right now, he needed to focus all his attention on the road.

He gently pressed on the brake as the road in front of him disappeared into a blur of white. He looked for any type of markers to show him where he needed to be.

There were too many unknowns in this area. Even though Dillon had driven this path many times, he hadn't memorized every inch of it. He hadn't remembered every turn and every drop-off. The lane was already narrow.

In different circumstances, he might pull off and try to wait the storm out. But the snow showers weren't supposed to be over until tomorrow. Forecasters hadn't even known that this system was going to come on this quickly, either.

Pulling off right now could be deadly. Especially if somebody else heading down the road wasn't expecting him to be there. Visibility was nearly down to zero.

Dillon glanced in his rearview mirror again and saw a brief glimpse of the car.

His heart rate quickened.

The vehicle was closer, probably only six feet behind them.

Was that on purpose? Dillon didn't know. But his gut told him he needed to remain on guard.

"Dillon?" Erin's voice sounded shaky beside him.

"Yes?"

"What's going on?" She still gripped the armrest.

"I'm just taking this moment by moment." He didn't bother to hide the truth.

"I don't even know how you're driving in this. It's completely white all around us."

"That's why I'm going slow. My Jeep has excellent traction." Those things were the truth. But there were many other hazards he didn't mention.

Just as the words left his mouth, he felt something nudge the car.

It was the vehicle behind them.

The driver was trying to run them off the road, wasn't he?

Dillon had to think quick if he wanted to walk away from this drive with his life—and the lives of those in his vehicle—intact.

As Erin felt the Jeep lurch forward, a muffled scream escaped.

Somebody *had* been following them.

And now somebody wanted to run them off the road.

Her thoughts swirled.

This couldn't really be happening...but it was.

She glanced behind her and could barely make out head-lights there. From what she could tell, this guy was gearing up to ram them again.

Next time, she and Dillon may not be so lucky. That driver might succeed and push them right off one of these cliffs.

It was nearly impossible to see what was about to happen. Erin had no idea if the Jeep was at the center of the road, if anybody was coming toward them, or how close they were to the cliff on one side of them or the river on the other.

She squeezed her eyes shut and began to pray even more fervently.

Dillon could be as experienced a driver as there was out there, but his skills would only get them so far in these circumstances.

Please, protect us. Guide us. I can't die. Not with Bella still out there. Please.

Scout let out a whine in the back seat. Erin reached back and rubbed his head, feeling his soft fur beneath her hand. "It's going to be okay, boy."

Comforting the dog helped distract her from her own fear.

The reprieve didn't last long.

The vehicle behind them rammed them again. This time, the Jeep careened out of control.

Erin gasped as they slid down the mountain road. The tires hit rocks and began to bump, bump, bump over them.

She squeezed her eyes shut as the bottom dropped from her stomach.

Where would they stop?

She didn't know. But she prepared herself to hit water. To hit a rock wall. To soar from a cliff.

To die.

SIX

"Hold on!" Dillon yelled.

Dillon fought to maintain control of the vehicle. But it was no use.

The icy road was winning.

Now he just had to work with the situation.

As he jerked the wheel, trying to avoid going off an unseen cliff, Erin gasped beside him.

The other vehicle revved its engine as it sped past them.

He strained to get a glimpse of who might be behind the wheel or what the vehicle looked like.

It was no use. All he'd seen was a flash of gray.

Finally, the Jeep slid to a stop.

Dillon let out a breath, halfway still expecting the worst. A sudden fall from the cliff or for the ground to disappear from beneath them.

But nothing happened.

His heart pounded in his ears as they sat there for a moment.

Then he glanced at Erin. "Are you okay?"

She let out a long, shaky breath. "I think so. You?"

He nodded. "That was close, to say the least. Did you get a glimpse of the vehicle when it went past?"

She shook her head, appearing disappointed she didn't have more to share. "All I saw was that it seemed to be gray. But everything…the snow was so thick that it was almost impossible and—"

"I know. You don't have to explain." He reached into the back seat and rubbed Scout.

The dog appeared to be okay still. They were *all* okay. That was good news.

But what waited for them next?

Dillon let out a long breath.

The three of them couldn't stay here. It was dangerous for any oncoming traffic, for starters. Plus, Dillon had no idea exactly where they were.

Had they skidded onto a pull-off on the side of the road? Had they hit a rocky patch of the road itself? He wasn't sure.

Based on the fact that he'd seen the car zoom past them on the right side, he could assume the roadway was there.

What would happen when Dillon started traveling down the road again? Was the other driver going to wait for them to pass and try these shenanigans again?

He wanted to say no. But he really had no idea.

"Should we call for backup?" Erin's voice cracked with fear.

He grabbed his phone and looked at the screen. It was just as he thought. There was no signal out here. Most places in these mountains didn't have a signal.

He frowned. "We're going to have to see if we can make it out of here ourselves. It's the best option of what we've got."

Erin rubbed her throat as if she were having trouble swallowing, but she nodded. "Whatever you think is best."

Dillon wished he knew what was best. There had been a time when he'd trusted his instincts. When his life had depended on doing so.

But after what had happened with Masterson, that was no longer the case.

He let out a long breath before slowly pulling onto what he hoped was the road. He waited for a moment, hoping for a break in the snow or the wind—something just enough to allow him to see where he was.

A moment later, he got his wish. The snow seemed to hold its breath and offered him a glimpse of the winter wonderland around them.

Dillon could barely make out a street sign in the distance—but it was something. That was where he needed to head.

At this rate, it would take him at least an hour to get to the Boone's Hollow police station, if not more.

He didn't care about how long it took, only that they arrived safe.

He began inching back down the road, ignoring the ache that had formed between his shoulder blades.

This wasn't the kind of weather people needed to be out driving in. Back when he'd been a cop, he'd seen way too many accidents happen in conditions like these. He didn't want to be one of those statistics.

Still, he pressed forward.

The good news was that the other car hadn't appeared again.

Maybe the driver had assumed they'd crashed. That would be the best-case scenario for them now.

Once they managed to get through this crisis, Dillon knew there would be another one waiting for them at the police station.

He never thought his day would turn into this.

He glanced over at Erin.

He was certain that she hadn't thought that, either.

Erin's relief was short-lived.

They'd finally managed to get off the mountain backroad and onto a highway. But now they'd pulled up to the police station. Now she was going to be facing another type of struggle.

You could run, a quiet voice said inside her.

She reminded herself again that, if she ran, she'd only look guilty. Besides, she had nothing to hide, nothing to be ashamed of.

As soon as Dillon parked the Jeep, she glanced over at him.

Something shifted in him also, almost as if arriving at the station had caused him to shift personas. Or was that only what Liam did?

Her emotions tangled with her logic until nothing made sense.

Was he getting ready to treat her like she was a criminal? Had he secretly needed to bring her in for questioning?

Erin didn't know the man well enough to say so. She only knew he was handsome and kind and brave. Not that any of those things mattered right now. There were so many more important things to worry about.

"Thanks for getting us off that mountain," she finally said instead.

Dillon nodded, his gaze still assessing hers. "It's no problem. I'm glad we're all okay right now. It was a close call back there."

That was an understatement. Erin's life had flashed before her eyes again—for the second time in one day.

He nodded toward the modest, one-story building in the distance. "Are you ready to head inside?"

She stared at the police building. It was still snowing, but at this very moment, it wasn't coming down hard. Memories flooded back to her.

Memories of bringing Liam lunch while he was on his break. Of the hope she'd felt when he'd first gotten the job.

Then she remembered how hostile it had all become when things went south. The uneasy feeling she'd felt whenever she'd stepped inside.

Was she ready to relive those moments? Not really.

That's why she'd gone to the park rangers when Bella

went missing, instead of the local police. But she'd known they would eventually get involved.

She didn't need to tell Dillon all that. He'd already carried enough of her burdens today.

She'd never answered his question. *Are you ready to go inside?*

"I suppose I'm ready," she finally said, wishing her heart wasn't beating so hard and fast.

Dillon stared at her another moment, something unspoken in his gaze. Erin wished she knew what he was thinking, but she didn't know him well enough to ask. Besides, he didn't owe her anything—definitely not an explanation.

"Let's go." He opened his door and a brisk wind swept inside.

Moving quickly, he retrieved Scout from the back seat. As he did, Erin climbed out and pulled her jacket closer as she ambled to the front doors of the station. The lot was slippery and snow still seemed to stockpile on the ground. The sudden darkness wasn't helping, either.

This place had so many bad memories. At one time, the building had seemed like a place of hope. When Liam first got his job here, it was like a dream come true for him. They'd even gone out to his favorite restaurant to celebrate afterward.

But Erin had never envisioned the ways that Liam would change. Not only had his personality shifted, so had the way he'd treated her. She wasn't sure what exactly had caused that change in him, but Erin had borne the brunt of his frustrations.

She continued to carefully plod over the icy surface, headed toward the front door of the building with Dillon by her side.

It certainly hadn't helped that Liam was a likable guy. He was the type of person who could make friends wherever he went. In fact, he would have made a great salesman.

Erin couldn't be certain about everything Liam must have said about her at work. But it was clear he hadn't painted her in a positive light around his colleagues.

That was why, when he disappeared, Erin was one of the first people they'd looked at.

The betrayal still hurt. At one time, these people had been her friends. In the blink of an eye, they'd turned against her. Sometimes, it felt like everyone in town had turned against her.

As she hurried toward the front door, Dillon lightly placed his hand on her back. His concern—or was it his touch?—caused her breath to catch.

His concern. It was definitely his concern that had caused that reaction.

It had been a long time since anyone had wanted to be associated with her. For someone like Dillon to go out of his way to offer a small measure of comfort and assistance touched her in surprising ways.

They reached the front door and Dillon opened it for her. Erin slipped into the warmth of the police building.

But the welcome of warmth was short-lived. As soon as she saw Chief Blackstone head toward her, a deep chill wracked her body.

The look in his eyes indicated that her troubles were just starting.

And, unfortunately, she already felt like she was at her breaking point.

Dillon watched as Chief Blackstone's eyes instantly darkened as soon as he saw Erin.

The man was in his early forties, with only a fringe of dark hair around the sides of his rectangular head. His burly frame and stiff movements made him an intimidating figure—for some people, at least.

The man obviously had a chip on his shoulder for the

woman. Dillon's curiosity spiked. Just what had transpired after Liam disappeared?

"Erin, I'd like to see you in my office." Blackstone's voice didn't contain even an ounce of warmth.

She nodded, looking resigned to that fact and like a lamb going in for the slaughter.

"Dillon, I'd like to talk with you also," Blackstone called. "Can you wait around?"

Dillon glanced at Erin, wishing he could go with her and shield her from some of what was about to happen. Because, based on the look in Blackstone's eyes, he was about to give her the third degree. Most likely, he'd show no mercy.

Why did he feel such a protective instinct toward the woman? It didn't make sense.

But he could feel the heartache she was going through right now. Plus, based on what had happened today and what he'd experienced with her, Dillon didn't believe she'd had any part in her daughter's disappearance. It just didn't make sense. She had no motive for harming her daughter.

Dillon planted himself near the door, still gripping Scout's lead. "I'll stick around."

Blackstone nodded to him.

Erin gave him one last glance before following the chief into his office.

Chief Blackstone cast a glance at Dillon before closing his door. Dillon clutched Scout's lead as he wondered exactly what was about to go down.

He hesitated a moment, unsure what to do with himself.

As he thought about everything Erin had already been through—about the grief in her gaze—something stirred inside him.

The woman had no one to stand up for her. No one to lean on.

That just wasn't right.

If Dillon's instincts were correct, she was about to experience another nightmare in the chief's office.

He couldn't let that happen.

As instinct took over, he started toward the chief's door. He knocked but pushed it open before Blackstone could answer.

"Yes?" A shadow crossed the chief's gaze.

"I'm wondering if I could stay in here and assist you with anything that you need to talk about."

Chief Blackstone narrowed his eyes. "Why would you want to do that?"

"I've been with Erin all day, so I can offer my perspective on today's events also. Including the fact that we were almost run off the road and her tires were slashed."

The chief stared at him a moment until finally nodding. "I suppose that's fine. As long as it's also fine with Erin."

Erin glanced at him and something that looked like relief flooded her face. "Yes, that's fine."

He stepped inside and closed the door. He and Scout stood in the corner, out of the way.

"Where were you when Bella disappeared?" The chief didn't waste any time before jumping right in and focusing his accusation on Erin.

Erin quickly shook her head as if the question had startled her. "Where was I? I was at work. I have a whole classroom full of kids who can verify that."

He glowered. "But what about before that?"

"Before I went to school?" She blinked several times as if his question didn't make sense. "I was getting ready to go to school, just like I do every day."

"And nobody was with you?"

She shook her head, and Dillon sensed her rising frustration.

"As I'm sure you know, the elementary school starts before the high school," Erin said. "So I left the house by seven that morning to head into school. Bella was in the bathroom getting ready when I left and that was the last time I saw her. I went through this with the park rangers."

The chief's expression showed no reaction—except maybe a tinge of skepticism. "You haven't talked to Bella since then?"

"That's correct. I've tried her cell, but she hasn't answered. I've texted her. Nothing."

"And your car was found parked beside the trailhead also…"

Erin's lips parted as if the chief's questions continued to shock her. "My car was only there because I drove to the area to search for her myself."

"Somebody said your car was there yesterday right after school hours."

Erin sucked in a breath, her eyes widening with outrage. "That's a lie. I didn't go there yesterday. I didn't even know that Bella's car had been found there until this morning. Who told you that?"

"It doesn't matter. I'm just telling you what a witness has come forward to say."

She swung her head back and forth in adamant denial. "Then somebody is trying to set me up. Are there security cameras there at the lot?"

Chief Blackstone shook his head. "I'm afraid there aren't."

"Well, you can talk to my neighbors. They'll tell you that I came home after school. That's when I realized that Bella wasn't there and I started making phone calls."

"I'd say that's a problem. We talked to your neighbors and none of them said they saw you."

"What?" Her voice trailed off.

Dillon felt a stab of outrage burst through him. "Are you accusing Erin of her daughter's disappearance?"

Blackstone's raised eyebrows showed annoyance at the question. "We're trying to cover all our bases here."

"Well, I can personally attest to the fact that her tires were slashed and someone tried to run us off the road. That's not to mention the fact that Erin was pushed off a cliff. If she was truly guilty, why did all those things happen?"

"That's a good question." The chief practically smirked. "One we need to look into."

Dillon's back muscles tightened. The chief obviously had a target on Erin's back.

If Blackstone was already convinced he knew what had happened, he wouldn't look at anyone else except Erin.

That didn't make things look promising as far as finding Bella.

SEVEN

Erin looked up and tried to offer Dillon a grateful smile.

She was glad he was there, even though she still wasn't sure why he'd barged into the chief's office. Still, his presence brought with it a strange comfort.

At first, she'd feared Dillon was one of the chief's minions. But the protective set of his jaw made her believe otherwise.

She hoped she wasn't wrong; that Dillon wasn't some kind of spy for the law enforcement head. Blackstone had so many people in his pocket that it made it hard for Erin to know whom to trust.

"Is there any other reason why you want to keep Ms. Lansing here?" Dillon's gaze locked with the chief's.

Chief Blackstone's eyes hardened. "We just wanted to hear her version of events again."

"I told you. So now, you tell me. Do you have any leads on Bella?" Erin rushed to ask, trying to keep the exasperation from her voice. But it was hard to do that when she felt like they were wasting valuable time. "Have you heard anything else? I'm so worried about her."

"No. Nothing yet." Chief Blackstone's expression—and tone—showed no emotion or regret.

Disappointment cut deep inside her. Erin had hoped for something more, even though she'd fully expected him to say those words. Once a person was guilty of something in this man's eyes, then they were always guilty. Always a suspect. Never to be trusted.

"Unless there's something else you need, I need to get her home." Dillon gripped her arm, nearly pulling Erin from her seat. "The weather is turning bad."

Erin's breath caught. Would this work? Would Dillon actually be able to get her out of here?

Chief Blackstone raised his eyebrows, a shadow darkening his glare. "*You* do? Is that right?"

Dillon shrugged. "Like I said, her tires were slashed."

Scout barked as if adding his agreement.

The chief nodded slowly, unspoken judgment lingering in his gaze. "I can get one of my guys to give her a ride home."

"That won't be necessary," Dillon said. "I don't mind."

Erin held her breath as she waited for the chief's response. Scout sat at attention as if he was also waiting.

Chief Blackstone's eyebrows flickered before he tilted his head in a nod. "Very well then. We'll be in touch if we have any more questions."

Erin wished the chief had said they'd be in touch if they had any more updates. But the way he'd worded the statement made it clear he still thought Erin could be guilty.

How could the chief think that? Did he hate her that much?

Right now, Erin just wanted to get out of there.

She stood and headed toward the door before the chief could ask anything else.

Without another word, Dillon directed her outside.

As she stepped into the lot, she noted that snow was still coming down but not as heavily as earlier. Still, the ground was covered with the icy, white flakes. The ride home would be slippery.

"Hello, Erin," someone said behind her.

She turned and saw Officer Brad Hollins standing there.

A friendly face.

He'd been a rookie who'd trained under Liam. The man had eaten at their house and come to cookouts. He was one of the few people who hadn't turned his back on Erin when everything went down.

"Hi, Officer Hollins." She paused. "You're looking good."

He grinned, but it quickly faded. "I'm sorry to hear about Bella. I'm keeping my eyes and ears open for any leads. I just wanted to let you know that."

"I appreciate it. Thank you."

She said goodbye before continuing to the Jeep. They all climbed inside. Only when the engine started did Dillon speak.

"Old friend?" he asked.

"He's one of the good guys. He's always been kind to me."

"Good. I'm glad to hear that. Listen, I'm sorry about that back there." Compassion wound through the strands of Dillon's voice.

Erin swallowed hard and glanced at her hands as they rested in her lap. What did she even say? If she overshared, would that make Dillon suspicious of her?

She finally settled on the obvious. "In case you can't tell, the chief doesn't really like me."

"Because of Liam?"

She nodded as she remembered the comradery the two men had shared. "Blackstone thought of Liam as a son."

"I see. So, Blackstone took it hard when Liam disappeared?"

"He did. He had tunnel vision and thought I was responsible for it. He was so convinced it was me, he hardly looked at any other possibility."

Dillon frowned. "I can see him doing that…"

She turned toward him and studied his face, his expression, for any sign that he was on Blackstone's side. "You mean you didn't fall under the chief's spell? Under Liam's spell?"

"I try, to the best of my ability, not to fall under spells." He offered a small grin.

Erin wanted to smile in return but she didn't. This was no time to find any kind of enjoyment out of her circumstances.

"Now, where do I need to take you?" Dillon asked.

She rattled off her address, which was located about ten minutes from the police station, just on the outskirts of town.

Using the same caution on the slippery streets as earlier, Dillon started down the road toward her place.

As the station disappeared from sight, at once she felt every ounce of her exhaustion.

What a day.

She needed to get a good night's rest so she could start again tomorrow. If it wasn't for the weather, she would keep searching tonight. But it would do no good, and she knew that.

"How long have you lived here?" Dillon's voice cut through the silence.

"I moved to Boone's Hollow when Liam and I got married, and he got a job on the force."

"Is that right? But Liam was a local, wasn't he?"

She nodded, surprised that he knew as much about Liam as he did. Then again, maybe she shouldn't be surprised. "He was. Born and raised in Boone's Hollow."

"I see. Where did you meet him? If you don't mind me asking…"

Her mind drifted back in time. "In college. Liam was studying criminal justice and I was working on my teaching degree."

"Do you teach at a local school?"

Erin shook her head. "I work two towns over. I switched after Liam went missing. It's a forty-minute drive both ways, but I figure it's worth it just for the peace of mind."

His jaw tightened. "I can't even imagine what that must be like. I'm surprised you haven't moved."

"I thought about it many times. And it's tempting. But Bella wants to graduate from high school here. Thankfully, she hasn't gotten as bad of a rap as I did. People still seem to like her because she's Liam's daughter." She frowned as she said the words.

It was a wonder they'd accepted Bella as much as they had, especially considering that Liam wasn't her biological dad.

The thoughts continued to turn over in Erin's head.

Finally, they turned onto the street she lived off of. It wasn't in a neighborhood but instead her home was a smaller cabin located on a back road. The woods surrounding the property offered her some privacy, which had been welcome the week that everything had happened.

But as Dillon pulled up to her house and his headlights shone on the front of it, she saw a message that had been spray-painted there.

It was the word "Killer."

The blood drained from her face.

Somebody had wanted to send a message, and it had worked.

As Dillon stared at the word painted on the front of Erin's house, the severity of the situation hit him once again.

Not only was this woman's daughter missing, but people in this town were bent on making it seem like Erin was responsible. He could only imagine the pressure Erin felt right now.

As Dillon glanced at her, he saw the tears well in her

eyes as she stared at the painted letters on her porch. What a shock it must be for her to see this.

"Let me make sure you get inside okay," he said.

She quickly wiped her eyes before waving her hands in the air. "You don't have to do that. You've already gone above and beyond."

"I'd feel better if I was able to check it out for you. I can't leave you here now when danger could be lurking just out of sight. I wouldn't be able to live with myself if something happened to you."

After another quick moment of hesitation, she finally nodded. "Okay then."

He took his key out of the ignition before climbing out and grabbing Scout from the back seat. Cautiously, he walked toward the front of the house, scanning everything around them as he did so.

He didn't see anybody waiting out of sight. But they still needed to be cautious.

"Stay behind me," he muttered as Erin trailed close to him.

He looked again at the letters across the front of her house. They'd been scrawled in red spray paint—of course. The color only added to the threatening effect.

How could someone do this? How could they think Erin was guilty without even knowing any details?

His stomach clenched at the thought of it.

The keys rattled in Erin's hand until finally she managed to open the door.

"Let me. Wait here." Dillon pushed himself in front of her and motioned for her to stay in the living room near the door while he checked out the rest of the place. He handed her Scout's leash, and Erin grasped it as if it were a lifeline.

Dillon checked out the house, but everything appeared clear. No threatening messages. Lurking intruders. Unsightly surprises.

As he met Erin in the living room, a fresh round of hesitancy filled him. He didn't want to leave her. She looked terrified with her wide eyes, shallow breaths and death grip on Scout's leash.

He wished he knew her better. Wished he was pushier.

But that wasn't his place. Not right now. Not when considering he'd only known her for less than twenty-four hours.

"Should I call the police?" Erin remained plastered against the wall, almost as if she were frozen in place.

Dillon let out a long breath as he considered her question. In ordinary circumstances, he would definitely say yes. But he'd seen the way the chief had spoken to Erin. Most likely, if she called for help, they wouldn't take her request seriously. Not only that, but no evidence as to who had done this had been left behind.

"How about this?" Dillon started. "I'll take a picture of the message that was left so we can record it as evidence. Then I'm going to clean it off."

"You don't have to do—"

"I want to." His voice remained firm, leaving no room for questions. "If you want to do something, how about you fix some coffee and maybe light a fire? After I finish cleaning this up, I'm going to need to warm up."

Erin stared at him another moment, hesitation in her gaze. Finally, she nodded. "Okay. If you don't mind, that would be a huge help."

She gathered the supplies he needed. Then Dillon went outside and did exactly as he'd promised. Scout stayed inside with Erin. She'd put some water in a bowl for him, and Dillon had pulled the canine's food from his backpack.

He knew Erin was in good hands with Scout. Not only was the dog an expert in search and rescue operations, Scout was also protective.

As Dillon scrubbed the spray paint, his mind went back to his own guilt. The accusations others had flung at him.

He knew what it was like to be guilty in the eyes of those around you. He knew what the weight of those accusations felt like. Maybe that's why he felt so compassionate toward Erin now. In some ways, he felt like he could understand.

As soon as Dillon finished washing the paint off, he stepped inside. The scent of fresh-brewed coffee filled his senses.

Erin waited for him to take his coat off before handing him a steaming mug.

"Smell's great. Thank you."

"I made a few sandwiches, too, just in case you're hungry." She nodded toward a tray she'd put together on the kitchen counter.

"That was thoughtful. Thank you." Now that she'd mentioned it, he was hungry. He hadn't eaten much all day.

He'd drink his coffee, eat a sandwich, and warm up a few minutes before heading back to his place.

But he doubted he'd get any sleep tonight as he wondered how Erin was doing…and if she was safe.

Erin was so grateful for Dillon. He'd truly been a godsend. If he hadn't been there for her today, she might not be alive right now.

Her throat tightened at the thought.

As she sat in a chair near the fireplace, her hands trembled. She attempted to take another sip of her coffee, but everything was tasteless. Enjoying herself was a luxury she didn't deserve right now, especially not when she thought about Bella.

Bella…

Erin continued to pray that God would protect the girl right now, whatever she was going through—whether Bella had been abducted or if she were wandering lost in the woods. Whatever the case, Erin only wanted her daughter to be safe.

However, she remembered that second set of footprints.

It looked like someone had abducted her daughter, just as she'd feared.

The hollow pit in her stomach filled with nausea at the thought of it.

"Tell me about Bella." Dillon leaned forward in his chair, his eyes fixated on Erin.

Scout lay between them, in front of the fire, his eyes closed as if he could finally relax for a little while. The dog's belly should be full, and the warmth of the fire seemed a welcome companion for all of them.

Erin set her coffee mug on the end table beside her. "I told you some basics earlier. But I guess what I didn't tell you is that Bella is adopted."

His eyebrows shot up. "Is she? I had no idea."

Erin nodded as memories flooded her. "She was ten when she came to live with me and Liam. An old friend from high school had a rough go at life and ended up in jail for quite a while. She personally asked me if I would adopt Bella, and, of course, I said yes."

"How did Liam feel about that?"

The day the adoption was finalized flashed back into her mind, replaying like an old film reel. "He was all in favor of it. At least, at first. But later, I couldn't help but wonder if he felt jealous."

Dillon narrowed his gaze. "Jealous because you were giving her more attention?"

Erin offered a half shrug. "Maybe. It never really made sense to me. I felt like I gave Liam plenty of attention. They both deserved all my attention, and I did the best that I could."

"It sounds like you're a good mom."

She shrugged, feeling another round of guilt wash

through her. "Sometimes I don't know. If I was such a good mom, then why is Bella not here with me now?" Her voice broke.

Dillon leaned toward her. "Sometimes in life, there are things out of our control. You can try to be a helicopter parent all you want, but there comes a point when you have to realize that some things are out of our hands."

"That's hard to stomach when you try to play by the rules and do everything right. And sometimes you try to play by the rules and do everything right, and everything still goes desperately wrong." She swallowed hard, feeling a knot form in her throat.

"Do you believe in God, Erin?"

Dillon's question nearly startled her. But Erin quickly nodded. "I do. I more than believe in Him. I try to follow Him."

"Good. Because that faith will sustain you now. Hold tight to it. Know that we have hope, not only in the way things turn out in this life, but also in the eternal."

His words caused a burst of comfort to wash through her. It meant a lot to have someone here who understood, who could remind her of those important things in life.

"I've been trying to cling to my faith. But it's definitely being tested right now, to say the least."

"I'll continue to pray for you. I know that prayer has helped sustain me through some of my toughest and darkest moments also."

She wondered exactly what Dillon meant by that. It sounded like there was more to the story.

Before she could respond, her phone buzzed. She started, wondering if it was a text either from Bella or about Bella.

Quickly, she looked at the screen.

But the same unknown number from earlier popped up. Along with another cryptic message.

You bring destruction wherever you go.

A cry caught in her throat. Why was someone so determined to make a bad situation even worse? Why did they want to try and be her jury and judge?

"Erin…" Dillon looked at her with a questioning look in his eyes.

Before she could say anything, a creak sounded on her porch.

Scout suddenly stood, his body tense as he looked at the door and began to growl.

Was someone outside?

Could it be Bella?

Or was it someone who wanted to make Erin suffer for sins they only assumed she'd committed?

EIGHT

Dillon felt his muscles bristle.

"Stay here," he told Erin.

From the look on her face, she wasn't expecting anybody. Hope and grief seemed to clash in her gaze as she stared at the front of her house.

If somebody was here for a friendly visit, they would have knocked.

Dillon instructed Scout to stay beside Erin before pulling out his gun and creeping toward the door. He stood at the edge of it and flipped the curtain out of the way.

A shadowy figure paced outside.

What was someone doing out there? Coming to leave another message? To finish what he'd started when his attempt to push Erin off the cliff hadn't been successful?

Moving quietly so his presence wouldn't be noticed, Dillon gripped his gun with one hand and the door handle with the other. He then threw the door open and stepped outside with his gun drawn.

"Freeze!" he ordered.

The man on the porch held up his hands. But there wasn't an apology in the intruder's gaze—only vengeance.

"Who are you?" the man demanded as he sneered at Dillon.

Dillon stared at the man. He didn't have the impression this guy was Erin's boyfriend or even a relative. Yet he seemed familiar with the house.

"I'm the one with the gun," Dillon said. "I suggest you answer that first."

The man narrowed his gaze. "I'm Arnold Lansing."

Realization hit Dillon. "You must be Liam's brother."

The man's scowl deepened. "That's right. Who are you?"

"I'm with the search and rescue crew. What are you doing here?"

"I came to see Erin. Do you have a problem with that?" Anger edged into the man's voice as if he silently dared Dillon to defy him.

Before he could respond, Dillon heard a shuffle behind him, and Erin appeared. Based on her body language, she wasn't happy to see Arnold. Instead, she crossed her arms and glared at the man.

"You're not welcome here." Her voice hardened with every syllable.

Arnold bristled as he stared at her. "This was my brother's house. I'll always be welcome here."

"Your brother's not here right now," Dillon said. "So I would rethink those words. If the lady says you're not welcome, then you're not welcome."

"My brother bought this property with his own money." Arnold's voice rose as he jammed his foot onto the ground.

"He bought it while we were married. As soon as I'm able to sell it and move somewhere else so I can get away from these bad memories, I plan on doing just that."

"Now, what are you doing here?" Dillon asked as he stared at Arnold.

Arnold's gaze remained on Erin, still cold and calculated. "I heard about what you did to Bella."

Erin adamantly swung her head back and forth. "I didn't do anything to Bella. I'm desperate to find her. If you were any kind of uncle to her, you'd be out there with me helping with the search efforts."

"Just like you did with my brother?"

"You know good and well I did not do anything to your brother." Erin's voice sounded at just above a hiss. "Liam outweighed me by a hundred pounds at least. What exactly do you think I could have done to him?"

"You're smart. I'm sure you could figure out something."

Dillon had heard enough of this exchange. He stepped forward, placing himself between Arnold and Erin. "I think it's time for you to leave."

"What are you going to do?" Arnold let out a sardonic chuckle. "Call the police?"

Dillon felt himself revolt. Guys like this were the kind who gave cops a bad name. And when one cop had a bad name, it damaged all cops.

"You need to go," Dillon repeated.

Arnold stared at Erin a moment longer before taking a step back. "Very well then. All the best. With everything. You're going to need it."

Dillon waited at the door until he saw the man drive away. Then he turned back to Erin.

What exactly was going on here?

There was clearly more to her story.

And the more he learned, the more he realized just how much danger she was in right now.

Erin pulled a blanket over herself but that didn't help her chill. The icy feeling came from down deep inside her.

As she rubbed her hands over her arms, she felt the scrapes on her palms from her fall down the cliff earlier today.

She was going to make it through this, just like Dillon had said. She just had to remember that her hope went beyond all these circumstances.

Dillon pulled his chair closer and sat in front of her, his studious gaze on her, worry rimming his eyes. "Are you okay, Erin?"

She nodded even though she felt anything but okay. Every part of her life had been shaken up, and she wasn't sure if she'd ever recover.

"Arnold's never really liked me that much, if you can't tell."

Dillon's regard darkened. "He has no right to treat you that way. How long has he been giving you a hard time?"

"Basically, from the moment we met. Who knows what Liam told him about me, for that matter."

"It doesn't sound like Liam treated you very well, either."

Erin shrugged, unable to fight the memories any longer. "He did at first. He was charming and sweet. But after we were married, that started to change. Then when we adopted Bella, it really changed. I was afraid he might lash out at her one day. As soon as I realized that was a possibility, I left him."

"I didn't realize that you were separated before he went missing."

"We were more than separated. We were divorced. And I got the house in the divorce, for the record."

Dillon leaned back, the thoughtful expression remaining on his face. "So why do people think that you're responsible for his disappearance?"

Erin rubbed her arms again and stared into the fire as more memories flooded her. "We were seen fighting the morning Liam disappeared. We got into a huge argument, and several people were around to hear it."

"How does that prove anything?"

"Apparently, in some people's minds, that means I did something to Liam. But I wouldn't have done that. Even though I don't always trust the legal system, I tried to go through the proper means of ending my relationship with him. Instead of enacting my own form of justice, I did everything the legal way instead."

"It doesn't sound like Liam was able to accept the terms of your divorce."

She stared into the fire, watching the flames dance. "He didn't want a divorce. But eventually he conceded, and it was finalized."

"How often does Arnold confront you like he did tonight?"

"It's random," Erin said. "I won't hear from him for months, and I'll think he's gone from my life. Then suddenly he'll show up, and I'll see him several times in a row."

Dillon frowned. "That's got to be hard."

"It is. I especially don't want Bella to have to see it or have any part of it. But Arnold even harassed her one time while she was at school."

Dillon seemed to stiffen. "What did he do?"

"He called to her through the fence at the school and told her that her mom was a killer. She was so upset…as you can probably imagine."

"That's terrible. Did you report it?"

Erin shrugged, no longer feeling disappointed in the local police. She'd simply accepted that they'd never be on her side. "No, it's like I said, the police believe I did something to Liam. They don't care about anything that I have to say."

"That's a shame. I'm sorry that you're having to go through all of this."

The sincerity of his words made Erin flush. "I appreciate that. But I suppose that I made my bed and now I have to sleep in it, as the saying goes. My friends never really liked Liam. Told me that I shouldn't marry him. I thought I knew better. And now look at me."

She wanted to laugh, but she couldn't. It wasn't a laughing matter.

Liam had slowly separated her from all those friends who hadn't wanted her to be with Liam. He'd told her lies about them. Told her they were just jealous. Eventually, in order to preserve her marriage, she'd pulled away from them.

Which was exactly what Liam had wanted.

She'd become isolated, with no one to talk to and no one to support her.

In other words, she'd been trapped and hopeless.

But adopting Bella had changed that.

"We all make mistakes," Dillon said. "What about that text you got right before we heard someone outside? What was that about?"

Erin found the message on her phone and showed it to him. His eyes widened as he read the words *You bring destruction wherever you go.*

"What an odd message for someone to send you," he muttered.

"What am I going to do, Dillon?" She heard the desperation in her voice, but she couldn't take it back. The emotion was raw—but it was true.

"First thing in the morning, we're going to get the search parties together again and we're going to look for Bella. We're not going to give up until we find her."

She let his words sink in and slowly nodded. "Okay then. But I doubt I'm going to get any rest tonight."

Dillon frowned before saying, "How would you feel if I slept on your couch? I just don't want to see any trouble come back here. Besides, the roads are bad, and it's late."

"I'm sure you have a life outside of this." His offer was kind, but he'd already done so much for her. Gone above and beyond. Done so much more than anyone could reasonably expect.

"I'm not married," Dillon explained. "And I have somebody who can help me with the dogs back at my place. My nephew lives there. I'll give him a call."

She nibbled on the inside of her lip for a moment as she

contemplated his offer. "Are you sure this won't be too much trouble?"

"I'm sure. In fact, I'd feel a lot better if you'd let me stay."

Erin stared at him another moment before nodding. This was no time to let her pride get in the way. Dillon staying here answered a lot of prayers.

"Okay," she finally said. "Thank you. I owe you big-time for this."

His gaze locked with hers. "You don't owe me anything."

Erin had brought Dillon a pillow and blanket so he could sleep on the couch. But he knew he wouldn't be getting much rest tonight. He had too much on his mind.

He paced toward the front window again and glanced outside at Erin's front yard. He had a strange feeling they were being watched right now.

Had the person who'd taken Bella come back to see what Erin was doing? Was this all out of some sort of twisted revenge against the schoolteacher?

What about Arnold? Could he be behind this? If Liam had resented Erin for adopting Bella, maybe Arnold wanted to give Erin some payback by taking Bella away from her now. Dillon wasn't sure if his theory had any validity, but he kept it in the back of his mind.

Scout stood from near the fireplace and paced over to him. The dog appeared more triggered than usual as he panted and seemed like he couldn't settle down.

Scout knew something was going on, didn't he?

Dillon thought about going outside to check things himself. But he knew that wouldn't be wise.

He didn't know what he was up against nor did he know this landscape. He was better off staying inside and being prepared for whatever might come. If anyone got too close to the house, Scout would alert him.

Instead, he decided to make a few phone calls about tomorrow's search and rescue mission. But first, he checked the weather. The snow was supposed to let up and pass by then.

Still, that didn't change the fact that everything was going to be covered in a layer of the icy precipitation. After what had happened today, they were going to need to be very careful. Not only would the trails be dangerous, so would the drive to get there.

Dillon glanced at the time and saw it wasn't quite midnight. Still, he knew Rick was a night owl. He called him to get a quick update on what happened today. Besides, Dillon could use someone to talk to, to bounce ideas off of.

"It took you longer to call than I thought it would," Rick answered.

"It's been a busy day. Any updates since we last talked?"

"I wish there were. But no, not yet. If the weather allows, we'll go back out tomorrow and keep searching the trails for Bella," Rick said. "We don't want too many volunteers in the forest right now because of the icy conditions. It could be dangerous."

That didn't surprise Dillon. They didn't want to add another tragedy to an already tense situation. "What about a helicopter?"

"We have one lined up to use tomorrow. How did it go with Scout? Did he stay on the trail?"

Dillon's mind drifted back to the moment they'd had to turn around. "I felt like we were so close to finding Bella today when we had to go back."

"It was a good thing you did because conditions got even worse. It was bad out there with the temperatures dropping so quickly." Rick paused. "I guess you know who she is now."

Erin's face flashed through his mind. "I do. But that doesn't change anything."

"I just want you to be careful."

"You actually think she did something to Liam Lansing?" Dillon honestly wanted to know his friend's opinion.

"I never cared for the man much myself," Rick said. "But a lot of people suspected her. You know the spouse or the ex is always one of the first people considered in an investigation like that one."

"It sounds to me like people in town didn't like her and wanted a reason to find her guilty."

"The community bonds are strong in Boone's Hollow," Rick said. "Everyone loved Liam, but Erin was still an outsider. I also know that Liam had a way of getting people on his side. Who knows what the truth is? It's usually somewhere in the middle."

"Usually. But sometimes that's not the case. Sometimes the truth squarely rests on one person's shoulders and not the other's."

"I can't argue with that."

"What about Blackstone?" Dillon continued. "Do you trust him?"

"I try not to deal with the man unless I absolutely have to."

That said it all as far as Dillon was concerned.

"Listen, I'm still filling out all this paperwork, but we're going to meet at 8:00 a.m. so we can start our search efforts again," Rick said. "Send me the quadrants where Scout last picked up on Bella's scent, and we'll start there. I'll send you more information first thing in the morning. Sound like a plan?"

"That sounds great. I have a feeling Erin will be coming along, too."

Rick didn't say anything for a moment. "Are you sure that's a good idea?"

"I'm sure I won't be able to keep her away. She's determined to find Bella—either with us or on her own. On her own, she might get herself killed."

"Okay then. As long as you know what you're getting into."

Did Dillon know what he was getting into? He wasn't sure.

But he wasn't going to change his mind now.

NINE

As Erin rode in the Jeep with Dillon and Scout the next morning, she prayed that today would be successful.

She'd hardly gotten any sleep last night as she'd prayed those words over and over. Prayer was the only thing she could rely on right now. Not only that, prayer was also the best thing she could do right now.

She needed to trust in God because He was the only one who could get her through this situation.

She'd heard Dillon on the phone last night. Heard him pacing. Heard Scout bark a couple of times.

When she'd asked Dillon about it this morning, he'd shrugged her question off. But she had a feeling that someone else had been outside her place last night.

Had Arnold come back? Had another member of Liam's family come by to make their presence known?

She had no idea.

She only knew that today was probably going to be just as treacherous as yesterday had been. Erin had tried to mentally prepare herself for that fact, but she wasn't sure she'd succeeded.

"The search and rescue team is hoping to get the copter out today." Dillon's calm voice cut through the silence.

A helicopter? Maybe that would find something. "That would be good."

"Even though it seems like winter is a bad time to get

lost—and it is—the good news is that without all the leaves on the trees, it's much easier to see things from the sky."

She supposed that could be a good thing.

She crossed her arms as she glanced at him again. "Is law enforcement still treating this as if Bella has run away?"

"My understanding is that they're exploring both options—that she could have run or that she could have been abducted. Until they have confirmation, that's what they'll continue to do."

"What about that second set of footprints?"

"It indicates she could have met someone. But that still doesn't mean she was abducted."

Erin rubbed her throat, knowing she couldn't argue with him. He was absolutely correct.

"Besides, if someone snatched her, you would have probably received a ransom call by now." Dillon glanced at her before turning his gaze back onto the road.

"I don't have money. I thought cases like that usually involved wealthy people."

"Sometimes, but not always."

"I just worry that someone abducted her, and that person has her in a car right now and is taking her as far away from this area as possible." Erin's voice cracked as emotions tried to bubble to the surface.

"That's a call that Rick and Blackstone will need to make. I know it's hard to trust Blackstone. We can go above him, if necessary."

Erin did a double take at him. "If you go above him, there's no way they're going to hire you to work search and rescue anymore. You'll be blacklisted in this town."

He shrugged. "Sometimes that's the cost of doing what's right."

"I don't want to cost you your career."

Dillon glanced at her. "I appreciate your concern, but I assure you that I can handle myself."

She nodded and stared out the window, feeling like every minute that passed, the mess around her grew. It was bad enough that Liam's disappearance had upended Erin's life. But now Dillon was willing to risk his career for this.

She admired the man for his stance, but she hated to think of more innocent people getting caught in the cross fire.

Finally, they reached the parking area near the trailhead. This time, no one had followed them, nor had Erin received any more threatening text messages. She took that as a good sign.

A brush of nerves swept through her as she climbed from the Jeep and merged with the rest of the search and rescue operation. Several new people had joined the team, people Erin assumed were volunteers, based on their clothing. A few people sent her strange glances.

Did they think she was guilty?

Erin knew there was a good chance the answer to that question was yes.

But she had to push past those opinions and keep her focus on finding Bella. That was the only thing that mattered.

She prayed that today would be successful. That today would be the day they found Bella. Her daughter had been missing for almost forty-eight hours now.

That was enough time for someone to have taken her far away from here.

Bile rose in Erin's stomach at the thought.

What if Bella was never found?

Dillon and Scout led the way down the icy trail. This was going to be trickier than he would have liked. But he knew time was of the essence right now.

More people had shown up to help search—but only experienced SAR volunteers.

They'd been divided into six different groups so they could cover more of the area. Dillon, Scout and Erin were on one team. Right now, they walked with Rick and two other rangers—Dan and William.

Later on, further down the trail, they would split up, but for now they all headed in the same direction.

It had been good to see the volunteers who wanted to help. The more of this wilderness they could cover, the better.

The teams threaded their way through the woods back toward the area where they'd been last night, the spot where the trailhead split and where Scout had lost Bella's scent.

Dillon had already decided that he would head down into the valley—that was unless Scout somehow picked up Bella's scent again.

He knew there were a few old hunting cabins out here and had to wonder if maybe the girl had somehow gotten inside one of those.

But this wilderness was so vast. Someone had gotten lost here one time and a search party had come out looking for him for two weeks, to no avail. People didn't realize how dangerous these mountains could be until they were in the middle of them. By then, it was usually too late.

Of course, Dillon didn't tell Erin that. She was dealing with enough harsh realities without him adding to her burdens.

As he glanced behind him, he noted that Erin was being a real trooper as she kept up with them. She wasn't complaining, though she was breathing heavy.

"How long have you had Scout?" she asked after she seemed to notice him glance back at her.

"Four years," he said. "Someone left him at the pound. As soon as I saw him, I knew he had to come home with me."

"Is it normal for dogs from the pound to become search and rescue dogs?"

He climbed over a downed tree before reaching back to also help Erin across. "They make the best search and rescue dogs, I'd say. Those dogs know they've been rescued and they just want to give back."

"That's really beautiful."

"It's true."

It was cold out here and slippery. Nothing about it was enjoyable. But it was necessary.

When they got to the area of the path where it split, Dillon nodded toward the trail leading into the valley. "This is where we part ways."

Rick nodded. "We need to stay in touch and make sure that everybody stays safe. Clearly, these conditions are treacherous, to say the least."

"We'll be careful," Dillon said. "And we'll be in touch if we need you."

With one final nod to each other, he, Scout and Erin began their descent into the valley.

He paused near a particularly rocky portion of the trail and held out his hand to help Erin down. As her hand slipped into his, a shock of electricity coursed through him.

Electricity? That made no sense.

He wasn't interested in dating or anything romantic. After his engagement had ended last year, he'd written off love for good. His fiancée had decided she couldn't handle a rough patch, and she'd left him.

He quickly released Erin's hand and they continued along the trail.

Just as they reached a relatively flat area, a new sound cracked the air.

Gunfire.

"Get down!" Dillon shouted.

He turned toward Erin, hoping he wasn't too late.

Erin ducked behind a boulder as another bullet flew through the air.

Why in the world was someone shooting at them? Was it a mistake? Had they been caught in a hunter's cross fire?

No, those bullets had been purposeful, Erin realized.

Someone *wanted* to hurt them.

Was it the same person who'd abducted Bella? If so, why would this person come after Erin and Dillon now?

So much didn't make sense.

"Stay down." Dillon crouched with Scout across the trail behind another boulder.

As he said the words, another bullet split the bark on the tree in front of the boulder.

Erin pressed her lips together, determined not to scream and give the shooter any satisfaction. But her pulse pounded in her ears and she could hardly breathe.

When would this nightmare end?

She glanced at Dillon again and saw he'd withdrawn his gun.

Her pulse pounded even faster.

As he held the weapon in one hand, he pulled out a radio with his other hand and called in what was happening. Erin assumed Rick and his team were a considerable distance away at this point. She was just thankful the radio was working. Her cell phone had no service out here.

She had no idea how this situation was going to end up playing out.

"He's getting closer." Dillon slipped his radio back onto his belt and peered around the boulder. "We're going to need to move."

Erin froze. The last thing she wanted to do was to move.

She felt safe behind the rock—at least, she felt safer here than she did running.

But she needed to trust Dillon's advice right now.

As another bullet rang through the air, she realized she had no other choice.

She glanced over at Dillon again and he nodded at the trail in the distance. "That path will be our best bet. It's going to be slippery, and you'll need to watch your step."

Erin nodded, trying to process everything that was happening and keep her head in the game.

"I'm going to stay behind you," Dillon continued. "Whatever you need to do, remember that we need to keep moving."

She nodded, but her brain felt numb, almost as if she even attempted to process all this, it would shut down.

Was this what Bella had gone through also?

She held back another cry, unable to think about that.

"Let's move," Dillon said. "We don't have any more time to waste."

As he said the words, another bullet pierced the air and Erin gasped. This guy wasn't letting up.

She wanted to peer over the rock, to see who it was and where the bullets were coming from. But she didn't dare.

As Dillon ran toward her, she rose from her hiding spot and darted down the slippery trail. Her breath came out in short, wispy gasps that immediately iced in the frigid air.

The first part of the trail was manageable. But as the path turned rocky *and* icy, her shoes practically skated on the slippery surface beneath her.

She hesitated, trying to keep her footing.

As she did, she felt another bullet whiz by. She sucked in a breath.

The bullet had practically skimmed her hair. It was that close.

This guy was following them, wasn't he? Hunting them?

He wouldn't stop until they were dead.

Erin held back a cry at the thought of it.

"You can do this, Erin," Dillon said behind her. "You just need to keep moving."

She didn't have the energy to respond. Instead, she kept walking, just as Dillon told her.

The ground in this area wasn't only icy, but the rocks were uneven. The terrain would be hard to navigate on a nice day when they weren't running for their lives. Today, it almost felt impossible.

You can do it, she told herself.

Erin kept moving…and moving…and moving.

As another bullet cracked the air, she sprang into action and darted forward. As she did, her foot caught on a rock. Her ankle twisted.

She gasped as she fell to the ground.

"Erin!" Dillon muttered as he rushed toward her.

She'd sprained her ankle, hadn't she? The pain coursing through her seemed to confirm her fears.

Despair built deep inside her.

No…not now.

Dear Lord…

How was she going to get out of this one?

TEN

Dillon leaned over Erin, trying to shield her from any oncoming bullets.

But this didn't look good. The way she grasped her ankle made it clear she was in pain.

He'd known it wasn't safe to run around in these elements. But the gunman had left them little choice.

Another bullet split the air behind them before hitting the ground several feet away.

Erin gasped as her eyes lit with fear.

Dillon leaned closer. "Can you put any pressure on your ankle?"

"Let me see." With Dillon's help, Erin tried to stand, but she nearly crumpled back onto the ground as soon as any weight hit her ankle.

Dillon was going to need to think of a way to get them out of the situation—and quickly.

Footsteps sounded—closer this time.

He gripped his gun and peered around the boulder.

He didn't want to use his weapon—but he would if he had to.

When he saw a figure dressed in black raise his gun, Dillon had no choice but to raise his own weapon. He quickly lined up his target and fired.

The bullet hit the man's shoulder and he let out a groan.

Dillon had just bought them some time—he didn't know how much.

That wound would slow the man down, but wouldn't necessarily stop him.

Dillon turned back to Erin. "I'm going to put my arm around you and help you down the rest of this trail. Then we're going to find shelter. We're going to get through this, okay?"

She glanced up at him, fear welling in her gaze. She nodded anyway.

Dillon slipped his arm around her waist. He let go of Scout's leash and let the dog walk in front of them. Then he helped Erin along the treacherous path.

He still held his gun in his other hand, and he craned his neck behind him, looking for any signs of danger.

There was nothing.

Not at the moment.

He needed to find one of those old cabins he'd been thinking about earlier. A cabin would offer them shelter from the elements and protection from this gunman—for a little while, at least.

The only thing that protected them right now were the bends and curves of the trail. Plus, the gunman seemed to have slowed down.

Erin drew in deep, labored breaths as they continued down the path. Dillon had to give her props, however. She was doing her best to keep moving.

"You're doing just fine," he assured her.

She nodded, but still looked unconvinced.

Dillon stole a quick glance behind him and thought he saw a flash of movement. Was that the gunman?

It was his best guess.

He knew that Rick and Benjamin were on their way right now. But he had little hope they'd get there in time.

As Dillon glanced ahead, he thought he saw a structure in the distance.

Was that one of the cabins he vaguely remembered being out here?

Going inside might buy them a little time. Plus, the structure would give them a place to hunker down until backup arrived. Erin needed to take some weight off her ankle.

"Do you see what I see?" Hope lilted in Erin's voice.

"That's where we're headed. Do you think you can make it?"

"I'll do my best," she said. "I'm sorry that I'm slowing you down."

"It's not your fault. You were only doing what I told you."

He kept his arm around her and helped her navigate the terrain. She let out little gasps, obviously in pain. But she kept going, kept moving. Her determination was admirable.

They continued over the rocky, uneven trail. At least it was flatter here, with no cliffs now that they were closer to the valley.

As the cabin neared, Dillon observed the small structure. It was probably less than five hundred square feet. Trees grew all around it, and junk had been left around the foundation—wood and cinderblocks and buckets, even a ladder.

Scout ran ahead and climbed onto the porch, almost as if he knew exactly what Dillon wanted him to do.

Moving as quickly as possible, Dillon climbed to the front door and pulled on it.

But it was locked.

He let out a breath.

Now they had to figure out plan B.

As Scout growled at something in the distance, Dillon realized they had no time to waste.

The gunman was getting closer and they were running out of time.

"Dillon?" Erin's voice trembled despite her wishes to stay strong.

"Give me a second," he muttered as he glanced around.

She couldn't believe they'd made it this far only to find the door was locked. What were they going to do now?

Certainly the gunman was getting closer and closer. What would the man do once he was near enough to shoot them point-blank?

A chill washed through her.

She couldn't bear to think about it.

And her ankle…she wished it didn't throb like it did. She wished she could put weight on it. But every time she tried, she nearly collapsed.

"I hate to do this but…" Dillon reached down and picked up an old board from the ground.

In one motion, he thrust it into the window and broke the glass. Using the same board, he cleared the shards from around the edges. Then he turned to her.

"You're going to have to climb through this."

Erin nodded, trying to imagine how that was going to happen. But this was no time to overthink things. She just needed to move.

Using his hands, Dillon boosted her through the window. She slid inside and landed on the couch below the window. A moment later, Dillon lifted Scout inside before climbing through himself.

Once he was inside, he didn't miss a beat. He paced to the center of the room and surveyed the area. "I need to get you away from these windows."

Moving quickly, he went to the kitchen table and turned it over. He then helped Erin behind it.

She nestled between the cabinets and table with her knees pulled to her chest. Scout lay beside her, almost as if the canine sensed she needed comfort. She reached over and rubbed his fur, grateful that the dog was here now.

She heard Dillon moving in the other part of the room

and something scraped across the floor. Was he moving furniture?

A moment later, Dillon sat beside her, his gun drawn and his posture showing he was on guard.

Her heart pounded in her chest.

Would they have a shootout? She hoped that wasn't the case. But certainly Dillon was preparing for what could be the worst-case scenario.

She continued to rub Scout's head as she waited for whatever was going to unfold.

As she did, her thoughts wandered. She remembered what Dillon had said to her when they'd reached the cabin. When he'd assured her that this wasn't her fault and that she had done her best.

The words had brought such an unusual comfort—an unusual comfort that surprised even her.

Liam…he would have lashed out at her. Told her everything was her fault. Blamed the situation on her and put it all on her shoulders.

It was what Erin was used to and what she'd been prepared to hear. But hearing the compassionate and rational words from Dillon reminded her that there were still good people in this world.

Not every man was like Liam—thank goodness.

"Are you still doing okay?" Dillon glanced over at her.

Erin nodded, probably a little too quickly. "I think so. What can I do?"

"Stay low and stay by Scout. I'll do the rest."

"But what if the gunman comes…?"

He locked gazes with her. "I'm just taking each moment as it comes."

Just as he said the words, a creak sounded outside.

Was the gunman on the porch?

Fear shot through her.

What was going to happen next?

*   *   *

Dillon's muscles tensed as he waited.

The gunman was clearly here. Even Scout sensed someone's presence. The dog's fur rose.

Dillon grasped his gun as he aimed it over the table, waiting to strike.

This wasn't the way he'd wanted things to play out. All he'd wanted was to find Bella. To make sure that the girl was okay. Now, somehow, it had turned into a confrontation.

He'd been in situations like this before. He'd trained to handle himself during standoffs.

As much as he'd like to believe there would always be a positive outcome, he knew that wasn't the case. One of his colleagues had been killed in a bank robbery a few years ago. That event had reminded him of the fragility of life.

Dillon didn't intend to share his thoughts with Erin. Not now.

She was already scared and on the verge of breaking, and he didn't want to add to that.

He waited, holding his breath as he prepared himself for whatever would happen. A shadow moved across one of the windows.

He'd moved a bookshelf in front of the broken window in the hope of slowing whoever was outside. If it were Rick or another ranger, they would have most likely announced themselves already.

That only left the gunman.

Dillon glanced around the small cabin. A loft stretched above them. There were four windows total. One by the bookshelf. One the shadow had crossed. And two other smaller windows on either side of the cabin.

Those two would be difficult to get to because the deck didn't span the sides of the cabin, which would make them harder to access.

So what kind of play would this guy make next?

"Dillon?" Erin sounded breathless as she said his name.

He put a finger over his lips, motioning for her to be quiet. Instead, she began to rub Scout's fur again.

The footsteps stopped.

What exactly was the man planning now? Did he have other tricks up his sleeve?

Dillon's heart thrummed in his ear.

He thought he'd put these high-octane days behind him. But part of him would always be a cop. It almost seemed ingrained in him.

Quiet continued to stretch outside.

Dillon wished he knew what the man was doing. What he was planning. Why he was after them.

Was this person who'd abducted Bella now determined to kill Erin? Why? Why abduct Bella first?

The details just didn't make any sense to him. But he'd need to figure that out later.

A new sound filled the air.

A creak.

This time, it came from the direction of the bookcase.

Did this guy know that they had come inside?

The gunman had been close enough that it wouldn't surprise Dillon if the man had seen them, if he'd spotted the broken window. Plus, he, Erin and Scout had no doubt left tracks in the snow, which would make it easier to follow them.

Dillon gripped his gun, still pointing it in the direction of the front door and the window beside it. Still bracing himself for the worst.

He heard another noise. It almost sounded like wood scraping against the floor.

The next instant, the bookcase crashed to the ground and a bullet fired inside.

ELEVEN

Erin swallowed back a scream.

The man was here.

And he was going to kill them.

She ducked and buried her face again, pulling Scout closer.

As she did, she heard Dillon fire. The smell of ammo filled the room and more fear clutched her heart.

How were they ever going to get out of this alive?

She began to pray furiously. *Dear Lord, help us! Protect us! All I want is to find Bella. She's the only thing that's important. But I need to stay alive in order to do that.*

More bullets flew and she heard wood splintering behind her.

Dillon fired back again.

How much ammo had he brought with him? How long could he hold this guy off?

Erin had no idea. There was nowhere else to hide.

The gunfire paused for another moment.

She held her breath, anticipating the man's next move. Waiting for more gunfire.

But there was nothing.

Her heart thumped so loudly that she was certain Dillon and Scout could hear the *thump, thump, thumps*.

Scout raised his head, almost as if he were also curious about what was going on.

Had the gunman regrouped? Was he headed to another

part of the cabin to fire on them from a different angle or take them by surprise?

Dillon's thoughts seemed to mirror hers. "Stay low," he murmured.

He still grasped the gun, and his shoulders looked tight. At least if Erin was stuck out here, she was with Dillon and not alone. If she'd been on her own, she'd most certainly be dead right now.

No more gunfire sounded…not yet.

But another sound filled the air.

What was that?

The noise was faint but getting louder by the moment.

Had the man planned something else? Was more danger headed their way as they sat there unassuming?

"Dillon?" Erin's voice cracked with fear.

"I hear it, too," he muttered.

A moment later, the sound became more clear.

Whomp, whomp, whomp.

Erin released her breath.

If she wasn't mistaken, that was a helicopter.

Was it from the search and rescue mission?

Even more so, had the sound scared the gunman away?

She hoped and prayed that was the case.

Just as the thought crossed her mind, she glanced at the floor and her breath caught.

She reached forward and picked up a pink scrunchie— one that had images of a laughing cat on it.

"Erin?"

"This is Bella's."

The rescue crew had found a clearing to land in. Another ranger met them there and had taken Dillon, Scout and Erin to a local hospital to have Erin's ankle checked while the rest of the team searched the cabin for evidence and the woods for the gunman.

Had someone snatched Bella and taken her to that cabin? Or had she wandered there by herself? It was still a possibility that she hadn't been abducted; that she'd just run.

They had too many questions and not enough answers at this point.

Dillon waited outside Erin's room, Scout beside him, until the doctor okayed her to leave. Surprise stretched across her face when she stepped out and spotted him in the hallway.

"Dillon…you didn't have to wait." She leaned down and patted Scout's head. "You, either, boy."

"How did you plan on getting home then?" Dillon raised an eyebrow, trying to add some levity to the situation.

Erin let out a sheepish laugh. "Good point. But really, I feel like I've turned your life upside down, and you don't even know me."

He shrugged, trying not to make a big deal of his decision. "You didn't ask me to do any of this, so you have no reason to feel guilty. How about if I give you a ride?"

"Is your Jeep even here?" More confusion rolled over her features.

"I had one of the rangers bring it by for me while the doctor was treating you." He paused. "I hope I didn't overstep, but I also had someone tow your car from the lot. My friend Darrel is going to take it into his shop and replace the tires for you."

"That was so thoughtful of you. Thank you." She offered a grateful smile.

Dillon glanced at her foot, which was now in a walking cast. "How are you?"

"The doctor said it's just a sprain. He wrapped it, and I can put a little weight on it for now. Nothing too strenuous."

"That's good news at least." They could both use some good news considering the events of the past twenty-four hours.

"It is." Erin paused and shoved her hands into her pockets as she turned to address him. "Thank you so much for everything that you did today."

He stared at her a moment. Stared at the lovely lines of her face. Her expressive eyes. The grief that seemed to tug at her lips.

He hadn't expected to be impressed. He'd expected a grieving, panic-stricken mother.

She was those things—of course. It would be strange if she wasn't.

But she also had a quiet strength, an unwavering determination, and a fragile vulnerability. She'd been given an unfair hand. She didn't deserve the scrutiny people had put her under. She needed the community's support right now.

She might not get that support from her neighbors now, but she would get it from him.

He rubbed his throat before saying, "I'm sorry we haven't been able to find Bella yet."

Erin's lips tugged into a frown. "Me, too. The more time that passes, the less the chances are that we're going to find her. I've watched enough TV shows to know that."

She sniffled, as if holding back a sob.

He wanted to reach out to her. To offer her some comfort. To tell her everything would be okay.

Instead, he settled on saying, "Don't give up hope."

"I'm trying not to." She ran a hand across her brow. "I really am."

Dillon nodded to the elevator in the distance. "Are you ready to go?"

"I am. More than ready to go, for that matter."

They silently started toward the elevator. There wasn't much to say. Dillon was still processing exactly what had happened. It would take a while to comprehend the scope of the danger they were in.

He helped Erin and Scout into his Jeep and then cranked

the engine. He felt like there were things that he wanted to say, he just wasn't exactly sure what those things were.

Part of him wanted to apologize, even though he knew none of this was his fault. But the situation had to be frustrating for her. Now it was already later in the afternoon.

They'd have to wait until tomorrow to search again.

"Are there any updates in the search for Bella?" Erin looked up at him, her eyes glimmering with hope.

He somberly shook his head. "I wish there were. But there's no new news."

She frowned again. "I checked my phone just in case there were any messages. I didn't have service in the mountains, but part of me hoped someone had left a message. Maybe Bella. Or, if she was abducted, then from the person who took her. The silence is maddening."

Against his better judgment, he reached over and squeezed her hand. "I know this has to be really hard on you. I'm sorry."

Erin glanced at his hand as it covered hers before offering a quick smile. "Thank you."

Scout barked in the back of the Jeep.

"I think Scout agrees with me."

Her smile widened. "He's a good dog."

Dillon pulled his hand back and gripped the gearshift. Immediately, he missed the soft feel of her skin.

He cleared his throat and turned his attention to Scout instead.

"You're getting hungry, aren't you, boy?" Dillon murmured.

Erin glanced back at the dog and rubbed his head. "Do we need to stop and get him something?"

"I packed some food for him, but I *am* out now."

"Do what you need to do. Scout is a hero as far as I'm concerned."

He stole another glance at her. "Are you sure you don't mind if we swing by my place?"

"Not at all," Erin said. "I'm in no hurry to get back home. Who knows what's waiting for me there?"

Dillon let her words sink in before nodding. "Okay then. I'll make sure that this doesn't take long."

Erin's eyes lit up as she stared at Dillon's home.

The mountain farm was complete with an old homestead and several outbuildings. With snow covering the property, it looked like a winter wonderland. No neighbors were visible for miles, just trees and gentle slopes.

The property looked like a slice of heaven.

"This is amazing," Erin said as she stepped from his Jeep.

Dillon climbed out and paused beside her. "I like it. It's my place where I can get away."

"Everybody needs a place like that, don't they?"

Scout barked in reply, and Dillon and Erin shared a smile.

Dillon nodded at a building in the distance. "How about I give you a quick tour?"

"I'd love one."

As they walked, Dillon held out his arm to offer some additional support. Normally, Erin might have refused, but not this time. This time, the last thing she needed was to sprain her other ankle or hurt herself in some other way.

Plus, she liked his touch.

When he'd touched her hand in the Jeep, she'd felt her insides go still. She'd liked it a little too much.

And that realization terrified her.

She wasn't interested in dating again, and she certainly wasn't interested in dating a cop again—or a former cop.

But she had to remind herself that not every cop was like Liam, despite what her emotions told her.

They walked toward a barnlike building. She wasn't sure what to expect inside. But when Dillon opened the door, various dog kennels and barking canines greeted her in the finished, heated space.

As soon as he closed the door behind them, warmth surrounded Erin—a welcome relief from the brittle cold outside. Dillon released Scout from his lead and let him run free. He stopped and greeted each of the dogs in their luxury-sized runs.

"These are the dogs I train," he explained.

Erin walked down the center aisle, peering at each dog as she did. They appeared to be remarkably cared for and happy.

"They all look amazing." She paused beside a husky and rubbed the soft fur.

"They are. They're working dogs. But they enjoy what they do, and they're good at it."

Erin straightened and turned toward Dillon. "It's good to do something that you love."

"Yes, it is," he said. "Do you enjoy your job as a teacher?"

Dillon's question surprised her. He hadn't gotten personal with her. Yet, in some ways, she felt like she'd known this man much longer than she actually had.

She thought about his question a moment before answering. "I do. I love working with kids. I feel like it's my calling in life." She glanced up at him. "How about you?"

"Same here. As soon as I started training canines, I knew that this is what I should be doing."

"Do you like doing this more than you liked being a cop?"

His face instantly sobered. "Maybe. It's different. I get to help people through this job. That's what I like most about it."

She smiled. "That makes sense. Now, let me meet these guys."

For the next half hour, Dillon took her kennel by kennel and introduced her to the various dogs inside. She rubbed each of their heads and talked to them for a few minutes.

This place seemed like a fantasy getaway to her. She couldn't even imagine what it would be like to live here. Bella would love this.

Her daughter loved animals even more than Erin did. In fact, she'd been asking lately if they could get a dog, but Erin had told her not now. With Erin teaching eight hours a day and having to drive forty-minutes to and from work, it just wouldn't be possible to give a dog the attention it would need.

Dillon paused once they reached the other side of the building and pointed to the outside door behind him. "Listen, do you mind if I run inside a moment?"

"Not at all."

As they stepped toward the door, it suddenly opened and a shadowy figure stood there.

Erin gasped and stepped back.

Was it the gunman? Had he returned to finish what he'd started earlier?

TWELVE

"Carson," Dillon said.

He instinctively felt Erin's fear and pushed her behind him.

But it was just his nephew.

As Carson stepped into the light, his features came into view. The boy was seventeen, with thick, dark hair and an easy smile.

"Erin, this is my nephew, Carson. Carson, this is Erin Lansing. Carson helps me take care of the dogs, especially when I'm gone like I have been."

Erin's hand went over her heart as if it still pounded faster than necessary after Carson's surprise appearance. "Of course. It's great to meet you."

Carson nodded at her. "Same here. Any success today looking for that girl?"

"Unfortunately, no," Dillon said. "But it's Erin's daughter who's missing."

Dillon knew he needed to put that information out there before Carson asked any questions that might come across as insensitive.

Carson's face instantly stilled with reverence. "I'm really sorry to hear about your daughter, ma'am."

"Thank you," Erin said. "I appreciate that."

"Wait…your last name is Lansing?" Carson asked. "Is your daughter Bella?"

A knot formed between Erin's eyes. "She is. You know her?"

"Not well, but we've met a few times. Have you talked to Grayson yet?" Carson stared at her, looking genuinely curious.

"Who's Grayson?" The knot on Erin's brow became more defined.

Carson's eyes widened as if he realized he'd said something he shouldn't have. He stepped back, almost as if he wanted to snatch his words back. He opened his mouth but quickly shut it again.

"Carson, who is Grayson?" Dillon repeated.

"I'm sorry, I thought you knew." Carson swallowed hard, his Adam's apple bobbing up and down.

"Knew what?" Erin's voice cracked with emotion, as if she were on the brink of tears.

"I've seen Bella around a few times at some football games between my school and hers. She's been hanging out with Grayson Davis."

Dillon sucked in a breath. He knew who Grayson Davis was. The whole family was trouble.

"What aren't you telling me?" Erin stared at Dillon, questions haunting her eyes.

"It's probably nothing." Dillon didn't want to alarm Erin for no reason. "I just know that Grayson's dad and grandfather—and even a couple of uncles—have been in prison before."

Erin's face seemed to fall with disappointment, and she squeezed the skin between her eyes. "What?"

He resisted the urge to reach out and try to comfort her again. That might be too much, too fast. "That doesn't mean he has anything to do with this. But you had no idea?"

She swung her head back and forth. "No, I even asked Bella if she liked anyone. She rolled her eyes and stared and told me there was no one."

"It's not unusual for teens to want to keep information like this from their parents," Dillon said before looking back at Carson. "Is there anything else that you know?"

"No, just that she was hanging out with Grayson." Carson shrugged. "I'm sorry I can't be more help."

"You're doing just fine, Carson," Dillon said. "But if you hear anything else, please let us know."

"Of course. Whatever I can do." The boy nodded, his gaze unwavering and assuring them he'd keep his promise.

"Let's get you inside." Dillon put his hand on Erin's back to guide her toward the door. "Then we'll figure out our next plan of action."

Erin followed Dillon into his home, yet he couldn't help but note that her eyes looked determined. He knew exactly what she was thinking. She wanted to go talk to Grayson Davis herself.

That could turn into an ugly situation.

They desperately needed answers before Erin did something she might regret.

How could Bella have been seeing someone and not told her? When had this happened? When had Erin's relationship with her daughter turned from easygoing and conversational to a bond riddled with secrets?

The questions wouldn't stop pounding inside her head until finally an ache formed at her temples.

She wanted her daughter back. She wanted her *old* daughter back. She wanted to turn back time and somehow erase this mess, this heartache.

"I know what you're thinking." Dillon's voice pulled her from her thoughts.

She jerked her head up as he stepped into the kitchen from the back hallway.

She leaned her hip against the counter there and waited. Normally, she'd be curious about his house or pictures on the fridge or the slight scent of evergreen permeating the air. But right now she could only think about Bella.

Erin stared up at Dillon. He'd claimed to know what she was thinking. "What's that?"

His gaze locked with hers. "That you want to talk to Grayson."

She crossed her arms, feeling a wave of defensiveness. "Can you blame me?"

Dillon shook his head, his perceptive eyes warm with compassion—and absent of the judgment she'd come to expect.

"Not at all," he murmured. "I'd say we should leave it to the police, but I'm beginning to think that's not such a great idea."

Erin released a breath she hadn't even realized she'd been holding. It felt so good to have someone who actually sounded like he was on her side.

"I'm going to leave Scout here with Carson, so he can rest. But if you'd like to go speak to Grayson, I'd like to go with you."

"You would do that for me?" Surprise lilted her voice.

"Of course. I'd want someone to do this for me if I were in your shoes."

Gratitude rushed through her, so warm and all-encompassing, it nearly turned her muscles into jelly. "I know I've said this before, but you've been a godsend, Dillon. Thank you so much for everything that you've been doing."

A compassionate smile pulled at his lips and his gaze softened. "It's no problem."

A few minutes later, they were back in his Jeep and heading down the road. Part of Erin felt like they'd been doing this together forever.

But it had only been a day since Dillon had rescued her from the cliff. Since then, so much had happened. Enough to fill a lifetime it seemed.

She just wanted this to be over with. She wanted to find Bella and try to sleep at night.

Being a single parent wasn't an easy task, but it was worth it. She would make whatever sacrifices necessary for Bella. But the past couple of years hadn't been a cakewalk, especially with Liam's disappearance and the cloud of doubt that had been hanging over Erin since then.

A few minutes later, they pulled up to Grayson Davis's house.

The place was an old two-story house with broken blue siding, a busted window, and piles of junk lining the porch and yard. It wasn't the nicest-looking place, not that it mattered to Erin. But she was glad Dillon was with her in case things turned ugly. She didn't know much about this family, but from the brief snippets she'd heard, the Davises could get rowdy.

Dillon glanced at her before offering an affirmative nod. "Let's do this."

They climbed out and Erin hobbled toward the door.

Before they even climbed the porch steps, the front door opened and a man stepped out, holding a shotgun.

"What do you think you're doing here?" he sneered as he stared them down.

Erin sucked in a breath as she observed the man. Probably in his sixties. Salt-and-pepper beard. Dirty button-up shirt. Old jeans. Hair that could use a good wash.

Then her gaze went back to his gun.

Was he planning to pull the trigger on them?

"Burt Davis," Dillon said. "Do you remember me?"

The man remained silent for several seconds until finally his eyes lit. "You were that cop who helped me find my Emmaline when she wandered off."

Burt's wife had dementia and was known to wander. Dillon and Scout had helped track her down when she'd once gone missing. They'd found her on the edge of a nearby lake. She'd been about to take a swim, despite the winter weather. If they hadn't found her when they had, she would have perished in that water.

"That's me."

Erin listened to every word Burt said, surprised at this side of Dillon. Not that he hadn't seemed heroic already. But hearing about him from someone else offered a different perspective—an affirmation.

Her respect for the man continued to grow.

Burt's shoulders softened. "What brings you by now?"

"We were actually hoping that we could talk to your grandson, Grayson," Dillon said.

Burt's eyes narrowed, not with anger but with what appeared to be resignation. "What's my boy done now?"

"Probably nothing," Dillon said. "Did you hear about the girl who went missing?"

He stared at Dillon, wariness in his gaze. "I did hear something about her while I was in town. What about her?"

"We heard Bella and Grayson were friends, and we're hoping he might have some information that will help us find her." Dillon kept his voice level and even.

"Is that right?" Burt stared at Dillon a moment, that skeptical look still in his gaze.

The man remained silent, chewing on something. Maybe bubble gum. Maybe tobacco. She wasn't sure.

But enough time passed that Erin was certain Burt was going to refuse to let them talk to his grandson.

Despair tried to well inside her again. Had all this been for nothing?

Finally, the man nodded and twisted his head behind him. "Grayson! Get down here. You have someone here who wants to talk to you."

Erin's lungs nearly froze. He was going to let them talk to Grayson!

Thank you, Jesus!

She couldn't wait to hear if Grayson had additional information to offer about Bella. She prayed that was what would happen, and that this lead might be the one that cracked the case in Bella's disappearance wide open.

Dillon sat at the dining room table. Erin sat beside him and Grayson hunched in his seat across from them. Grayson's granddad stood behind him with his arms crossed and his eyes narrowed, almost as if he dared Grayson to say something he didn't approve of.

Mountains of leftover meals and trash littered the table between them. With it was the scent of rot mixed with old socks and recently cooked collard greens.

Dillon stared at the boy.

Grayson Davis was sixteen with blond hair that he kept cut short. His build was stocky enough that he could play football. He had a thin stubble on his chin, and his gaze focused on the table instead of making eye contact with anyone in the room.

"Thanks for meeting with us," Dillon started, keeping his voice pleasant.

There was no need to start this conversation as if they were enemies. As they sat there, Dillon felt Erin's nerves in her quick movements and shallow breaths.

Thankfully, she was letting him take the lead right now. They didn't want to spook the boy and make him go silent.

"What's going on?" Grayson swallowed hard, his eyes shifting from Dillon to Erin then back to Dillon again.

"We understand that you are friends with Bella Lansing," Dillon said.

Grayson rubbed his hands on his jeans and nodded. "Yeah, we talk."

"When was the last time you talked to her?"

Grayson ran a hand through his hair. "I'm not sure. Maybe two days ago."

Dillon watched the boy carefully, looking for any signs of deceit. "You are aware that she's missing, right?"

Grayson nodded. "I know. I heard. I keep hoping to hear that she has been found."

"Why haven't you come forward to the police yet if the two of you were friends?"

Grayson sighed. "I don't know. I guess because I didn't have anything to tell them. I didn't have anything to offer. Plus, with my family's reputation, I was afraid that they would look at me as a suspect."

"You care about Bella, don't you?" Erin's voice sounded calm and soothing.

Grayson stared at her for a moment before nodding. "Yeah, I do. But she knew you wouldn't approve."

Erin sucked in a breath, his words seeming to shock her. "Is that what she told you?"

"She said that she's not allowed to date. But the two of us really like each other."

"Did she tell you anything that might have indicated that she was in danger?" Dillon asked.

Grayson shifted again, rubbing his hands across his jeans as if he were nervous.

He definitely knew something. The trick would be getting him to share.

"I don't know."

Dillon leaned toward him, clearly about to drive home a point. "Grayson, if there's anything you know, it's important you tell us. We need to find her, and you may know something that will help us do that. You're not in trouble. We are just looking for information."

Grayson remained quiet but sweat had beaded across his forehead.

"You can trust him," Burt said. "Dillon is one of the good guys."

Grayson looked at his granddad and nodded, his eyes still darting all over the place as if he were nervous.

Finally, he looked back at Dillon and Erin. "The day before she went missing, Bella told me she felt like she was being watched."

Erin sucked in a breath beside him. "What else did she say?"

Grayson shrugged. "Not much. She tried to laugh it off and say she was being paranoid. She talked about how much people in this town hated you guys. I think she assumed it was probably just somebody from Liam's side of the family."

Dillon made a note of the fact that Grayson had said Liam instead of her dad. How exactly did Bella view Liam Lansing? He'd ask Erin later.

"No one approached her or did anything?" Dillon continued to press. "Was it just a feeling or was there any action to justify it?"

Grayson rubbed his throat again. "She said she felt someone watching her a couple of times, but she never saw anyone nearby. If anything else happened, Bella didn't tell me."

"Do the two of you text or email each other?" Erin asked.

Grayson nodded, his eyes misting. "I've been trying to talk to her since she left for school two days ago. But I haven't heard back. That's when I knew something was wrong."

Grayson's voice cracked and he wiped beneath his eyes.

He was fighting tears, wasn't he? He really cared about Bella. That was obvious.

Dillon nodded and glanced at Erin. "Anything else?"

Erin shook her head, her eyes lined with grief. "No, but thank you for sharing what you did, Grayson. I'm glad that my daughter has a friend like you."

Relief seemed to fill his gaze at Erin's approval. "I'll let you know if I hear anything else."

As they started toward the door, Burt joined them.

He leaned close to Erin and whispered, "If I were you, I would have killed Liam, too."

Erin froze and glanced at the man, alarm racing through her gaze. "I didn't kill him."

His expression remained unapologetic. "I wouldn't blame you if you did. I had a couple of encounters with him. That man thought he was above the law."

"Yes, he did." Erin's words sounded stiff, as if she were hesitant to agree.

"But if you didn't kill him, then my bets are on the Bradshaws." Burt nodded as if confident of his statement.

Dillon's mind raced. The Bradshaws were a deeply networked family in this area who had drug connections. Dillon suspected they grew pot and sold it, but police were still trying to prove it. Basically, they were trouble, and everyone in these parts knew it.

Dillon put his hand on Erin's arm. He had to get her out of here. Not only did they need to process everything they'd just learned, he could tell she was uncomfortable with where this conversation was going.

"Thank you again for your help," he told Burt and Grayson.

But just as they stepped out the door, a truck drove past. The passenger leaned out the window, his baseball cap pulled down low.

As they watched, the man tossed something from the window.

The next instant, the front yard exploded in flames.

THIRTEEN

"Get down!" Dillon yelled.

The next thing Erin knew, he threw her on the ground and his body covered hers.

An explosion sounded in the front yard before flames filled the air along with the scent of smoke.

Erin's mind could hardly keep up. What had just happened?

She lifted her head and saw fire spreading across the grass in the front yard. She heard a truck squealing away.

The flames appeared to be contained to a small patch of grass. Leftover snow had prevented the fire from spreading.

That was good news.

But it could have turned out a lot differently if she and Dillon had taken just a few steps into the yard.

Dillon rolled off her and also glanced back. "Is everyone okay?"

Burt and Grayson nodded, still looking like they were in shock as they stood inside the doorway.

"What just happened?" Erin muttered.

Dillon rose to his feet before reaching down and helping Erin stand. She brushed imaginary dust from her jeans, mostly so she could forget the tingling feeling she'd felt when her hand touched Dillon's.

She especially didn't trust any tingly feelings or mini firework explosions.

But something about Dillon felt different. Still, she'd be wise to remind herself to keep her distance right now.

"My guess is that it was a bottle bomb." As Dillon scowled at the scene outside, he pulled his phone out and called the police.

"Do you really feel like they'll do anything?" she asked after he ended his call.

"It's hard to say. But we do need to report it." He knew what she was thinking: that the police here weren't reliable anyway.

"Did anybody recognize that truck?" Erin glanced around the room, but everybody shook their head.

"At least I got a partial of the plates," Dillon said. "But everything happened so fast that I wasn't able to memorize the whole thing."

She shook her head and shivered as the explosion replayed in her mind.

Who would be behind this? The same person who took Bella?

Again, nothing made sense. This whole thing was a nightmare she couldn't seem to wake up from.

She glanced at the front yard again and saw that the flames were gone, leaving smoke, a wide black circle in the lawn, and a few scraps from the bomb itself.

If Erin had to guess, the person who'd done this probably hadn't wanted to kill them. They'd simply wanted to send a message.

What was that message? Was it that Erin wasn't welcome here in Boone's Hollow? That they still thought she'd had something to do with one of these crimes?

It was hard to say. A bad feeling lingered in her gut.

The feeling only worsened when she saw Chief Blackstone pull up several minutes later.

Would he still give her a hard time? Would he ever be on her side, be someone she felt as if she could trust?

She had no idea.

But it was going to take all of her energy and mental strength to get through this next conversation.

"I'll run the plates and see if we get any hits." Chief Blackstone glanced in the distance at Burt before looking back at Dillon.

They all stood in the driveway outside. Three police cars had arrived on scene, and the other officers were collecting evidence and questioning people.

"What are you guys doing here anyway?" Chief Blackstone asked.

"Can't we just pay a friendly visit to some of the town folk?" Dillon didn't want to give this man any more details than he had to.

For some reason, he'd never really liked Blackstone, but his respect had been decreasing steadily ever since this investigation into Bella's disappearance started.

"It's just that you all don't seem like the type who'd hang out with each other." The chief spoke slowly, as if he were purposefully choosing each word. "Unless maybe you're conspiring together."

Dillon felt irritation prickle his skin. "Chief, respectfully, you know that Erin had nothing to do with Bella's disappearance. When you look at all the pieces of the puzzle, it doesn't make sense that she'd do something like this. Besides, how would you explain all the threats that have been made toward her if that was the case?"

Blackstone shrugged. "I like to look at every angle. Maybe she set this up so she wouldn't look guilty."

"What possible reason could she have for wanting to make her daughter disappear?" He didn't bother to keep the exasperation from his voice.

"That's an excellent question. But I heard her girl was giving her a hard time lately. Someone who killed her own husband might be willing and able to do the same to her daughter, too."

Dillon felt Erin tense beside him. Her uptight body language and quick breathing clearly indicated she could pounce at any minute. He didn't want to put her in a position that would only make her look more guilty.

He gently touched her arm, silently encouraging her to remain quiet.

He understood her anger. He was angry also.

"You know that doesn't make sense." Dillon kept his voice even and diplomatic—for the time being, at least. "I know Liam was your friend and that you need to figure out what happened to him. But you need to expand your pool of suspects outside of Erin."

Blackstone narrowed his eyes and pressed his lips together, not bothering to hide his aggravation. "It sounds like she's got you under her thumb."

"I'm just looking at the evidence. Objectively. That's what you should be doing, too."

Chief Blackstone scowled and took a step back. "You best watch your tone if you want to get any more jobs around here."

Dillon heard the underlying threat in the man's voice, but Dillon wasn't one to be deterred. His sense of right and wrong was stronger than any threats that could be made against him.

Dillon crossed his arms, unfazed by the chief—and determined to let the man know that. "By the way, any updates on that body that we found in the woods?"

"Not yet," the chief said. "It's still with the medical examiner. In the meantime, we'll look into what happened here tonight. But, based on the lack of evidence, I doubt we're going to figure out who threw this bomb. It was probably just some kids trying to play an innocent prank."

"Bombs are never an innocent prank." Dillon's voice hardened.

"Then maybe this isn't about you guys. Maybe this is about those two." Blackstone nodded toward Burt and Grayson as they stood near the garage and listened. "They like to hang out with unsavory types."

"You don't know what you're talking about," Burt called, his gaze daring the chief to defy him.

Dillon turned back to the chief, not liking how this conversation had gone. "Chief Blackstone, I'd appreciate you looking into this matter and taking it seriously."

The man's eyes narrowed. "Need I remind you that I don't take orders from you?"

"Don't be that guy, Chief Blackstone."

The chief stared at Dillon a moment before frowning and walking back to his car.

Dillon hoped that he had laid enough pressure on him that the chief might think twice about how he proceeded. But given the chief's nature, that wasn't a sure thing.

Erin stared out the window, replaying everything that had happened, starting with that conversation with Chief Blackstone.

How could the man be so rude? Such a jerk? And how had he gotten away with it for so long?

She believed in cops. Believed that they did good work. She hated the fact that a couple of bad ones could make all cops look bad, even when that wasn't the case.

But once certain people got into positions of power, like Blackstone had, it felt nearly impossible to change that. To oust them from their positions. And because that was the case, the power trips just seem to keep growing.

Chief Blackstone's was the biggest one of all right now.

"Listen, I know you don't know me that well," Dillon started beside her. "I don't want this to sound weird. But

I don't think you should stay at your place by yourself tonight."

Erin froze at Dillon's words. She knew exactly what he was getting at.

Her place wasn't safe.

She wasn't safe.

Erin didn't want to stay by herself, either. But short of leaving town to go stay with family, she didn't have many options. There was no way she would leave this area with Bella still missing.

Dillon had stayed on her couch last night, but she couldn't ask him to do that again. It was too much.

"I'm sure I'll be fine." She didn't sound convincing, even to her own ears.

"How would you feel about sleeping in the spare bedroom at my place? Carson and I will be there, along with all the dogs, of course. You'd have your own space and most people wouldn't even know that you're staying out there."

He raised a good point. Everybody would assume she was staying at her place. Maybe that would allow her to get some rest so she could start fresh the next morning.

"Are you sure you really don't mind? You're going deeper and deeper with me, and I'm afraid that it's going to ruin things for you here in this town."

He ducked his head until they were eye to eye. "Erin, I know it probably feels like everybody here hates you, but I have a hard time believing that's true. Anybody who knows you can clearly see you have a good heart. That you're a good person. Just because a few people—a few loud people—bad-mouth you, don't think they speak for everyone."

Something about his words caused her cheeks to warm. He sounded so sincere, so much like he was speaking the truth. She hadn't expected to crave hearing an affirmation like that. His words brought a strange sense of comfort to her.

"Thank you." Her throat burned as the words left her lips. "I really appreciate that. If you don't mind, I think I will take you up on your offer. I'd feel better if I wasn't at that house by myself tonight."

"Let me just run you past your place so you can pick up a couple of things then."

A few minutes later, she'd packed a small overnight bag and was back in the Jeep with Dillon and Scout. They headed back to his place, another day coming to an end.

Another day without Bella.

Erin continued to pray that her daughter was safe and unharmed. But every day, her prayers felt more and more frail, like she was losing hope that her requests would actually be answered in the way she wanted.

She didn't want to lose faith.

But it was becoming more and more of a struggle.

FOURTEEN

Dillon got Erin settled in the spare bedroom at his house before returning to the living area and starting on some dinner.

He was famished. He'd grabbed a quick sandwich while at the hospital earlier. But certainly Erin was hungry also. Today's events had made him build up an appetite.

He didn't have much to eat, but he could throw together some chicken-and-potato stew. It was one of his go-to staples, and it sounded especially good on such a cold day.

Erin emerged from her room a few minutes later with her hair wet and wearing fresh clothes.

He had to drag his gaze away from her.

He hadn't expected that reaction.

He'd known from the moment he'd met Erin that she was an attractive woman. A very attractive woman. The more he'd gotten to know her, the more he'd been impressed with her character as well.

He'd meant what he had told her earlier. Anybody who had the privilege of actually getting to know Erin had to know she couldn't be responsible for the events that had happened. It was a shame she'd been painted in such a negative light.

He continued to stir his stew as she sat across from him at the breakfast bar. "Dinner?"

"I figured that we both needed to eat," Dillon said. "Carson, too."

She pushed a wet strand of hair behind her ear.

"Thank you for everything you've done." Her voice sounded raw—but sincere—as she said the words.

"I'm just sorry I haven't been able to do more. I want to find Bella also." He bit down, meaning what he'd said. He wasn't going to feel any peace until they had some answers.

"Where do you even think she is right now?" Erin asked. "Do you think she's in the woods? Or did she simply start in the woods? Did she go there to meet somebody who ended up snatching her? If that's the case, where did this person take her?"

"I wish I had those answers for you. But I do know that people have cabins out in those woods where they can live off the land and never be seen. When I was a cop, we assisted park rangers with a search and rescue mission when this woman thought her husband had disappeared. Turned out that instead of divorcing her, he'd run away. He'd lived off-grid for three years before anyone ever found him."

"Wow," Erin muttered. "What did you think when Burt said that the Bradshaws could be responsible? Are you familiar with them?"

"I've heard of them. A lot of people suspect they have a drug enterprise going on in their home. But without any evidence, the police haven't been able to act."

"I see."

Dillon cast another glance at her. "Did you ever suspect that your husband got himself too deeply into a case and disappeared because somebody wanted to silence him or exact revenge?"

"I've tried to think of every angle. But the circumstances of it all were just strange—as was the timing. Especially considering it happened right after a huge fight we had out in public."

"Who initiated the fight?"

"He did. He thought I was seeing someone else, and he told me I shouldn't do that."

"He was the jealous type, huh?"

She frowned and nodded. "To the extreme. We had Officer Hollins over once, and he accused me of flirting with him when I laughed at one of his jokes."

"That doesn't sound healthy."

"It wasn't. All of our fights seemed to go back to him wanting to control me. When things got physical…that's when I knew I had to get out. I couldn't put Bella through that. I couldn't let her see the way he treated me and think that it was okay."

"Leaving him sounds like it was the right thing. I'm sure it also took a certain amount of bravery."

She shrugged. "I don't know about that. But I felt like a burden had been lifted after I'd made the choice. He didn't make it easy on me, unfortunately."

"I can imagine."

Dillon tried to store away every detail just in case it became important later.

He stirred the stew one more time and realized it was close to being done. He was about to grab some bowls when suddenly Scout stood and growled at the front door.

Dillon abandoned his food and pulled his gun out instead.

After everything that had happened, he couldn't take any chances.

"Stay back," Dillon said. "Let me make sure that trouble hasn't found us again."

Erin backed deeper into the kitchen.

Not again.

It just didn't make any sense. Why couldn't this person leave her alone?

She watched as Dillon crept to the window and peered

out. Scout stood at his side, on guard and ready to act at the first command.

"Do you see anything?" Her voice trembled as the words left her lips.

"There's a flashlight in the woods," he said.

She sucked in a breath. Somebody really was out there. Of course.

Scout didn't seem like the type of dog who would react otherwise.

Why would someone be back there? What was this person's plan?

Dillon turned to her, his muscles tight and drawn, as if he were ready to act. The hardness in his eyes surprised her. This whole situation was beginning to get to him as well, wasn't it?

"I'm going to go check it out," he announced.

Alarm raced through her at the thought of him being out there with this person. "Dillon...you could be hurt."

"This needs to end," he said. "Somebody is stalking and threatening you. The situation is bad enough without adding those elements to it."

She couldn't argue with that statement. But... "I don't want you getting hurt. Too many people have already been hurt."

His determined—and undeterred—gaze met hers. "I'll be careful. I'm going to go out the back door and sneak around the other side of the woods to see if I can take this guy by surprise."

"Do you really think that will work?"

"I don't know, but it's worth giving it a shot." He paused. "Carson!"

A few minutes later, his nephew appeared from upstairs. "Yes?"

"I need you to stay here with Erin and keep an eye on her. You know where the guns are, right?"

Carson stood beside Erin and nodded. "I do. What's going on?"

"Somebody is outside, and I need to figure out who."

Carson stiffened. "Understood. Be safe."

"Always." Dillon nodded at Erin, giving her some type of silent reassurance that everything would be okay.

She wished she felt as confident. But she didn't. Not with so much on the line right now.

Carson went to the closet and opened a safe inside. He pulled out a gun and paced toward the window. He remained there, watching everything outside.

"Do you still see somebody out there?" Erin asked.

He didn't answer for a moment as he stared outside. "Yes, somebody with a flashlight is out there. I can see them moving."

She rubbed her throat, fighting worst-case scenarios.

"My uncle knows these woods better than anybody." Carson seemed to sense her anxiety, to read her mind. "He was a good cop. Competent. He won't put himself in unnecessary danger."

Erin closed her eyes and began lifting prayers. She hoped that Carson was right.

Because her feelings for the man had apparently grown much more quickly than she had ever imagined possible.

Dillon moved carefully through the woods. He couldn't risk giving away his presence. Not if he wanted to take this person by surprise.

And that was exactly what he wanted to do.

He'd meant what he'd said inside. It was time to put an end to this. This trauma had gone on for far too long.

Besides, if the person in the woods was the same person who'd taken Bella, then Dillon needed to sit him down and demand answers.

None of this made sense to him. None of these games.

Now it was time to find some answers.

He slipped between the trees, watching his every step. If he stepped on one twig wrong, it could mess up everything.

He quietly walked through the woods at the back of the property, skirting the edge of those woods and carefully remaining out of sight.

The person he'd spotted had been lurking near the front of his property. The flashlight Dillon had seen had indicated movement.

Was this person looking for a good vantage point to spy on Erin? Or was the reason someone was out here even more deadly? Perhaps the intruder was searching for the best position to pull the trigger.

Anger burned through Dillon's blood at the thought.

Erin didn't deserve to go through this. If Dillon could do anything to stop it, he would. It was the same reason that he was determined to leave in the morning and to begin search efforts for Bella again. If the girl was out in the Pisgah National Forest, Dillon wanted to find her.

He gripped his gun, his muscles tense as he wondered exactly how this would play out. Though he'd given up being a cop, another part of him would always be a cop. Would always want to look out for people who needed help. To be a voice for the voiceless.

He continued forward, snow crunching beneath his boots. As the temperature dropped, everything was becoming icy again. The threadbare trees didn't allow much cover. But he was deep enough in the forest that he could maintain his distance.

He rounded the curve of the trees, headed toward the front of the house where he had seen the light.

As he did, he paused.

Where had the trespasser gone? Enough time had passed that the person could have walked deeper into the woods or closer to the driveway. Dillon couldn't afford to walk into a situation not knowing what was happening around him.

He held his breath as he waited, watching for that flashlight he'd spotted earlier. Listening for any telltale footsteps.

If he'd wanted to risk it, he could have turned on his own flashlight and shone it on the ground to search for any footprints. But that was a risk he couldn't afford to take. He couldn't give away his presence.

He continued to wait and listen.

Still nothing.

As he waited, he wondered how the person had even gotten here without his noticing a vehicle.

If he had to guess, the intruder had probably parked on the side of the road and then cut through the woods.

Dillon would check that out later, if necessary.

For now, maybe the man had moved farther away.

Dillon crept forward a few more steps, trying to find a different vantage point.

But as he did, a stick cracked behind him.

The next thing he knew, something hard came down over his head and everything began to spin.

FIFTEEN

Erin stood at the window and stared out the crack between the curtain and the wall. She knew that Dillon wouldn't want her standing that close. Especially if bullets were to start to fly again.

Whoever was behind these threats was certainly persistent. In fact, he was relentless.

Could it be Liam? If so, where had he been hiding out the past year?

But when she remembered the body they'd found with his necklace on it, she knew that wasn't the case. That had to be Liam, right? Who else would it be?

Could Liam's family be behind everything that was happening? Or had Liam made someone mad and now this person was trying to get revenge on Liam's family as some type of ultimate payback?

Erin had no idea, but she didn't like any of this.

"Are you doing okay?" Carson stood on the other side of the window, gun in hand.

She shrugged. "I guess as well as can be expected."

"It sounds like you've gone through a lot."

"It feels like I've gone through a lot."

Carson glanced outside again before saying, "Dillon used to be one of the best cops out there, you know?"

"Is that right?" Erin really wanted to ask what happened, but she figured it wasn't her business. Maybe, if she were lucky, Dillon would tell her later.

"It seems like every cop has that one case that gets to him," Carson said, still keeping an eye on the window. "My uncle went to find a missing hiker. His team searched everywhere but didn't find him. A day after they called off the search, the man's body was discovered within a half-mile radius of where my uncle searched. He's beat himself up over it ever since."

Erin soaked in each new detail, a better picture of Dillon forming in her head. "Certainly it wasn't his fault. He seems very thorough."

"He would have probably realized that eventually," Carson said. "But the family of the hiker who died began to attack my uncle. They sued the police department, and Dillon became the poster child of botched rescue operations. He was the face that they put with their grievances."

She let out a small gasp. "That couldn't have been easy."

"It wasn't. He was engaged at the time, but his fiancée couldn't handle the pressure. She broke things off with him. Talk about a hard time."

Erin shook her head, unable to understand how somebody could leave someone they loved in the midst of turmoil. "I can only imagine how difficult that had to be for him."

Carson kept one eye on the front yard as he talked. "It definitely changed him. But I truly believe he's doing what he loves right now. He's really good with dogs and training them. Plus, I think that in some way it helps him to feel like he can make amends for the mistakes that he blames himself for."

The new insight into Dillon painted him in a different light.

In some ways, Erin could understand exactly where he was coming from. She had lived under the weight of accusation. It wasn't a fun place to be, and people rarely came out the same on the other side.

"If you don't mind me asking, how long have you lived with your uncle?"

"Two years," he said. "He's not really my uncle, but he's my father's best friend. My mom left us when I was thirteen and my dad started drinking pretty heavily. He needed help. Uncle Dillon paid to send him to rehab. He's still trying to get his life back together, to be honest. Uncle Dillon said I could stay here for as long as necessary."

"I'm sorry to hear about all that, but I'm glad you have someone like Dillon in your life." Again, her perspective on Dillon changed—in a good way.

He was a good man. It wasn't just a mask he wore around her.

Her admiration for the man grew.

Erin's gaze went back to the window, and she wondered what was happening outside. She was going to give Dillon five more minutes. Then she would push past Carson and go check on Dillon herself.

What if something was wrong? What if he needed them?

He had done so much for her. There was no way Erin was going to leave him in his time of need, especially since she was the source of all this trouble.

She crossed her arms over her chest and waited.

Five minutes.

That was all.

Then she was going to have to take action.

Just as Dillon felt everything spinning around him, a shock of adrenaline burst through him and he sprang into action.

He swirled around and saw a man in a black mask standing in front of him with a shovel in his hands.

He braced himself for a fight before muttering, "I don't think so."

As the man swung the shovel at him again, Dillon

ducked. His shoulder caught the masked man in the gut, and they crashed to the ground.

As another wave of nausea rushed over Dillon, the man flipped him over. The guy's fist collided with Dillon's jaw, and pain rippled through him.

But Dillon still had more fight in him left. This was far from over.

He grabbed the guy and shoved him backward. Dillon's hand went to the man's throat as he pinned the intruder to the ground.

The man grunted and thrashed beneath him. Whoever he was, he was strong, and Dillon had to use all in his energy to keep the man pinned.

If only Dillon could see who was on the other side of that mask. But if he shifted his weight to pull it off, he feared the guy would take advantage of his disheveled state and get the upper hand.

"Where is Bella?" Dillon demanded.

The trespasser grunted.

In one motion, the man shoved Dillon off and burst to his feet.

Dillon stood just in time.

With his hands in front of him, the man rammed Dillon into the tree.

His head spun.

Dillon straightened to go after the man again, but before he could, the man took off in a run.

Dillon staggered forward, still not ready to give up. But as everything swirled around him, he realized he wasn't going to make it if he chased this guy.

That blow to his head was making him light-headed and nauseous.

He started to take one more step forward just out of stubborn determination.

As he did, he crumpled to the ground.

He'd been so close to finding answers. So close.

But he'd let the man get away.

"I'm going out there." Erin stepped toward the door.

Carson moved in front of her, blocking her path. "I can't let you do that. I promised my uncle that I wouldn't."

"He might need our help."

"He can handle himself." Carson's voice contained full confidence in his words.

"He's been out there too long. What if he's hurt?" Her voice trembled with emotion. She was honestly worried about Dillon.

Something flashed in Carson's gaze. Was that fear? The realization that she might be right?

"You stay in here." Carson's voice hardened with surprising maturity. "I'll check."

"I'm going with you," Erin insisted. "There's no way I'm letting a teenager go out there and get hurt on my account."

He stared at her a moment before marching to the closet. He pulled out another gun and handed it to her. "Do you know how to handle one of these?"

She stared at the small handgun and nodded, her throat suddenly feeling dry. "I do."

"Good. Bring it with you. It's fully loaded. Use it if you need to."

A shiver of apprehension raced down her spine. Erin really prayed that she didn't have to use this. But if it came down to Dillon's life or someone else's?

She knew that she had to protect these people who had protected her. She would aim for a shoulder or a knee or something nonlethal. She could do this.

As she walked with Carson toward the back door, another surge of apprehension rippled up her spine. She really had no idea what she was doing right now. She only knew she had to help Dillon.

"We're going to skirt around the backside of the property, just like my uncle did," Carson said. "We don't want to make ourselves easy targets for this guy if he's still out there."

Erin nodded and gripped the gun in both hands.

With one more nod from Carson, they both stepped outside into the dark, tranquil night. She scanned everything around her, looking for a sign of anything that might have happened. Dark woods stared back at her, looking deceitfully peaceful with the white snow covering the branches and ground.

Everything seemed still and quiet.

Carson motioned for her to follow, and they took off in a run toward the trees. Once they reached the cover of the woods, they followed a small path around the edge of the property.

The temperature had dipped close to zero, and it felt every bit like it. Snow crunched beneath her feet no matter how hard she tried to stay quiet. Her nose already felt numb, as did her fingers.

But those were the least of her concerns. Dillon was her main focus right now.

As they neared the area where they'd seen the flashlight, Carson put a finger over his lips, motioning for her to be quiet. They slowed their steps as they crept forward.

Erin kept her gaze on everything around her, looking for any signs of trouble.

She saw nothing. No one. No lights. Nor did she hear anything.

Exactly what had gone on out here?

What if that man had grabbed Dillon just like someone had grabbed Bella?

A sick feeling gurgled in Erin's gut at the thought of it.

She continued forward and, with every step, the tension in her back muscles only increased.

Erin had hoped they would have found Dillon by now. That he would have offered an explanation for what was taking so long and then ushered them back into the warmth and safety of the house, giving them a good lecture in the process.

But that wasn't the case.

Her thoughts on Dillon, Erin nearly collided into Carson's back. He let out a breath in front of her, and that's when she knew that something was wrong.

She peered around him and spotted Dillon on the ground. Not moving.

Alarm raced through her. Was he dead?

Oh, God. Please...no!

Dillon startled when he heard a noise above him. But as he tried to sit up, pain shot through his skull.

At once, everything rushed back to him.

The intruder in the woods. The one who'd hit him with a shovel. Who'd pushed him into the tree. Had ultimately gotten away.

Or had he?

Dillon felt the shadow over him and raised his fists, ready to fight.

"Wait! It's just us, Dillon."

Slowly, Carson's face came into view. Erin stood beside him, worry in her gaze as she looked down at him.

Dillon scowled as he rubbed the back of his head. "What are you guys doing out here? I told you to stay inside."

"We came to check on you," Carson said. "It looks like it's a good thing we did."

He rubbed the back of his head again, wishing that it didn't hurt as badly as it did. There was no way he could pretend that he wasn't in pain. No way that he could pretend nothing had happened out here.

Carson took one of his arms and Erin the other as they helped him to his feet.

"Where's the person who did this to you?" Carson demanded, his gaze hardening with anger.

"He got away. I tried to catch him, but we ended up in a fistfight."

"You obviously hurt your head." Erin stared at him, worry still lingering in her gaze.

"I'm fine." He brushed her concern off with the shake of his head.

"You don't look fine." Erin wrapped her hand around his arm so she wouldn't lose her grip. "We need to get you inside and check your head for injuries."

Dillon knew better than to argue at this point. Besides, his head pounded with every new line of conversation. The sooner he could get this over with, the better.

He dropped an arm over both of their shoulders, and they helped him through the woods and back into the house. Scout greeted him with a wet nose as soon as he stepped inside, letting out a little whine to let him know he'd been worried also.

He rubbed the dog's head before sitting on the couch. Erin hurried across the room and grabbed a glass of water, handing it to him and insisting he take a drink.

He complied.

Even as he did, all he could think about was that man. Dillon had been so close to catching him, to finding answers.

Just like he had been so close to finding Michael Masterson.

Guilt seemed to dogpile on top of his regret and he squeezed his eyes shut.

"Let me see the back of your head," Erin said. "Carson, can you get him some ice for his face?"

Carson hurried into the kitchen.

As he did, Erin moved to the back of the couch and leaned over him. "I don't see any cuts. But you might have a concussion. We should take you to the hospital."

He started to shake his head when everything wobbled around him again. "I'll be fine."

"I think she's right." Carson returned and handed an ice pack wrapped in a dishtowel to his uncle. "It couldn't hurt to be checked out."

"I'm telling you, I'm fine. I'm going to have a headache, and I need to watch myself when I go to sleep tonight but, otherwise, I'm going to be okay." He pressed the compress against his cheek.

He didn't miss the look that Erin and Carson exchanged with each other. They were both worried about him. He supposed he should be grateful he had people in his life to worry over him. Some people didn't have that privilege.

"How about some coffee?" Erin asked. "Would that make anything better?"

"That sounds great." The caffeine would help him stay awake, which he knew was important right now. Plus, he needed some space.

A few minutes later, she brought him a cup before lowering herself beside him on the couch. Her wide-eyed gaze searched his. "What happened out there?"

As tonight's events filled his thoughts, he closed his eyes, wishing he could have a replay. But that wasn't always possible in life.

Instead, he sighed before starting. "The guy must have heard me coming. He hit me in the back of the head with a shovel. I thought I was coming out ahead until he pushed me into a tree. Everything went black around me. The last thing I remember is him running away."

"Did you get a good look at him?" Erin asked.

Dillon frowned. "Unfortunately, I didn't. He was wearing a black mask, and it was dark outside. I couldn't even tell you his eye color."

"What about his voice?" Carson asked. "Was there anything distinct about it?"

"I already thought about that. I wish I had something to report to you guys. I really do. But there's nothing. I even tried to ask him where Bella was, but he just grunted in response."

"If he wasn't involved in this, then he would have denied it, right?" Erin's voice contained a touch of fear that mingled with hope.

"I definitely think he has something to do with what's going on. I don't know if he's the person who grabbed Bella or not. But this is all connected. We just need to figure out how."

Erin's hand went over her mouth as she squeezed her eyes shut. "I shouldn't be here. I'm putting you in danger."

The thought of her leaving and being on her own right now caused a strange grief to grip his heart.

"I don't want you to leave." The surprisingly raw and honest words surprised even him. And Erin, too. Clearly, because her eyes widened. "I'd just feel better if you were here where we can keep an eye on you."

"But if these attacks continue and you're constantly in the line of fire…"

His gaze locked with hers. "I'm in the line of fire because I put myself there. You leaving won't take me out of that position now. Do you understand?"

She stared at him another moment, and Dillon wasn't sure what she was going to say. Part of him thought that she might just up and leave.

He held his breath as he waited to see what her response would be.

SIXTEEN

If Erin were smart, she'd leave. If she really cared about Dillon, Carson and Scout as much as she thought she did, she'd get out of here before any more damage could be done.

But as she stared at Dillon now and saw the sincerity in his eyes, everything in her wanted to stay.

She knew it was selfish. She didn't want to do anything that she would regret. But she felt certain that if she went back to her house tonight, things wouldn't end well. The person who was pursuing her wasn't letting up. The only way this would end would be with her dead.

She licked her lips before nodding at Dillon as he sat on the couch, compress still against his face. "If you don't mind, I will stay. But the moment you want me gone, you let me know, and I'm out of here. I'm serious."

Something that looked close to relief flooded Dillon's gaze. "Good. I think you're making a smart decision."

Erin reminded herself that Dillon's reasons for wanting her to stay were purely professional. Nothing about this case was personal. She needed to remember to keep her walls up as well. Just because she felt safe with Dillon didn't mean anything.

Quickly, she stood and went into the kitchen to check on the stew. "Would you like some? I think it's done."

"Maybe some food is just what the doctor ordered."

"You stay there. I'll get it ready." She found some bowls

and spoons. A few minutes later, she had the table set for three.

Erin wanted to pretend like this was just a normal dinner with new friends, but she knew it was anything but. They were together right now simply because they wanted to survive.

After praying, they all dug into the warm meal.

Erin took her first bite of the stew and the flavors of nutmeg and garlic washed over her taste buds. "This is delicious."

She hadn't known what to expect.

"It's my mom's recipe," Dillon said. "She's quite the cook—and comfort food is her specialty."

"Where are you parents now?" she asked.

"They retired down in Florida. I still get to see them several times a year, though."

"That's nice."

"How about you, Erin?" Dillon asked. "Where are you from?"

"I grew up closer to Raleigh, but Liam and I met in college. He was from this area, so we moved here."

"This is God's country," Carson said. "At least, in my eyes that's what it is."

Erin smiled. "No one can deny it's beautiful out here."

They chatted about the area as they finished their meal, and then Erin cleaned up while Dillon moved to the couch, still looking worse for the wear after the confrontation in the woods.

As the dogs began barking outside, Dillon glanced at Carson. "Would you mind checking on the dogs?"

"No, sir. I'll do that now." Carson grabbed his coat and started toward the back door.

"Be careful out there," Dillon called.

His words were a reminder of the danger they were all currently in.

As he left the room, Erin sat beside Dillon on the couch and felt the tension stretch between them.

Now that her emotions over what happened were settling down, she had to wonder what they were going to talk about. She sucked in a deep breath, deciding to address the unspoken issues they were both certainly thinking about.

She cleared her throat. "Are you sure you don't want to call the police and tell them what happened tonight?"

Dillon's expression tightened. "No, they're not going to do anything. First thing in the morning, I'll go out and investigate for myself."

He really didn't like Blackstone, either. Why did Erin find so much comfort in that thought?

She pulled her legs beneath her and leaned against the couch as she turned to Dillon. "Have you heard anything about the search and rescue operations for Bella tomorrow?"

"Rick told me they're going to take the helicopter out again and that there will be more search and rescue teams. I'll take Scout out and see if he can pick up her scent again. At least we have a basic idea of what direction Bella traveled in."

Erin nodded, trying not to show her anxiety.

Dillon shifted closer to her before lowering his voice. "Erin, I haven't been in your exact shoes. But I feel like another part of me knows what you're going through."

She stared at him, curious about what he might share. Was this concerning what Carson had told her? About his ex-fiancée who'd left him?

"How so?" she finally asked.

He lowered his compress and put it on the table as a far-off look flooded his eyes. "A lot of people turned against me when one of my search and rescue missions went south. Even my fiancée ended up leaving me because she couldn't take the pressure of it."

"I'm sorry to hear that."

"I deal all the time with people who have missing loved ones. I feel like I live their experiences with them sometimes."

Spontaneously, she reached forward and grabbed his hand. "I can only imagine."

As they looked at each other, their gazes caught.

Their grief had bonded them, hadn't it? They'd both been through ordeals that only the other could understand.

Erin still marveled at the fact that Dillon was so unlike Liam. He was a breath of fresh air—and he brought her a renewed hope.

"Erin?" His voice sounded scratchy as he said the word.

"Yes?" Was she imagining things or was he leaning closer?

The next moment, he reached forward and pushed a lock of hair behind her ear. His gaze almost looked smoky with emotion—and the look in his eyes took her breath away.

It wasn't just attraction there. It was genuine care and concern.

His thumb brushed across her cheek as he moved in closer.

She closed her eyes, anticipating what might happen next.

Until a new sound cut into the moment.

Dillon's phone.

He pulled back, seeming to snap out of the impulsive moment.

Instead, Dillon excused himself and grabbed the device from the table.

Erin tried not to feel disappointed.

It was best that kiss hadn't happened. The interruption was probably a godsend, a reminder that she was better off going solo rather than getting tangled in a bad situation again.

So why did it feel like Dillon would never create a bad scenario in her life?

* * *

Dillon saw Rick's number on the screen and his breath caught.

His heart still pounded out of control from the near kiss. It only accelerated more when he realized his friend might have an update.

He answered and put the call on the speaker. "Rick, I'm here with Erin. She's listening."

"Perfect," Rick said. "I just wanted to let you know that a hiker on a different trail found a shoe that I believe belongs to Bella."

Dillon's breath caught. "What trail?"

"Gulch Valley," Rick said.

Dillon frowned as he pictured the layout of trails in the park. "That's on the other side of the park."

"I know." Rick's voice sounded somber. "It doesn't make any sense."

Dillon shook his head as he tried to think through this newest update. "Scout couldn't have been that wrong. Bella was definitely in the part of the forest that we searched."

"I agree. But how did her shoe end up nearly twenty miles away?"

Dillon bit down as he imagined various scenarios. None of his theories rose to the surface, however. "That's a good question."

"It's a possibility that someone took her shoe and left it as a means of misdirection," Rick said.

"Do you think somebody would do that?" Erin's voice sounded wispy with surprise.

"It's hard to say for sure," Rick said. "We've involved several other local police departments in our search, including the guys from Boone's Hollow. Chief Blackstone said his guys were going to search that area tomorrow as well and see if they could pick up on anything."

"I'm glad he's doing something," Dillon muttered.

They ended the call with a promise to keep each other updated.

Then silence stretched between them.

As the back door opened, Carson wandered inside. "The dogs are fine. I'm not sure why they started barking."

"That's good news, at least." Erin stood and rubbed her hands down the sides of her pants as if she were nervous. "Now that Carson is back, I think I should probably be getting some rest."

Dillon nodded, wondering if something had spooked her. Had he said something? Or was it just this situation?

"I'm going to get Carson to stay awake with me for a little while," Dillon finally said. "I probably shouldn't go to sleep right now after my head injury."

"That's probably a good idea. Do you need me to—"

Dillon shook his head before Erin could finish the sentence. "I'll be fine."

Erin stared at him a moment, questions lingering in her gaze.

Maybe the two of them needed a little time apart. Their emotions had grown quickly, fueled by the danger around them. The last thing he wanted was to do something in the heat of the moment that they would both later regret.

"Carson and I have got this," Dillon insisted. "You get your sleep."

Erin stared at him a moment longer before nodding. "Okay then. I'll talk to you in the morning."

"I'll see you then."

But as she disappeared down the hallway, he couldn't help but wonder what kind of trouble tomorrow would hold.

As Erin laid in bed, she couldn't stop thinking about the kiss she'd almost shared with Dillon.

What would it be like to open herself up to somebody

again? Part of her felt thrilled at the possibility and another part of her only felt fear.

Liam had been the only guy she'd ever dated, and she hadn't dated anyone since he'd disappeared. She'd had no desire to.

But something about Dillon was different. He was gentle. Respectful.

Then again, Liam had been those things at first also. People said you never really knew a person until you went through the hard times with them. That was when their true colors seemed to appear.

Erin had to agree with those words.

She frowned at the memories.

It was a good thing that the kiss had been interrupted. Erin needed to slow down. They both did. Their emotions were clearly out of control.

But another part of her felt like there could be something special there between her and Dillon.

As she punched her pillow, trying to get comfortable, she tried to put any thoughts of Dillon out of her mind. The only person she needed to think about right now was Bella. To engage in any type of romance while her daughter was missing would be uncouth.

That was right.

Until Bella was found, romance was totally off the table, even with someone like Dillon.

Besides, who knew what was going to happen once this was all over. What if Bella wasn't found? Just like Liam hadn't been found.

Or Bella might need help after she was rescued. Erin's life might be devoted to counseling sessions as she tried to help Bella deal with the aftermath of this ordeal. That *had* to be Erin's first priority.

As she turned over in bed again, a noise in the corner of the room caught her ear.

She froze.

What was that?

Sometimes, new houses had different sounds, she reminded herself. Had the heat kicked on? Had a branch scraped the window?

Erin listened, desperate to hear the sound again so she could confirm the noise was mundane and nothing to be worried about.

All was quiet.

She waited a few more seconds, trying to write off the sound. Maybe sleep would find her. Maybe her brain would turn off. Maybe she could stop worrying so much over something so trivial.

Liam had always said Erin liked to make big deals out of nothing.

He'd used the word *trivial* quite a bit. Now, even the thought of that word made Erin's insides tighten as bad memories began to pummel her.

She turned over, determined to get some rest.

But just as she did that, the noise filled the room again.

The next instant, somebody pounced on top of her and a hand covered her mouth.

SEVENTEEN

Erin felt tension pulsing through her as the intruder pinned her down.

She froze, unable to move, unable to defend herself. All she wanted to do was panic.

Who was in her room? How did he get in here?

Even worse: what was he planning?

"You're not going to get away with this," a deep voice muttered in her ear. "Do you understand me?"

Erin remained frozen, unable to react or respond. Her heart thudded in her ears at a rapid pace.

"I said, do you understand me?" he repeated, his voice a growl.

Erin forced herself to nod. The man's hand clutching her mouth made it impossible to speak.

"You deserve to suffer," he continued. "You deserve everything you've got coming for you."

Her blood went cold. Why was this man doing this?

He didn't seem interested in hurting her—only in making her suffer.

But why?

Did this go back to Liam?

"Don't make me tell you again. And yes, I have more in store for you. Ending it like this would be too easy."

What was this guy talking about?

Maybe Erin didn't want to know.

"I'm going to slip out of your room," the man continued. "If you make a sound, I will kill Bella. Do you understand me?"

Kill Bella? *This* was the man who'd taken her? Why had he broken into Dillon's house? Just to threaten her like this?

Her chill deepened.

"I said, do you understand?" His rancid breath hit her ear.

Erin nodded again, more quickly this time.

"Good, because I'm going to be watching. One wrong move and she's dead."

A cry caught in Erin's throat at the thought.

The next instant, the weight of the man's body lifted from her.

Erin pulled in a deep breath, relishing the gulp of air as it filled her lungs.

In a flash, the man opened a window and rushed out.

A cool wind swept through the room.

Otherwise, everything was quiet.

Erin waited, her pounding heart the only sound she heard.

Had that really just happened? It still seemed like a nightmare.

She waited several minutes and tried to compose herself. She knew she needed to move. But she couldn't seem to force her body into action.

Get up, Erin. You're wasting time. Push through the fear!

Finally, she threw her legs out of bed. Her limbs trembled as adrenaline claimed her muscles.

She rose to her feet and peered out the window.

But the man was gone.

Erin had to get Dillon. Had to tell him what had just happened.

She only hoped she could make it out of this room in time.

Dillon straightened from his position on the couch as he heard footsteps rushing down the hallway. Carson sat in the chair across from him, so that had to be Erin.

Was she having trouble sleeping?

When he saw the expression on her face, he knew something was wrong.

He rose, worry pulling taut across his back muscles. "Erin?"

"A man…was in…my room." She clung to the wall as her red-rimmed eyes stared at him.

Even from across the room, Dillon could see her shaking.

He darted toward her and slipped an arm around her waist. He led her to the couch and lowered her onto the cushions before she collapsed.

"A man was in your room? Here at my house?" Had Dillon heard her correctly?

"He went out the window. He's gone now." Her voice broke as if she fought a moan.

Dillon looked at Carson, who'd also risen to his feet. "Did you see or hear anything?"

"No." He shook his head, his stiff shoulders indicating he was on guard. "Not a single thing."

Dillon turned back to Erin, desperate for more information. "What did he say?"

She drew in a shaky breath. "He said I wasn't going to get away with this, that I deserved to suffer, and that I deserved everything I had coming to me."

Concern pulsed through him. He couldn't believe Scout hadn't picked up on the stranger's scent. But the evening had been hectic. He had noticed the canine whine once, but he'd assumed it was from the chaos around them.

"Anything else?" Dillon asked.

"He said he had more in store for me, and that ending it like this would be too easy. Before he left, he said he would be watching, and if I made one wrong move, Bella would die." Her voice broke as a sob wracked her body.

Dillon put an arm around her shoulders before pulling her to him in a hug.

He didn't say anything for a moment. He just held her, comforted her. Carson set a box of tissues beside them, and Erin grabbed one to wipe her face.

She drew in another breath and seemed to compose herself for a moment. "What am I going to do?"

"That's what we need to figure out," Dillon muttered. "Why would someone go through the trouble of breaking in just to tell you that?" Dillon asked.

"It's like he said—he wants to make me suffer. To let me know that I have no control, yet all of this is my fault." Erin's voice broke as if she held back a cry.

Her words settled on him. They made sense—in a twisted kind of way at least.

"That was why that man was outside the house earlier," Dillon mumbled.

Erin sucked in a quick breath as she stared up at him. "Do you mean that he drew us outside just so somebody else could sneak inside?"

"That's my best guess. That's the only thing that makes sense."

"But *none* of this makes sense. Why would the person who abducted Bella go through all this trouble?" She pressed the tissue into her eyes again.

The truth slammed into Dillon's mind. How had he not seen this before?

"That's because this isn't about Bella," Dillon muttered. "This is about you, Erin."

Realization spread through Erin's gaze and she nodded. "You're right. This *is* about me. I'm the actual target here, aren't I?"

Dillon almost didn't want to agree with her, but he had no choice. Erin had to know what she was up against.

"What am I going to do, Dillon?" Her wide eyes met his, questions filling their depths.

His heart ached for the woman.

He reached forward and squeezed her hand. "I don't know. But I'll be here with you to help you figure it out."

Erin startled awake.

Where was she? What was going on?

All she felt was a cold fear that pierced her heart.

Danger seemed to hang in the air around her.

"It's okay," a deep voice murmured beside her.

Erin jumped back even farther.

Who was that?

She glanced up and her eyes slowly adjusted to the darkness.

Dillon's face stared back at her.

Erin let out a breath. She must have fallen asleep on the couch. Had her head been on his shoulder?

Her cheeks heated at the thought of it.

The events of last night flooded back to her and she shivered. Especially when she remembered the man who'd been in her room—the person who wanted to strike fear into her heart.

He had succeeded. He'd taken away everything that was precious to her. Erin's sense of security. Her peace of mind. Her faith in humanity.

Most of all—he'd taken away Bella.

She held back a cry.

The only thing the man hadn't taken was her faith in God, but even that felt like it was on shaky ground lately. This situation was definitely a test of her faith.

Dillon shifted beside her before softly murmuring, "I didn't want to wake you."

Erin raked her hand through her hair and nodded. She

vaguely remembered Dillon holding her as they'd sat on the couch. She remembered resting her head on his shoulder.

She must have fallen asleep.

She rubbed her throat as she felt another wave of self-consciousness. "I'm sorry… I didn't mean to…"

"No need for apologies." Dillon glanced at her, his eyes warm and almost soft. "I'm glad you were able to get some rest."

She studied his face for a moment, wondering how his concussion was—not to mention his swollen cheek. She wasn't the only one suffering here.

"How about you?" She studied his face. "Do you feel okay?"

"I'm fine."

He shrugged, but Erin knew that meant he hadn't gotten any rest. He was simply trying to play it off, and maybe he was even worried that Erin might feel guilty over all that had happened.

He was always so considerate of her feelings, a fact she deeply appreciated.

"What time is it?" Erin rubbed her eyes again, wishing she didn't feel so groggy.

"Almost 6:00 a.m."

She let out a breath. She must have been out. On a subconscious level, she had realized she was safe with Dillon so close.

Her cheeks heated at the thought.

"I can't believe I slept that long," she murmured.

"You must have needed it."

She couldn't argue with that point. "Have you heard any updates?"

Dillon shook his head. "Unfortunately, no."

Erin pushed herself to her feet, needing a moment to compose herself. "Would it be okay if I hopped in the shower real quick?"

Dillon's perceptive eyes met hers. "Go right ahead. Maybe that will make you feel better."

She wished something as simple as a shower had that power. But all she wanted right now was Bella.

She needed her daughter.

With every day that passed, her worry only grew.

And there didn't seem to be an end in sight.

She only hoped today might provide some answers.

EIGHTEEN

Dillon instructed Carson to stay inside the house to keep an eye out for trouble. While Carson was on guard, Dillon put his boots and coat on before going outside to search for any evidence of what happened last night.

Just as Erin had told him, footprints came from the window near her bedroom.

Anger zipped through his blood at the thought of what had happened. The person behind this was brazen—a little too brazen for his comfort.

Yet the man hadn't wanted to hurt Erin. He'd only wanted to scare her. To draw out her suffering.

He pulled out his phone and took some pictures of the footprints, using a dollar bill for size. Then he continued following the footprints.

The steps led into the woods. As Dillon crossed into the tree line, memories of being whacked in the head with that shovel filled him. Each thought made his muscles tense.

His head still throbbed, but he felt better today than he had yesterday. He was grateful to be alive. He'd known people who'd lost their lives after taking blows like that.

He continued into the woods, but the footsteps became harder to follow under the brittle canopy of branches above. They'd protected the ground below, preventing snow from reaching it. Without as much snow here, the tracks weren't as obvious.

As Dillon crossed through the small patch of woods to

the street on the other side, he spotted tire prints on the edge of the road. Just as he'd expected, someone had pulled of the street, parked there, and then done their dirty deed.

This whole thing didn't make sense to Dillon.

Why go through so much trouble just to teach Erin a lesson? What kind of logic was this person following?

Unless there was something he was missing.

Dillon frowned.

He had to get to the bottom of this and soon.

Dillon headed back to the house. He'd need to change and get ready also so he could meet the rest of the search party. He hoped that maybe they could find some answers today.

Not only for Bella's sake, but for Erin's well-being also.

How many more hits could she take?

He didn't know, but she'd had more than her fill.

Erin glanced up as Dillon stepped back into the room. She quickly flipped a piece of bacon on the griddle.

"I hope you don't mind," she said. "But I figured we could both use our energy today."

"No, not at all. It smells great." He stomped his boots to get the snow off as he closed the door behind him. After hanging his coat on a rack, he strode toward her.

Erin hadn't been sure if she should cook or not. She hadn't wanted to overstep.

She'd taken a quick shower and hadn't bothered to dry her hair. At least she had clean clothes on, and she'd brushed her teeth. Despite her doubts, Erin felt a little more alert than she had earlier.

"Anything new outside?"

When Carson had told her that Dillon had stepped out, Erin had figured he was looking for clues. But as she'd prepared breakfast, she hadn't been able to stop thinking about what Dillon might have discovered.

"I found footprints and tire prints." Dillon paused near her. "I took pictures of them, just in case."

"At least it's something." Erin wasn't sure what else to say. It wasn't exactly like she'd been expecting Dillon to catch the person responsible.

Dillon pulled out a barstool across from the kitchen island cooktop and sat down. "Can I help?"

She shook her head as she flipped another piece of bacon. "I'm fine. You can just take it easy. In fact, if you want to go get ready, our food should be done by the time you change."

He nodded and stood—almost seeming reluctant do so.

As Erin watched him walk away, her throat tightened.

Something about this arrangement felt a little too cozy. Why was Erin letting her emotions get the best of her like this? The rush of attraction she felt for Dillon threw her off balance, especially given everything else that was going on.

"Life can be pretty confusing sometimes, can't it, Scout?" She glanced down at the canine who sat at her feet, probably hoping she'd drop some food on the floor.

He raised his nose in the air and sniffed in response.

Just as she'd predicted, Dillon had finished getting ready just as Erin pulled the eggs off the burner. A few minutes later, they sat across from each other at the small dining room table, Carson joining them. After Dillon prayed, they all dug in.

Erin was especially touched by the prayer he had lifted for Bella.

Be with Bella. Keep her safe as only You can do, Lord. Wrap Your loving arms around her and give her comfort. Most of all, help us find her.

But as soon as she took her first bite, Dillon turned toward her. The serious look in his gaze indicated that something was wrong.

"Rick called just as I got out of the shower," he started.

She wiped her mouth before leaving her napkin on her lap. "And?"

Dillon's face tightened as if he were having trouble forming his words.

That couldn't be good.

"Bella's other shoe was found," he finally said. "It was located about five hundred feet from the first one."

Erin stared at him, trying to read between the lines. Trying not to jump to worst-case scenarios. Trying to stay positive.

But she had to ask… "Is that a bad sign?"

He pressed his lips together, the ends pulling down in a frown, before he finally said, "There was a small amount of blood on it."

Dillon practically inhaled his breakfast.

There was no time to waste.

As soon as he took his last bite, he stood and turned to his nephew. "Carson, I'm going to need you to utilize all that training we've been working on. You need to take Scout out there in the search for Bella."

Erin's breath caught beside him. "Why wouldn't you go? I hear you're the best."

"You're not going to be able to walk those trails." He nodded at her twisted ankle.

"Then you can go without me," she insisted.

He shook his head, knowing that wasn't going to work out for multiple reasons. "I don't want to leave you alone. Not after everything that has happened. It wouldn't be safe."

"But finding Bella is more important than my safety!" Her voice rose with each word, a haunting desperation floating through the tone.

Dillon leaned forward and squeezed her hand. "I know what you're saying. But I have another idea for us. I'd like to go talk to the Bradshaws."

Her face went still as she seemed to process that thought. "Why do you want to do that?"

"Because Burt mentioned them, and he's right. Liam worked a case against that family that could have left them with a lot of resentment toward Liam. Maybe they're the ones who did something to Liam. And maybe that wasn't enough. Maybe they want to do something to Bella also. I think we should talk to them. I'd like to do it myself and not leave it to Chief Blackstone."

Erin stared at him a moment, her eyes glimmering with uncertainty, until finally she nodded. "Okay then."

He turned his gaze back Carson who stood in the doorway. "Do you think you can handle this?"

Carson nodded quickly. "I can do it. I know I can. Thank you for trusting me with this."

"We've been through all these drills before. I have total confidence that you'll be able to handle the situation. There are going to be a lot of teams out there searching today. I heard the park service put out a call for volunteers."

"Is anyone from Boone's Hollow coming out to help?" Erin rubbed her throat as if anticipating the worst.

"I'm not sure. But I know that people from the surrounding counties are coming. There should be a good group there to scour the woods."

"I am grateful for that at least." But her voice still sounded tight.

"While they handle the search and rescue operation side, we're going to talk to the Bradshaws and see if we can get any answers from them. I know we don't need to waste any more time here. I think this is our best option."

She stared at him a moment before nodding. "Then let's do it."

NINETEEN

Erin stepped from the hallway, still gripping her phone and reeling from the conversation she'd just had. When her phone had rung, she'd stepped away for privacy.

"Erin?" Dillon glanced at her as he stood at the front door waiting.

"Bella's best friend, Gina, just called." Erin rubbed her temples as the conversation replayed in her mind. Each time made her feel like she'd been punched in the gut.

"Is everything okay?" Dillon's forehead wrinkled as he stepped closer to her.

"Gina told me the police brought her in this morning for questioning. And she..." Erin drew in a shaky breath.

Dillon squeezed her arm. "It's okay. Take your time."

Erin gulped in a deep breath, trying to keep her composure even as panic raced through her. "She told them Bella and I had been fighting lately and that I'd threatened to kick Bella out of the house."

Dillon continued to wait for her to finish, no judgment on his face. "Okay..."

She squeezed the skin between her eyes. "Bella and I have been fussing with each other recently, but it's just been the normal type of parent-teenager argument that happens. I did tell Bella that she needed to straighten up, but I had no intention of kicking her out or putting her on the street."

"So why did Gina tell the police that?"

"She said they kept pushing her. She said that she knows

I'm a good mom, but the police kept pushing her to say something. Finally, she cracked." Erin closed her eyes, willing herself not to cry. There had already been too many tears.

And tears wouldn't help her find Bella. This was no time to feel sorry for herself. That would only waste time.

Concern filled Dillon's gaze. "Is that all she said?"

"She said she had the impression the police were going to bring me in for questioning again." Her voice trembled as unimaginable scenarios raced through her head. "They're going to arrest me, aren't they?"

"A verbal argument between you and Bella doesn't give them probable cause for arresting you."

Her gaze met his. "But I already have a target on my back. Who says these guys are going to play by the rules?"

"I know what you're getting at. You think they're looking for an excuse to put you behind bars."

"They've wanted to for over a year."

"We are not going to let them arrest you," Dillon finally said.

She shook her head. "I don't see how we can stop them."

"Right now, we're just going to keep doing what we'd planned on doing."

"Are you sure?" Tension threaded through her voice.

Dillon nodded. "I'm sure. Now, let's keep going. We don't have any time to waste."

Erin nodded, but her thoughts still raced.

How could Gina have said that? How could the police have kept pushing her until she did? Now she was just going to look even more guilty than she already did. People in this town were going to have another reason to hate her.

Just once Erin had thought things couldn't get worse, that's exactly what they seemed to do.

Dillon typed the Bradshaws' address into his GPS. The family consisted of three brothers—Bill, David and Samson. Each was a powerhouse in his own way, and people in town knew it was best not to mess with them. Mysterious incidents would happen if they did—slashed tires, smashed car windows, unexpected fires.

But nothing could ever be traced back to the family, though everyone knew they were guilty.

Their place was a good thirty-minute drive from here.

As he headed down the road, his thoughts continued to race.

He wondered how Carson and Scout were doing. He wanted to call to get an update, but he didn't want to interrupt the operation, either. They would contact him if they needed to.

Meanwhile, he hoped that he wasn't leading Erin right into the line of fire. He knew this family wasn't safe, but he also knew he couldn't leave Erin alone.

In an ideal situation, he would have brought backup. But since Dillon wasn't officially a cop anymore, there was no one to ask to come with him. Plus, with the suspicion that had been cast on Erin, he wasn't sure how many of his friends would be willing to help. Especially if it meant risking their career.

"Tell me about when you adopted Bella," he started.

Erin glanced up, her gaze still looking strained. "I was friends with Bella's mom in high school. Her name was Stephanie. She didn't have a good home life and had gotten involved with drugs and more of the party crowd. But I used to always help tutor her in math, so we became friends, I suppose."

"Okay…"

"We lost touch for a long time," Erin continued. "Then Bella ended up in my first-grade class. I knew her mom was having a hard time. I could see it in her eyes, and I'd heard through the grapevine that social services was on the verge of taking Bella away from her."

"What happened next?" Dillon glanced in his rearview mirror, feeling like they were being followed again. He didn't tell Erin. Not yet.

"One day, out of the blue, I got a phone call from Stephanie. She was hysterical, and I could tell that she was on something. She asked me if I would take care of Bella for her. She said she needed to go get help."

"And you said yes?"

"I did. I love Bella. Even when she was just my student, I thought she was a great kid. So I told Stephanie that her daughter could come live with me and Liam."

"What happened next?"

"Stephanie tried to get help, but it was too late. She called me again and said she wanted me to adopt Bella, that she couldn't handle being a mom anymore. I tried to convince her to keep getting help, tried to encourage her that she could change. But Stephanie wouldn't listen and insisted that Bella needed to be with me, that I was a good person. I didn't know what to say."

"What did Liam think?" Dillon asked.

"At first, he was supportive. I think it made him look good that we'd taken in a little girl and helped her out. He liked the accolades he got because of that. In fact, when I mentioned to him that we could adopt her, he was all in favor at first. I don't think he really realized what he was saying yes to."

"Was Bella troubled?"

Erin sucked in a deep breath. "She'd had a rough past, and of course that affected her. It would affect anybody. But we were working through it. Bella isn't a bad girl by any means. Like I told you earlier, it's mostly her anxiety that gets to her."

"And eventually Liam realized that and held it against you?"

Erin nodded. "His fuse just kept getting shorter and

shorter. I thought he might change if we had a child in the house. That it would awaken a gentler side of him. I was wrong. He only escalated and things got worse and worse."

"But Liam never hurt Bella?"

"No, I made sure of that," Erin said. "Bella was the reason I ultimately decided I couldn't stay with Liam. I couldn't risk him ever hurting her."

"What about Bella's birth mom? Did she totally disappear after that?" Dillon glanced in his rearview mirror again. Somebody was definitely following them. The vehicle maintained a steady distance behind them.

Erin rubbed her throat as she stared out the window. "Once the adoption was finalized, I never saw her again. I still wonder what happened to her. Where she ended up. If she is still alive."

"How about Bella? Does she ask about her?"

"She did when she first came to live with me. But over the years, the questions faded. I'm sure she still thinks about her mom, though. Who wouldn't? But perhaps she got tired of hearing the same answers."

"I'm sorry to hear that. I can only imagine that must have been really hard on her."

"It was. I hate to see a child go through that. I did what I could—I'm *doing* what I can—to give her a good life. But in so many ways, I feel like I failed her also."

He shot a quick glance at her, curious about her words. "What do you mean?"

"Maybe I should have said no to the adoption. Part of me feels like I took her from one bad situation and I put her in another." Her voice caught.

"But you did everything that you could to protect her." He understood the guilt—even if he thought the guilt wasn't justified. It just added more pain to an already difficult situation.

"Bella is gone now. Whether she ran away or if she was

abducted, either way, it kind of feels like I fell down on the job, doesn't it?"

Dillon squeezed Erin's hand, wishing he could offer her some more comfort. "I know it might feel like that now, but you have to know that's not the truth."

Before she could respond, Dillon looked into the rear-view mirror again and saw that the car was still there.

Somebody was definitely following them.

And it was time to end this.

Now.

Erin sucked in a breath as the Jeep suddenly skidded to a halt. The back of the vehicle fishtailed until the Jeep blocked the road.

Her eyes widened. What was happening?

She knew by the stiff set of Dillon's jaw that something was wrong.

When she glanced back, she saw a red pickup behind them.

They were being followed again, weren't they?

Not only that…but that truck looked familiar. Where had she seen it before?

"Stay here," Dillon growled.

He grabbed his gun before stepping from the Jeep and storming toward the person following them.

"Get out of the car with your hands up."

Erin held her breath as she waited to see what would play out.

After several minutes, there was still no movement.

This wasn't good. What if the driver opened fire? Or what if that person decided to ram them?

There were so many unknowns.

A moment later, the truck door opened.

Her heart throbbed in her chest.

Then a familiar face came into sight.

That's why Erin had recognized that truck.

It was Arnold, Liam's brother.

She lowered her window so she could hear what happened next.

Arnold raised his hands in the air as he scowled at Dillon. "Let's talk this through."

"You didn't seem interested in talking when you were following us just now."

Erin climbed from the Jeep and stood behind Dillon. "What are you doing, Arnold? Do you have Bella?"

He pulled his head back in shock. "Why would I have Bella?"

She started to lunge toward him when Dillon stuck his arm out to stop her from going any closer.

"Why would you do this to me? Why would you take her?"

"I didn't take Bella," Arnold said. "Why would I do that?"

"Why are you following us right now?"

He sneered. "Isn't that obvious?"

"Clearly, it isn't obvious," Dillon said. "Now, why don't you give us some answers before I take you in?"

"Last I heard, you weren't a cop anymore."

"That doesn't mean I can't march you down to the police station so they can question you there. Don't think that I won't do it."

Arnold stared at him another moment, as if trying to ascertain if he was bluffing.

He must have decided that he wasn't because he finally spoke. "I didn't take Bella. I may not like you, but that doesn't mean I want to hurt the girl. Besides, everybody knows *you're* the one who did something to her."

Fury sprang up inside her, and she fisted her hands at her sides. "Arnold, you have to know me good enough to know I'd never do something like that."

His gaze locked with hers. "You did something to my brother."

Erin's throat burned as emotions warred within her. "You know that I didn't do anything to your brother. He was the one who hurt me."

Arnold's gaze darkened. "Then you just had to exact revenge on him, didn't you?"

"If you knew he was hurting me, why didn't you try to stop him?"

Arnold's shoulders bristled. "It wasn't my place. He said you got what was coming to you."

The burning in her throat became even greater. More tears welled in her eyes, but Erin held them back. She wouldn't give Arnold the satisfaction of seeing her cry.

"You're saying that you're not the one who took Bella?" Dillon's voice sounded hard and unyielding.

Arnold crossed his burly arms over his chest. "I didn't take Bella. That's ridiculous."

"And why are you following us now?" Dillon continued.

"Because I need to let Erin know she's not going to get away with this."

Realization dawned on her. "You're the one who's been sending me those text messages, aren't you?"

Arnold said nothing.

"You probably left that message painted on the front of my house also. And you're the one who threw that bottle bomb at us."

His nostrils flared. "I just want to see justice for my brother."

Dillon bristled beside her. "Threatening Erin isn't the way to do it."

She heard the anger—and protectiveness—simmering in Dillon's voice.

"I can't let her get away with it," Arnold growled as he glowered at them.

"I think you know, if you look deep inside yourself, that Erin isn't guilty of this," Dillon said. "Now, you're just hindering our search for Bella. You're hindering our search for an innocent sixteen-year-old girl who's probably been abducted. I hope you can live with yourself knowing that."

Arnold's gaze darkened again, but he said nothing for a few minutes. "I didn't do it. I have chronic obstructive pulmonary disease. You know I do. There's no way I could have carried out a plan like this. Besides, I was at a doctor's appointment in Asheville the day she disappeared."

Erin let his words sink in. That seemed provable enough.

But she still didn't like this man and didn't want him around. He was dangerous in his own way.

"If I see you around one more time, I'll be calling in all the favors I'm owed by the local law enforcement community." Dillon's voice sounded hard, like he wasn't someone to be questioned. "Don't think I won't do it. Do you understand?"

Arnold stared at him a moment before nodding. "Understood."

TWENTY

As they continued down the road, Dillon's pulse raced.

That man had a lot of nerve.

He wished he had the power to arrest him now. But they had more important matters to attend to. At least they now knew where those texts had come from along with the message on Erin's house.

Was Arnold the person who'd tried to run them off the road? Dillon's gut told him no. He'd thought that vehicle had been gray, and this man's truck was clearly a bright red.

Was he the one who had been in the woods? Who'd thrown the bomb?

"Are you doing okay?" He glanced at Erin.

Certainly, that whole conversation had shaken her up. It would shake anybody up.

She crossed her arms over her chest and shrugged. "Hate can do horrible things to people, can't it?"

"Yes, it can. I'm sorry you have to be on the receiving end of that."

Before they could say any more, Dillon's phone rang and he saw that it was Rick.

He hit the talk button, and the man's voice came out through his Jeep's speakers.

"Hey, Rick," Dillon started. "I'm here with Erin."

"Good. I can talk to both of you at once. There are a couple of updates I want to give you."

"What's going on?" Dillon waited, hoping for good

news. But by the sound of his friend's voice, he wasn't sure that's what they were going to get.

"First, I just heard through the grapevine that Blackstone got a warrant to search Erin's house. He's probably going to take her computer and look for any evidence that she may have done something to Bella."

A muffled cry escape from Erin beside him.

Dillon frowned.

Another hit. How many more could she take?

"I also wanted to let you know that we got our official report from the medical examiner," Rick said. "The body that we found in the forest that day wasn't Liam's."

Erin gasped. "What? But the necklace..."

"It appears that somebody placed the necklace on the body. Maybe they did that just to throw us off."

"Then whose body was it?" Dillon asked.

"It belonged to a drifter named Mark Pearson. He went missing about fifteen months ago, not long before Liam went missing."

"How did he die?"

"It looks like he had a head injury. He was known for his involvement in drugs. That probably played a role also."

"Thanks for letting us know."

"Where are you now?" Rick asked.

"We're headed to see the Bradshaws and give them a visit."

"The Bradshaws? Be careful. They're not a family that you want to mess with."

Dillon's spine tightened at his friend's reminder. "I know. We'll watch our backs."

"If you need anything, let me know."

Dillon rubbed his jaw. "We will."

Erin's heart continued to race.

That body wasn't Liam's.

She still didn't have confirmation about whether he was dead or alive.

Sometimes, she just wanted an answer. Living with the unknown was too hard. At least if that had been Liam's dead body, she could put that part of her life to rest.

Now the possibility still remained that he was alive and out there somewhere.

Otherwise, things didn't make sense. Why would Liam have run away and hidden? For this long, too?

He was the type of person who loved people. He loved being the center of attention, and he wasn't the type who wanted to hide in a cave for an indefinite period of time. If he was doing that, he was desperate.

"What are you thinking?" Dillon's voice snapped Erin from her thoughts.

"I'm just trying to process all this."

"I understand."

"I can't believe the police are searching my house. Then again, I shouldn't be surprised." She rubbed the sides of her arms, suddenly feeling chilled.

"That's pretty standard in investigations like this," he said. "They always look at family first."

She shook her head, feeling half numb inside. "They're not going to find anything—unless somebody has planted something."

A sick feeling filled her gut. What if that were the case? Given everything else that had gone wrong, it did seem like a possibility. Somebody wanted to make her look guilty. This could just be another way of making her suffer.

"Let's not think about that. Let's wait and see what happens next."

She nodded, knowing she had no choice but to do exactly that.

Dillon pulled up to a house that was set off the road on a long lane. The log cabin, which looked almost like a lodge, had probably cost a pretty penny. Yet despite its massive appearance, the place wasn't well cared for. Too much trash was outside. Too many cars in the driveway. The lawn was too unmanicured.

As Dillon parked the Jeep, he turned to Erin. "Stay here while I talk to them. Whatever you do, don't get out."

Erin heard the warning in his voice and knew that he wasn't messing around.

But before Dillon could even open the door, gunfire rang through the air.

"Get down!" Dillon shouted.

They ducked below the dash as more bullets filled the air.

The Bradshaws were shooting at them.

Dillon could feel the adrenaline pumping through him.

He drew his own gun as he tried to figure out his next move.

He hadn't come this far to leave now. But he didn't want to put Erin in danger, either.

At a pause in the rounds of ammunition, Dillon raised his head. "I'm just here to talk!"

"Who are you?" one of the men yelled back.

"My name is Dillon Walker."

"What do you want?"

"I want to talk to you about Liam Lansing."

Silence stretched as he waited for the man's response. Finally, the man said, "What do you want to know?"

"We want to know if you know what happened to him," Dillon said.

"Why would I know that?"

Dillon raised his head again. "Look, can we just talk? Without any guns?"

The man was silent another moment until he finally said,

"Come up to the porch. But don't try anything or there will be consequences."

Dillon glanced at Erin again. He didn't like this and knew things could go south fast. "Listen, if anything happens, I want you to get behind the wheel and drive away as fast as you can. Do you understand?"

"Dillon…" Her voice cracked with worry.

His gaze met hers. "I mean it. I don't want you getting hurt. Bella is going to need you when she's found. Do you understand?"

Erin stared at him, emotions filling her gaze until she finally nodded. "Okay."

He climbed out and started toward the house.

As he did, he felt the tension thrumming inside him. Would this guy do what he had said? Criminals in general couldn't be trusted. Dillon hoped he wasn't walking into an ambush.

Bill Bradshaw stepped onto the porch, a shotgun in his hands. The man was in his fifties, with short silver-threaded hair and a hooded gaze.

He was well seasoned in his life of crime. He had whole networks of people working for him. Even though his home wasn't well maintained, it probably had cost more than a million dollars. Money wasn't an object for him. His drug business clearly paid well.

"What do you want to know about Liam?" Bill asked, a cold, hardened look in his gaze.

"His daughter is missing," Dillon said.

"I heard that. But I still don't know what this has to do with me."

"We're wondering if there's a connection between their disappearances."

Bill raised a shoulder and scowled. "Why would I know?"

"I heard that you have some bad history."

"He tried to arrest us, if that's what you're talking about." Bill's eyes narrowed. "Do you think I killed him?"

"We have no idea what's happened. But we wonder if Liam's disappearance is somehow connected with the disappearance of his daughter Bella. Bella's mom is worried sick, and I'm just trying to find some answers."

The man stared at him, his eyes narrowing even more. "You were one of those state cops, weren't you?"

The fact that this man knew that fact didn't surprise Dillon. Bill probably studied all the local police departments so he would know what he was up against in case something tried to come between him and his drug operations.

"Is there anything you know that might help us to find him?" Dillon asked.

"I don't want that guy found. I don't help cops."

"So you don't know anything?"

He continued to stare at Dillon.

He *did* know something, Dillon realized. But what?

"Now I need you to get off my property," Bill growled.

"Just a few more questions—"

"I need you to get off my property now."

Dillon stared at him and heard the warning in his voice.

But as he took a step back, more gunfire rang out.

He spotted one of the Bradshaw sons in the window— holding a gun.

Dillon needed to get out of there. Now.

TWENTY-ONE

Erin heard more bullets being shot and gasped.

She'd promised Dillon she'd leave at the first sign of trouble.

A promise was a promise.

But she couldn't leave him here. He'd be a sitting duck.

Quickly, she climbed into the driver's seat, trying to remember everything she could about driving a stick shift. She'd learned in high school, but that seemed like a long time ago now.

With her hand on the gearshift and foot on the clutch, she managed to get the Jeep into first gear.

She nibbled on her bottom lip and had to make a quick split-second decision.

Leave or help Dillon?

It was a no-brainer.

Releasing the clutch and pressing the accelerator, she charged toward the house in front of her.

She wasn't leaving Dillon behind.

As she got closer to Dillon, she slowed and opened the door. "Get in!"

Dillon's eyes widened, but he dove inside.

Before he closed the door, she did a quick U-turn and charged back down the lane.

As she did, a bullet pierced the back glass, shattering it.

But as long as she and Dillon were okay, that was all that mattered.

Keeping her foot on the accelerator, Erin shifted the gears again and drove as fast as she could to get away from the house.

She had to keep Dillon safe and she had to stay alive in order to help Bella. Those were her only two goals right now.

She turned back onto the street just as Dillon sat up and jerked on his seat belt.

"I told you to leave," he muttered.

"I did leave. I just picked you up first."

He shook his head before a laugh escaped.

A laugh? That wasn't what she had been expecting.

"You have a lot of guts, Erin. Don't let anybody ever tell you that you don't."

"I'm glad you made it out okay. But did you find out anything in the process?"

His eyes softened with concern. "Not really. They definitely know something, but the Bradshaws aren't going to share what it is."

"I remember overhearing a few things and thinking that Liam and this family were mortal enemies. Maybe *they* did do something to Liam."

Dillon leaned back. "Did the police ever look into them?"

"It's hard to say." Erin let out a sigh. "What now?"

"Let's head back into town, and maybe stop to grab a quick bite to eat in the process."

"But first, we're going to switch seats. No way am I going to try to drive this up the mountain."

He grinned. "I think you're doing a pretty good job."

"Then I need to stop while I'm ahead."

What Erin had done was risky. But it may have saved his life. If she hadn't had the nerve to drive by and pick him up, he could be dead right now.

What she had done had also meant that she could have been hurt. And that wasn't okay.

As she pulled off onto the side of the road, Dillon climbed out to switch seats with her. As their paths crossed behind the Jeep, he paused and grasped her elbow.

"Thank you." His voice came out throatier than he had intended.

Her cheeks turned a shade of red. "It's no problem. You would have done it for me."

"You're right. I would have."

Their gazes caught and, for a moment, all he wanted to do was lean down and press his lips into hers.

The urge surprised him. It was so unexpected.

All of this was.

A search and rescue case had turned his life upside down once. Now it appeared that another case might turn his life upside down again. Maybe it wouldn't be in a bad way this time.

Right now, he needed to concentrate on finding Bella.

Dillon cleared his throat, wishing it was that easy to also clear his thoughts.

"It's cold out here," he finally said. "We should probably get back in the car."

Erin stared up at him, something swirling in the depths of her eyes. She felt it, too, didn't she? Dillon had a feeling she was in the same boat that he was.

She wasn't looking for a relationship. It sounded like the one relationship she'd had in her life had put her through the ringer.

He swallowed hard again before stepping back. "Let's get inside. You've got to be hungry. Maybe we'll grab a quick bite to eat and then we can keep looking."

Erin seemed to startle out of her daze as she nodded at him. "Sounds like a plan."

They both climbed back into the Jeep, and he took off down the road.

As he did, his thoughts raced.

It seemed as if they could rule out Arnold as being involved. But Dillon would guess that whoever was behind this wasn't a stranger. This seemed too personal for that. It wasn't about money; when a stranger was involved in a crime like this, it was usually for financial reasons. Erin clearly did not have much cash.

So if they ruled out Arnold, who did that leave? Could the Bradshaws be involved? It seemed like there was a good chance, but what would their motive be?

There was still a lot they needed to figure out.

He stared at the road in front of him. There was another town near, one adjacent to Boone's Hollow. Dillon knew of a diner where he and Erin could grab a quick meal before they continued looking for more answers.

Part of him was looking forward to spending more time with Erin and getting to know her even more.

What would the future hold when this was over?

Dillon didn't know. But he did know that the most important thing was that when this was all over, Bella was safe.

Erin glanced at the restaurant in front of her. Surprisingly, she'd never been here. She wasn't much for going out to eat, not when she could cook things on her own. Besides, that was the way Liam liked it, and she'd tried to respect his wishes.

"They have great BLTs if you're interested," Dillon said.

"That sounds great." As if in response, Erin's stomach rumbled. She was clearly hungrier than she'd thought. Maybe all this danger had worked up an appetite.

It had certainly worked up questions within her.

As soon as they stepped inside, the scent of comfort

foods filled her senses. Was that roast beef? Gravy? Maybe even chocolate?

She couldn't be sure, but whatever the scents were, they were alluring.

"What do you think?" Dillon glanced at her. "Do you want to sit down for a few minutes and regroup? Or should we get this to go?"

Erin glanced at her watch. "I suppose that if we can eat something quickly, we can stay."

It was always good to recalculate and figure out the next step. Plus, this wasn't Boone's Hollow. Maybe she could grab a bite to eat without everyone scrutinizing her like they did back in her hometown.

The waitress led them to a seat in the corner and handed them laminated menus. But Erin didn't even need to look at it. She would get a BLT just as Dillon had suggested. That selection sounded good.

She glanced around the outdated but friendly-looking restaurant before turning back to Dillon. "Do you eat here a lot?"

"Not really. But on occasion I want a meal that reminds me of Grandma's. When I do, this is where I come."

Erin wanted to engage in simple chitchat, but her heart wasn't in it. Not when so much was on the line.

Instead, she said, "Can we review everything we know?"

"Of course." Dillon shifted across from her.

Erin's mind raced through everything as she tried to sort through her thoughts. "So this is what we have so far. Bella disappeared when she went to school three days ago. Her car was found in a parking lot near a trailhead. A body was found on the trail, but it belongs to a drifter and doesn't appear to be connected to the case other than the necklace found on the corpse."

"Correct," Dillon said.

"Meanwhile, Arnold sent me threatening texts as well

as left a message painted on the front of my house," she continued. "He also threw that bomb."

"Also correct."

"One of Bella's shoes was found twenty miles away, at a different section of the park. Five hundred feet from that, her other shoe was found. In the meantime, there's been no real contact."

"That sounds accurate."

She frowned and nibbled on her bottom lip for a moment. "Somebody's also been trying to run us off the road, watching us from the woods, they've shot at us, and that man was in my room last night."

Dillon reached across the table and squeezed her hand. "Unfortunately, all of those things are correct. Someone certainly is weaving a tangled web."

"Yes, they are. And when you put it all together, what do you have?"

"That's the million-dollar question. Who could possibly be behind this?"

His question hung in the air.

Erin heard the door jangle open behind her and glanced over her shoulder.

The person who stepped inside made her eyes widen.

She pulled away from Dillon's grasp and stared at the woman.

"Erin?" Dillon said from across the table. "Do you know that person?"

Erin nodded, her thoughts still reeling. "That's Stephanie. Bella's birth mom."

TWENTY-TWO

Dillon felt himself bristle as Erin stared at the woman who'd stepped into the restaurant.

He had a feeling he knew who this woman was.

Stephanie—Bella's birth mother. The two looked like each other and this woman was in the right age range.

As if to confirm his gut feeling, Erin muttered, "Stephanie?"

He was right. So what was Stephanie doing there?

He tensed as he waited to see what would happen next.

The woman's gaze latched on to Erin. Stephanie had obviously known Erin was there and had come to find her. But how had she known that? Had she been following them?

His muscles tightened even more at the thought.

The woman ambled toward their table now.

She had straight blonde hair that was pulled into a sloppy ponytail, and wore faded jeans and an oversized sweatshirt. The gaunt expression on her face, combined with her thinning hair and dull eyes, seemed to indicate a history with drug abuse—in Dillon's experience, at least. Her red-rimmed eyes showed grief…and maybe more.

"Erin…" She paused at the edge of their table, her hands fluttering nervously in the air.

"Stephanie." Erin's eyes widened with surprise. "What are you doing here?"

"I… I needed to talk to you. I heard what happened and…"

"Of course." Erin scooted over in the booth and patted the space beside her. "Have a seat. Let's talk."

Stephanie carefully perched herself there, but her body language seemed to indicate she could run at any minute. Her muscles were stiff. Her gaze continually drifted back to the window. Her fingers flexed and unflexed.

Dillon leaned forward to introduce himself. "I'm Dillon, a friend of Erin's. I'm trying to help her find Bella."

Stephanie frowned and nodded. "I know. I've been keeping an eye on things ever since I heard the news about Bella. I know that probably sounds strange, and I don't want to come across as creepy. I just didn't know what to do or if I should approach the two of you or not."

Erin reached over and squeezed the woman's arm. "We're doing our best to find Bella. I promise we are."

Stephanie used the sleeve of her sweatshirt and rubbed beneath her eyes as if wiping away unshed tears. "I know you are. I know that the scuttlebutt around town is that you may have done something to Bella. But I know that's not the truth."

"I would never hurt her." Erin's voice caught.

"I can't believe people would say that you would. I know you love her."

Erin placed a hand over her heart as relief filled her gaze. "I can't even tell you how relieved I am to hear you say that. I know you trusted me with your daughter, and I'd never want to let you down."

Stephanie sniffled and stared out the window before drawing in a shaky breath. "Giving Bella up was a hard decision. But I know that it was the right one, even with everything that's happened."

"So why did you come find me now?"

Stephanie ran a hand over the top of her head. "I want to do whatever I can to help. I don't just want to sit back and pretend like this doesn't affect me."

"You haven't heard anything, have you?" Dillon asked. "Or seen anything?"

"No. I wish I had something to offer you. But I don't."

Disappointment filled his chest cavity, even though he'd expected that response. "I understand."

"We need to find her." Stephanie's voice cracked as her gaze connected with Dillon's. "What if she's hurt? What if someone took her?"

"That's what we're trying to figure out," Dillon assured her.

"Or what if she's just like me? What if she ran, trying to escape all her problems?" Her expression pinched with pain.

Her words hung in the air.

Her questions were valid. There were a lot of variables in place here.

And time was quickly running out.

As Erin and Dillon headed back down the road, Erin's thoughts wandered.

On one hand, it was a relief to know that Stephanie didn't blame her for what had happened. That Stephanie thought she was a good mother. That she didn't regret her decision to let Erin adopt Bella.

On the other hand, the fact that Stephanie had shown up now of all times made Erin cautious. She hadn't seen the woman in years. Stephanie had smelled slightly of alcohol and cigarettes. And she'd looked so nervous.

Was that because Bella was missing? Or was there more to the story?

"That was surprising," Dillon said beside her, almost as if he could read her thoughts.

"You can say that again."

"I hate to ask this, but I feel like I need to. Do you think

Stephanie could have anything to do with Bella's disappearance?"

Erin blinked as she processed his question. "I don't think Stephanie's the violent type, if that's what you're asking."

"No, but do you think there could be more to this?"

The implications of his question hit her. "Wait...you think that maybe this is all a scheme? That Stephanie wants Bella back, so she snatched her?"

Dillon shrugged. "It makes sense, and it wouldn't be the first time that something like that has happened."

Erin swung her head back and forth. "I just can't see her doing that."

"The timing is uncanny."

"I can't argue with that. But I just don't know... I don't want to think she's capable of doing something like that."

"I just want you to be careful," Dillon said. "It's hard to know who to trust with everything that's happened."

"I know. And I appreciate your concern."

Silence stretched between them for a moment.

Finally, Erin glanced back over at him. "Where are we going?"

"I need to swing by the house and check on the dogs since Carson isn't there. It will only take a few minutes."

She nodded. "Of course. Have you heard any updates?"

"Unfortunately, no. But everyone is still searching. That's good news."

Erin stared out the window, trying not to be bothered by the conversation. But she knew Dillon had to ask about Stephanie's sudden appearance. He wasn't the type to skirt around the fact that Stephanie could have ulterior motives.

A few minutes later, they pulled up to his house. Erin scanned the buildings and woods around them to make sure there were no signs of danger. Everything looked clear.

For now.

After all that had happened, they had to be careful. Danger could be hiding around any corner.

Dillon parked his Jeep and turned to her. "Let's do this. And then we'll figure out our next steps."

Erin nodded, but tension still coursed through her.

She was growing more and more anxious by the moment.

Dillon escorted Erin inside so she could freshen up. Once he'd secured the doors and made sure everything was safe, he headed outside to the kennel to check on the dogs.

As he did, Erin slipped into the bathroom and stared at herself in the mirror. This experience seemed to have aged her. She didn't remember dark circles beneath their eyes before. Didn't remember looking so tired or her hair looking so dull.

She leaned against the sink and closed her eyes. *Dear Lord, please help Bella right now. Help us to find her. Lead us to her. Please. I'm desperate, and I'm sorry for those times that I've doubted You. Because right now, I know I'm not going to get through this without You.*

After muttering, "Amen," Erin opened her eyes and splashed some water in her face before wiping it dry with a towel. She'd promised Dillon she would wait inside until he came back just as a precaution.

As she wandered toward the living room, her phone buzzed.

She looked down at the screen and the words that she saw there made her blood go cold.

If you want to see Bella alive, meet me at the Buckhead Trailhead. Come alone. Or else.

Her heart pounded in her ears. Was this for real?

Erin knew that it was. The number wasn't the same one Arnold had used to send her those other threats.

This had most likely been sent by the person who'd abducted Bella.

Erin nibbled on her bottom lip as she thought through her options. Clearly, she didn't have a vehicle here. Her own car was in the shop, the tires being replaced.

Maybe she should just tell Dillon. Maybe he could help her figure something out.

The instructions were explicit. The sender had said Erin had to come alone.

And the penalty if she didn't?

Bella would be hurt—or worse.

It was a risk she couldn't take.

But how was Erin going to meet anyone without a vehicle?

As the question fluttered through her mind, her gaze fell on the keys Dillon had left on the kitchen counter.

The keys to his Jeep.

She swallowed hard before glancing out the window to where the dog kennel was located.

Dillon was still inside. Still out of sight. Still occupied.

Erin thought about her decision only a moment before grabbing the keys.

She could slip outside and borrow his Jeep.

Dillon would be angry with her. Erin knew he would be. Really angry.

But she had to do this for Bella.

She had no other option.

Before she could second-guess herself, Erin started for the door.

She prayed this was the right choice.

TWENTY-THREE

As an unexpected noise sounded in the distance, Dillon rushed from the kennel.

As he did, he saw his Jeep pulling from the driveway.

His Jeep?

He darted toward his house, praying that Erin was safe.

After searching inside, he knew she was gone.

Realization spread through him.

Erin had taken his Jeep, hadn't she? Why would she do that?

Was she setting out to find Bella on her own?

The thought of her doing that sent concern ricocheting through him.

There had to be more to this story.

But Dillon didn't have time to ponder that. Right now, he needed to catch her and find out what was going on.

He darted to his desk and pulled the drawer open. After riffling through paperclips and notepads, he finally found what he was looking for.

The keys to a truck he kept inside his barn.

He grabbed them before sprinting outside, yanking the barn doors wide, and climbing into the old truck.

After a few tries, the old truck engine finally rumbled to life. He eased through the open doors and made his way to the end of his driveway, he headed to the right, the same direction Erin had traveled.

But a few minutes later, when he reached a T in the road, Dillon realized he had no idea which direction she'd gone.

He contemplated his choices for a minute.

If he went to the left, it would lead him to the national forest where Bella was last seen.

If he had to guess, that was the direction Erin had headed.

Dillon jerked the wheel that way. As he did, he prayed—prayed that Erin was safe. That she would use wisdom. That God would protect her.

What could have happened to lead her to do something like this? Whatever it was, certainly Erin didn't realize what kind of situation she might be getting herself into right now.

Most likely, she was headed directly into danger. Whoever had taken Bella wouldn't stop until they got what they wanted. Dillon feared that what this person wanted was to make Erin suffer more and more.

It looked like Erin might be giving them that opportunity.

Now the challenge would be figuring out exactly what part of the national forest she might have headed toward. The place was large—500,000 acres—with uncountable trailheads. There was no way Dillon would be able to cover them all.

He had to figure out what he was going to do…and fast.

Erin felt the sweat across her brow as she headed down the road.

She prayed she was making the right choice. Prayed she wasn't making a bad situation worse.

What if she was playing right into the hands of the person who'd taken Bella? She knew there was a good chance she was.

But she'd sacrifice whatever necessary if it meant Bella would be safe.

She wiped her forehead with the sleeve of her sweat-shirt before shifting gears as the Jeep climbed higher up the mountain.

It had been a rough ride. But she was doing okay.

Now she just needed to make it up this mountain.

And find the Buckhead Trail.

She should have looked up an address before she'd left, but she hadn't thought about it. She'd had to leave right then before Dillon stopped her. She'd had no time to waste.

Dillon...she frowned. She hadn't realized until now just how much she truly cared about that man.

But she did.

Even though it was crazy that her feelings had grown so quickly in such a short period of time, that's exactly what had happened.

Dillon had been a rock for her. He'd cared about her when no one else had. And he hadn't doubted her story.

She wiped beneath her eyes.

Please, Lord, keep him safe. Don't let my decision hurt him. Help him forgive me.

She muttered an amen and then pulled herself together. Right now, Erin had to concentrate on Bella. Everything else she would deal with later.

What would the person who'd sent her the text do when Erin arrived? Take her to Bella? Kill her on the spot?

She had so many questions, so much that didn't make sense.

There were too many possible players in this scheme, and Erin didn't know which one might be behind this.

Whoever it was wanted to make Erin pay. She just didn't know what mistakes this penance was for.

Her hands gripped the wheel, white-knuckled.

The mountain road was steep, and as she traveled to a higher elevation, the air became cooler. The road became icier.

You can do this, Erin!

She gave herself a mental pep talk. But the higher she climbed, the more her anxiety grew.

She should have told Dillon. Coming alone had been a bad idea. With every turn of the wheel, that seemed more and more clear. But there was no going back now. Erin doubted she even had any phone reception at this point.

More sweat beaded across her skin.

Finally, she spotted a sign on the side of the road.

Buckhead Trail.

It was only a mile away. She was getting closer.

She continued up the mountain, shifting gears and praying she could figure this out.

Finally, she reached the parking area for the trail.

She was here.

Erin let out a breath, even though she knew her trouble was probably just beginning.

The person who'd texted her had said for her to come alone. It was too late to change her mind now.

She'd followed the instructions and played by the rules.

Now maybe she could get Bella back.

She parked the Jeep and sat there a moment, her heart racing.

What next?

She glanced at her phone, but it was as she'd expected. She didn't have any reception.

How would she get her next set of instructions?

She leaned back and waited, her heart pounding in her ears.

Waiting would be the hardest part, especially if she started to second-guess herself.

As another car pulled into the parking lot, she sucked in a breath. Who else was here?

Her eyes widened as the vehicle came into focus.

It was a police car.

The cops were here?

Had they tracked her down so they could arrest her?

She pressed her eyes closed.

No.

Not now.

Not when she was so close.

Dear Lord...what am I going to do?

As she saw the door open and someone step out, she braced herself and tried to figure out how to handle this situation.

With every mile that went past, Dillon's worry grew.

Where had Erin gone? What had happened to make her do this?

Dillon only prayed he found her in time.

So far, he'd checked out every road that pulled off from this main one. But the task was tedious and taking too much time.

If only he knew where Erin was.

If he had more time, he could search his Jeep's GPS to see where the vehicle was located. But to do that he would need to go back to his house. For now, he would keep searching in his truck.

There were entirely too many pull-offs in this area. Working this way would take forever. But he had little choice right now.

He studied each of the various trailhead signs as he passed, wondering if Erin may have decided to go search by herself. With her ankle being sprained and conditions being what they were, it sounded like a terrible idea.

Plus, he'd just heard while checking on his dogs that another snowstorm was headed this way. The last thing Erin needed to do was to be stuck on this mountain during a storm in her present condition.

He had to admire her determination as a mom. He knew

that mothers were protective of their kids, and Erin had proven that to be true.

Dillon hoped there was a good solution for the situation, one where Bella would be rescued and Erin would be okay.

He shook his head as he pulled onto another lane branching from the main road that wound through the mountains.

Erin should have told him what was going on. She should have never left on her own.

Just as those thoughts raced through his head, he spotted a vehicle in the distance.

His breath caught.

Was that his Jeep?

He pressed the accelerator harder as he headed toward it. Quickly, he pulled up behind it and then rushed to the front doors. He already knew what he would most likely find inside.

He was right.

Nothing. No one.

Erin wasn't here.

He bit back a frown.

He glanced around at the trees surrounding him.

Where had Erin gone?

As he stepped back, he spotted another set of tire tracks in the space beside the Jeep.

Erin had met somebody here.

But who?

Could Arnold really be guilty? Was he working with someone to teach Erin a lesson?

Or what about Stephanie? What if she really was involved?

Or there was always the Bradshaws. They had a long history of crime and violence.

He wouldn't put anything past that family.

It almost seemed like there were too many possible suspects.

There was no way Dillon would be able to track down all these people on his own.

He was going to need to call in backup.

As soon as he got phone reception, he would talk to Rick and find out what his friend could do to help.

Because something was majorly wrong here.

And if Dillon didn't get to the bottom of it soon, he feared Erin may not make it out of this situation alive.

Erin felt her throat tighten as she sat in the back seat of the police cruiser. She'd tried to explain that she couldn't leave. Tried to convince the officer that this was a mistake, that she was innocent.

But Officer Hollins hadn't listened.

Instead, she'd been placed in the back of the police car like a criminal.

Panic fluttered up inside her as the officer backed out and started down the road.

"How did you find me?" Her voice squeaked as the words left her lips.

"We've been watching you." Hollins glanced back at her. "Be glad I'm the one who finally tracked you down and not Blackstone. He's furious, and he has a major chip on his shoulder."

"He's had a chip on his shoulder for a long time." Erin shifted and glanced out the window.

As she did, more panic rose in her. How was she ever going to find Bella now? Her one opportunity had slipped away. She hated the helpless feeling swirling inside her.

"Hollins, you've got to listen to me." She leaned forward so he could hear the desperation in her voice. Her argument hadn't worked the first time, but maybe it would now. "If you don't let me meet the person I was supposed to meet, they're going to do something to Bella."

"What do you mean?" Officer Hollins glanced back at her in the rearview mirror.

"I got a text saying I had to meet whoever had taken Bella at that location. If I'm not there, I don't know what's going to happen to her."

He continued to stare at the road ahead. "I can send an officer out."

"You can't do that. It had to be me." Her voice came out higher pitched and louder with each word.

"I told the chief that I would bring you in. He'll figure something out."

"You know that's not true. You know he thinks I'm part of this." Despair bit deep into her.

"You're just going to have to trust us."

But that was part of the problem. Erin *didn't* trust them. It was why she'd had to take matters into her own hands.

Erin squeezed her eyes shut. She desperately wished that Dillon was there right now. He would know what to do.

But she'd made the decision to go without him, and now she had to live with it.

She hoped this wasn't the biggest mistake of her life.

She slowly opened her eyes again, trying to regain her focus. "What are you going to do with me?"

"I'm going to take you into the station for questioning. The chief said he found something on your computer."

Alarm raced through her as questions collided in her mind. "On my computer? There was nothing on my computer."

Had Erin been set up again? When would the hits stop coming?

"I'm just telling you what I heard," Hollins said. "I'll do everything I can to make sure Blackstone handles this in the right way."

At least Officer Hollins had picked her up. At least he was one of the good guys.

But there was so little positive Erin could see in this situation.

As Hollins turned off the street onto another road, Erin's spine straightened. "This isn't the way to the police station."

"I just need to make a quick stop first."

"A quick stop? Where?"

"You'll see."

But as Hollins said the words, a bad feeling grew in Erin's gut.

There was more to the story, wasn't there?

The truth nagged at her, but she didn't want to face it. Didn't want to think she could be right.

Instead, she braced herself for whatever would happen next.

TWENTY-FOUR

As soon as Dillon got reception, he called Rick and gave him the update. Rick promised to keep his eyes open and to alert the other park rangers that Erin might be missing. He also told Dillon there were no updates out on the trail and that the teams were going to head back soon.

It was a double set of bad news.

Before he ended the call, Dillon asked one more question. "Is Blackstone with you?"

"No, he's not out here today," Rick said. "He said he's manning the station. Why?"

"I'll explain later."

Dillon knew exactly where he needed to head next. He had to talk to Blackstone and let him know what was going on. Even if the man didn't take him seriously, there was no way Dillon could find Erin on his own. He needed help.

As he continued down the road, Dillon made a few more phone calls. He let his colleagues with the state police also know what was going on so that everybody could have their eyes open for Erin.

A bad feeling brewed in Dillon's gut as he thought about the possibilities of what had happened.

What if the person Erin had met in the parking lot was the same person who had taken Bella?

It was clear this person wanted to make Erin suffer. If Bella's abductor had been able to finally snatch Erin, maybe this would fulfill the last step of his plan.

Yet there were other things that didn't make sense. The person behind this had the opportunity to grab Erin after breaking into Dillon's house. Why hadn't he? Maybe he had some kind of weird timing he wanted to follow.

It was hard to always predict how criminals thought. But in this case, this guy obviously had some type of agenda.

And Erin was at the center of it.

Dillon's gut clenched as he thought about it.

Finally, Dillon arrived at the police station. He quickly threw the truck into Park before hurrying inside. He bypassed the reception area and barged right into Chief Blackstone's office.

The man looked up at him and narrowed his eyes when he saw Dillon standing there.

"Can I help you?" Blackstone's voice sounded tense with irritation.

"Erin is missing."

His eyebrows flickered up. "Is she missing? Or did she sneak away to go check on Bella?"

Anger surged through Dillon. "You know Erin's not responsible for this. You just want to make her pay because Liam disappeared."

"You don't know what you're talking about."

"It's as plain as day that that's the case. I think somebody may have taken Erin. Most likely the person who took Bella."

Blackstone tapped his finger on his desk. "Why would they want both of them?"

"Clearly, it's because someone has some type of agenda. I need your help."

Blackstone shrugged. "I'm not sure what I can do. Most of my guys are out on the trails right now, looking for Bella. If Erin had just told us where she had taken her…"

Dillon slammed his hand onto the chief's desk. "You need to listen to me. Somebody took Erin and Bella, and we've got to find them before it's too late. Do you under-stand that?"

The chief stared at him for another moment. "I hear what you're saying."

"And what are you going to do about it?" Dillon hated to speak to the chief like that, but being nice wasn't cutting it with this man. He had to let him know he meant business.

Blackstone rose from his seat. "I'll let my other guys know what's going on, and they can be on the lookout."

At least that was something. But Dillon needed more. "Can you try to trace her cell phone signal?"

He stared at Dillon a moment, and Dillon braced him-self for whatever he was going to say.

But finally, Blackstone nodded. "Let me see what I can do."

As Hollins pulled off onto a side road, Erin's heart went into her throat.

"Where are you taking me?" she demanded. Her fingers dug into the seat beneath her as tension curled her muscles.

"It's like I told you. I just need to make a quick stop."

"Hollins…"

"Stop asking questions." His voice hardened.

As soon as she heard his words, Erin realized her worst fears were true.

Hollins was part of this somehow, wasn't he?

She leaned toward the plastic divide separating them. "You don't have to do this."

He didn't bother to look at her. "I don't know what you're talking about."

"I thought that you were my friend."

One of his shoulders tensed, rising slightly as he sat there. "You did wrong by Liam."

Wait… Hollins was doing this to honor his friend? Was

that what this was all about? "Hollins...you don't know this whole story. You only know what Liam told you."

"You adopted Bella and then you kicked Liam out of the house. You took everything he'd worked so hard for. Liam tried everything to get you back."

"There's more to that story," Erin rushed to insist.

She glanced at the door handle, wanting to grab it and yank it open. But she knew the door was locked, and she couldn't open it from the inside.

There was no way out of this car.

She tried to push down the panic that wanted to bubble up inside her.

"I'm sure you're going to say he treated you badly," Hollins said. "That's what people always say."

"But Liam *did* treat me badly. I'm not even just talking about yelling at me. He hurt me, Hollins."

His jaw tightened. "He would never do that. He's a good man."

"Whatever you think you need to do right now, you don't have to do it," Erin told him, praying she might be able to convince him to change his mind.

"Yes, I do."

Erin swallowed hard, trying to think through ways she might convince him to change his mind. No good ideas hit her. Maybe she needed more information first.

"Are you the one who broke into Dillon's house and threatened me?"

He finally glanced over his shoulder and shrugged. "I wanted to send you a message."

"Why not just kill me there and get all of this over with?"

"Kill you?" His eyes widened. "You think that's our goal?"

Erin didn't miss the fact that he'd used the word *our*. Who else was a part of this? "What else would you want to do?"

"Plenty. You'll see. You're asking too many questions."

"Hollins..."

"Enough!" He sliced his hand through the air. "Enough talking. Anything else you want to know, you're just going to have to wait. Understand?"

Erin leaned back in her seat and stared at the forest as they traveled deeper and deeper into the woods.

How could Hollins be involved in this? Did he really want to make Erin pay this badly for what he perceived as a slight against his friend?

How was she going to get herself out of the situation? Especially considering the fact that she wouldn't be able to run, not with her hurt foot.

Hollins pulled to a stop at the end of the lane.

There was nothing in front of them.

They were miles and miles into the heart of the Pisgah National Forest, she realized. Clearly out of cell phone range. Where nobody else would be around for miles and miles.

Nausea gurgled in her stomach.

There was no one out here to help her, she realized.

Erin was going to have to rely on her own skills if she wanted to get out of the situation alive.

As promised, Blackstone had pinged Erin's cell phone, but it was out of range. Instead, Dillon had tried to follow the tire tracks away from that parking area. But in the lower elevations, the snow had faded and so had any tire tracks.

He'd only been probably ten minutes behind Erin, however. So if someone had picked her up, Dillon would have passed them—and he hadn't passed anyone on his way up the mountain.

The questions only made his temples pound harder.

There was only one way he could think to find her. It was a long shot. But it might work.

Dillon called Carson and told his nephew to meet him at the parking area where his Jeep had been found.

Normally, in situations like this, search and rescue dogs could follow a scent on foot. But considering the treacherous mountain road, the fading daylight and approaching storm, that wouldn't be safe.

Instead, Dillon had grabbed a piece of clothing Erin had left at his place and then met Carson and Scout near the Buckhead Trailhead.

As soon as he saw Scout, he squatted on the ground and rubbed his dog's head. "You ready to work?"

Scout leaned into his hand.

"I need you to find Erin," Dillon continued. "Can you do that?"

Scout raised his nose as if he understood the question.

Without wasting any more time, Dillon let Scout sniff Erin's sweatshirt.

A few minutes later, the dog raised his nose into the air and sniffed. Scout began pulling Dillon back toward the entrance of the parking area.

Dillon knew the chances were slim, but he was going to give it a try.

With Carson driving, Dillon would sit in the front seat with Scout. He'd put the window down and let Scout reach his nose out.

They slowly took off down the road.

Dillon hoped the dog would remain on the scent.

They crept back down the mountain. Dillon knew the next turnoff wouldn't be for another mile, but as they passed a section of woods, Scout began to bark.

Carson tapped the brake. "What do you want me to do?"

Dillon peered between the trees. "It looks like there's a service road right here that's just barely big enough for a vehicle to go through. The way the tree branches fall in front of it, it's nearly impossible to see from the road."

"I didn't notice it," Carson said.

"Let's see what happens. Turn here."

Carson did as he'd said, and they pulled down the narrow lane.

Just as Dillon had thought, the space was barely wide enough for them to fit through, and some of the overhead branches scratched the roof of his Jeep. Dillon would worry about that later.

Slowly, they continued along the gravel lane.

It was possible that Erin and whoever had taken her had gone down this lane before Dillon arrived. It was probably the right distance away that Dillon wouldn't have seen them.

His heart pounded harder. Maybe he was onto something.

Because he desperately wanted to find Erin.

In the short amount of time they'd known each other, he'd realized there was something special about her. He needed to find her and tell her that. He needed to stop holding on to the hurts of his past relationships and open himself up to more possibilities for the future. Possibilities with Erin.

There was a lot that needed to happen first.

Starting with finding Erin and Bella.

The task nearly felt insurmountable. But for Dillon, failure wasn't an option.

At the end of the lane, Carson pulled a stop.

Right behind a police cruiser.

Carson nodded to the vehicle. "Do you know who that belongs to?"

Blackstone's face flashed in Dillon's mind.

But Dillon didn't think the police chief could have gotten here in the time since they'd spoken. Was the chief working with somebody? Had he sent one of his guys here to take care of business?

It was a possibility.

In other circumstances, Dillon would call in the car to

see who it belonged to. But out here, he had no phone reception.

Scout barked out the window at the car.

He was still on the scent.

That meant Erin had been here recently.

"We're going to have to go the rest of the way on foot," Dillon said.

Carson nodded beside him. "I want to help. Just let me know what I need to do."

Erin nearly stumbled down the trail as Hollins gripped her arm. He wanted her to move faster than she possibly could.

The trails were too steep. Too slippery. Her ankle was too weak.

He didn't care about that. All he cared about was that she kept moving forward.

So that's what Erin tried to do.

But every time she breathed a gulp of air, her lungs hurt. It was so cold out here and the wind was only getting stronger and cooler by the moment.

If her gut instinct was right, a storm was headed this way. It was the only way to explain the sudden drop in temperature and why such a sharp breeze had stirred.

"Where are you taking me?" Her words came out between her gasps for air.

"I told you to stop asking questions."

"You're not like this," she told him. "You like doing the right thing. I can see it in your eyes."

His eyes narrowed. "Sometimes the right thing isn't black or white. Sometimes you have to go off course in order to do the right thing."

What did that mean? Could she break through to him? She was going to keep trying.

"I don't know what you think the right thing is, but I assure you that this isn't it," Erin said. "I'm innocent in all of this. I don't care what anyone has told you."

Blackstone's face flashed in her mind. He'd put his officer up to this, hadn't he? As vengeance for Liam's disappearance. It was the only thing that made sense.

"Just keep moving," Hollins muttered. "You're not going to change my mind on this."

"Do you have Bella?" Erin's voice cracked as the question left her lips.

"I said, no more questions."

"Please, I have to know. Is my daughter okay?"

He didn't say anything for a moment until finally blurting, "She's fine. Now, keep moving."

As Hollins shoved her forward, Erin nearly stumbled. Her knee hit the boulder in front of her and pain shot through her. She winced but didn't have any time to recover.

Hollins kept his grip on her arm and urged her down the path. "We don't have much time. The weather's going to turn bad."

"It's not too late to turn around now." Erin knew he wouldn't listen to her, but she felt like she had to try anyway.

"Keep moving," he grumbled.

With her shoulders tight, Erin did just that. She kept moving forward.

Finally, a cabin came into view. Yellow lights glowed from the windows.

The whole place looked like it was less than a thousand square feet, and there was no smoke coming from the chimney. It was probably cold inside.

But this was clearly where Erin was heading.

Hollins dragged her up the steps and opened the door.

The figure waiting for her there took Erin's breath away.

TWENTY-FIVE

"Liam?" Erin blinked as she stared at his oversized form.

He still looked basically the same, except now his blond hair had grown longer and a beard and a mustache covered part of his face.

But his eyes…they were still cold and calculating enough to send a shiver through Erin.

"Are you surprised to see me?" His words sounded full of malice as a mix of satisfaction and dark amusement mingled in his tone.

She tried to back up but Hollins caught her and pushed her forward. "I thought you were dead."

"That's the point. Everybody is *supposed* to think that I'm dead."

Hollins shut the door behind her, and the brisk wind disappeared for a moment.

They couldn't use the fireplace. From a distance, the smoke would have drawn too much attention. Instead, piles of blankets were on the couch and there was an electric heater. If she had to guess, this place was solar-powered.

"Why do you want people to think you're dead?" Erin stared at Liam, still unable to believe he was standing in front of her.

"It's a long story," he muttered.

Her gaze wandered around the room, looking for any signs of Bella. Looking for any signs of what was going on here.

Nothing caught her eye.

"Why did you bring me here?" Erin drew her gaze back up to meet Liam's. She needed answers. Would he offer her any? "Why have you done all of this?"

He stepped closer and ran his finger down her arm. "You're here because you're mine. If you thought that you were just going to divorce me and walk away and I was going to pretend like none of this happened, then you were sadly mistaken."

She cringed and tried to back up. But Hollins was still there, holding her in place. "So you're just going to live out the rest of your days here? Pretending that you're dead?"

"Maybe. But for now, I'm safe here."

Her breath caught as more realizations raced through her mind. "You got yourself in some type of trouble, didn't you?"

His gaze darkened. "That's not important. What's important is that you're here now. Our little family is back together."

"Where's Bella?" Erin demanded.

He nodded at Hollins. Hollins took his cue, walked over to a door off to the side and opened it. A moment later, Bella nearly tumbled to the floor.

As soon as Bella spotted Erin, tears flooded her eyes. She drew herself to her feet and darted toward Erin. "Mom!"

"Bella!" Erin threw her arms around her daughter as tears flooded her eyes. "I was so worried about you."

"I'm so sorry, Mom," Bella breathed. "I should have never gone without you."

Erin had so many questions for her daughter, but now wasn't the time to ask them.

Now was the time to figure out how she and Bella were going to get out of this seemingly no-win situation.

With an arm still around Bella, Erin turned back to

Liam. "Now that you have us both here, what are you going to do with us?"

His eyes sparkled with some kind of unspoken plan. "I thought we could just settle down and live like the perfect little happy family for a while."

Was he serious?

There was no amusement in his gaze. That realization terrified her.

"There's nothing happy about the situation," Erin reminded him.

He nodded at the window. "There's a snowstorm coming, so you might as well get comfortable. We have a lot of catching up to do."

A sickly feeling trickled in Erin's gut.

Liam really had lost his mind, hadn't he? Who exactly had he gotten himself into trouble with—enough trouble that he'd had to hide away from the rest of the world?

Liam had been perfectly content to let people think that Erin had done something. It was one way of making her pay for divorcing him.

Erin had to figure out how she was going to get out of the situation.

She had no time to waste.

Dillon and Carson followed the trail as Scout pulled them along.

Erin had definitely come this way. Dillon had no doubt about it.

As they walked, a smattering of freezing rain fell between the branches above them. Conditions were only going to get worse and worse.

They had to find her and soon.

Dillon looked at his phone. He still had no reception. Thankfully, he'd told his state police officer friends as well as Rick where they were heading. Maybe they would know to follow this trail just in case they needed some backup here.

Dillon paused Scout on the path and sucked in a breath. Carson nearly collided into them. "What's going on?"

Dillon put a finger over his lips. Then he pointed to the ground. "Look at all the footsteps here. If Erin came this way, she either had an army with her or people were following her."

Carson's eyes widened. "But there were no other cars in the parking lot."

His nephew raised a good point. "There's probably more than one way to get to this trail. Either way, we need to be on guard. We don't know exactly who we're up against here."

Carson nodded and they continued, quietly making their way down the trail. They had to watch their steps to make sure they had no more injuries. That was the last thing they needed to slow them down.

Dear Lord, please be with Erin now. Keep her safe. Protect her. Bella also. Guide our steps and help us to find them.

The deeper they headed into the valley, the rockier the trail became. They weren't moving as quickly as Dillon would have liked, but he reminded himself that slow in actuality meant fast. Being careless would only make them trip up, and he couldn't afford to do that.

As something in the distance caught his eye, he paused. "It's a cabin," he muttered.

Carson stopped beside him. "Do you think that is where Erin is?"

"It's my best guess."

Scout would get a nice reward later for leading them here.

Dillon kept his hand raised in the air, motioning for Carson to remain still. Then he scanned everything around him.

He spotted three men hiding in the brush in the distance.

If he wasn't mistaken, they had guns in their hands—guns that were aimed at the cabin.

Best he could tell, they hadn't spotted him, Carson or Scout yet.

Dillon would have to be careful as he planned his next move.

Erin still held Bella as they stood facing Liam.

"I still don't understand why you're doing this," Erin said.

"You don't have to understand." He sneered at her. "You just need to be pretty."

Erin narrowed her eyes. "You're the one who called and told the police chief that my car was on the trailhead on the day Bella disappeared, weren't you?"

His grin was answer enough for her. "I wanted them to scrutinize you. I wanted you to feel the heat."

"I'm guessing you sent Hollins into the woods near Dillon's place? He was the one who broke into Dillon's home." She glanced at Hollins as he stood guarding the door, his face expressionless.

"I just wanted to send you a message. I understand you and Dillon were getting pretty cozy."

She shook her head. No doubt, that had only upset him more. But Dillon was the last thing she wanted to talk to Liam about.

"Everything still doesn't make sense," Erin continued. "You had opportunities to snatch me, if that's what you needed to do. Why go through all the trouble of taking Bella and then sending me those threats?"

"I've always liked playing games with you."

She sucked in a breath. His words were true. He'd tested her, left dishes in the sink just to see if she'd wash them, rearranged drawers to see if Erin would straighten them.

And if she hadn't met his expectations…then she'd paid for it.

So Liam had taken Bella, knowing that would make her suffer the most. Then he'd sent Hollins to keep an eye on her. To threaten her. To let her know there was more to come.

Enjoying her mental anguish was just a small gratification for him.

The thought made disgust roil in her stomach.

Erin turned her thoughts back to the present. She surveyed the cabin, trying to find any means of escape.

But even if she and Bella managed to get away, there was no way the two of them could navigate these mountains. It would be dark soon. Freezing rain hit the roof. And Erin's ankle and leg throbbed.

She looked at Liam again. "What are you going to do with us now?"

"Right now, I want you to sit down and be quiet for a few minutes. There's been way too much talking for my comfort."

Erin took Bella's hand and led her to the couch.

"Hollins, keep an eye on them," Liam ordered.

"Yes, sir."

Liam disappeared into a different room while Hollins stood guard with his arms crossed over his chest. As he did, Erin turned to Bella.

"How are you?" she asked, looking Bella over. "Did he hurt you?"

With tears rimming her eyes, Bella shook her head. "No, he just scared me."

"How did he even lure you away?"

"Someone left me a message on a piece of paper saying that I needed to meet at the trailhead, that your life was in danger. But when I got there, I saw Officer Hollins. He told me he was going to take me to you."

Erin's eyes flickered to Hollins, and she scowled.

"Instead, he led me down the trail. Liam was waiting for us. Hollins left me with him, and Liam insisted I had to come with him. He had a gun. He made me walk down these trails and over cliffs until we got to this cabin."

Erin's heart lurched into her throat as she imagined what Bella had been through. "I'm so sorry that happened to you. We've been looking hard for you."

"I know you have. I knew you wouldn't give up."

Erin wrapped her arms around Bella and held her. "You have no idea how worried I was."

"I love you, Mom. I'm sorry you're here with me now, but I'm glad to see you at the same time." She sniffled.

Erin didn't let go. "I know, sweetie. I know."

"What are we going to do?"

Erin glanced around the cabin again. "I wish I knew. But we'll figure out something. We just need to be brave."

"I wouldn't do that if I were you," Hollins muttered.

He'd clearly been listening to their conversation.

"How did you get involved with this?" Erin asked. "I always thought you were a good cop."

"Liam trained me," Hollins said. "He told me what you were like. He told me about the conspiracies against him. Told me I couldn't believe anything."

"Conspiracies about what?"

"About—"

Before he could finish, the window shattered.

A bullet had flown through that window.

Someone was outside, and they were shooting at them.

It couldn't be Dillon. He wouldn't be that careless.

If Liam and Hollins were inside, then who could possibly be behind the gunfire now?

TWENTY-SIX

When Dillon heard the gunfire, he knew he had to spring into action. There was no time to waste.

He pushed Carson back and handed him Scout's lead. "Stay here."

Carson nodded and ducked behind a boulder.

Crouching low, Dillon moved closer to the cabin. He gripped his gun, prepared to use it if necessary.

Aiming carefully, he took his first shot. He hit one of the men in the shoulder.

The man let out a yelp before falling to the ground.

One down. Two more to go.

But he knew those two remaining guys could do a lot of damage.

Especially now that they knew Dillon was there.

Just as the thought raced through his mind, a bullet split the bark on the tree beside him.

Dillon was going to have to get closer. Those guys were going to breech that cabin, and there was no telling what would happen then.

As he crept closer, another bullet flew through the air.

Before he could duck out of the way, pain sliced his arm.

Dillon let out a gasp.

He'd been hit.

"Get behind the couch!" Liam yelled. "Now!"

Erin heard the anger in his voice and rose. Wasting no

time, she shoved the couch from the wall and pulled Bella back there with her.

More bullets continued to fly.

As they did, Liam pulled out his gun and crouched beneath the window.

Things began to click in Erin's mind.

Liam was hiding because he'd made someone mad, wasn't he? Likely, it was the Bradshaws.

Now he had no choice but to hide out or they were going to kill him.

It made sense.

"Mom…" Bella's wide eyes stared at her.

Erin squeezed her hand and held her close. "Just stay low."

More bullets flew.

What was going to happen if the gunmen outside got inside? Would they all be goners?

It was a good possibility. At least Liam appeared to want her alive for a little while.

As more bullets flew, Erin heard someone gasp. She raised her head enough to see Hollins drop to the floor.

He'd been hit in the chest. Blood filled his shirt.

She swallowed back a scream.

Just as Erin thought things couldn't get worse, someone burst through the door. When she heard Liam mutter something beneath his breath, she knew they were in trouble.

The gunman was inside.

Dillon glanced at his biceps.

The bullet had grazed his skin.

He might need a few stitches, but otherwise he was going to be okay—other than the pain from where the bullet had sliced into his arm.

As he saw the gunmen moving toward the cabin, Dillon crept closer. One man approached the door while the other stood back.

Dillon got in place behind the tree and then aimed his gun. When he pulled the trigger, the bullet hit the one man in the shoulder and he fell to the ground.

Now it was just the gunman at the door.

And whoever else was inside.

As Dillon heard another bullet fire, a scream sounded from inside.

His heart pounded harder. Was that Erin? Was she okay?

He had to get closer.

He darted toward the back of the cabin. There was a window there, and he should be able to see inside.

Remaining low, he crouched beneath it and peered inside.

Liam stood there, his back to the window.

He was alive.

Dillon sucked in a breath.

And the man was probably behind most of this chaos.

Dillon would deal with it later.

He continued to scan the interior of the cabin. He spotted two people huddling behind the couch.

Erin and Bella…

They were okay!

Relief filled him at that realization.

Thank you, Jesus!

But he had other issues to address first…starting with the fact that Bill Bradshaw stood in front of Liam with his gun raised.

The Bradshaws were also involved in this. They'd probably been hunting Liam this whole time. Somehow, when Erin came here, she must have led them right to Liam.

While Dillon didn't care what happened to Liam, he couldn't risk something happening to Erin and Bella.

"You thought you were going to get away with this," Bill muttered.

"How did you find me?"

"I've been following that state cop and your ex-wife ever since they came to my house," Bill said. "I figured they might lead me to you, and I was right. Now, I need you to put your gun down."

Liam's nostrils flared. "That's not going to happen."

He turned his gun toward Erin. "Then I'll shoot them first."

"I don't care if you shoot them," Liam said. "But you're not walking away from here alive."

"You've been trying to find evidence to take my family down, haven't you?" Bill said. "But you got in with the wrong people. You're not going to get away with what you've done."

Dillon continued to listen. What exactly had Liam done?

"I didn't do anything," Liam insisted.

"You stole money from us! Money you found during a police operation. Then you tried to bribe us."

Liam said nothing.

But suddenly everything made sense.

Liam had tried to blackmail a crime family. They'd probably put a bounty on his head, and he'd been forced into hiding.

Except, Liam was too much of a narcissist to simply disappear. He'd wanted his old life back—one way or another. That's why he'd come after Erin and Bella.

In the blink of an eye, Bill shifted his gun toward Liam and pulled the trigger.

Erin screamed.

Liam collapsed on the cabin floor.

Bill had shot him, Dillon realized.

"Now it's your turn," Bill grumbled, his gaze on Erin.

Wasting no time, Dillon rose, aimed, and pulled the trigger.

But not before Bill also fired his gun.

Erin huddled with Bella behind the couch, praying they'd stay safe.

When she glanced up, she spotted someone peering in the window.

Was that… Dillon?

Her breath caught.

It was! He was here!

He was okay.

Thank you, Jesus.

But what about everybody else? What was happening inside this cabin?

Erin dared lift her head even more.

When she did, she saw both Liam and Bill Bradshaw on the floor. They'd both been shot.

"Stay here," she whispered to Bella.

Quickly, Erin darted from her hiding space. Both men were still alive, their chests rising as they breathed. If they were alive, that meant they were still dangerous.

She kicked the gun away from Liam before he could grab it from the floor. Instead, she darted across the room and snatched the weapon herself. She needed to have it on hand, just in case.

At the thought, Bill raised his head and moaned.

Her eyes rushed to the ground.

His gun was still at his fingertips. One move and…

She knew she didn't have time to grab the gun.

Before she could figure out what to do, men in SWAT uniforms invaded the cabin.

"Police! Put your hands up!"

The state police. They were here.

The gun fell from her hands, clattering on the floor as relief filled her.

Erin nearly collapsed to the floor herself.

But before she could, arms caught her.

She looked up and saw Dillon there.

As the police took over the scene and a paramedic checked Bella, Dillon folded her into his embrace.

This was finally all over.

She melted in his arms.

"Are you okay?" Dillon muttered.

"I am now that you're here."

He pulled her closer. "I was so worried. You shouldn't have left without me."

"I know. It's a long story. I'll explain later."

Dillon's gaze was full of warmth as he pulled away just enough to lock gazes with her. He gently placed a kiss on her cheek, one that assured her everything would be okay.

"We'll have time to talk later," he said. "I hope we'll have a lot more time for talking together."

A grin spread across her face.

Erin liked the sound of that.

She glanced over at Bella again. Right now, she had to concentrate on her daughter.

But she and Dillon would definitely finish this conversation later.

TWENTY-SEVEN

"This is like my dream come true!" Bella hurried from dog kennel to dog kennel so she could meet all the canines at Dillon's place.

As she did, Erin and Dillon stood back and smiled as they watched her.

Seeing her bounce back after such a horrific ordeal was wonderful. Erin had been anxious that what had happened would set Bella back—and in ways, it had. The healing process would take time.

But overall, Bella was doing so well.

A month had passed since Bella had been rescued. Liam and Bill Bradshaw were now behind bars, as were their henchmen. In the midst of the media blitz about everything that had happened, Blackstone had been in the hot seat over his handling of the case. That had eventually led to the mayor firing him and offering Dillon the job. Dillon had turned the position down.

He liked what he was doing here apparently. As he should.

He was a great dog trainer, and the work he did was valuable.

Dillon wrapped his arm around Erin's waist and pulled her closer.

"I think Bella likes it here," Erin murmured, still watching her daughter. They'd purposely waited a while before bringing Bella here. They hadn't wanted to rush things.

But, so far, Bella and Dillon had really hit it off. Seeing Dillon come to their rescue had only helped their quick bond.

"I think she does, too," Dillon muttered.

Scout deserted the bowl where he'd been lapping up water and wandered toward them. As he did, Erin knelt on the ground in front of the canine. "And how are you doing today, boy?"

She rubbed his head as the dog leaned into her.

Thankfully, Scout hadn't been hurt in the middle of the shootout. Carson had kept him safe.

"I think he likes you," Dillon said.

"You led Dillon to me, didn't you?" Erin murmured. "You helped save my life. Thank you, boy."

She'd already thanked the dog numerous times, showered him with attention, and even brought him some bones.

Erin gave Scout one more head pat before rising again.

As she did, Dillon caught her in his arms. He stole a glance over his shoulder as if checking to see if Bella was still occupied.

When he saw that she was, he planted a kiss on Erin's lips. "In case I haven't told you this yet, I'm so sorry about everything that happened. But I'm so glad this path led me to you."

Erin's heart warmed as she stared into his warm eyes. "Me, too. You've been a real godsend, Dillon Walker."

He leaned forward and kissed her again.

"I love you, Erin Lansing," he told her.

Erin grinned. "I love you, too."

"Am I going to have to tell you two to knock it off again?" Bella called from the other side of the building.

They laughed before turning to her, arms still around each other.

Bella strode toward them, her eyes on Erin. "It's actually nice to see you happy. You never looked like this when Liam was in your life."

Erin's smile faded. "You're right. I didn't."

Until she'd met Dillon, Erin didn't know what a good relationship could look like. She was so grateful God had brought him into her life.

She looked forward to their future together...a future complete with Bella and Scout.

* * * * *

Experience action-packed mystery and suspense in the K-9 Search and Rescue series:

Search and Defend *by Heather Woodhaven*
Following the Trail *by Lynette Eason*
Dangerous Mountain Rescue *by Christy Barritt*

If you enjoyed this exciting story of suspense and romance, pick up these other stories from Christy Barritt:

Hidden Agenda
Mountain Hideaway
Dark Harbor
Shadow of Suspicion
The Baby Assignment
The Cradle Conspiracy
Trained to Defend
Mountain Survival

Available now from Love Inspired Suspense!

Find more great reads at www.LoveInspired.com.

Dear Reader,

Thank you so much for reading *Dangerous Mountain Rescue*. I hope you enjoyed getting to know Dillon, Erin and Scout as much as I did.

Like the characters in my book, have you ever been painted in a negative light? Have untrue accusations been thrown at you?

The Bible says in Colossians that God had rescued us from the darkness and brought us…redemption.

I love the word *redemption*. It means that we've been saved from sin or error. It means forgiveness.

Erin and Dillon both felt an oppressive sense of accusation throughout the story. Their pasts came with seemingly impossible burdens. But in the end, they overcame those obstacles and found the freedom they sought.

We can do that, too, when we rely on God and trust in His plan for us and our future.

Until next time!
Christy Barritt

COMING NEXT MONTH FROM
Love Inspired Suspense

DETECTION DETAIL
Rocky Mountain K-9 Unit • by Terri Reed

Protecting an alleged arsonist was not what K-9 officer Nelson Rivers and accelerant-detection dog, Diesel, expected from any assignment. But when a gunman targets Mia Turner, Nelson will need to figure out if she's guilty or innocent—before she's hunted down.

HIGH-RISK RESCUE
Honor Protection Specialists • by Elizabeth Goddard

Surviving a shoot-out is not how Hannah Kahn planned to start her new job. But when her boss is killed, she'll have to rely on Ayden Honor—her boss's bodyguard and her ex—to outrun the mysterious mercenaries now intent on chasing her...

ABDUCTION IN THE DARK
Range River Bounty Hunters • by Jenna Night

When kidnappers force their way into her house to abduct her nephew, Tanya Rivera will do anything to protect him, even if it makes her their new target. Teaming up with bounty hunter Danny Ryan, who is tracking one of the men, might be her only chance at evading their clutches and keeping everyone safe...

WITNESS IN PERIL
by Jodie Bailey

Narrowly escaping an attack by a man wearing a US Marshals badge, estate lawyer Ivy Bridges flees to the one man she can trust—her ex, Special Agent Jacob Garcia. And discovering her child is *his* daughter makes him even more determined to stop the killer on her heels.

MOUNTAIN MURDER INVESTIGATION
Smoky Mountain Defenders • by Karen Kirst

While attempting to expose a cheating ring at the university that has left one student dead, architecture professor Aiden Ferrer turns to ex-fiancée mounted officer Raven Hart for help—except she thinks he's dead. Will they be able to outrun a murderer *and* their feelings?

CANYON SURVIVAL
by Connie Queen

When Annie Tillman wakes on a cliff with amnesia, two small children at her side and someone shooting at her, she knows she must run. Former FBI agent Riggs Brenner rescues them and now he's her best hope of surviving in the canyon—and recovering her memories.

LISCNM0222

Get 4 FREE REWARDS!

We'll send you 2 FREE Books plus 2 FREE Mystery Gifts.

Love Inspired Suspense books showcase how courage and optimism unite in stories of faith and love in the face of danger.

FREE Value Over $20

New dangers. New enemies. New adventures.

SHARDS OF ALDERAAN

While visiting the remains of their mother's home, Jacen and Jaina encounter a long-lost enemy of the Solo family . . .

DIVERSITY ALLIANCE

Everyone is searching for Bornan Thul, but the young Jedi Knights may be too late—for their true enemy is about to show its shockingly familiar face . . .

DELUSIONS OF GRANDEUR

As the search for Raynar Thul's father continues, the young Jedi Knights turn for help to a dangerous source: the reprogrammed assassin droid, IG-88!

JEDI BOUNTY

Lowbacca has gone to the planet Ryloth to investigate the Diversity Alliance. And the other young Jedi Knights have discovered one truth about the Alliance—you either join, or you die.

THE EMPEROR'S PLAGUE

It's a race against time: the young Jedi Knights must find and destroy the Emperor's Plague before it can be released. But they first must face Nolaa Tarkona. And her very lethal hired hand, Boba Fett.

continued . . .

And don't miss the thrilling "Rise of the Shadow Academy" cycle of Young Jedi Knight novels . . .

HEIRS OF THE FORCE

The *New York Times* best-selling debut of the young Jedi Knights! Their training begins . . .

SHADOW ACADEMY

The dark side of the Force has a new training ground: the Shadow Academy!

THE LOST ONES

An old friend of the twins could be the perfect candidate for the Shadow Academy!

LIGHTSABERS

At last, the time has come for the young Jedi Knights to build their weapons . . .

DARKEST KNIGHT

The Dark Jedi student Zekk must face his old friends Jacen and Jaina—once and for all.

JEDI UNDER SIEGE

The final battle between Luke Skywalker's Jedi academy and the evil Shadow Academy . . .

STAR
YOUNG JEDI KNIGHTS
WARS®
THE EMPEROR'S PLAGUE

KEVIN J. ANDERSON
and REBECCA MOESTA

BOULEVARD BOOKS, NEW YORK

STAR WARS: YOUNG JEDI KNIGHTS:
THE EMPEROR'S PLAGUE

A Boulevard Book / published by arrangement with
Lucasfilm Ltd.

PRINTING HISTORY
Boulevard edition / January 1998

All rights reserved.
®, ™ & © 1998 by Lucasfilm Ltd.
This book may not be reproduced in whole or in part,
by mimeograph or any other means, without permission.
For information address: The Berkley Publishing Group,
a member of Penguin Putnam Inc.,
200 Madison Avenue, New York, New York 10016.

The Putnam Berkley World Wide Web site address is
http://www.berkley.com

Make sure to check out *PB Plug*, the science fiction/fantasy newsletter, at
http://www.pbplug.com

ISBN: 1-57297-331-5

BOULEVARD
Boulevard Books are published by The Berkley Publishing Group,
a member of Penguin Putnam Inc.,
200 Madison Avenue, New York, New York 10016.
BOULEVARD and its logo are trademarks
belonging to Berkley Publishing Corporation.

PRINTED IN THE UNITED STATES OF AMERICA

10 9 8 7 6 5 4 3 2 1

*This one is especially for all the fans:
the devoted readers who have made this series so
successful and who have enjoyed the adventures of
Jacen and Jaina, Tenel Ka, Lowie, Em Teedee,
Zekk, and Raynar as much as we have.*

acknowledgments

This is the final book in the second story series of the Young Jedi Knights. We are indebted to the imagination and helpfulness of many other people, including *Star Wars* writers A. C. Crispin, Mike Stackpole, Vonda McIntyre, and Dave Wolverton, not to mention George Lucas. Sue Rostoni, Allan Kausch, and Lucy Wilson offered their help and support at Lucasfilm Licensing; Ginjer Buchanan and Jessica Faust ran the gauntlet at Boulevard Books; Lillie E. Mitchell, Catherine Ulatowski, Angela Kato, and Sarah Jones at WordFire, Inc. kept a thousand details working smoothly; and Jonathan Cowan remained our primary test-reader.

THE EMPEROR'S PLAGUE

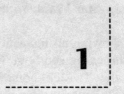

1

AFTER DAYS OF recuperation, Jaina Solo steadied herself on the edge of the bacta tank, dripping. Programmed to be courteous, the Too-Onebee medical droid helped her out.

Slippery fluid from the healing tank trickled from Jaina's hair and bare skin onto the floor, where it gathered in iridescent puddles before flowing into a drain by her feet. The bacta smelled healthy. Even beneath the brief strips of medical wrap she wore, every square centimeter of her flesh tingled with renewal.

Cautious at first, she planted her feet on the floor and tested her strength before letting go of the droid's green metal arm. Her legs had not supported her full weight for several days now and she wasn't quite sure they would hold her.

Confident at last, Jaina stretched luxuriously, then looked down at herself. Her skin was pink and new, showing no indication of the burns and injuries she had recently suffered during their escape from the Twi'lek homeworld of Ryloth. For a moment Jaina wondered if the whole ordeal had merely been a nightmare—the capture of the young Jedi Knights, laboring in the spice mines, the mad flight from Diversity Alliance guards through winding catacombs, the brutal heat of Ryloth's dayside.

But it was all real. Definitely real.

"Glad to see you're feeling better," a warm voice said close behind her.

Jaina whirled. "Zekk!"

"In the flesh—more or less, that is," he said. He held out a sheet of white absorbent cloth and helped Jaina drape it around her shoulders. "You looked like a roasted nerf sausage when I picked you up a few days ago," he said, snugging the soft material around her. "Now I can hardly tell you were burned."

Jaina smiled at her friend. His long hair, a shade lighter than black, hung at the nape of his neck neatly tied with a thong. His dark clothing was rumpled, as if he had slept in it; the shadowy smudges beneath his emerald-green eyes attested to a lack of sleep.

"I thought you were part of my dream," Jaina said. "I kept thinking that I was waking up, and I would see your face, kind of distant and blurry . . . but always there."

The centaur girl Lusa wrapped a sheet around the

dripping form of Raynar at another bacta tank nearby. She remarked, "Zekk hasn't left the medical center since all of you went into the tanks."

Jaina smiled at Zekk. He shrugged, as if embarrassed. "I don't get out much these days. Training to be a bounty hunter kind of puts a crimp in your social life. Besides," he added, "old Peckhum's been off on a supply run, so I didn't see much point in going home for a visit."

Raynar toweled off his spiky blond hair and blinked groggily at Lusa.

Zekk continued, "Anyway, I'm not the only one who's been haunting the medical center. Lusa was here practically around the chrono. Your parents and Master Skywalker came in every couple of hours. And Threepio kept bustling in to check on us and to bring us meals." He smiled. "I remember when he wanted to fit me with a fancy new suit for that important state dinner your mother hosted."

"That was a long time ago," Jaina answered softly, tugging her own clothes on.

"That was the same night I was captured by the Shadow Academy," he added, then paused a moment as a troubled expression crossed his face.

The centaur girl Lusa offered Raynar a clean set of garish colorful robes that displayed the scarlet, purple, orange, and gold colors of the noble Thul family from Alderaan. Of late, Raynar had been wearing more drab and serviceable Jedi clothes, but now he accepted the fresh garments gratefully.

"Lowie and your little brother were here, too," Lusa said.

"Anakin wasn't a bother, was he?" Jaina asked.

Zekk looked amused. "Far from it. I learned a thing or two from watching him. With the Force, he looked inside the controls of each of your bacta tanks, then made some suggestions to Lowie on how to improve their performance."

Zekk's voice sank to a whisper as he glanced over at Lowbacca, who was helping the warrior girl Tenel Ka out of her bacta tank, while the medical droid assisted Jacen. "Lowie and Anakin spent hours optimizing the diagnostics relays on each of the bacta units. They ran a physiology-specific calibration on all the bacta regulators, while Lusa and I overhauled the nutrient monitors."

"Are you sure all that was really necessary?" Jaina said, shaking her head. Her bacta-wet hair hung close against her face. "I feel fine."

He gave a wry grimace. "I think Lowie feels guilty you all got hurt on Ryloth, since *he* was the reason you went there in the first place."

"I'm just glad that we're all back together and safe," Jaina said. Then she smiled ruefully. "Guess I owe you another one, huh?"

"Maybe you'll get a chance to even up the score," Zekk said. "Our battle with the Diversity Alliance isn't over yet."

Tenel Ka dried herself with the absorbent cloth Lowie handed her, then let the damp material drop to the floor. By now she had learned how to do just about everything quickly and efficiently, even with only one arm. She felt energized and alert, and she couldn't wait to get out of the medical center and do some calisthenics or go for a run across the rooftops of Coruscant.

Her thick red-gold hair clung in damp clumps around her bare shoulders, but it would not take her long to tame it into her customary warrior braids again. Turning her cool gray gaze to inspect Jacen, she was relieved to see that the frostbite, cuts, and bruises her friend had sustained on Ryloth's frozen nightside had left no lasting damage.

Jacen's unruly brown curls were plastered flat to his head by bacta fluid, and his brandy-brown eyes told her that he was rested and strong again. He flashed Tenel Ka a lopsided grin that made him look like his father, Han Solo. "I'm glad to see that we're all *bacta* normal again," he said. He raised his eyebrows at the pun, as if waiting for her response.

Tenel Ka kept her face expressionless, though deep inside she was glad that their ordeal had not changed Jacen's sense of humor. "This," she said, "is a fact."

Later, Zekk tinkered with the *Lightning Rod*, readying it for his continuing search for Bornan Thul. Running diagnostics gave him something to do while Raynar and his mother Aryn Dro Thul—who had just arrived on Coruscant with the entire Bornaryn fleet—spent some long-overdue time talking in private.

Tenel Ka had gone to see her parents Isolder and Teneniel Djo, newly arrived from Hapes. Her wily grandmother Ta'a Chume, who was also on Coruscant, had been using her spies to uncover further disturbing evidence about Diversity Alliance activities.

At the same time, Lowie and his sister Sirra had gone to visit with their uncle Chewbacca, while Jacen, Jaina, and Anakin were enjoying a private family meal with their parents.

That gave Zekk a few hours to himself.

He could hardly begrudge the families some time alone together. He knew how difficult it was for General Han Solo and Chief of State Leia Organa Solo to find the time to relax with their Jedi-trainee children. Even so, Zekk thought as he cleaned the life-support recirculation modules, he couldn't help being a little jealous. He was left out of all those warm family gatherings, since he had no relatives of his own. Zekk sighed.

Just then a gruff voice drifted up the *Lightning Rod*'s boarding ramp from outside. "I hope you're taking good care of this fine ship, boy. Not giving you any trouble, is she?"

Zekk dropped the replacement intake filter and

bounded toward the entry hatch as a grizzled old spacer trudged up the ramp.

"Peckhum!" Zekk exclaimed. The older man returned Zekk's greeting with a bear hug, and Zekk's spirits soared. Now he was truly at home; *this* was his family.

Raynar still couldn't believe that his mother had risked coming out of hiding. Now both he and Aryn Dro Thul stood on the highest balcony of the Bornaryn headquarters building, overlooking a broad plaza that bustled with people.

"This view was one of the reasons Bornan and I chose this building for our headquarters." His mother wore her midnight-blue gown shot with silver and belted with a sash in the colors of the House of Thul. Her fingers toyed with the sash and her lips curved in a faint smile. "Somehow I feel closer to your father just standing here."

At the heart of the plaza, a fountain with hundreds of tiers burbled, trickled, gushed, and spouted. The spectacular display reminded him of the Dro family's Ceremony of the Waters, a tradition from their Alderaanian heritage. For the millionth time since his father's disappearance, Raynar found himself wishing that his whole family could be together again, and that he had remembered to enjoy those times more in the past. . . .

"He's in danger, you know," Raynar said.

Without looking away from the fountain, Aryn nodded. "Tell me what you've learned."

Raynar took a deep breath, then let it out slowly. "It all started with the Twi'lek leader, Nolaa Tarkona. Dad was negotiating some trade agreements with her when he disappeared."

Her gaze still fixed on the fountain, Aryn nodded. "Bornan was planning to meet with her at the Shumavar trade conference . . . but he never arrived."

"Dad decided to disappear, but he had a good reason. Nolaa Tarkona's interplanetary political movement, the Diversity Alliance, was supposed to bring nonhuman species together to right the wrongs of the past. Unfortunately, Nolaa decided that the only way to right those wrongs was to destroy all humans."

"But why should she have singled out Bornan?" Aryn asked.

"An alien scavenger named Fonterrat discovered an Imperial storehouse that held a plague that could kill humans specifically. Fonterrat offered to sell the information to Nolaa Tarkona, but he refused to deal directly with her. Instead he insisted that she send a neutral party to meet with him on an ancient planet called Kuar."

"And so Nolaa Tarkona sent Bornan?" Aryn said.

"Right. As far as we know, Dad traded a time-locked case full of credits for a navicomputer module that had the location of the plague storehouse in its memory. Just a simple exchange. Dad was supposed to deliver the navicomputer to Nolaa Tarkona at the Shumavar conference. He'd probably never have known what he was carrying—but at the last minute I guess Fonterrat confessed it to him."

Still looking down at the bustling plaza far below, Aryn Dro Thul shook her head. "That scavenger could have been exaggerating about the plague."

"He wasn't," Raynar said. "Early in his negotiations with Nolaa Tarkona, Fonterrat gave her at least one sample. Nolaa used that sample to booby-trap his payment. At Fonterrat's next stop, an all-human colony on Gammalin, the plague killed everyone. The colonists locked him up before the plague killed them, and Fonterrat died in a tiny jail, since no one was left alive to take care of him. If Nolaa Tarkona ever gets her hands on that plague, the entire human race will be destroyed. So, ever since he got the navicomputer from Fonterrat, Dad has been on the run, trying to keep it from her."

Aryn's shoulders drooped. "That sounds like your father—but why didn't he simply destroy the module, or bring the information here to Coruscant?"

"It's not that easy," Raynar said. "We know that some members of the Diversity Alliance have infiltrated the New Republic government. A Bothan soldier wearing a New Republic uniform even tried to kill Lusa on Yavin 4. Maybe Dad suspected the information wouldn't be safe if he delivered it here."

"Yes, your father has always had good people instincts," Aryn agreed.

"Then he probably also guessed that Nolaa Tarkona would stop at nothing to get that plague—with or without the navicomputer. When Jacen, Jaina, Tenel Ka, and I were prisoners on Ryloth, we learned that she wants to release that plague and infect every last human in the galaxy."

"I wish I were there to help your father," Aryn said.

"I wish I could help him too," Raynar said, taking his mother's hand a bit awkwardly. It felt strange at first, but he had come to realize in the past months how easy it was to lose the things and the people that you cared about. "I'm glad you came out of hiding, Mom," he said.

Aryn Dro Thul stood tall, straightened her shoulders, and looked into Raynar's eyes. "Sometimes we simply have to face our worst fears," she said. "You've shown so much courage since your father disappeared. I'm very proud of you, you know."

Raynar sighed. "I guess facing our fears is a part of growing up."

His mother raised her eyebrows at him. "Maybe. Even so, it never gets any easier."

With a contented smile, Leia Organa Solo gazed slowly around the meal table in the Solo family's quarters of the Imperial Palace. It was still hard to believe that her husband and three children were here at home, all at the same time. She allowed herself to enjoy the moment, though it had taken a galactic crisis to bring them together.

"More nerf sausage, Master Jacen?" See-Threepio offered. "It is a particular Corellian favorite."

"Maybe just one," Jacen answered. Leia noted that Jacen was taller than she had remembered. It amazed her to see how the twins and Anakin changed each time they returned from their studies at the Jedi academy.

After serving Jacen, the gold protocol droid turned to Jaina. She held her hands over her plate, as if to protect it from Threepio's enthusiastic service. "Couldn't eat another bite," Jaina protested.

"Over here, Goldenrod," Han said, holding out his plate for more. "These are just like the ones Dewlanna used to make for me when I was a kid."

Anakin smiled sympathetically at his brother and sister. "I have a feeling you're going to need all your strength when you speak to the New Republic Senate tomorrow morning."

"*Tomorrow?*" the twins asked in unison.

Leia nodded. "I've scheduled a special meeting of the New Republic Senate. I'd like you and your friends there to present your findings. I think the whole galaxy needs to know what the Diversity Alliance has been planning."

2

THE NEW REPUBLIC Senate chambers were full to overflowing. Jaina looked uncertainly through the door into the immense, crowded room and then back at her mother. The Chief of State shrugged. "We had a vote coming up on several major issues, so I requested full attendance today. I haven't seen some of those senators and delegates in months."

Tenel Ka said, "Perhaps they heard of our intention to discuss the Diversity Alliance."

"More than likely," Leia admitted. "I know you all understand how much is at stake here."

"If you want, I could loosen up the crowd with a joke." Jacen waggled his eyebrows. Leia turned toward him with a startled look, but Jacen held up his hands in a placating gesture. "Hey, I was just kidding!" Beside him, Lowie and his sister Sirra both rumbled deep in their Wookiee throats. "Okay— bad timing, I admit," Jacen said. "It's just that we all seem so tight and edgy."

"You're right," Jaina said, drawing a slow deep breath and letting the Force flow through her. A wave of calm clarity washed the worry from her mind. Around her, the other companions also used Jedi relaxation techniques, with varying degrees of success. Her father and Chewbacca, along with her uncle Luke, the Jedi historian Tionne, and Kur, the Twi'lek politician rescued from exile on Ryloth, had already taken their seats toward the front of the Senate chambers.

"Well then, what are we waiting for?" Jaina asked.

Much later, an hour after they had finished telling of their adventures and delivered their alarming news, it still wasn't over.

Jaina grew defensive as yet another representative stood up to take the floor. She could sense her brother's bafflement at the response with which the Senate had greeted their announcement. Tenel Ka, as usual, was stolid and alert, probably scanning the crowd for any signs of trouble.

Only Chief of State Leia Organa Solo seemed perfectly calm, as if she had expected the reactions of the senators and delegates. She looked around the room with a practiced ease, seeing everything, listening to everyone, gauging the reactions of her audience. Jaina bit her lower lip, willing herself to be more like her mother, ordering herself to listen with an open mind to the squeaking Chadra Fan senator.

"And so, it is not the members of the Diversity Alliance who should be censured—rather, these willful *human* children need to be taught respect for legal governments," Senator Trubor concluded, triumphantly swiveling his triangular batlike ears.

Alarmed, Jaina looked over at Luke Skywalker, hoping the Jedi Master would react to these accusations. But already it seemed as if too many humans had spoken out. Luke met Jaina's gaze, giving her his silent support.

Without comment, Leia nodded and announced the name of the next speaker. "Senator J'mesk Iman."

The small cherub-faced Tamran steepled his fingers at chest level and bowed slightly. J'mesk Iman's expressive brows rose as he spoke. "Forgive me if I have misunderstood the situation, but it is not the habit of the New Republic to meddle in the affairs of local governments, is it?" J'mesk Iman spread his hands in a traditional gesture his people used when offering peace. "Perhaps this could all be viewed as a cultural misunderstanding. From an objective point of view, what these young Jedi did might be described as well-intentioned but ill-advised. There should be no need to consider it an act of outright espionage."

Jaina shifted uncomfortably at the ambassador's benign condemnation. Her brother flinched, and she sensed rather than heard a growl forming deep in Lowie's throat. The black streak of fur over his eye bristled.

"Since the children's arrival was neither announced nor authorized—since it was, in fact, covert," Iman continued, "the government of Ryloth had ample reason to view it as an act of aggression."

"But we explained what we were doing there," Jacen objected. "The Diversity Alliance was holding Lowie against his will. And they still threw us into their spice mines."

Iman fixed them all with a serious look and cocked his head to one side. When he answered, though, his voice was not unkind. "Yet had any of you *requested* their government's permission to enter its headquarters?"

"No," Jaina answered truthfully. "But we never intended any harm. We just wanted to get our friend back."

"Even so, since your mission was not a diplomatic one, and not sanctioned by any government, you placed yourselves under the jurisdiction of local laws by trespassing as you did. I do not believe even the New Republic could allow such an intrusion without punishing the perpetrators. It is only natural that any government should want to deter others from doing what you did."

Jaina bit her lower lip. She knew there was no way to refute the ambassador's logic.

"But what about the spice mines?" Raynar asked. "We were taken prisoner, turned into slaves."

"Very well, then. How long did you spend in the spice mines?" Iman asked.

Jaina answered, "We didn't have chronometers with us."

"Very well, a few days, then? A harsh punishment perhaps for highborn youngsters such as yourselves, but not outside the realm of reason. Were you denied food or water or sleep?"

Jaina grimaced at the memory of the fungus they had been expected to eat and the foul-tasting water they had been offered, but she shook her head. Raynar took a sudden interest in studying the floor near his feet and said nothing. "But they never released us," Jaina pointed out. "Lowie had to help us escape."

The ambassador steepled his fingers at his chin and smiled. "And yet here you all are, alive and well. So allow me to summarize. You broke into the headquarters of a well-respected political movement. The legal planetary government sentenced you to a short term of unpleasant yet not unjustifiable punishment—long enough for you to learn a valuable lesson, we can hope. Then, before you had served your complete term, your friends, who at the time were *working* for the Diversity Alliance"—at this, Iman's brows rose expressively—"released you from captivity and assisted you in departing from Ryloth without further punishment. And during all that time, the only true injuries you sustained were as a result of the ill-advised paths you chose when leaving."

Jaina drew in a deep breath and held it for a long moment before releasing it. It wasn't fair when the story was presented that way.

At this point Lowie spoke up in a series of rumbles, barks, and growls. Em Teedee made a throat-clearing sound to be sure he had the attention of the entire assembly and then provided a translation.

"Master Lowbacca does not choose to dispute your interpretation of the events surrounding his associates' arrival and departure from Ryloth. He does, however, wish to clarify two facts. First: the current government on Ryloth does not necessarily represent the Twi'lek people"—at this point, the overthrown leader Kur stepped forward and nodded his confirmation—"And second: during the time they were held by the Diversity Alliance, Master Lowbacca, his sister Mistress Sirrakuk, and the centaur girl Mistress Lusa all noted a distinct antihuman sentiment that had the potential for expressing itself with some violence."

A salmon-colored Mon Calamarian female with glossy blue-silver robes approached the floor, her large round eyes swiveling to study the audience. J'mesk Iman yielded his position, and Leia announced the new speaker with a sense of relief. "Ambassador Cilghal, please speak."

Cilghal, one of Luke Skywalker's first Jedi students, nodded to Leia and stood tall. "I do not believe any government is sacred. It may well be, as my colleague has said, that nothing more happened on Ryloth than a juvenile infraction of local laws and the punishment of that infraction." A murmur of approval ran through the Senate.

"*However*," she continued, "if the government of Ryloth and the Diversity Alliance are peaceful and do no more than work in the interests of their members, then they should have no objection to a visit by diplomatic inspectors. This would, of course, be prearranged and approved through appropriate channels with their government. Some of the charges against the Diversity Alliance are indeed troubling and warrant our attention. Therefore, I propose a simple fact-finding mission.

"The delegation should consist of a representative mixture of species and include a few members familiar with the government of Ryloth"—Cilghal nodded to the Twi'lek Kur—"and the Diversity Alliance." Here she gestured with a broad flipper-hand toward the Wookiees and Lusa. "If we find no evidence of wrongdoing, as some of my colleagues expect, then this inspection will be the simplest method of putting the matter to rest."

From the corner of her eye Jaina saw her mother relax considerably. Taking a cue from her, Jaina ordered her muscles to unknot themselves. The Chadra Fan senator Trubor approached the floor again, but from the small smile of triumph on Leia's face, Jaina knew there was no longer any doubt of the outcome: a team of investigators would soon be on its way to Ryloth.

Then they would find undeniable proof of Nolaa Tarkona's schemes.

3

ZEKK HAD NOT expected it to be so easy, especially not after the debacle in the Senate hall. "What?"

"I *said*, 'Of course.' When do we leave?" Raynar answered.

Zekk had anticipated several tedious meetings with Aryn Dro Thul, explaining why her son should accompany him on the dangerous quest to find Bornan Thul. Zekk already knew *how* to find the fugitive, since he had placed a tracer on Thul's ship a week ago, but he had no reason to believe Bornan Thul would willingly return with him, or even listen to reason.

That was why Raynar had to come along.

The Alderaanian boy clasped his hands behind his back and began pacing up and down the length of the battle-scarred *Lightning Rod*. His bootsteps echoed in the large repair bay. "I can be ready in a few hours, if that's not too long," he said with an eager expression.

Zekk shook his head and tapped a hydrospanner against the ship's hull. "It'll take me at least that long to finish here. Less than that if Jaina can help us—and if I know Jaina, wild gundarks couldn't keep her away."

As it turned out, Jaina also recruited her twin brother, as well as Tenel Ka, Lowie and his sister Sirra, and of course Em Teedee. In addition, she offered to accompany Zekk and Raynar on their rescue mission to serve as navigator, copilot, or anything else they might need.

"No, Jaina," Zekk told her in a gentle but firm voice. "Raynar's one of two people in the galaxy that Bornan Thul is likely to trust. I need him with me, but I'm not risking anyone else."

Jaina tried to hide her hurt by turning toward the navigational console and double-checking Em Teedee's connections. "Run the usual diagnostics, Em Teedee," she said. "And don't forget the special ones I asked for."

"Certainly, Mistress Jaina," the little droid replied. "But do you believe it's absolutely necessary to—"

"Just *do* it, Em Teedee," Jaina broke in with an edge of impatient urgency. Then she turned back to Zekk. "I understand exactly how dangerous this situation is. Whether you find Raynar's father or not, you're probably on the Diversity Alliance's most-wanted list by now. And you're definitely considered fair game for bounty hunters, since you turned against them and helped Bornan Thul escape before."

A pair of Wookiee voices bellowed from the cargo bay, and Jaina yelled back, "I think Tenel Ka and Jacen have the sealant patches. They're outside working on the hull."

Zekk placed his hands on Jaina's shoulders, shook her gently. "There's a chance Raynar and I won't make it back. He *has* to go, and so do I—but I won't put you in that kind of danger."

Jaina looked past him out the cockpit viewports, pretending an interest in the Sorosuub ion skimmer that had just cruised into the docking bay. What gave Zekk the right to decide whether or not she could put herself in danger? Her hands clenched and unclenched a few times.

"If that plague gets loose, none of us will be safe anyway," she pointed out, still trying to make him see reason. "There's a lot at stake, and everyone's taking risks. Lusa and Sirra and Uncle Luke are all going on the inspection team headed for Ryloth. They'll *all* be in danger. So will you. You'd stand a much better chance of coming out of this alive if I came along, you know." A long silence stretched between them.

"I don't know if you can understand this," Zekk said at last. He pulled her closer to him—a move that surprised Jaina. His voice was tight with emotion. "I made some choices back when I joined the Shadow Academy—the wrong choices. I was willing to put the whole New Republic at risk just to prove to myself that I was as good as you and your family. All I managed to prove to myself was how wrong I was.

"I came close to killing you once, because Brakiss had convinced me—or I had convinced myself—that you thought I was unworthy. Now the New Republic is in jeopardy again, and I'm one of the few people who can do something about it." He gave a mirthless laugh. "Funny thing is, this time I don't feel like I have anything to prove. I just need to know that you're safe, that your family's safe, that old Peckhum's safe. I want to make sure that humans, Wookiees, and all other species are safe from anyone who rules by murder and hate . . . or because they have something to prove."

Zekk pulled back, and his emerald eyes bored into Jaina's. "I'm going to try to save Raynar's father. But if I can't, I'll do whatever I can to keep the galaxy safe—whether it means blowing up his ship, or my ship . . . or everything."

Jaina sensed the fierce determination in Zekk. Her eyes filled with tears, and she tried to blink them away. Yes, she understood. She understood only too well, and she knew there would be no changing Zekk's mind. She unclenched her fists, slid her arms around his back, and squeezed him tightly.

Jacen's upside-down face appeared in one of the side viewports. He dangled from the roof of the *Lightning Rod*, making faces at his sister, and pointing to where Raynar and Lusa stood in front of the ship, also sharing a goodbye embrace. Jacen's upside-down eyebrows raised and lowered comically.

"Well then," Jaina said, somewhere between a laugh and a choke, "what are we waiting for? We have a ship to get ready for its most important flight ever. You got everything we need, Em Teedee?"

"Yes, indeed, Mistress Jaina."

Zekk pressed his cheek against hers. "Thank you," he whispered.

Raynar leaned over the navicomputer console and fine-tuned his lock on the tracer frequency. "Looks stable this time," he reported. "The beacon hasn't cut out or faded."

Zekk nodded. "Good. Your father's not making any more hyperspace jumps right now. Let's hope he decides to stay put for a while."

"Should I calculate a route to these coordinates?" Raynar asked.

Zekk had spent the past day filling in the gaps in Raynar's star-piloting education. The blond-haired boy now felt competent to set a course, calculate hyperspace jumps, and operate some of the weapons systems. Zekk had even let him fly the *Lightning Rod* for a couple of hours.

"Go ahead," Zekk said as he watched the boy enter the coordinates and plot the route. "You're not a half-bad copilot, you know?"

Raynar flushed with pride at Zekk's expression of confidence. "Thanks for taking the time to teach me. I guess I've always been so used to people doing this stuff for me that I never thought to learn it for myself. Actually, I'm surprised Jaina didn't insist on coming along to be your copilot."

Zekk grimaced. "She did." He paused for a long moment, as if considering how to say something unpleasant. "I told her I didn't want her along . . . because we might not make it back."

"We *have* to make it back," Raynar said with a stubborn optimism he hadn't known he possessed. "I promised Lusa. Besides," he added, flashing Zekk a calculating glance, "you don't expect Jaina to stay out of trouble just because you're not around, do you? Who'll come to her rescue?" As Raynar leaned forward to fiddle with the navicomputer, he heard a soft chuckle from Zekk.

"You're right. We *will* have to make it back." With that the dark-haired young man flicked a few switches and plunged the *Lightning Rod* into hyperspace.

They traveled in companionable silence for a few hours. Finally, Zekk shook himself from a deep reverie. "Speaking of convincing people not to come along, how did you talk your mother out of trying to come with us?"

"It was easier than I expected," Raynar said. "I told her that if a couple of Jedi couldn't bring my father back safely, then two Jedi and a business-woman wouldn't be any more likely to succeed."

Zekk's eyebrows raised slightly when Raynar said *two Jedi*.

Raynar added, "She knows that if anything happened to my father and me, she's the only one who can run Bornaryn Trading. She has a responsibility to all of those clients and employees. Anyway, I think it made her a bit happier just to learn that my father had a good reason for running. He was trying to protect us all."

"And now we've got to protect *him*," Zekk said, looking down at the navicomputer. "Here we are." He nodded to Raynar when the *Lightning Rod* dropped out of hyperspace.

Raynar's breathing sped up, and his heartbeat pounded in his ears. After a long, long search, he was finally going to see his father again.

"Uh-oh," Zekk said as normal space resolved into clear focus around them. "Looks like your father's not just taking a break—he's got uninvited guests."

Raynar swallowed hard as he surveyed the scene before him. His father's ship was here, all right. But so were two other ships: Boba Fett's vessel *Slave IV* and another craft he didn't recognize. He flicked on the comm system. "Dad, it's me, Raynar. Zekk and I are here to rescue you."

A split second later, both bounty hunter ships fired on Bornan Thul.

4

EVEN THOUGH HE recognized the *Lightning Rod* as the ship flown by ambitious young bounty hunter Zekk, Bornan Thul decided he couldn't be choosy—not anymore. With both Boba Fett and the other bounty hunter Shakra firing on him, he either had to trust Zekk or sacrifice himself and blow up his ship.

But Bornan wasn't ready to self-destruct. Though it would obliterate the deadly knowledge he carried, the plague storehouse itself still existed; Nolaa Tarkona would keep searching for it. For him, the deciding factor was hearing his son's voice. *Raynar* was traveling with Zekk!

He toggled the comm system to SEND. "I'll come over in the escape pod, Raynar. But I can't leave anything behind here. Just give me a minute . . . and stay clear of my ship."

Bornan swallowed hard and, with trembling fingers, engaged the destruction subroutines he had hoped he would never need. Cutting the time as close to the edge as he dared, he set the count-down.

Inside the claustrophobic ship, he could hear his damaged engines whining as they looped energy overloads back into themselves. The cockpit temperature gauges crept into the red with astonishing speed.

Without wasting a second, Bornan Thul grabbed the precious navicomputer Fonterrat had given him and ran for his ship's single escape pod. The module that had caused so much distress contained the coordinates for the Emperor's munitions storehouse, the laboratory asteroid where Evir Derricote had developed plague organisms specific to races the Emperor had found troublesome.

Derricote had created many diseases—including the one that would kill only humans. But even the Emperor had not dared to release the horrific scourge. Palpatine wanted to destroy only trouble-some groups of humans, such as the Rebels—not the entire race. Nevertheless, the Emperor had left an immense storehouse filled with plague can-isters. This navicomputer module held those coordinates, and Nolaa Tarkona desperately wanted that knowledge.

Bornan Thul had vowed to die before letting such a terrible weapon fall into the hands of the Diversity Alliance. He had flown to the abandoned storehouse himself and seen that it was indeed as terrible as he had imagined. More terrible, in fact. He hadn't found a way to destroy the place single-handed, and he couldn't risk approaching the New Republic. Nolaa Tarkona had too many converts, too many spies, among the alien members.

It would take only one stolen vial of the plague released into a major spaceport . . . and the New Republic would be lost.

No, Bornan Thul knew that until the entire storehouse was destroyed, he had to keep the location of the biological weapons depot a secret from everyone. And so he had taken the navicomputer module—*and vanished*.

It had worked . . . until now.

Red lights flashed in the cockpit, and klaxons squawked. He cradled the module, knowing that everything else would become space dust in a few minutes, including his ship's own computer.

As he clambered into the escape pod, Bornan Thul glanced over his shoulder for one last look around the little ship that had served him so well during his months on the run. But he was startled to see activity lights flashing on his systems console—more than just the self-destruct sequence. His ship's memory banks were being split open remotely.

Someone was slicing into his computer!

Thul paused in dismay. Certain illegal technology allowed illicit users to rip data directly from other computers. He had intended to destroy his vessel before anyone could get close to it—but it might already be too late.

Too late.

"I hope you're ready for me, Zekk," he muttered. His escape pod should take him to safety before Boba Fett or the other bounty hunter could latch onto him. He sealed the hatch and hit the launch button.

Acceleration threw him back against the small padded seat, and Bornan Thul held on while the lifepod ejected. As the predatory bounty hunters moved into position, he looked out the small round porthole, hoping the right ship would retrieve him first.

While Boba Fett's *Slave IV* raced after the dwindling escape pod, the bounty hunter Shakra sat in her bare cockpit considering another alternative, another way to achieve her goal. Her reptilian frill plumped with excitement and her large slitted eyes narrowed as she made her choice. She accelerated toward Bornan Thul's newly abandoned ship.

She would get aboard and tear out his computer banks with her own sharp-knuckled hands.

Most of all, Shakra hoped to find something Boba Fett might have neglected. The bounty and the fame she'd receive from Nolaa Tarkona were the incentive that drove her ambition—but the reward of knowing she had outsmarted Boba Fett would be nearly as sweet.

She docked her little craft against Bornan Thul's empty vessel and used robotic grapplers, magnetic sealers, and powerful blasters to rip her way into the abandoned ship. She didn't care about causing damage. All that mattered to her was the information she might find inside.

Shakra came aboard like a predator stalking a wounded creature. She looked from side to side, scanning the decks, observing the cockpit, tasting the air with her forked tongue. Through the front windowports she watched Fett's ship closing in on the escape pod, while the newly arrived *Lightning Rod* raced to intercept.

They had left Shakra alone with this craft, and she hoped to make a killing.

Alarms flashed in the cockpit. The engines groaned, rumbled, and whined as power built up. Her hard lips expressed her distaste in a scaly frown. Her slender black tongue flicked out. The air tasted hot, angry. Apparently, this craft had sustained more damage during the attack than she had expected. But anything that remained was now hers.

She let out a long hissing laugh, and her slit pupils widened as she contemplated which files to steal first.

Abruptly her attention fixed on the engine diagnostics, the power levels, the heat exchangers that blazed a silent warning: a countdown. Her frill shot up in astonishment and alarm.

Thul had set his ship to self-destruct!

She whirled about, her fanged jaws wide open as she gasped in the hot recycled air. The timer showed only seconds remaining.

Crying out like a coward, Shakra fled toward her ship, glad that none of her brood-mates could see her reaction. If only she could get far enough away from the blast zone! Her clawed feet scrabbled on the deckplates. Through the hole in the hull up ahead she saw her own ship, her escape—

Just as she reached the opening, Bornan Thul's craft exploded like a supernova, obliterating Shakra, her ship, and itself, along with any residual information its computers might have carried. . . .

As Zekk jockeyed into position to cut off Boba Fett's ship, he looked grimly at the *Lightning Rod*'s weapons systems. He had shot at and chased the masked bounty hunter before, but in each case Zekk had had the element of surprise, and he had fled before the firefight could get too intense. Fett outgunned him by a significant margin.

"Get the tractor beam on that escape pod," he said to Raynar. "We don't have much time."

"Which is the tractor beam?" Raynar said, looking frantically at the control panels. "We haven't covered that one yet."

Zekk dodged and rolled the *Lightning Rod*,

skimming past a volley of laser fire from Boba Fett. "That one!" he said, jabbing quickly at a control panel in front of the copilot's chair. He fought his impatience with Raynar's lack of training. The blond-haired young man was just as interested in rescuing his father as Zekk was in surviving this encounter.

Slave IV came in shooting. Bornan Thul's voice came over the comm system. "If you're going to rescue me, you'd better do it quickly."

"I got him!" Raynar yelled as he successfully locked on the tractor beam. Boba Fett cruised toward them, ready to snatch the escape pod directly from their grip.

At that moment, without warning, Bornan Thul's ship exploded in a nightmare of blinding white that washed across space in an expanding sphere.

"Hang on!" Zekk swung the *Lightning Rod* around to shield the escape pod just as the shock wave struck. Fett's ship was knocked into a dizzying spiral.

Zekk barely held position, nudging his thrusters to keep the *Lightning Rod* balanced. "We're still here. We're still intact," he said.

"So am I," Bornan Thul shouted over the comm system. "But I won't be for long unless you get me aboard."

Fett recovered quickly and came after them again, angry now. Zekk fired, but his weapons were much weaker than the bounty hunter's. He fed all available power to his shields but still felt the pounding of Boba Fett's blasts. He checked to see if Raynar had drawn the escape pod into the cargo bay yet.

"What's this alarm light mean?" Raynar asked.

"It means our shields are failing!" Zekk said.

Suddenly, another ship soared out of hyperspace, emerging from the glare of Bornan Thul's self-destructed vessel. Without pausing to take aim, the new ship fired immediately upon Boba Fett. Bright streaks of fire sprayed space and struck *Slave IV*.

"Yee-ha!" Jaina Solo's voice crowed over the comm system. "Take that, Boba Fett—and don't mess with our friends!"

Zekk fired his own weapons again in tandem with the *Rock Dragon*'s second full-powered volley. Fett, seeing himself clearly at a tactical disadvantage and not knowing if other ships might soon arrive, broke off his attack. He sent one brief comm burst as he wheeled about. "I have what I need." Then he vanished into hyperspace.

"Nice turnabout, Jaina," Zekk said, with a tense smile. "About time you came to rescue *me* for a change!"

The *Rock Dragon* pulled alongside, and Jaina's chuckle came through the comm system. "Kind of a family tradition. Dad did the same thing for Uncle Luke at the Death Star, you know. Anyway, couldn't let you keep thinking you're the *only* one who can pull off a surprise rescue."

Raynar was relieved, nervous, and exhilarated all at the same time. At the moment, nothing was more important to him than getting down to the cargo hold, where the retrieved lifepod rested. He ran to be reunited—at last—with his father.

5

THE SHARP SCENT of ozone and metal drifted up from the escape pod, along with a crackle of static electricity from the recently disengaged tractor beam. Raynar could hear the chugging of the pod's life-support systems mixed with the whine of the *Lightning Rod*'s sublight engines as Zekk maneuvered to dock with the *Rock Dragon*.

He had never heard or smelled anything so wonderful. The harsh glare of the cargo hold's glowpanels was cheering, welcoming. Everything seemed brighter, sweeter, fresher to him than it had for nearly a year. The galaxy would soon be set to rights. His father had returned.

With shaking fingers Raynar pressed the hatch release, and the heavy top panel popped open with a *whoosh* of depressurization. Giving a joyful cry of welcome, Raynar leaned into the pod—only to find a blaster aimed straight at his heart.

•   •   •

Jaina was the first to stumble through the airlock from the *Rock Dragon*. Setting his external sensors to full alert to keep an eye out for unwanted visitors, Zekk threw aside his crash webbing and bounded out of the *Lightning Rod*'s cockpit and into the crew cabin.

He twirled Jaina in a happy hug while they both laughed with relief, but then he growled, "I thought I told you you couldn't come with me!"

Jaina knew he was trying hard to sound stern, but she could hear the pleasure in his voice. She pulled back and favored him with a Solo grin. "Since when have you ever done anything *I* wanted *you* to do?" She gave an unladylike snort. "I'm just as worried about your safety as you are about mine, you know."

"All right," Zekk admitted, "I'm glad you came. But I still don't know how you found us."

Jaina shrugged and grinned again. "Trade secret."

"Hah!" Jacen said, appearing in the airlock with Tenel Ka behind him. "Some trade secret. More like a sneaky droid, if you ask me." Lowie also emerged from the airlock in a flurry of ginger fur and full-throated Wookiee bellows.

"Why, if you're referring to *me*, Master Jacen, I'll take that as a compliment," Em Teedee said, zipping past him into the crew cabin on his microrepulsor jets.

"This is a fact," Tenel Ka said. "You are an excellent 'sneaky' droid."

Zekk looked accusingly at Jaina. "What did Em Teedee do?"

"When we were helping you with your pre-flights," she stammered, "I kind of, um, had Em Teedee download the frequency and encoding for the tracer you used on Bornan Thul's ship."

"Hey, it was a good thing, too," Jacen picked up where his sister left off. "After we saw the delegation off to Ryloth, we all had this feeling that something was about to go wrong."

Lowie woofed and brushed at the back of his neck to indicate the tingle of danger they had sensed.

"Mom must have felt it too," Jaina said, "because when I told her you were going to need our help, she didn't even try to argue. She was glad she had some Jedi she could send on such an important mission—even if two of them *were* her own kids."

Tenel Ka nodded. "Her one stipulation was that we send her a message if we required reinforcements." She raised an eyebrow and looked around at her friends. "Do we require reinforcements?"

"Not if Bornan Thul made it out intact with his navicomputer."

"Or managed to destroy it," Zekk added. "We'd better go down to the hold and find out."

"Don't shoot, Dad—it's me!" Raynar said.

His father, looking haggard and wary, glanced

around but did not lower his blaster. "Are you a hostage? Have you been coerced into helping a bounty hunter or the Diversity Alliance?"

"No, Dad. Zekk may have worked as a bounty hunter, but he's a . . . a friend." Raynar was surprised to note as he said it that this was true. Zekk *was* a friend, and the dark-haired young man had risked his life more than once for each of them. "He believes what you told him about all humans being in danger. He wanted to help you, so he came to get me—he figured you wouldn't trust him alone."

Bornan Thul's haunted eyes closed for a moment, and he nodded. "Your . . . friend was right. I wouldn't have trusted him." Raynar's father lowered the blaster and extended a hand for his son to help him out of the escape pod.

Raynar had thought about this too long to be embarrassed anymore, although his family had rarely engaged in physical contact when he was growing up. Even before his father's feet were firmly on the deckplates, Raynar threw his arms around Bornan in a fierce hug. And his father, perhaps because he was unsteady, or perhaps because he'd also had months to reflect, did not hesitate in returning the embrace.

Only the sound of his friends' footsteps descending into the cargo hold brought Raynar back to reality. His father flinched and reached for his blaster, instantly suspicious again.

"These are my friends, too," Raynar said, and introduced them one by one. "They're all Jedi trainees, except of course for Em Teedee, who is the best miniaturized translating droid ever to be retrofitted on Mechis III—and a pretty good navigator to boot."

"Speaking of navigators," Zekk said, "what about the module Nolaa Tarkona wanted so badly? Was it onboard your ship when it blew up?"

Bornan Thul pointed into the emergency pod. "No, I brought it along. It's here with me."

Raynar felt giddy with relief. "Then you don't have to run anymore," he said. "All we have to do is destroy the information."

His father's mouth formed a grim line. All the blood seemed to drain from his once-round cheeks. He shook his head. "It's not that simple. Before I got into the escape pod I noticed that the computers on my ship were all being accessed at once. I don't know how, but someone was slicing into them remotely."

"Ah. That would probably be Boba Fett," Zekk said.

"He did that to the *Rock Dragon* when we were in the rubble field of Alderaan," Jaina explained, then looked questioningly at Bornan Thul. "But you have the navicomputer *with* you. Boba Fett couldn't have sliced into it."

"You don't understand." Bornan's voice rasped as if it were painful for him to speak. "I *knew* that even if I destroyed this navicomputer Nolaa Tarkona would never stop looking for the weapons depot. That's why I went there myself, hoping to destroy it. I couldn't find a way, though, so I left again, planning to buy supplies and weapons so that I could return to blow up the storehouse."

Raynar blanched. "But that means that the location of the plague storehouse —"

"—was in your ship's own automatic navigation log before it blew up," Jaina finished for him.

"In that case," Zekk concluded, "Boba Fett has the information. And he won't hesitate to give it to Nolaa Tarkona."

6

NOLAA TARKONA GRITTED her sharpened teeth when she learned of the impending arrival of the New Republic inspection team. Her hirelings had failed to find either Bornan Thul or the location of the Emperor's plague storehouse. And now she was being pushed against the wall.

Her glorious political movement was in grave danger. Her finest plan, her highest expectations, had been thwarted—so far. The Diversity Alliance might never be able to unleash its storm of vengeance to obliterate the human race in punishment for the evils of the past. She had tried, and she had failed, because of one missing piece of information. Her hopes of liberating all oppressed species had collapsed like an imploding star.

Even so, Nolaa did not intend to give up willingly. She would make her mark in blood if nothing else. When pushed to the wall, some creatures turned very vicious indeed.

She summoned Rullak, the Quarren representative, and Kambrea, the Devaronian female whose wily ways had allowed her to move up quickly in the ranks of the Diversity Alliance. Kambrea had recruited many members, both from her own race and from other downtrodden species. Nolaa also sent for Corrsk, her reptilian Trandoshan general wounded in combat by the young Wookiee who had betrayed them and fled back to his cronies in the New Republic.

She looked stonily at her three generals as they came forward. All had increased in rank since the untimely death of her wolfman Adjutant Advisor, Hovrak. "The New Republic is sending a team to inspect Ryloth," Nolaa said, "and we must choose whether to surrender meekly, or fight to the death. We can either be cowards or martyrs—and I know which I must choose."

She didn't ask for their decision. She knew Corrsk would fly into a battle frenzy, but Rullak and Kambrea were not quite as determined to lay down their lives for a dream. They had come to the Diversity Alliance to gain personal glory, and Nolaa doubted they would sacrifice their own blood for the cause.

"We've gathered arms, weapons, explosives," Nolaa pointed out. "We have a few fighting ships, enough for a small armada. And we have sufficient weaponry and devoted soldiers to make a stand here. We can fight! We will lure the unsuspecting

New Republic team into our catacombs and slaughter them. Then we declare Ryloth neutral—exempt from human law—and refuse to grant them any further access."

Kambrea looked astonished. "But they will never let you get away with that. They will force their way in, howling for revenge!"

Nolaa stiffened. Her tattooed head-tail lashed back and forth. "We have the power of righteousness on our side. If we become martyrs, the whole galaxy will see how humans treat any resistance to their domination."

Kambrea took a step backward. The Quarren fidgeted, his face tentacles quivering. Corrsk stood like a towering statue. "Kill humans," he said in his gargling voice.

A signal alerted Nolaa, and she felt cold inside. She hadn't expected the human team to arrive for another day, at least—but it would be just like them to attempt to catch the Diversity Alliance unawares.

One of the Duros command system operators signaled her. "Esteemed Tarkona, Boba Fett's ship has arrived. He bears urgent information for you."

"Boba Fett!" She did not allow herself to hope. The masked bounty hunter had already reported failure too many times. Still, he would not have come without good reason. She waited for the *Slave IV* to enter the landing bay and for Fett to be escorted into her presence.

Ignoring the guards, the masked bounty hunter

strode directly up to Nolaa Tarkona, his shoulders squared. In one gauntleted hand he carried a data cylinder. The slitted visor showed nothing of his face. It was difficult to read his body language, but Nolaa thought she detected a swagger of pride that had been missing the previous times he had come to her.

"We cornered Bornan Thul," Fett said without any greeting. "He escaped in a small lifepod and triggered his ship to self-destruct."

Nolaa wanted to strangle something, some*one* nearby. "So he got away again? You dare to report another failure?"

"No," Fett said. He held up the data cylinder. "Before his ship exploded, I sliced into his computers and drained the files. I sorted through them during my flight here." He handed the cylinder to her. "Thul took Fonterrat's navicomputer with him, but he went to the place you seek—five days ago. His ship's own log carried the precise co-ordinates."

Barely able to contain her excitement, Nolaa snatched the cylinder, raised her clawed fingers, and motioned for a data reader to be brought to her. A Talz guard hustled up with the apparatus. She inserted the cylinder and began scanning files. Her rose-quartz eyes flicked from side to side.

Finally Nolaa bared her sharp teeth in a broad

grin. "Yessss," she said. "It *is* here. This changes everything." Leaping out of her stone chair, she called the other generals to her side. Then she instructed her Sullustan clerks to pay Boba Fett the full bounty from the Diversity Alliance coffers.

"Our business is finished then, Nolaa Tarkona," Fett said.

"Yes. Yes, of course." She waved impatiently to get rid of him so that she could discuss Diversity Alliance plans with her generals in privacy.

When Fett was gone, she gathered Corrsk, Kambrea, and Rullak around her. "Assemble the armada—all the ships we have. Nothing will stop us now. Corrsk, you and Rullak come with me. We'll go directly to the storehouse and take as many plague samples as we want. Kambrea, you will remain here to deal with the New Republic inspectors. Delay them until we can unleash our final solution."

"*Me*?" the Devaronian said in alarm. She lifted her pointed chin so that her curved horns tilted backward. "But what can I say to them? How will I answer their questions?"

Nolaa scowled at her. "Use your imagination. Clear away anything that might arouse suspicion. Remove the slaves from the spice mines and find volunteers to work there. Hide all the weapons storehouses. Make sure the team spends most of its time in our happy, tame Twi'lek cliff cities. That should convince them everything's in order."

"But how long will I have to keep them distracted?" Kambrea said.

"Not long," Nolaa Tarkona answered, gesturing for Corrsk and Rullak to follow her. "Once we reach the plague storehouse and get what we need, we'll never have to worry about humans again."

7

JAINA'S MIND KICKED into high gear as the implications of Bornan Thul's words struck home. Somewhere in the galaxy was a secret storehouse that held a plague lethal to humans. Raynar's father had actually been there, but hadn't managed to destroy it. And very soon the asteroid's location would no longer be a secret. If Boba Fett already had the information, Nolaa Tarkona would have it, too.

"Hey, I don't get it," Jacen said. "If you found the plague, why couldn't you destroy it?"

"Was the facility heavily guarded?" Tenel Ka asked.

All eyes turned back to Bornan Thul. He looked down at the deckplates, as if ashamed. "From what I could tell, the weapons depot was an old Imperial research facility. It was completely abandoned. But I couldn't blast through its outer domes with the weapons I had on my little ship."

"Ah. Aha," Tenel Ka said. "Then you were unable to enter."

"No . . . I got in," Thul said, "as Fonterrat had before me. I don't think the Imperials expected many intruders—its location was highly classified. Inside, though, I found the facility's vaults locked. I've no idea how Fonterrat got into any of them to get his samples." He sighed. "Unfortunately, the only weapon I had with me was my blaster, and I was all alone." He ended with an apologetic shrug. "Not much chance destroying an entire munitions depot that way."

Jaina shook herself and stood up straighter. "Well, you're not alone now," she said.

Lowie roared his agreement and then woofed a few times for emphasis. "Master Lowbacca wishes to point out that you now have several trained Jedi to assist you. And, if I might be so bold," the little droid added, "I myself am quite accomplished at interfacing with strange computers, analyzing cyberlocks, retrieving encrypted data, and so forth. And, now that I have been upgraded, I am fluent in over sixteen forms of communication."

The forlorn expression on Raynar's face wrenched Jaina's heart. "But we can't go to that asteroid, Dad. We were supposed to bring you back to Coruscant as soon as we found you. Mom's waiting for you there, and the Chief of State needs to hear what you found."

"No time for that anymore," Zekk said. "As soon

as Nolaa Tarkona gets a report from Boba Fett, she'll be on her way to the plague storehouse."

Raynar set his mouth in a stubborn line. "I'll have to figure out a way to get a message to Mom, then. And we promised to signal for reinforcements right away if we needed them."

"They'll have to meet us at the plague storehouse," Zekk said. "There's no time to waste."

Jaina nodded to Bornan Thul. "We've got to download the coordinates from your navicomputer module right away into both the *Lightning Rod* and the *Rock Dragon*. Then we'll let our mom know where we're going."

"Wait. Even if Nolaa Tarkona already knows the location of the storehouse," Zekk said, "we can't just broadcast it over the hypercom."

"Then encrypt the message and send it immediately," Tenel Ka said.

A look of hope dawned on Bornan Thul's face. He looked at Raynar. "Did anyone manage to break our family's proprietary codes while I was in hiding?"

"I don't think so," Raynar said. "Tenel Ka says it's one of the best encryption systems she's ever seen."

"If anyone else had broken that code, I'm sure I'd have heard about it by now," Zekk added. "After all, *I* couldn't break it when you had me send those messages for you."

"Then we'll transmit to your mother through

Bornaryn headquarters on Coruscant," Bornan said, rubbing his hands briskly together. "First we send a message. Then we blow up a weapons depot."

"Hey, just another day's work for a bunch of Jedi trainees," Jacen said.

Lowie barked a call to action.

"But what if we can't do it by ourselves?" Raynar asked.

"Then we'll just have to hope the New Republic reinforcements arrive in time," Jaina said.

In a blur of activity, Bornan Thul composed his message while Raynar entered coding subroutines with Em Teedee's assistance. Jaina and Zekk downloaded the coordinates to their respective vessels' navicomputers and calculated hyperspace routes to the isolated depot. Jacen, Tenel Ka, and Lowbacca made a quick check of each of the ships' subsystems. In no more than five minutes, the message was sent, the *Rock Dragon* and the *Lightning Rod* were decoupled in space, and the ships made the jump to hyperspace.

As it turned out, it took six separate hyperspace jumps and twice as many hours to get to the weapons asteroid. There was no more direct route available. Fonterrat had found the place by accident, and they had to follow his wandering path.

"I can see why no one just stumbled on this place," Jacen commented as Jaina brought the *Rock*

Dragon in toward the lumpy asteroid on a parallel approach with the *Lightning Rod*.

"Looks like a wormy piece of half-eaten fruit," Jaina observed. Beside her Lowie woofed and pointed with a furry arm to a cluster of transparisteel blisters on the surface of the asteroid.

"*Rock Dragon*, this is the *Lightning Rod*," Raynar's voice came over the comm speakers. "My father says there are several single-ship docks on the outer edge of the central dome. We can land without being seen by any other visitors."

"Automatic laser cannons or anything else we ought to know about?" Jaina asked.

"Thul says no," Zekk replied. "I guess this asteroid's secrecy was the best security system the Imperials thought they'd ever need. Just pick an airlock and dock to it."

Lowie gave a suspicious rumble, but did not comment further as he guided the *Rock Dragon* toward the cluster of domes.

"All right then," Jaina said, "we'll meet you inside."

8

THE NEW REPUBLIC inspection team arrived in a heavily armed escort frigate, flanked by ceremonial squadrons of X-wing and B-wing fighters. The starfighters were supposedly just for show, but Leia Organa Solo wanted to make it clear that she meant business and would tolerate no delays or resistance from the Diversity Alliance. Given the serious nature of the charges that had been brought, Leia refused to waste time on political games.

Standing on the bridge of the escort frigate, Luke Skywalker looked down at the harsh, mountainous planet of Ryloth. The Twi'leks lived in excavated tunnels and cliff cities in a band of twilight between the baking day and the frozen night. The inspection team would tour Ryloth's cities, searching for any evidence of Nolaa Tarkona's misdeeds.

Beside the Jedi Master, Lusa stamped a forehoof nervously. The centaur girl had twice escaped from the clutches of the Diversity Alliance. They had brainwashed her, taught her to hate all humans. She was loath to return, but believed it was her responsibility. Lowbacca's sister Sirrakuk growled quiet encouragement; she herself had been taken in by the Diversity Alliance before she broke away and helped the young Jedi Knights escape.

Kur, the exiled Twi'lek leader, kept silent watch at the bridge windowports. As he stared down at the swirling coppery colors of the blazing daylit hemisphere, his head-tails twitched. Luke sensed that for Kur there could be no happy homecoming. Kur had been defeated by Nolaa Tarkona, though she had refused to let him die, as was the tradition of vanquished head-clan members. Instead, she had sent him out to survive in the glacial cold of night. Now, he was returning, accompanied by humans and New Republic soldiers.

The small bat-faced Chadra Fan senator, Trubor, marched haughtily up to Luke, his squeaky voice indignant. "Jedi Master Skywalker, you had best hope we find substantial evidence to back up the accusations of those young troublemakers." He put his small hands on his narrow hips. His triangular ears swiveled from side to side to pick up subsonic vibrations. Wide nostrils flaring, he blinked his tiny black eyes. "I've long known that Chief of State Organa Solo was concerned about the agenda of the Diversity Alliance, but it is not for the New Republic to make judgments on what beliefs people should or should not hold."

"I agree," Luke said, "but we must take action if an extremist group has kidnapped innocent hostages, taken slaves, and threatened to spread a plague so powerful it could wipe out an entire species."

With a tiny furred hand, Trubor rubbed his forehead in disbelief. "That story is as ridiculous as the propaganda the Empire used to spread."

"We'll see soon enough," Luke answered in a mild tone that nonetheless held power and conviction.

He turned to find even-tempered Ambassador Cilghal, whom he had trained at the Jedi academy, by his side. A Mon Calamarian like Admiral Ackbar, Cilghal had huge fishlike eyes and a salmon-colored head. She spoke calmly, looking down at the Chadra Fan senator. "I intend to keep an open mind. I will observe with my own eyes, and no one—not you, not Master Skywalker—will tell me my opinion. I will decide for myself, as I hope you will do."

"Of course, of course," Trubor said. He waved his hands, then scurried off the bridge, somewhat flustered.

A signal chimed on the escort frigate's comm system, and the glowering image of a female Devaronian flickered to life on the hologenerator. Her horns were polished and decorated with what appeared to be golden glitter. Though she spoke with forced amiability, her eyes were hard and suspicious.

"Welcome, representatives of the New Republic. I am Kambrea. Although your worries are completely groundless, we will bow to your demands and allow you to scrutinize our private cities."

Luke stepped forward into the range of the hologenerator. "When may we schedule an audience with Nolaa Tarkona? We would like to discuss certain matters with her."

"The Esteemed Tarkona was called away on urgent business, and I have been left in charge." She huffed. "An important political movement such as the Diversity Alliance cannot grind to a halt simply because a handful of human children decided to make up stories about us."

Cilghal now stepped forward and spoke in quiet, calming tones. "It is the nature of justice that we must investigate any accusation of such magnitude."

"Perhaps you should investigate crimes committed by humans with the same zeal," Kambrea snapped.

"A crime is a crime, no matter who commits it. I assure you we will be impartial and study the facts. Will you escort us, or shall we find our own way around Ryloth?" Cilghal said, sliding smoothly into a change of subject.

"I'll transmit a homing beacon to one of our main

cities," Kambrea said. "I will meet you there. Follow the beacon precisely, or you risk activating our planetary defense systems." Immediately on the heels of this veiled threat, she switched off.

Luke piloted the transport shuttle from the escort cruiser. The shuttle bore an equal mixture of humans and aliens acting as New Republic escort guards. Lusa, Sirra, and Kur went with him, as did Cilghal, Senator Trubor, and the other members of the inspection team.

When he passed from the daylight side over into the dark, cold night, Luke fought against the turbulence caused by extreme temperature variations. Around him, team members peered out the viewports, awed by the dramatic landscape, where hot, blurry whirlwinds of heat storms whipped across the border into the night and blasted ice from cracks in the frozen mountains. The peaks looked like a dragon's spine.

The beacon directed Luke's shuttle to the mouth of a vast cave in one of the main cities the Twi'leks had built in ancient times. By Ryloth's standards, the cliff city was a huge metropolis.

The shuttle landed in a high-ceilinged grotto where various other ships were docked: unmarked supply craft, small personal vehicles, massive ore haulers for ryll mining activities.

Kambrea came out to meet them, surrounded by a cadre of heavily armed and surly-looking guards—piglike Gamorreans, white-furred Talz, and a brutish, one-eyed Abyssin. *Odd*, Luke thought. *Nolaa Tarkona's group includes no Twi'leks, even though this is their own world.* Perhaps in her takeover, Nolaa Tarkona had killed most of those who had previously wielded power. People like Kur.

"We're here to cooperate." Kambrea's brittle voice broke into Luke's thoughts. "But this is not a holiday outing. Simply tell us what you need to see, and we will show you. You'll quickly realize that your government's accusations are baseless. We view this visit as a form of harassment— a punishment because our politics do not agree with those espoused by your Chief of State."

"Believe me," Trubor said, "we will be open-minded and fair to the Diversity Alliance. Not everyone agrees with the former Princess Leia of Alderaan."

Cilghal kept her own counsel. Lusa and Sirra came out of the shuttle behind the honor guard. Kur emerged last, blinking his eyes and sniffing the air of the tunnels with apparent unease.

Kambrea studied the group, and a storm crossed her face. "The New Republic insults us. Are *these* to be our judges? Lusa, who was cast out of the Diversity Alliance because her incompetence caused three of our ships to crash, killing all aboard?"

Lusa reared up in astonishment. "That's a lie!"

Kambrea looked next at Sirra. "And this *Wookiee*

sabotaged our supply storehouses. She destroyed medicine and food containers being sent to refugee worlds, while her brother Lowbacca meddled with our computer files!" The alien guards beside her shifted restlessly and let their hands stray toward their weapons.

Sirra bristled and growled. Luke laid a hand on her furry arm.

Finally, Kambrea looked at Kur. "And this—the greatest dishonor by far. A humiliated Twi'lek, defeated and exiled during the liberation of Ryloth."

Cilghal said, "Then it's true that Nolaa Tarkona sent him to die in the cold wastes?"

Kur hung his head in shame at hearing his disgrace spoken of so openly. Luke could sense the resentments boiling in each of his fellow team members.

Kambrea lifted her pointed chin. "Surely you know the Twi'lek custom: if any member of the head clan dies or is overthrown, the remaining members sacrifice themselves by going out into the Bright Lands to die. That is the way it has been for centuries. After Kur's defeat, he proved himself a coward. He insisted on fleeing out to the cold wastes in hopes of surviving. You offend us by bringing him back here, where he has no place." The Devaronian snorted. "Saboteurs, incompetents, and cowardly exiles—is this the best team you could find to investigate us?"

"We chose the members we felt were necessary,"

Luke said. "Show us the areas we've asked to see, and we'll make our own observations."

Kambrea spun about, shoulders rigid. Her guards clustered close around her. "Very well—follow me. You are about to see one of the most wonderful cities the Twi'leks ever built."

THE SILVER SPECKS in Aryn Dro Thul's gown swirled around her like a spiral galaxy as she rushed into the comm center at Bornaryn headquarters. "Are you certain the message is for me?"

"No doubt about it," the comm officer said, standing up and making way for her at the console. "The proprietary encryption is layered," he said. "I was only able to decode the first level that addressed it to Lady Aryn Dro Thul."

Aryn did not allow her hands to shake as she deftly input her authorization to decode the message. It was trilevel-encrypted, which meant that it must be from either her son or her husband. Not even Bornan's brother Tyko Thul possessed authorization for the third level of encryption.

The comm officer discreetly activated his console's privacy field. Aryn barely noticed when the soundproof and light-scattering security field formed around her.

Realizing that this message might contain news she did not wish to hear, she cued it up to play immediately. Her husband's voice was accompanied by a sphere of light that pulsated with a variety of ever-changing colors and an audible pattern of harmonics from which Aryn's musically attuned ears gleaned more information than Bornan's words could possibly have expressed in so short a time.

"My dearest wife. I greatly regret that my work here is not finished and I cannot return to you. I received two shipments that will delay my return." The sphere of light pulsated with two colors side by side, representing Bornan and Raynar together. The vividness of the hues meant that they were both in good health. Around the edges, bright splashes of color indicated the presence of other friends. At the same time, the music told her through a series of harmonizing tones that her husband and son were happy—but the music skipped a beat or two, then paused on an open chord that symbolized something missing from that happiness: her presence.

"There is no urgency to this message. I am completely alone and need no help," Bornan's voice went on. Pastel colors wove through the sphere of light, intertwining and then reversing their colors. *So,* Aryn thought as she recognized the code, *the exact opposite is true.* Someone was already there helping, but Raynar and Bornan needed reinforcements. Urgently. An undulating low tone warned of danger and the possibility of traitors around her.

"You are a strong-willed woman, my love, and I cannot tell you what to do—but I believe you know what I ask." Squiggles of alternating color indicating friends and enemies alike began at the outer edges of the sphere and rippled inward to converge on a single point. It meant that he needed her to bring help to a single location, and that the enemy might already be on its way. The music became a precise arpeggio, and in her mind each individual note became distinct, relaying to her a series of numbers. Coordinates—a map that would take her to her husband.

"Until I see you again, remember that I love you," Bornan ended. Light-swirls of sincerity and regret surrounded a bright core of love. A musical note of tenderness rang out a single time. And suddenly the message was gone—music, lights, words . . . everything.

Aryn Dro Thul did not waste time replaying the entire message. She fixed the notes of the arpeggio firmly in her mind, deleted the message, and switched off the privacy field. Coming to a swift decision, she stood and nodded thanks to her comm officer. Then she swept out of the room and headed toward the Imperial Palace. She had to see Leia Organa Solo.

"So you believe your husband found the source of the plague, and he needs our help immediately?" Leia said, leaning forward to study Aryn Dro Thul's serious expression. The two women sat together in the Chief of State's private office.

Aryn nodded. "From the way his message was formatted I would guess he already has several people helping him in addition to our son—your children perhaps?"

Leia nodded. "It sounds like they all found each other."

"He indicated that they need even more help," Aryn said. "But Bornan seemed to be concerned about spies and traitors."

Leia smiled grimly. "Don't worry. We'll send them some trustworthy reinforcements, if I have to hand-pick every member of the team myself. And my husband, General Solo, will lead the mission personally."

10

THE EMPEROR'S OLD weapons depot was a labyrinth of pressurized domes, tunnels, and sealed chambers where unimaginable mechanisms of death lay stored.

Since the isolated asteroid station had, as far as they knew, no large docks or entrance points, the *Rock Dragon* and the *Lightning Rod* were forced to dock against separate domes. The cargo hatches sealed against the airlocks, and the seven companions gathered inside the silent, abandoned station.

Low rock ceilings and tunnels plated with metal made the confined chambers feel like a prison. Jacen looked all around, sniffing the air, which was none too fresh. Other than the scavenger Fonterrat and Bornan Thul, he guessed that no one had set foot here for decades.

Now Thul looked sickened. "I wish Fonterrat had never stumbled on this place."

Raynar stood close to his father. "I wish the Emperor had never even *thought* of making this asteroid into a weapons storehouse." The older man looked down at him with a sympathetic smile.

"Well, what are we gonna do about it?" Jaina asked.

Zekk stood next to her, his face grim. "We'll destroy the depot, of course. Isn't that why we're here? Nolaa Tarkona's probably on her way already."

"First, we must find where the plague itself is stored," Tenel Ka said. "Then we can neutralize it."

Jacen nodded vigorously to show that he agreed with the warrior girl. But then, he usually did.

Bornan Thul took a step forward, placing himself in the lead. "Follow me. I found it before, but I couldn't get inside." He swallowed hard. "At the time, there didn't seem much chance Nolaa Tarkona would ever get here. I thought there might be another solution."

"We're here to help you this time," Raynar said consolingly. "We can solve this problem if we work together." Squaring his shoulders with determination, he marched beside his father through the enclosed corridors.

The artificial gravity generators still functioned on the tiny rock in space. The companions passed through a central complex where curved transparisteel domes overhead showed a sprawling view of an endless starfield, studded with the occasional floating mountains of asteroids in space around them.

At one time, Jacen knew, Star Destroyers had come here to stock up on weapons. They carried stormtroopers and munitions to oppressed worlds so that the Empire could squeeze its iron fist even tighter.

Here in this station, Evir Derricote had tested and stored his most deadly creations, diseases against which no blaster could defend. Derricote had released the Krytos plague on Coruscant just after the capital world had fallen to the Rebels. Because the disease struck only nonhumans, its spread caused a great deal of friction among the member races in the Rebel Alliance.

Now, in a frightening turnabout, it seemed the opposite was about to happen. In order to get her revenge against humans, Nolaa Tarkona wanted to release the ultimate plague—a disease even the Emperor had considered too terrible to use—so she could strike down all of humanity.

But the young Jedi Knights would never let that happen. Jacen picked up his pace.

After hesitating at an intersection of corridors, where half-open bulkheads seemed ready to crash down on them, Bornan Thul said, "This way to the central chamber." He led them through another dome to a large blast-shielded airlock that blocked their way.

Though the door was closed, the controls were not passworded. Bornan Thul worked the keys easily, sliding the long-silent airlock door open. The next corridor held more secure airtight interlocks. Thul operated door after door, until finally they entered a central hub, the core of the asteroid depot.

"This is the chamber of horrors," he said.

Jacen hovered near Tenel Ka's shoulder, gasping in awe as he stared through broad panels of transparisteel that looked down into the main room. Raynar remained beside Bornan Thul. Zekk and Jaina stood next to each other, while Lowie, taller than the rest, peered over their heads.

Behind the sealed windows, Jacen saw a vast room where row after row of tanks and cylinders stretched to the far side of the chamber: small canisters, large tubes, vats, gurgling spheres. Each was filled with bubbling, evil-looking liquid. Refrigeration racks full of tiny vials and flasks covered one entire wall, floor to ceiling. Every last container held a colorful mixture that was deadly to one species or another.

Jacen could hardly believe his eyes. "There's enough contamination in there to wipe out every living creature in the galaxy!"

Lowie growled in agreement. Em Teedee chirped, "I do believe you're right, Master Jacen. I could make a reasonably precise estimate, if you like. Given the rate at which the human plague organism spread on Gammalin, and assuming each of the plagues could as easily be passed from one member of a targeted life-form to another, I should venture to guess that—"

"We understand, Em Teedee," Jaina cut him off, but she could not tear her eyes away from the transparisteel window. "We understand all too well."

Doors marked with an ominous skull and DNA symbol to denote the deadly virus gave access to the chamber. The two-way intercom system would have allowed for communication between Imperial workers inside the sealed chamber and stormtrooper guards on the outside.

But Bornan Thul did not go near the entry. "We shouldn't risk setting foot inside just yet," he said. "If any one of us were exposed to that human plague . . . we could all die before we have a chance to destroy anything."

Zekk frowned. "No. We didn't come here to die. Any ideas on how to demolish the storehouse? The place looks pretty secure. Could we use blasters to break all of the cylinders?"

Bornan Thul shook his head. "No, that would merely spread the plague. We'll have to expose it to space."

"To accomplish that, we must turn this entire asteroid to dust," Tenel Ka said.

"Hey, sounds reasonable to me," Jacen said.

"Shouldn't we get started before Nolaa Tarkona arrives?"

"We don't know how much of a head start we have on her," Raynar pointed out. "We've got to hurry."

"Well, what are we waiting for?" Jaina said. "Any suggestions?"

Bornan Thul raised his eyebrows. "This *is* a weapons depot. The Emperor stored munitions here as well as biological weapons. The plague canisters are in this central chamber, but I'm fairly certain that some of the other bunker rooms contain thermal detonators, explosives, space mines, heavy demolitions equipment."

"Yeah . . . we could use stuff like that," Jaina said with a twinkle in her eye.

Jacen let out a low whistle. "Sounds just like what we saw Nolaa Tarkona hiding in the tunnels of Ryloth."

Tenel Ka gave him the faintest of smiles. "Those stockpiles produced rather gratifying explosions." Jacen looked at her and flashed a grin, remembering how they had escaped from the ryll mines.

"If we wipe out every speck of this plague," Raynar said, "Nolaa won't pose much of a gallactic threat anymore."

Bornan Thul strode to a side doorway, unsealed it, and led the way to a tangential corridor inside the asteroid. Jacen paused for one long moment, feeling a shiver down his spine as he looked at all the cylinders filled with the deadly plague, then turned to hurry after his companions.

Thul took them to where a heavy, blaster-shielded door blocked his way. "I think this is one of the main weapons vaults," he said. "All the munitions should be in there, but . . ." His shoulders slumped. "Unfortunately this one has security coding. I was never able to get in to see if I was correct."

Tenel Ka snatched at her lightsaber handle and flicked on the turquoise energy blade. "A Jedi Knight could find a way in."

"Excuse me," Em Teedee said quickly, "but perhaps I could manage the code? I have had some experience with Imperial systems."

Jacen paused, his hand on his lightsaber handle. "Let him try, Tenel Ka. We can always use our lightsabers later."

The warrior girl agreed. "I will save my weapon for the real battle."

Jaina hooked up the leads in Em Teedee's case to the door control systems. The little droid's golden optical sensors glowed and pulsed as his computer brain worked through the encryption levels. With a *thunk* and a hum, the locks unsealed themselves and the door slid open.

"Quite masterful, if I do say so myself," Em Teedee stated, sounding insufferably pleased with himself.

The young Jedi Knights drew together. Bornan

Thul and Zekk moved closer as they gazed into a room filled with explosives, detonation packs, sonic grenades, and every form of compact destruction Jacen had ever heard of. The shelves of demolition equipment seemed to go on and on.

"I think that'll be quite enough firepower," Zekk said, crossing his wiry arms over his chest.

Tenel Ka nodded and whispered, "This is a fact."

11

WHEN NOLAA TARKONA'S armada arrived at the plague storehouse, the Twi'lek leader could barely contain her excitement. She gripped the bridge rail and leaned forward as the Wookiee woman Raabakyysh guided the flagship into orbit high above the small asteroid.

Nolaa's single head-tail thrashed from side to side, while she observed the expressions of her crew through the optical sensors in the stump of her other head-tail. She saw anticipation, eagerness for battle, and a bloodthirsty desire for vengeance upon the cursed humans.

The asteroid depot itself was small and nondescript, studded with pressurized domes. Slash marks showed where excavation had shaped the giant rock. The place looked abandoned, though the numerous domes and airlocks and hollow bays offered plenty of hiding places for small ships. She had feared she might encounter an entire guardian fleet of New Republic warships—but she had beat them all. She had arrived first.

"The human-killing virus is down there," she said. "It is the only weapon we need for our ultimate victory. Raaba, you will command my armada while I go down personally to make sure we get everything we need. Corrsk, Rullak, come with me. Bring guards . . . and plenty of weapons. I'm not in the mood for further delays."

Nolaa spun about as Raaba proudly took her seat in the flagship's command chair.

The Diversity Alliance guards suited up, belted blasters to their waists, and prepared to go down to secure the Emperor's plague.

After docking to an isolated dome at the pole of the asteroid, Diversity Alliance guards stormed out of their ships. They marched through mazes of interconnected corridors, weapons raised and ready to shoot anything that moved.

Nolaa fervently hoped her soldiers wouldn't blast any of the plague cylinders in their enthusiasm. She didn't want to waste the precious deadly substance. She walked with brisk footsteps, her dark robe swirling, her body armor confining but protective.

This place stank of humans. It had been built by the human Emperor, used by human scientists, guarded by human stormtroopers. The twisted biologist Evir Derricote had worked here—also a human. But in a way *he* hadn't been so terrible. . . . Derricote had, after all, devised the means for bringing about the extinction of his own race.

"Spread out," Nolaa said sharply. "This is a small asteroid. It shouldn't take long to find what we need." Directing Rullak and Corrsk each to take a team of guards, she herself took charge of the third group. "And remember, this was a munitions storehouse." She turned back with a smile, flashing teeth that had been filed to delicate points. "Keep an eye out for anything else we might find useful to our cause."

They split up, each choosing a different hallway. As Nolaa's group passed through pressurized doors, she saw how foolish the Imperials had been for not installing better security or identification locks. It made her task almost too easy. She and her soldiers marched down the stone-floored corridors, casting a critical eye at the metal walls, the interlock doors, the decades-old technological enhancements.

Someone with less finely attuned senses might have thought this place similar to the comfortable Twi'lek tunnels on Ryloth—but to Nolaa Tarkona it had an entirely different feel. This had been made by humans, dug out as a pit in which to store weapons, not a civilized place for a species to grow and expand.

The soldiers fell into step with her; the pounding of their hard boots echoed in the chill, sluggish air. They explored each alcove and side passage under the pressurized domes, searching for the place Fonterrat had described—the chamber that contained the plague. It held the future of the Diversity Alliance, and the death of the human race.

They came to a series of small cells. Each had been sealed and marked as contaminated and hazardous. Curious, Nolaa peered through the thick transparisteel windows at what seemed to be secure pens, each with a cot and a refresher unit but few amenities.

Inside lay the desiccated, plague-ridden corpses of various aliens. She saw the remains of a Quarren, a Wookiee, a Twi'lek, and many other species that were unidentifiable because of the advanced decomposition. Test specimens for other genetically engineered diseases, targeted at specific alien species. Here, before her eyes, was clear-cut evidence of the horror Evir Derricote had intended to inflict upon nonhuman species.

Any glimmer of pity that might have remained in her for all humans who were about to die faded in an instant. Nolaa Tarkona could not wait until the murderous species was eradicated entirely.

"Pick up the pace," she said. "Let's find that plague and get out of here. The Diversity Alliance has important work to do."

On the flagship, Raaba growled orders, insuring that the other ships in the Diversity Alliance armada fell into line. The asteroid field was sparse but still held hazards for clumsy navigators or inexperienced pilots. Raaba wanted their cluster of ships to act like a military fleet, to pull together like a well-trained force. Attitude was essential.

They cruised above the weapons depot, and she growled for two outlying vessels to tighten up the formation. While Nolaa Tarkona was on the asteroid, Raaba intended to keep the armada alert. They had no reason to anticipate any resistance, of course—or that New Republic forces might come after them—but Raaba would not be taken by surprise.

Lowbacca and Sirra had already done that to her. . . .

Leaning back in her command chair, Raaba scanned the asteroid below. She used the ship's high-resolution sensors to study the pockmarked surface, analyzing the structural refinements Imperial engineers had added: the blister domes and bunker outcroppings, the fuel station, the numerous small docking ports.

Then, as she focused in on what seemed to be an anomaly, she sat up with a growl and stared at the image before her eyes, unable to believe what she saw. In an instant she recognized two small craft nearly hidden in the rocky shadows beside the domes: the *Rock Dragon* and Zekk's ship, the *Lightning Rod*.

She leaped up from her command chair with a

startled roar. The young Jedi Knights were already here! They had arrived at the weapons depot before the Diversity Alliance.

Raaba toggled the communications system, sending a tight-beam transmission directly to Nolaa Tarkona. She had to warn her leader that she might be walking into a trap.

12

THE YOUNG JEDI Knights emerged from the munitions bunker, each carrying a pack that held enough explosives to blow up a substantial portion of the depot.

As they'd realized what they were about to do, their lighthearted camaraderie had turned to grim determination.

When Bornan Thul narrowed his eyes, inspecting the companions, Jacen was worried the man might dismiss them as a bunch of kids caught in a dangerous situation. But instead, Raynar's father saw bravery there, and a dedication to purpose. He obviously considered them all, including his own son, to be real Jedi Knights.

Jaina dug in her pack to take inventory of the explosives, the detonators, and the space mines she had stashed there. "We'll have to find strategically vulnerable areas on the asteroid. It'll take plenty of explosives, carefully positioned at specific structural weak points, to bring this place down."

"We will find the weaknesses," Tenel Ka said.

"Let's split up into teams," Zekk suggested. "We can go off in different directions and plant more explosives in less time. I want to slag this depot and get out of here before anything goes wrong."

"If anything *does* go wrong, though," Jacen said, "we'd better agree to rendezvous in our ships out in space."

"An excellent suggestion, Master Jacen," Em Teedee said at Lowie's side. "I, for one, will be glad to have this Diversity Alliance business over with so that we can get on with more pleasant pursuits."

Lowie patted the little translating droid as if in commiseration. He barked and chuffed an alarming suggestion, which Em Teedee passed along. "Master Lowbacca suggests that since he is the only nonhuman in this group, *he* should be the one to plant explosives inside the plague chamber."

Jaina exclaimed, "We can't let you go in there by yourself, Lowie!"

"Lowbacca is correct," Tenel Ka said. "If the rest of us are exposed, we are doomed. He may be immune because he is not human."

"Hey, I think we'll all encounter sufficient dangers in setting our own explosives," Jacen said, understanding the grim truth behind Lowie's realization.

Somberly, they went in separate directions, carrying their explosives. Lowie trudged toward the central plague chamber, Em Teedee clipped to his belt. Zekk and Raynar stayed with Bornan Thul, who was still loading up at the munitions storage room, while Jacen, Jaina, and Tenel Ka went off to disperse their detonators at structural weak points in the domes and tunnel junctures.

As they hurried, Jaina scrutinized the tunnel walls, corridor intersections, and pressurized domes. She hesitated outside the doorway to one of the overhead domes, unslung her pack, and withdrew a heavy disk, a space limpet mine. Holding the mine against one of the metal walls, she pushed a button to activate its magnetic seal. With a *clank*, the mine attached itself to the wall.

She looked over at her brother and Tenel Ka, raising an eyebrow. "These limpet mines used to be sent out like a cloud into space. If one attached itself to the hull, it could blow up an entire Corellian corvette."

Tenel Ka grunted in appreciation. "Devastating," she said.

"The only problem was, they clung to *anything* metal in the vicinity. They used no discrimination routines, and several *Victory*-class Star Destroyers ended up victims of their own space mines."

"Serves them right," Jacen said.

"It is always tragic when warfare causes unintended casualties," Tenel Ka pointed out. "Even Imperial ones."

"Well, if we destroy this depot, the Emperor won't cause any more casualties," Jaina said. She activated the space mine, and its lights winked green: READY FOR DETONATION.

She went farther down the wall of the dome and planted another mine on the opposite wall. "That should take care of this dome," she said. "Now let's move on to the next one."

Jacen followed, planting detonators at the branchpoints of corridors. Once they set off all this destruction, nothing would remain of the asteroid but a rock as dead as it had been before the Empire set foot on it.

Lowbacca hesitated outside the doorway to the central plague chamber. This airtight room contained more death than he had ever seen in one place: sealed transparent cylinders filled with multi-colored liquids, vials of plague solutions, nutrient baths teeming with virulent organisms.

It was his responsibility to destroy them all, and he carried high-temperature incinerating explosives to do the job. It wouldn't do just to crack open the vials and disperse the liquids. He had to make sure the explosion was hot enough, with incandescent heat from a dozen thermal detonators, to annihilate the virus that had been created to kill human beings.

"Well, Master Lowbacca, it does no good to wait," Em Teedee scolded. "It's high time we went inside and plant the detonators. The others are counting on us."

Lowie growled something, and Em Teedee huffed. "I am *not* being impatient. Just because I'm a droid and can't get a plague doesn't mean I don't understand the dangers. I can well imagine computer viruses, you know."

Rather than endure more of the droid's talk, Lowie worked the airlock controls, assisted by Em Teedee's rapport with the computer systems. The air within the pressurized chamber was kept sterile, and backup systems and fail-safes prevented any possible leaks.

Lowie stepped inside, his fur bristling with apprehension. The metal floor felt cold against his feet, and the air smelled harsh and disinfected. He looked around at the tubes and spheres of deadly solution and planned his strategy. He left the pressure door open behind him, not relishing the prospect of being trapped inside the lethal chamber. Then he cautiously walked in among the towering cylindrical tanks.

He moved slowly, carefully, until he finally snapped himself out of his daze and removed the thermal detonators from his pack. He was a Jedi Knight, and he had a threat to wipe out.

He placed his first set of heat explosives under the largest of the bubbling tanks in the center of the room; then he spiralled outward, ducking down, moving like a machine as he planted one detonator after another.

He didn't want to think about the swarming virus behind the thin walls of transparisteel. He didn't want to smell the reprocessed air. He just wanted to be out of here and destroy it all behind him.

As he planted another set of detonators, though, he noticed a marking near the base of the tube labeling the solution inside—KRYTOS PLAGUE, MULTIPLE SPECIES, SLOW-ACTING. Lowie stiffened, recognizing this disease that had harmed so many aliens, including Wookiees, just after the fall of the Empire.

So . . . this plague storehouse held far more than just the human-killing plague after all!

Lowie now turned his attention to the other tanks and vials, inspecting their labels. The colored solutions contained numerous deadly agents. Label after label made his blood run cold. GAMORREAN, SLOW-ACTING. QUARREN, FAST-ACTING. WOOKIEE, SLOW-ACTING. TWI'LEK/CALAMARIAN, VARIABLE VIRULENCE.

Lowie realized that if Nolaa Tarkona got her hands on all of this, not only could she destroy humans, but she could also threaten every other race in the galaxy! The leader of the Diversity Alliance could assert her power over any species in a way that even the Emperor had not dared to do.

Lowie planted his remaining detonators as fast as he could, then rigged up a central explosive controller, which he placed near the main containers in the middle of the room. He would be very glad to get out of this place. Not even he was safe in here.

• • •

After the other young Jedi Knights went on their way, Raynar stayed beside his father inside the munitions bunker. Zekk put his hands on his hips and looked up at the remaining explosives, blasters, and detonators.

"Still plenty left here to cause quite a bit of destruction," he said.

Bornan Thul went to work opening cases and linking detonators, preparing to trigger the remaining explosives. "If we set off all these," Thul said, "we'll put this entire asteroid into a spin."

"I'd rather not be here when that happens," Raynar said.

His father looked down at him with an understanding smile. "We won't be, Raynar," he said. "I'll make sure you get out of here safely."

Bornan Thul worked hard to arrange boxes, linking up blast points for sympathetic explosions. His son dutifully opened more cases, while Zekk moved from one to another, making connections, checking timers, and setting the stage for the biggest explosion he could imagine.

"If Jaina can find enough structural weak points to booby-trap, then this should take care of the weapons depot once and for all," Zekk said, confident in his friend's abilities.

Bornan sighed. "I should have found a way to do this myself a long time ago."

"We're finished here," Zekk said, impatient to

get moving again. He grabbed several explosive packs to take with him. "We'll plant these along the way," he said, "then pick up Lowbacca back at the central chamber."

13

WITH EACH EXPLOSIVE she planted, Jaina felt the metal-lined hallways seem to close in on her. At her direction, Jacen set timed explosives in alternate places, while Tenel Ka drew her lightsaber and sliced partway through support beams or disabled safety interlocks.

"Blaster bolts! When this place blows, it's really going to blow," Jacen observed. "Hey, how many thermal detonators does it take to blow up an Imperial weapons depot?"

"Ah. Aha," Tenel Ka said, responding to Jacen's attempt at humor as if the question were a serious one. "The answer is obvious."

Jaina finished setting the time delay on her detonator, moved farther down the corridor, and began setting up the next one. "Okay then," she said, rising to the bait, "how many thermal detonators *does* it take?"

Still holding her lightsaber, Tenel Ka shrugged eloquently. "All of them, of course."

Jacen chuckled. "Yeah. I think you're right. We—"

"Wait." Tenel Ka held up her hand for silence. She listened, then switched off her lightsaber so its hum would not mask any other noises.

Jaina heard the sound and sprang to her feet. "Company?"

Tenel Ka backed a few steps down the corridor toward Jaina and Jacen, alert and looking in the direction from which the sound had come.

"Uh-oh," Jacen said, rubbing the back of his neck. "Something tells me that whoever our visitors are, they didn't arrive on the *Lightning Rod* or the *Rock Dragon*."

Jaina bit her lower lip as she felt the same tingle of warning. "The Diversity Alliance?"

"This is a fact," Tenel Ka said. "We must stay ahead of them in order to complete our mission."

But before the three young Jedi could move, several figures rounded a corner far down the hallway. A furry white Talz and a tentacle-faced Quarren were in the lead. They all recognized the Quarren, whom they had seen on Ryloth with Nolaa Tarkona. Lowie had told them his name.

"Rullak," Jaina said. Before Nolaa Tarkona's henchmen took another step, the three friends ran in the opposite direction down the corridor. Behind them the Quarren burbled a command and fired his blaster. The energy bolt spanged harmlessly off a metal wall and deflected into the ceiling, where it left a small, smoking hole.

"Excellent," Tenel Ka said as they ran.

"*What*?" Jacen asked. Another shot zinged past without touching them. "They're trying to kill us!" He ran full tilt toward an intersection of corridors.

"Yes, excellent," Tenel Ka said, moving into the lead beside him. Her long red-gold hair and warrior braids streamed out behind her. "Because Rullak's aim is terrible."

A third blaster bolt hit the floor several meters behind them, and Jaina realized that Tenel Ka was right. Jaina still carried a concussion grenade under one arm and a microdetonator in her hand. Risking a glance behind her, she noticed that the alien guards had not gained any ground. She had already set the detonator in her hand. Without stopping, she reset the timer with her free hand, activated the microdetonator's magnetic backing, and smacked the explosive against one of the metal walls, where it clung.

Then, pulling the concussion grenade from under her arm, she armed it and dropped it to the floor as Jacen and Tenel Ka disappeared around a corner ahead. Jaina barely managed to dive to the floor around the corner before the first of her explosions went off.

Jacen and Tenel Ka dragged Jaina back to her feet as the second blast shook the corridor. "Those were only minor explosions," she panted. "Won't hold 'em long."

"Hurry then," Tenel Ka urged, switching her lightsaber back on and taking up her position in the rear as they pelted down the hallway. Sooner than they might have hoped, Diversity Alliance guards reappeared behind them, pursuing with renewed vigor. Blaster bolts—this time from several weapons—pinged and sizzled around them. Tenel Ka, running backward now, used her lightsaber to deflect any shots that came close.

"This way," Jaina said. She turned down a branching corridor just as a blaster bolt hit close to the floor at Tenel Ka's feet, forcing her to jump.

When a second blast zinged off the corridor wall beside her, Tenel Ka threw herself backward, brought up her lightsaber, and deflected the bolt—but not without a price.

Unable to regain her balance in time, Tenel Ka tried to pull herself forward again to land on her right leg, but her foot encountered a loose chunk of plasteel broken free from the ceiling. Her foot slipped, and the ankle turned at an angle it had never been meant to assume.

One of the guards saw her loss of balance and shot past the Quarren toward Tenel Ka. Knowing her leg would not hold her anyway, the warrior girl relaxed her body and allowed it to fall, so that the energy bolt sizzled harmlessly over her—a hair's breadth from the breastplate of her lizard-hide armor. Tenel Ka tucked and rolled as she hit the floor, having the presence of mind to switch off her lightsaber as she tumbled a few meters to avoid more blaster fire and—even with only one arm—displaying her prowess as a fighter.

Jacen stepped out of the corridor in front of her, his lightsaber blazing to deflect the enemy fire. "That way," he yelled, jerking his head to indicate the corridor from which he had come. Pushing off from the metal wall behind her, Tenel Ka launched herself into the side corridor in a tumbling roll.

During calisthenics she'd often used such maneuvers to bring herself out of a defensive position, back to her feet, and ready to go on the offense. This time, though, when she came out of the roll with both feet planted beneath her, a jolt of pain lanced upward from her right ankle. She bit back an outcry. She could not afford to draw Jacen or Jaina's attention away from their own defenses by causing them concern for her.

"This way," Jaina's voice hissed. Jaina stood farther down the corridor at the control panel to a safety interlock, where a vaulted portal was set into a bulkhead. Jacen backed around the corner beside Tenel Ka, still deflecting blaster bolts.

"Come on, you two," Jaina called. Her brother turned and ran, grabbing for Tenel Ka's arm. She gritted her teeth and pounded down the hallway next to him, ignoring the spear of pain she felt every time her right foot touched the ground.

Moments later they were through, and Jaina swung the heavy portal shut behind them. "I set an entry code on the emergency interlocks," she explained, "but I don't know how long this'll hold them."

Tenel Ka ignored the flaring pain in her right leg, tuning it out as if switching off a faulty comlink. "Perhaps our situation calls for desperate measures," she said.

14

INSIDE THE PLAGUE chamber, Lowie planted his last thermal detonator and set the controls. He stood up, satisfied with his work, and growled at the insidious storehouse of destruction. He looked around one last time, surrounded by a forest of tall, bubbling cylinders.

Suddenly he felt a chill as his Jedi senses brought him to full alert. He was no longer alone in the room.

Lowie heard no change in the background hissing and burbling, no muffled conversation—but he did feel an unaccustomed stir in the air currents. From the center of the crowded equipment room he couldn't see the outer walls. In fact, he could see very little except barricades of tubes and canisters. But as he listened, his fur prickling against his skin, he heard a grating, rasping breath . . . heavy footfalls that came slowly, stealthily.

As if something were stalking him.

Lowie's fingers drifted to his lightsaber. His muscles tensed, and the dark streak on his forehead stood upright in an intimidating brush.

Danger, he sensed, *danger*. He held himself utterly still.

Then Em Teedee said in a whisper that sounded louder to Lowie than his uncle losing a hologame, "Master Lowbacca, I do believe there's someone else—"

Lowie jumped backward, startled, and planted a ginger-furred hand over Em Teedee's speaker grille. But it was too late. He heard a roar and the scrape of claws on the cold floor as the giant reptile Corrsk marched around the corner, his fang-filled jaws open as wide as their hinges would allow.

His hiss was like a boiler explosion. "Time to die, Wookiee!" Corrsk drew a huge blaster, wrapping his scaly fingers around its grip.

Lowie ignited his lightsaber with a throbbing *snap-hiss*. "Master Lowbacca, you mustn't allow him to shoot at you in here!" the droid said. "Any blaster fire could break open one of the plague canisters!"

Lowie roared to acknowledge that he was fully aware of the danger.

Licking the scaled edges of his mouth with a long tongue, Corrsk nodded and reholstered the blaster with a gleam of pleasure in his cold yellow eyes.

The Trandoshan came at Lowie, his bare claws extended.

Lowie ducked behind two cylinders as Corrsk lumbered after him, growling with anger but also expressing joy in the hunt. Em Teedee was absolutely right—he had to get the Trandoshan out of the plague chamber so that their fight would not cause accidental damage.

Lowie ran full-out in a long-legged sprint across the slick metal floor. After gaining some distance, he deactivated his lightsaber, afraid of what a careless blow against one of the cylinders might do. He heard the Trandoshan follow, crashing . . . and then the reptile fell silent, stalking him again.

Lowie slipped between two large canisters that contained the human-killing virus. The fluid-filled transparisteel felt very cold against his back. He growled quietly for Em Teedee not to voice a word. The little droid flashed his optical sensors to show he understood the order. The Wookiee listened, but heard nothing.

He stepped out, cautiously peering around. He gazed down a long corridor filled with identical-looking tubes of plague solution. The chamber door remained open, inviting him to dash out into the corridors. He had not sealed it, thinking to leave himself a clear path for escape—but he had inadvertently made it easy for Corrsk to come in and stalk him.

If Lowie could get out the door and lock it behind

him, he could perhaps trap the Trandoshan inside.
But then another realization struck him—Corrsk
could not possibly be on the asteroid alone. He must
have brought the Diversity Alliance with him!
Perhaps Nolaa Tarkona herself was already in the
plague depot.

Lowie moved as silently as he could, ready to
dash for the doorway. Suddenly, with an exploding
roar, Corrsk lurched out from where he had hidden,
waiting for Lowie to head toward the chamber door.
The Wookiee's Jedi senses warned him in the same
instant, and he leaped aside.

The giant reptile, however, wrapped his muscular
arms around Lowie in a murderous bear hug. Lowie
struggled and roared, but his arms were pinned at
his sides. He looked down to see a smooth, waxy
scar on the scaled arm, the remnants of the lightsaber gash Lowie had dealt him during their previous battle, when he had caused a tunnel ceiling to
fall down on Corrsk.

The Trandoshan should have died then, but the
monster was just too *mean* to die so easily, Lowie
thought.

Lowie could not move his arms, could not bunch
his muscles or draw his lightsaber. He was helpless.
Corrsk snarled a hot, wet breath against his fur-
covered ear. The sharp teeth were close, close
enough to rip out Lowie's neck if they wished, but
Corrsk was enjoying his victory too much. He
tightened his grip.

Lowie's ribs creaked; his muscles strained. His

lungs wanted to burst because he could not draw a breath. He could not reach his weapon—so instead, with a final bestial wheeze, Lowie used the primal weapons he still had available to him. He opened his mouth wide and sank his Wookiee fangs deep into the Trandoshan's scaled shoulder, biting down with all the force he could muster.

Leathery skin ripped, and greenish-black blood spurted into Lowie's mouth as he bit down hard again, snarling. Corrsk drew in a long hiss of shock and pain and loosened his grip just enough for Lowie to snap both of his arms sideways, breaking free of the embrace. Without taking the time to draw his lightsaber, he spread both of his hands and clapped them like cymbals against the Trandoshan's flat earholes.

Corrsk staggered back, disoriented and shaking his head. Lowie broke away and ran as fast as he could. He had no need to be quiet now, no requirement for stealth.

Corrsk howled after him, but Lowie made his best speed toward the door. The Trandoshan, finally giving up his attempt to savor the kill, drew his blaster and fired. Lowie ducked, and the energy bolts struck the metal walls of the plague chamber. Luckily, the ricochets dissipated, and the secondary bolts struck none of the plague canisters.

"Run, Master Lowbacca, run!" Em Teedee urged. For once Lowie did exactly what the translating droid told him, without the least thought of argument.

The reptilian charged after them, bellowing in fury.

15

BACK IN THE tunnels on Ryloth, Luke Skywalker had to admit that the Diversity Alliance had done a good job of sanitizing its operation.

Kambrea surrounded herself with armed soldiers to match the New Republic honor guard. All business, eager to get rid of her unwanted visitors, the Devaronian led them through a large Twi'lek city and spoke of how the once-bloodthirsty race had risen above violence to form peaceful collectives.

The inspection team stood in a vast cavern hollowed from the mountain's heart. The rubble itself had been used to construct tall buildings like warrens hugging the grotto walls. Twi'lek families and clans lived and worked inside the stone-walled dwellings, going about the shadowy business of Ryloth—much of which was now devoted to promoting and assisting the Diversity Alliance.

Luke watched everything, absorbing details. The Calamarian ambassador Cilghal stood next to him, also observing, though he could not read any expression on her fishlike face. Kur, the exiled clan leader, spent most of his time staring at the floor, as if afraid to gaze at the cave city.

Trubor, the Chadra Fan senator, seemed impressed by Twi'lek society. The rodentlike creature scuttled around, making appreciative noises every time Kambrea pointed out newly erected dwellings, prisons that punished corrupt slavers who had once captured Twi'lek females renowned for their dancing skills. Nolaa Tarkona's own half sister Oola had been sold as a dancing girl and killed by Jabba the Hutt. The underground commerce in sentient beings had now been halted.

Kambrea turned her horned head to Luke Skywalker. "So you see, the Diversity Alliance takes a stance, not just against human oppression, but against oppression in all its forms."

"Very admirable," Luke said, but made no other comment.

Lusa and Sirra followed the group, remaining together. The centaur girl was skittish, barely able to face her fear at being in the realm of her greatest enemy. She was immensely relieved that Nolaa herself was not there to confront them. However, the question remained as to where the Twi'lek leader was, and what she was up to.

Luke noticed the hateful sidelong glances Kambrea flashed at both Lusa and the young Wookiee girl. The Diversity Alliance did not tolerate betrayal: a Bothan assassin had already tried to kill Lusa on Yavin 4, and though the alien soldier insisted he had no connection with the Diversity Alliance, Luke could sense otherwise.

Kur followed meekly, offering no commentary. He seemed ashamed to set foot in the cliffside cities again, though occasionally he looked longingly at the tall rock-walled buildings and the hardworking people that had once been part of his clan. The Twi'leks looked down at him with cold hatred. They despised Kur—but Luke couldn't tell whether it was because he had been banished . . . or because he had failed them and let Nolaa Tarkona take over.

After a day of being shown the glories of Twi'lek civilization and all the changes Nolaa Tarkona had wrought, Senator Trubor whined in exasperation. "I see no evidence of all the horrors those children claimed," he said. "The New Republic is a diverse group of worlds, with many species—not just humans, but Chadra Fan and Calamarians and Wookiees and all manner of intelligent races. I am insulted that Chief of State Organa Solo would pit us against each other so soon after we formed our government and drove out the hated Empire—the *human* Empire, I might add."

"I won't argue with you the terrible nature of the Empire," Cilghal said calmly. "But we must continue to look. Remember, we are seeing only what Kambrea wishes to show us."

As Sirra growled, Lusa added her own comment with a snort. "Yes, we need to see the ryll mines. Take us to where slaves excavate the mineral for Diversity Alliance profit. Then we'll see what Nolaa Tarkona's really doing."

Kambrea brushed nervously at one of her curved horns, then let out a long sigh. "The ryll mines are in a different portion of the mountains, but we can take our tunnel transport system, if you really insist on seeing them."

"We insist," Luke said. "This is an inspection team, not a guided walk for tourists."

Kambrea sighed again. "Come with me." She looked over her shoulder, fixing a cold glance on Lusa. Then she returned to Cilghal and Trubor with a more placid expression. "Remember, though, it's an industrial area for rock excavations. It's not pretty—but you'll see that we have no captive humans. All of our workers are willing laborers." She laughed, and the sound made it clear that Kambrea was not accustomed to laughing. "Certainly not slaves!"

They boarded a high-speed transport train that shot them southward beneath the spine of mountains. As they held on to their seats, the New

Republic honor guard looked nervous: this would be a perfect place for an ambush, if the Diversity Alliance decided to turn against them. The alien guards seemed just as uneasy as the humans, though, finding themselves in the awkward position of having to question their own prejudices.

When the high-speed train stopped, the air grew colder, picking up a breeze from increased air circulation. The glowpanels overhead flickered, then grew brighter. Kambrea looked up to the rocky ceiling, where conduits rose upward through sloped tunnels to the mountain peaks high above.

"A heat storm just passed over the surface," she said. "We receive most of our power and air circulation from wind turbines erected on the twilight borderline. The shifting temperatures create the terrible storms that drive our turbines."

"We know," Lusa said. "Our friends were trapped outside in one of those storms after they escaped from slavery in your ryll mines."

Kur stepped forward. "Yes, I rescued them out in the cold, and took them to where their ship could take them away from your oppression."

Kambrea looked at them coldly. "So you say."

The Diversity Alliance soldiers grumbled, and the human guards reached for their weapons, ready to fight. Cilghal raised her flipper hands. "So let us see the mines. We wish to inspect the work conditions there."

Kambrea hesitated, then turned, ignoring the previous exchange. She led them into a large cavern where scores of Twi'leks were busily hammering out chunks of rock, seeking veins of the precious mineral buried deep in the mountain.

The Rodian crew boss stood around waving his sucker-tipped fingers and giving orders. Luke saw the large polished eyes, the narrow flexible snout, and the warty head; he remembered the inept bounty hunter Greedo who had tried to capture Han Solo in the Mos Eisley cantina. Luke hoped all Rodians weren't so gullible. This shift boss seemed to be doing a good job keeping his workers in line.

Twi'leks scurried over the walls using sonic hammers; others dangled from the ceiling in harnesses as they chipped away at fungus-covered stalactites.

"They're all Twi'leks!" Lusa said in astonishment.

"Of course," Kambrea answered, "volunteer labor from the cliff cities. Ask any one of them— they work here and get paid well. In fact, people wait in line for this opportunity." She laughed again in her broken-glass chuckle. "We have no need to take slaves. Besides, Twi'leks work harder than weakling humans, especially human children."

"I've seen enough," Trubor squeaked, putting his hands on his tiny hips. He perked his wide, fanlike ears around as if listening for hidden prisoners, cries for help. "There is nothing the least bit suspicious in all these tunnels. I, for one, must say that Nolaa Tarkona's concerns about of human prejudice and intolerance seem to have a very firm grounding— especially with what the New Republic has demonstrated here."

Luke used his Jedi senses, but could detect no struggling human prisoners. He hoped that Nolaa Tarkona hadn't ordered their immediate execution upon learning of the inspection team's visit.

"Is there nothing else we can show you?" Kambrea said.

"Yes!" Lusa snapped. "Show us everything you have hidden."

The Diversity Alliance guards stiffened, but Cilghal proved calmer. She turned to Sirra. "Is there anything specific you suggest?"

Sirra growled something, a suggestion, and the Calamarian ambassador turned to Kambrea. "You wouldn't mind if we looked at your loading dock, would you?"

"Certainly not," the Devaronian answered with a huff. "As I've said repeatedly, we have nothing to hide."

Luke's senses prickled as Kambrea led them to one of the main shipping and receiving bays. Stacks of crates stood tall against one wall. Bulky alien workers and numerous droids lifted the crates, catalogued them, and loaded them into small transports.

"You see," Kambrea said with a gesture, "food and medicinal supplies for alien colonies, settlement worlds the New Republic has abandoned."

"Very commendable," Cilghal said.

Trubor emphasized the point further. "The New Republic cannot help every world, though we wish we could. The Diversity Alliance serves a good purpose by assisting those we cannot."

Sirra growled curiously as she strode over to the wall of crates. Luke watched her carefully. The Wookiee seemed to know exactly what she was doing.

"I hope you're satisfied," Kambrea said, intent on Trubor. "There's nothing to warrant the treatment we have received. We trust you'll return to your New Republic and report our displeasure to your government."

Sirra gave a challenging bellow. As everyone turned to look, she balled her furry fist and punched in the side of a supply crate marked FRAGILE: MEDICINAL SUPPLIES—URGENT. The container split open.

Kambrea yelped in astonishment, and Sirra stood

back as the crate cracked, groaned, and then spilled packaged blaster power-packs and handheld laser rifles out onto the floor.

At that point, all chaos broke loose.

16

JAINA TROTTED UP the metal-lined corridor beside Tenel Ka and Jacen. Looking back over her shoulder she saw that the emergency interlock still held Rullak and his Diversity Alliance guards. She couldn't tell how much longer the barrier would last, though.

A moment ago it had sounded as if Tenel Ka might have a plan. "Exactly what kind of drastic measures did you have in mind?" Jaina asked.

"Speed is essential," Tenel Ka replied, and picked up her pace. Her expression flickered with physical pain, but the warrior girl did not falter or slow down.

"Yeah, I think we can all agree on that," Jacen panted.

At the next branching of corridors, Tenel Ka said, "This way!" and turned so quickly that Jaina had to pivot on one foot to make the turn, causing her to fetch up sharply against the wall.

Jacen grabbed her left arm and pulled her forward again. "Come on, Jaina. So what's the rest of the plan, Tenel Ka?"

Jaina willed her legs to keep moving. "Kind of hard to have a committee meeting while we're"—she gasped—"while we're on the run."

"Almost there," Tenel Ka said, turning left again at the next intersection.

Jaina sped up and hoped that Tenel Ka really did have a plan.

"Almost there," Jacen echoed, trying to encourage Jaina. "Hey—almost *where*?"

Tenel Ka skidded to a stop without warning, and Jacen collided with her, forcing him to throw an arm around her to keep her from falling down. Jaina overshot the intersection by a few steps before she managed to stop.

"We must set explosives here," Tenel Ka said.

Jaina's mind quickly switched to analytic mode and her gaze swept the walls, ceilings, joints, and supports of the intersection. "Structural weak points there, there, and here." She pointed to each location as she swung her knapsack from her back and rummaged around for the larger thermal detonators. She tossed one to her brother, who caught it easily and began setting it up where she had indicated. Jaina set another one by herself.

"If my sense of direction serves me, the *Rock Dragon* is docked just over one hundred meters from here," Tenel Ka said. "Set the timers for three minutes."

Jaina blinked at the other girl. "But the blast from these detonators is going to be *huge*—"

"—and we won't be able to get far enough away from the blast unless we do a full takeoff in the *Rock Dragon*," Jacen finished for her.

"Exactly, my friends."

Shaking his head, Jacen positioned his detonator and set the timer. Jaina rigged her second and third detonators, lobbed one at the warrior girl, and situated the remaining one for maximum damage.

"Hey, we can't leave Zekk and Lowie and—"

"We will take off only for a few minutes," Tenel Ka said, catching the detonator with her one hand and thumbing it into position, "then return to a different point, free of pursuit."

As one, the three young Jedi Knights began to run down the corridor toward the *Rock Dragon*. Jaina put on a burst of speed which barely kept her ahead of the clock that ticked down each second in her mind. The passageway seemed to stretch endlessly ahead of them.

"Almost there," Jacen chanted as they ran.

Jaina's entire concentration focused on the effort of placing one foot in front of the other without slowing down. *Left, right, left, right, left, right.*

An airlock hatch swung open right in front of her. Through her haze of exhaustion she glimpsed her brother's face streaming with perspiration as he held the hatch open for her. "Don't stop now, Jaina!"

She couldn't have stopped then if she had tried. She bolted straight through the hatch into the *Rock Dragon* without even thinking about where she was going. She dove into the pilot's seat, and her hands instantly began moving across the console controls. There was no time for mistakes.

In the back of the *Rock Dragon* Jacen slammed the airlock shut, and Tenel Ka was already beside Jaina, slapping the engine power to full. Jaina checked her chronometer and knew there was no time to wait for her brother to get into his crash restraints.

Uncoupling from the asteroid dock, she threw the *Rock Dragon* into full reverse. Repulsorjets kicked the *Rock Dragon* free a split second before the asteroid began to shudder from the shock of the explosions. In the back, she heard Jacen stumble and fall with a loud *thunk*.

Flames and shattered rock sprayed out of the dome and docking area, but the Hapan passenger cruiser shot away at full power.

"Hey, no need to worry about me—I'm fine." Jacen scrambled into the cockpit as the *Rock Dragon* pulled away from the tiny asteroid.

"You are bleeding," Tenel Ka observed.

Jaina looked back in alarm to see a large discolored lump forming on the side of her brother's forehead. Blood trickled from a ragged gash beside his eye. Jacen shrugged a shoulder and pulled his crash webbing around him. "Builds character."

Beneath them, an angry, fiery glow marked the site of the detonation. "We'll wait another minute until all the aftershocks have died down," Jaina said. "Then we'll find a new place to dock."

"There," Tenel Ka said, pointing to a dock far below. Jaina nodded.

Jacen said, "Uh-oh. We're not alone out here."

Jaina looked out the windowport at a cluster of ominous ships racing toward them—the Diversity Alliance armada.

17

FROM SPACE, RAABA watched the weapons depot like a ravenous hawkbat waiting to pounce on a juicy rodent. The chocolate-furred Wookiee was well aware of the honor she held by being in charge of the Diversity Alliance fleet. Nolaa Tarkona trusted her, and Raaba would not let her leader down.

Keeping the fleet in attack-ready formation, Raaba took them around the asteroid again and again, altering their course each time so that they got a view of the plague storehouse from every angle.

The human ships were still down there, but one was no longer docked at the asteroid.

She looked at the ship glinting in the reflected light of the distant sun. The sight sent a meteor storm of conflicting emotions through her. She had first seen that Hapan passenger cruiser on Kuar, where she had found Lowbacca and explained to him why she had faked her own death. Then, more recently, the *Rock Dragon* had appeared on Ryloth. Lowie and Sirra had stolen the ship, rescued their human friends, and left Raaba behind.

Deep inside, Raaba grudgingly admitted to herself that she was glad the humans had not actually died in the ryll spice mines. Still, it had been hard for her to accept that her lifelong friends Lowie and Sirra could so easily abandon her in order to save other friends, especially humans.

Yet a part of her could not help but understand. After all, *she* would have done the same for either Lowie or Sirra. And, taking the responsibilities of command seriously, she knew she would willingly risk her life for any of the Twi'leks, Talz, Devaronians, Bith, or other Diversity Alliance members who worked around her with such dedication.

Raaba knew her duty to the Diversity Alliance. The *Rock Dragon* could not be allowed to interfere with their plans. She had informed Nolaa Tarkona of the intruders, and the Twi'lek leader had promised to deal with them appropriately.

Raaba swallowed hard. Lowie himself might be on the *Rock Dragon*, and even if he wasn't, his human friends were surely aboard. But her loyalty was clear—at least she thought it was. She couldn't let her emotions or sentimentality get in the way. She had thought about this for part of an hour, ever since she had spotted the ships, and she had to come to a decision.

Sitting down in her command chair, she ordered the front viewscreen's magnification to be increased. She swung a console into position in front of her, then ordered half the weapons systems to be switched to her control. The Ugnaught weapons officer complied, and Raaba took careful aim on the *Rock Dragon*. She could not betray Nolaa Tarkona, but for the sake of their friendship, she would do this one thing for Lowie—even if she never had the chance to tell him about it.

Raaba's fingers depressed a firing stud. Her shot narrowly missed the Hapan cruiser. She knew she had to be cautious: she only wanted to disable the ship, not destroy it. She took another shot and scored a good hit, though the *Rock Dragon*'s defensive shields held admirably.

Suddenly a third shot exploded against the hull of the *Rock Dragon*—but Raaba had not fired again. The Ugnaught weapons officer turned to grin at her, obviously waiting for Raaba to commend him on his excellent shooting.

She commanded the crew to wait, but another blast lanced out, this time directed by the security console on the other side of the bridge. Seeing her actions, everyone had decided to take a potshot.

No! Raaba wanted to cry. *Do not destroy the ship!* But she knew she had no reason to give the command. Nolaa Tarkona's orders had been specific. Shoot to kill. Take no prisoners.

"Maybe this wasn't such a great idea after all," Jaina muttered, throwing the *Rock Dragon* into a spin to avoid a new volley of fire from the Diversity Alliance armada. "How many?" she gasped.

Jacen's voice was tense. "I'd say thirty—maybe forty ships."

"Standard Old Imperial attack formation," Tenel Ka added in clipped tones. "Use the asteroid as a shield."

"Full sublight," Jaina snapped, pulling the ship into a tight curve around the asteroid. "I guess we won't be getting back down there as soon as we planned."

Jacen leaned forward to help Tenel Ka yank the power levers into position, and all three passengers were thrown backward in their seats. The ship shot out of range as laser fire speared through space behind them. Within seconds Jaina had managed to put the bulk of the depot asteroid between the *Rock Dragon* and the Diversity Alliance fleet.

"Not much of a shield for us," Jacen pointed out.

"Those ships will not fire on the asteroid as long as Nolaa Tarkona is down there," Tenel Ka said.

The flagship of the Diversity Alliance armada appeared around the edge of the asteroid, and Jaina dodged back into the asteroid's shadow for cover again. "I don't know how much longer we can keep this up," she said. A moment later her heart skipped a beat as Diversity Alliance ships appeared around the edges of the asteroid from three directions simultaneously.

The split armada triangulated and converged on the *Rock Dragon*. The young Jedi Knights' ship shuddered as turbolaser fire struck the hull, further weakening their shields.

Jaina zigged and zagged. Bright fire lanced under, above, and to either side of the ship.

Then—suddenly—their path was cleared. More ships streaked overhead, emerging like missiles out of hyperspace. New Republic ships—at last!

A wild cry of exhilaration sounded over the comm speakers, followed by a Wookiee roar of challenge. Jacen and Jaina gaped briefly at each other in astonishment. "Dad?" Jaina said.

"Chewie?" Jacen asked.

"Half of the New Republic fleet," Tenel Ka said. The warrior girl was not exaggerating. An entire cavalry of friendly vessels had dropped out of hyperspace to engage the Diversity Alliance attackers. A few of Nolaa Tarkona's ships, apparently not yet ready to give up their quarry, began firing again at the *Rock Dragon*. A moment later one of those ships exploded into a fireball in space behind them.

Han Solo's voice came over the comm speakers again. "I suggest you kids get to safety while we handle the heavy artillery out here."

"But Dad—Lowie and Zekk and Raynar are still on the asteroid!" Jaina objected as turbolaser fire exploded uncomfortably close to their port shields. "We're just heading back there."

Chewbacca roared so loudly over the speakers that sparks flew. Han Solo spoke grimly, communicating both his concern for his children and his high estimation of their competence. "Just stay clear of the crossfire," Han said. "Wait for an opening, but until then, stick close to the *Falcon*."

Tenel Ka pointed out, "Until the Diversity Alliance armada is under control, our safest alternative is to stay with the New Republic fleet."

Jaina swerved to avoid another turbolaser blast. Then, with a determined whoop, she pulled the *Rock Dragon* alongside her father's ship.

18

JAINA'S BLAST IN the subsidiary dome rocked the entire asteroid. The eruption destabilized the munitions depot, knocking out several artificial gravity generators in distinct sections.

The shockwave threw Lowbacca to his knees as he fled from Corrsk down a long corridor. The walls shook, and suddenly the tug of gravity went slack and the floor and ceiling spun around him. The Wookiee lost his footing and tumbled, disoriented in the weightlessness.

He banged against the wall, flailing his furry arms and legs. Em Teedee clanged on the metal plates with a loud ringing sound. Lowie's ears popped from a surge of decompression elsewhere in the asteroid.

At the other end of the corridor, Corrsk lurched through an open pressure door, unbothered by the shift. His entire attention was focused on his prey.

The Trandoshan aimed his blaster at the Wookiee—but an aftershock threw him to one side. His shot streaked past Lowbacca and struck the airlock at the tunnel juncture.

Alarms rang out after the explosion created a violent decompression. With a grunt, Lowie surged toward the end of the hall, but he was too late. Automatic systems slammed the blast doors closed, sealing off and compartmentalizing sections of the asteroid to stop the loss of air.

The heavy door closed shut just as Lowie reached it, pounding his hairy paws against the unyielding surface. He was trapped in a dead end, facing the reptilian hunter.

At the far end of the corridor, Corrsk gave a dry rasping laugh, like sandpaper on a raw wound.

Lowie didn't intend to give the predator the satisfaction of an easy kill. He drew his lightsaber, and its molten-bronze blade blazed brightly as he bounced from one wall to the other, as if dancing on marionette strings. The asteroid's natural gravity was barely enough to keep his feet touching the floor.

Corrsk blasted at him again, and Lowie leaped up, hitting the ceiling, ricocheting back down at an angle to the wall, and then springing off again. He took the initiative and lunged toward the Trandoshan. Blaster bolts streaked in another haywire pattern, and Lowie swung his lightsaber in the air for intimidation. Its humming, buzzing sound was like a swarm of deadly insects in the enclosed tunnel.

"No escape," the Trandoshan gargled.

Lowie growled something untranslatable in response. He was concerned about his friends, about the explosion that had just rocked the asteroid, about Nolaa Tarkona and the plague—but right now, despite all his training as a Jedi, the primary force surging through him was a bestial hatred of this reptilian species that had slaughtered hundreds, maybe thousands, of Wookiees, taking their fur as trophies. The Trandoshans were Lowie's natural enemies, and he did not intend to become a prize pelt for Corrsk.

Corrsk braced his blaster and fired again, but Lowie ducked out of the way. The bolt singed the metal wall near a control panel for the environmental systems and the pressurized doors.

Lowie crashed into the tall reptilian, and they grappled, hammering at each other. He did not simply strike Corrsk dead with the lightsaber as he could have. He resisted that—for now—but he doubted there could be another end to this battle. He snarled, and the Trandoshan hissed back at him.

During the fight, the catch holding Em Teedee onto Lowie's prized syren-fiber belt snapped, and the little droid sprang free, using his microrepulsorjets to bob into the air. "Master Lowbacca, please be careful—I could have been seriously damaged!"

Lowie rammed the Trandoshan into the wall, and

Corrsk struck back, pushing hard and driving Lowie across the corridor. The low gravity made resistance futile, and they bounced and caromed like foam balls in a spin-dagat tournament.

Lowie saw that on the other side of the sealed pressure door the dome had been ripped open, leaving only the vacuum of space. He could not take the time to find a different way out; he would have to go back the way they had come.

Many corridors reeled out behind them, but other pressure doors had locked down as well—and right now all he could see was the blazing hatred in Corrsk's eyes; all he could smell was the sour breath of half-digested raw meat that clung between the Trandoshan's teeth.

They continued to fight. Lowie backed off, raising his lightsaber. The Trandoshan fired his blaster, and Lowie deflected it. Corrsk fired again, stepping closer, raising his weapon.

Lowie had no room to move. As the Trandoshan prepared to push the firing stud again, Lowie had no choice but to slash with the lightsaber, severing Corrsk's arm high above the elbow.

The reptilian roared, but before his amputated arm could fall to the floor, he reached out with his other hand and grabbed his detached wrist, trying to snatch the blaster pistol from its twitching grip.

"It will regenerate," he said.

Em Teedee flew free, spinning up and over to the control panel on the wall. The little droid bounced against it, pushing buttons with his casing. As Corrsk stood up and lunged, a hot blast of steam came from an environmental control nozzle in the ceiling.

The reptilian yowled in surprise, and Lowie bent over, pushing against the floor and springing outward. He crashed full force into the Trandoshan's torso, knocking him backward. Corrsk spun end over end in the low gravity, leaking black blood from the broken cauterized stump of his arm.

Lowie fought to regain his footing, his balance. He wasn't accustomed to struggling in near-weightlessness. Em Teedee wailed, "Over here, Master Lowbacca! I'm over here, if you're trying to find me."

Lowie was more interested in the control panel itself. As he drifted past, he snagged the square box, then held on to a sturdy support pipe that ran up the wall.

Staggering and unable to catch his footing, Corrsk drifted to the back of the passageway and slammed into the pressure door on the opposite end. Still clutching his severed limb in his good hand, he tried to wrestle the blaster pistol away from the reflexively clenched dead fingers.

At the control panel, Lowie frantically worked to analyze the Imperial codes and the buttons used for fail-safe mechanisms.

Corrsk succeeded in prying his blaster free from

his dead hand's grip and held it out in his left hand, aiming at Lowie.

Lowbacca punched in the final sequence and disengaged the airlock mechanism, which popped open the pressure door.

The metal bulkhead slid aside right behind Corrsk. He snarled and reached out to grab for support, but his arm was no longer there. Suddenly, with a wail, the vacuum of space ripped him away. The Trandoshan flew backward into open space.

Air gushed out, swooping and cold. Lowie fought to lash his syren-fiber belt around the support pipe, which held him firmly in place against the wall.

"I'm being pulled out!" Em Teedee wailed, fighting a losing battle with his microrepulsorjets at full power, being sucked away in the vacuum.

With one hand Lowie snagged the little translating droid as he frantically used his other hand to punch the buttons that would seal the door again. Air roared around him.

As atmosphere rushed from the compartment, Lowie managed to get the door shut again, sealing Corrsk outside. The towering Trandoshan drifted up and out into airless space, still flailing feebly in outrage.

Lowie grabbed the power conduit connected to the control panel and yanked it free. Sparks flew. Then emergency power sources flickered on, and the artificial gravity generators cycled, adding normal weight to the room again. Debris crashed to the floor.

"Oh, my. That was a close call," the little droid said as he bobbed in the air, released from Lowie's grip. Lowbacca slumped down to the cold metal deck, feeling weak from the battle. His stomach clenched and he fought to control his feelings after having just killed a sentient being, even one as despicable as Corrsk. Lowie clipped Em Teedee back into place.

He looked in both directions down the corridor. The heavy pressure door behind him had also sealed shut . . . and he had just ripped out the power conduit.

He groaned in dismay. Now he would have to rig a way to fix the controls, or he would never get back to the central plague chamber and complete his mission.

19

THE ROCKING EXPLOSION also caused Raynar to slip and stumble, and thus lose his grip on the delicate munitions he carried.

Zekk reacted quickly. He sensed the instant danger and snatched the explosives from the Alder-aanian boy's hands, catching and cradling them before Raynar could drop them to the floor.

"I hope that wasn't an accident from one of our team," Bornan Thul said.

Raynar looked about, his face pale in its texture of fear. "Maybe we're under attack!"

Zekk held the explosive pack carefully, trying to control his trembling. He shook his head. "That was Jaina. She's all right, but something's gone wrong." He marched forward. "We'd better find Lowie quick and make sure he's set the detonators in the plague chamber. Then we can all get off this rock before anything else happens."

Raynar swallowed hard and followed him. "Unless some disaster has already taken place."

They dashed down the curving corridors from the munitions chamber back to the central room that stored the plague canisters, pausing only briefly to plant the last of their explosives at strategic points. Pressing his lips together in a grim line, Zekk fixed the linked detonation transponders so they could set off all the bombs at once.

Zekk's Jedi senses tingled. Despite his ordeals of the past, he was no longer entirely reluctant to use the Force, especially in a situation where those skills might mean the difference between life and death.

He pulled himself up short and looked at Raynar; they could both sense danger around the corner. Bornan Thul eased past them, taking the lead. "We can't waste any time."

As soon as he turned the corner, though, Bornan Thul nearly ran into a lumbering Gamorrean guard, who appeared to be lost. The guard grunted at him in surprise and blinked stupid-looking eyes. Bornan Thul snatched out the blaster pistol he had taken from the munitions room and shot the guard twice before the piglike brute could make a move.

Raynar gasped. "I can't believe how fast you reacted!" he said to his father. "You protected us all."

Bornan looked at the dead Gamorrean and sighed. "I used to be a merchant lord. My entire battlefield was in trade negotiations. I was able to pull a faster trick than even the great Lando Calrissian." He drew a long, heavy breath, and then shook his head. "At one time I thought I could sell sand to Jawas—look at how I've changed."

Raynar put a comforting hand on his father's arm. "Maybe it's because you're concerned with more than just the Bornaryn fleet this time. Maybe you're thinking on a much broader scale, and your priorities have changed."

Thul looked at his son and smiled. "That's very perceptive, Raynar."

Zekk looked down at the fallen Gamorrean guard and urged them to move again. "I admire your reactions, Bornan Thul." He tossed his long dark hair behind him. "This means we're not alone on the asteroid. Nolaa Tarkona and the Diversity Alliance must be here already."

They hurried along the corridors as rapidly and as cautiously as they could. They reached the plague chamber without incident, but they did not see Lowie when they surreptitiously peered through the transparisteel windows into the collection of plague containers.

Instead, they looked down in astonishment to find Nolaa Tarkona standing triumphant in the middle of the chamber. She held a control box, the central connector for all the incinerators and thermal detonators Lowie had dispersed among the plague cylinders. Her single head-tail thrashed, making the tattoos ripple. Flashing her pointed teeth and looking utterly confident, Nolaa disconnected the explosives.

Bornan Thul watched with cold anger on his face. Raynar stifled a soft moan of despair.

Zekk gritted his teeth. "Looks like we need to try something else then—if it isn't already too late."

Surrounded by hundreds of liters of concentrated death, Nolaa Tarkona experienced the thrill of long anticipation, the payoff of years of searching. At last she had a weapon to exterminate the human vermin for all time. Then alien races could be free. They could work together. They could reclaim their stolen worlds and live with all the glory they were meant to have.

As she stood among the transparisteel containers, she breathed the oh-so-clean-smelling air, sterilized and disinfected. But she knew something was terribly wrong. The sealed door had already been opened, and her guards scoured the plague chamber, searching for evidence of sabotage. They had shouted in outrage when they found dozens of incinerators and thermal detonators strung together, planted at strategic points.

Nolaa had moved to the center of the room and found the control box. She could smell Wookiee in the air, and she knew that Lowbacca, one of the great traitors to the Diversity Alliance, had been here already. He wanted to destroy this stockpile in the war for alien freedom.

With her rose-quartz eyes, she studied the control box now that she had disconnected the sabotage devices. Then she yanked out the remaining cables before tossing away the useless box. It made a resounding, satisfying clang on the metal floor. Nolaa glowered down at it, her sensitive head-tail twitching.

The Twi'leks had an extensive but subtle language that depended on the movements of their head-tails. But she had only Diversity Alliance soldiers beside her, none of her own Twi'lek people to understand her thoughts and her emotions.

No race could truly comprehend the downtrodden hopelessness the Twi'leks had endured—centuries of slavery, technological inferiority, hellish environmental conditions, even treachery from their own race. Now that she had control of the Emperor's plague, though, Nolaa could become the savior of aliens everywhere, and she relished that position.

As she glanced at the various liquid solutions, Nolaa saw other test plagues, hideous viruses targeted to nonhuman species—the biological weapons Evir Derricote had developed and tested on those hapless alien prisoners they had found sealed in the small cells.

These other plagues certainly had potential as well. The Diversity Alliance could free all non-human races by spreading one kind of plague . . . but in the aftermath, she was certain to encounter further resistance, struggles against her benevolent rule by various commando groups from different species. She might have to deal with strongholds that resisted their own liberation, and these biological solutions would give her an edge against the Wookiees, the Calamarians, and other races that might prove troublesome. She had to take samples of these other plague organisms as well.

With the optical sensors mounted in the stump of her severed head-tail, she saw a flash of movement behind the transparisteel windows above. Someone spying on her. She set her sharpened teeth on edge. A part of her already knew who the intruders were.

Nolaa took a deep breath and stifled the anxious twitching of her head-tail. She was not worried. She had gotten here in time to secure the plague samples. She had plenty of soldiers with her, all armed with blaster rifles.

The little Jedi saboteurs had been foiled in their plan, and Nolaa would bide her time. They would come to her. Then, with all the plague solution she would ever need, and with the human meddlers all dead, she could begin the great work of her life.

20

USING HIS POWERFUL fingers as tools, in addition to Em Teedee's cables and diagnostics for leads and crossovers, Lowie managed to hot-wire the inner door. The sealed pressure barrier hissed open, finally allowing him to run back toward the central plague chamber. At least he didn't have to worry about Corrsk anymore, and the gravity here was normal again.

Farther along, he encountered another barricade, more sealed doors. Lowie groaned, disconcerted. His fingers still ached from prying open the previous control panel, and now he had to work his way through a second one. He had no idea how many other pressure doors had automatically closed behind him after the explosion.

"Now then, Master Lowbacca," Em Teedee said, "we mustn't lose patience. We must be cautious and persevere. We have a mission to complete. I will offer whatever assistance I can."

Lowie fully understood the implications. Nolaa Tarkona might even now be making her way off the asteroid with the deadly plague samples, and he knew he had to stop her.

The companions each had their separate missions, but he cared too much for his friends not to worry about them, all the same. First, though, he had to get past this door.

Lowie dug his hard claws into the screw bolts holding the cover plate on the access controls. He twisted with his fingers, and one of his claws cracked, but the screw finally turned, and he pried it away. After loosening another, the plate came away sufficiently that he could just bend it aside, ignoring the other two screws.

Impatient, he studied the wires, circuit boards, and cyberfuses. This control setup was more complex, governing four different automatic doors in the adjoining passages. He dug his fingers into the nest of electronics and jammed wire leads through Em Teedee, connecting one circuit to another. He took the final cable and without double-checking, jabbed it into position, just as Em Teedee squealed, "No, Master Lowbacca, not—"

Sparks flew as two incompatible linkages short-circuited. The control panel blazed, as a small fire erupted. Black smoke spewed up, stinking of insulation, burned plastic, and melted wires. Lowie yanked the wires away, but it was too late.

"Oh, my!" Em Teedee wailed. His voice warbled

up and down, quickened then slowed. "I think all my circuits are scrambled. What day is it today?" Then he made strange bleeping noises as he ran a diagnostic and bypassed his damaged circuits. "Ah, there! Much better. Please don't do that again, Master Lowbacca. You must be more cautious."

Lowie gave a long sigh as he looked at the blackened panel. He would never be able to operate the door controls now. He had ruined them. He stepped back.

At the very least, he could use his lightsaber to hack his way through. Lowie gripped the weapon in his right paw, finding the power stud with his thumb. But before he could activate the energy blade, a loud booming sound came from one of the other sealed bulkheads.

"Oh, dear," Em Teedee wailed. "Perhaps it's the Diversity Alliance firing upon us. What if they break through and take us prisoner? What if it's that horrible Nolaa Tarkona?"

The Wookiee ignited his lightsaber, this time ready to fight. The crash came again. It sounded like something immensely heavy, metal against metal, like a relentless battering ram.

The bulkhead buckled outward, and convex mounds appeared in the center of the heavy door, as if someone were punching fists into a thin sheet of dough. After another slamming crash, the hinges groaned.

Lowie stood with his feet planted apart, his lightsaber raised in a fighting stance.

After enduring three more heavy strikes, the blockading door broke free of its supports and toppled into the corridor with a crash like an explosion. Out of the sparks from tearing metal, and the shadows of smashed and flickering glowpanels in the ceiling, a giant angular shape lumbered into the intersection.

Lowie froze as he recognized the blinking red lights on the conical metal head, the broad durasteel shoulders, the arms, torso, and legs made of impenetrable metal tubing. The framework created a body somewhat resembling a human's, but it was clearly a droid—an assassin droid.

"My, how very unexpected!" Em Teedee said. "IG-88! What are you doing here?"

The assassin droid clomped forward, raising its scarred durasteel fists and arming grenade launchers and built-in blaster rifles.

"What is he doing?" Em Teedee said testily. "IG-88, don't you recognize us? I wonder if he's been this sluggish ever since Jaina reprogrammed him back on Mechis III."

The assassin droid did not seem the least bit impressed by Lowie's lightsaber. Instead, IG-88 paused, swiveling sensor eyes toward them, and then lowered his own weapons.

"Ah, very good. You do know who we are," Em Teedee said.

The towering droid's lights flashed, and Lowie wondered if Em Teedee could understand them as some sort of communication.

"I know why he's here, Master Lowbacca," Em Teedee said. "Mistress Jaina reprogrammed IG-88 to search for Bornan Thul. His assignment was to find Raynar's father and stay as his bodyguard, following his wishes, or at the very least protect him from harm."

Lowie slowly lowered his lightsaber when the assassin droid made no threatening move. The Wookiee and IG-88 stood motionless, regarding each other.

"We've tried to keep our own mission quiet, but with the numerous ships involved, some comm traffic must have gotten through. IG-88 could well have picked up the evidence that Bornan Thul was here, and he came to complete his mission! We're saved, if he'll protect all of us."

Lowie grumbled skeptically.

"Come along with us, IG-88. You can help," Em Teedee said to the big droid. "We're supposed to meet Bornan Thul near the chamber where the plague cylinders are stored. But these doors have gotten in our way. Could you assist us in removing them?"

Lowie still held his deactivated lightsaber, ready to cut away the door if necessary. But IG-88 clomped forward to the partially opened but frozen barricade that blocked them from the central chamber. He planted his metallic feet on the floor, adjusted his stance for traction, and then grabbed the blast door.

Servomotors whined; straining gears and metal joints squealed. IG-88's durasteel arms and torso flexed ever so slightly, bending with the immense strain—an then the pressure door groaned and snapped. Through metal fatigue the hinges simply broke away, and IG-88 shoved the wreckage aside.

"Very good," Em Teedee said. "Now do let us hurry. We can assist you in finding Bornan Thul."

IG-88 plunged ahead into the corridor, fearing no Diversity Alliance soldiers or any other obstacle that might slow him down. Lowie followed, knowing that at least they wouldn't have any further trouble with bothersome doors.

21

MEANWHILE, BACK ON Ryloth, as soon as Sirra exposed the Diversity Alliance's secret cache of weapons, Kambrea screamed at the top of her voice, "Guards! Stop them before they kill us all!"

Kambrea's words provided exactly the right provocation for the already-tense guards. Her soldiers whirled about in search of a target. The Gamorreans, slower-witted than the others, simply opened fire without aiming.

Several blaster bolts struck near Sirra and the stockpile of contraband weapons. Luke Skywalker threw himself backward, his Jedi reflexes ready and tight as a spring.

"Stop shooting! Stop shooting!" Senator Trubor squeaked, but nobody listened to him.

Lusa galloped across the loading bay and knocked Sirra aside as a volley of bolts struck a small box of packaged hand blasters, detonating it. The explosion shoved them all backward. They scrambled to keep their balance.

"Don't let them leave!" Kambrea shouted. "They can't escape!"

Under a barrage of alarms, dozens of Diversity Alliance soldiers raced in. Luke felt a deep sadness as he ignited his lightsaber and prepared to fight. Most of these soldiers, he knew, had been swayed by Nolaa Tarkona's words and struggled against enemies who did not need to be enemies. They knew nothing about the circumstances here, only that they felt threatened.

Kambrea's soldiers shot in a cross fire across the loading bay. New Republic guards fell back with their own weapons blazing. Two human escorts stood next to Kur, protecting him as they held their blaster rifles, ready to fight to the death. Another blast ricocheted off the ceiling, and broken stone rubble pattered down around them.

Cilghal stepped up to Luke, her lightsaber glowing. She looked at him with her large round eyes. "Even though I'm an ambassador," she said, "I always carry my Jedi weapon with me."

Luke raised his energy blade beside his former student. "Diversity Alliance soldiers!" he called. "We did not come here to fight. Surrender now, and the New Republic will punish only the treacherous members of your organization."

"You mean like me?" Kambrea shouted. "And

Nolaa Tarkona? These humans want to destroy us all! We must fight for our lives!"

Outraged, the alien fighters redoubled their blaster fire.

Lusa and Sirra had taken shelter behind one of the ships. Sirra dug in a broken container marked MEDICINAL SUPPLIES and drew out a blaster of her own. She squatted, carefully picking her target.

Three brutish Abyssin set aside their heavy spiked clubs and hauled out energy rifles as they hunkered behind a small skimmer. Sirra watched the one-eyed soldiers preparing to fire on the New Republic troops. Flashing her fangs in a grim smile, she lined up her blaster crosshairs with the fuel module of the tiny ship. Here in the landing bay, the skimmer would have no shields, no protection. She fired at full strength.

The fuel pod exploded nicely. The Abyssin were blown back with the rain of shrapnel.

Diversity Alliance soldiers continued to stream in, increasing their firepower. A human soldier died with a smoking blaster hole in his chest. When a Gamorrean guard lumbered forward to check on his kill, another human soldier cut down the piglike creature in turn.

The entire grotto was filled with sounds of weapons fire, explosions, ricochets, screams of terror, and howls of pain. Luke realized how outnumbered they were—and their enemies were increasing moment by moment.

Kambrea kept herself sheltered near a barricade of weapons crates stacked high behind her. The Devaronian female had all the firepower and ammunition she would need to hold off assailants for many days.

She gestured with a clawed hand, trying to attract the attention of her fighters, pointing toward Sirra and Lusa, who huddled in scant shelter near the small craft. "Get those two! They're traitors to the Diversity Alliance. *They* brought all this upon us!"

As the weapons fire turned toward his two young charges, Luke knew he had to help protect them. Sirra shot her own blaster, but she couldn't possibly hold off the entire barrage. Ambassador Cilghal ran beside Luke toward where Lusa and Sirra were making their last stand. With crossed lightsabers Luke and Cilghal intercepted the blaster fire, deflecting energy bolts into the stone walls and occasionally into enemy attackers as well.

Lusa, boiling with frustration and wanting to strike a blow against the radical group that had caused her so much misery, saw Kambrea hiding behind the wall of weapons crates.

From where he stood, Luke Skywalker could sense the centaur girl tapping into the Force. He knew Lusa had great potential to become a Jedi, but she was untrained, did not know what to do—and so she could not control the surge she directed at Kambrea. Her rippling tug made the wall of heavy crates shake, tilt . . . and finally topple down.

The Devaronian had only time to look up and see the avalanche of weapons containers falling toward her. Kambrea roared and tried to squirm away, but she was far too late.

Tons of heavy crates fell on top of her, burying the provisional leader of the Diversity Alliance.

Seeing Kambrea killed, the Diversity Alliance soldiers, who were still duped as to the actual cause of the fight, let out a howl of outrage, roaring vows of revenge. Their blaster fire increased. More soldiers rushed in. It looked as if nothing could stop the complete obliteration of the New Republic inspection team.

The bloodlust and anger bottled in the grotto grew even higher, as everyone fought for their lives, for revenge, or for political ideals. On the other side of the chamber, left unattended except for two small Sullustan guards wearing the uniforms of the New Republic, Senator Trubor crawled along, trying to stay under cover. He squeaked, "We surrender! We surrender! It's the only way!"

The small Chadra Fan stood up, waving his hands—and two of the Gamorrean guards, seeing only someone they knew as their enemy, targeted him. Both shot the senator. Little Trubor died with a high-pitched squeal as he tumbled backward into the hands of the helpless Sullustan guards, who dragged his body away. The New Republic soldiers cried out in anger.

Unexpectedly, the Twi'lek refugee Kur stood up,

shook away the restraining hands of his two New Republic escorts, and strode into the thick of the firefight. He seemed willing to die, or convinced of his own invincibility.

Standing out in the open, in the middle of the chamber, he held up his clawed hands. "You must cease firing. All of you!" His voice was stronger and prouder than anything Luke had expected.

Several more blaster shots rang out; a Gamorrean guard fired at him and missed—but more rapidly than Luke would have thought possible, the blaster-fire tapered off and then fell silent. Kur looked at the barricaded fighters in the bay, squaring his shoulders. His head-tails thrashed with agitation, and he tried to meet them all with his piercing gaze.

"Aliens have shed alien blood!" he shouted in a tone of voice that expressed horror to all present. He gestured down at the dead Chadra Fan senator. "But for what? Did you gain peace? Freedom from tyranny? No! The search for revenge has only brought you death and given you cause to distrust each other. Isn't this exactly what the Diversity Alliance promised to *prevent*?"

Kur paused and stared at all the fighters, who were huddled down for shelter. But they were listening now, and not shooting.

"Look around you. This time there is no scape-goat—no excuse to blame the killing on one species or another. All races must stop trying to place the blame for the injustices of centuries gone by—and begin working together." He held up a fist. "*As equals*. We must build from the present, not resort to savagery because of the past."

As he looked at all of them, he swelled with pride. Luke felt the strength in the air, felt that Kur had regained his self-confidence.

In a brave gesture, Cilghal switched off her lightsaber and stepped away from her shelter to stand next to Kur. Luke went out to join her, willing the others to come out as well.

Several of the Diversity Alliance soldiers, idealistic aliens who fought for what they believed was right and knew nothing of Nolaa Tarkona's other plans, also tossed down their weapons and came forward.

"We must talk together," Kur said. "Only that way can we find peace."

Luke looked at the exiled refugee. Though Nolaa Tarkona wasn't there, and Kambrea had already been killed, he sensed that the Twi'leks had found a powerful new leader.

22

IN ORBIT AROUND the insignificant-looking asteroid, the Diversity Alliance armada and the New Republic fleet battled for the right to continued existence. Violent explosions from blasted warships punctuated the blackness all around, made all the more eerie because of the silence of vacuum.

Raaba might have been watching a hologram of an event that had occurred long ago. No smells of flaming gases or singed flesh reached her nostrils. No expanding ball of heat threw her backward or scorched her chocolate-brown fur. No thunderous detonations burst painfully upon her eardrums.

Yet to Raaba, who had never witnessed such death and destruction of those she knew, space itself seemed to shudder at the savagery—and that shudder she felt all the way to her bones.

The Ugnaught gunner on her bridge crew clipped a New Republic X-wing with a lucky shot. Raaba's crew cheered as the little ship blossomed into an expanding cloud of hot gas and debris on the front viewscreen. The cheers died to grim murmurs when a few seconds later one of their own midsize transports disintegrated in slow motion before their eyes.

Raaba paced the deck behind her tactical officer. She continued to issue orders, forcing a calm and steady tone into her voice that she did not completely feel. She couldn't allow herself to panic. If she lost control, even more lives could be lost.

Raaba ordered her comm officer to contact Nolaa Tarkona on the asteroid and inform her that the entire armada was now under attack. Raaba had hoped not to bother her leader again, especially not with bad news, but the senseless losses being suffered by the Diversity Alliance left her little choice. Most of the pilots in the Alliance armada already wanted to retreat. Raaba could smell the terror that a dose of true combat had injected into the veins of her crew.

"I'm sorry, Captain, there's no response from the Esteemed Tarkona," the comm officer told Raaba. "We picked up a couple of explosions on the surface just before that Hapan ship took off. We have not been able to reach her since then."

Another New Republic fighter exploded and vanished into insignificance in the vastness of space while Raaba looked on. A growl of rage and protest built in her throat.

What did this fighting gain them? One moment a human enemy died, the next it was one of her compatriots. Talz, Bith, Ithorian, Sullustan, Ugnaught, Rodian, Kushiban, human—what did it matter? *People* were dying!

Raaba could not let this go on much longer. Facing the tactical officer in charge of the armada, she gave him simple, strict orders: he was to draw the New Republic fleet away from the asteroid but engage them as little as possible, keep losses to a minimum.

Raaba herself would go down to the weapons depot to fetch Nolaa Tarkona. If their leader was alive, Raaba would bring her back within the hour, triumphant. If Raaba had not returned by then, the tactical officer must retreat to Ryloth and await further orders.

The tactical officer, a short, fearless Sullustan named Ma'thu, started to object, but Raaba growled that her orders could be countermanded by no one but Nolaa Tarkona herself.

With that, the chocolate-furred Wookiee sprinted off the bridge toward the docking bay, where her skimmer *Rising Star* awaited. If luck was with her, she could make it to the asteroid in less than five standard minutes.

After today's events, however, she could no longer be certain that luck was with her.

23

BORNAN THUL STOOD outside the central storage chamber, cold with anger and sick with despair. Nolaa Tarkona had found the human-killing plague at last, and now she had in her grasp the means to destroy everyone. And it was his own fault for not taking care of it sooner.

Bornan knew what he had to do.

Hunkered next to Zekk and Raynar, he took a deep breath. He reached out to squeeze his son's shoulder. "Lowbacca isn't in there—or if he is, Nolaa Tarkona's already dispatched him. I have to go in and finish setting the explosives myself."

Raynar looked at him with wide eyes. His moon-round face flushed with astonishment. "But you can't! It's dangerous in there. All that plague—"

"I know, and we can't risk letting it get out. I have to stop Nolaa Tarkona."

"We'll go with you," Zekk said. "The three of us can fight her together."

Bornan Thul stared at the hardened, dark-haired young man. "That would risk all of us, and it's not worth the cost." He stopped to look at Raynar. "I've already put the galaxy in danger. I can't do even worse by getting you killed."

He gave his son a quick hug, and Raynar clutched him tightly. "But I just found you again, Father. Don't go in and get yourself killed."

"I don't intend to," he said. "I sincerely hope I come out alive, but I have to seal the door behind me. I can't let any of that plague get loose."

Sweat beading on his forehead, Bornan Thul gripped the blaster pistol with which he had killed the Gamorrean guard. He slid along the wall, keeping low so that he couldn't be seen through the observation windows. Then he ducked over to the heavy door, flashing one last glance at the mournful face of his son before he slipped inside the deadly chamber.

He clutched the blaster, hoping against hope that he wouldn't have to fire it. Any stray bolt could easily shatter one of the plague canisters. Thul reached up and worked the controls until the heavy airtight door hummed and moved sideways. With a hiss it slid shut, then compressed against its contamination-free doorjamb. He knew he couldn't remain hidden after all that noise, so he dashed into the forest of plague cylinders, taking shelter between the canisters.

Nolaa Tarkona cried out. "So the vermin are here

at last—hoping to save themselves from the fate they deserve. Rullak, see that they don't escape!"

Bornan Thul slipped between the nearest bubbling cylinders, seeking shelter. He heard the pounding feet of guards, and he shrank into the shadows. As he peered around the curve of the transparisteel cylinder, he saw Raynar's look of horror through the window above. The boy stared in at his father and the armed guards lunging toward him.

Thul crouched low and scuttled between a pair of bubbling cylinders, skirted a scarlet-filled sphere, and ran down the next aisle of liquid-filled tubes. Guards charged after him. He caught only a glimpse of burly alien forms as he wove in and out. He stopped, breathless and panting, beside a coolant station whose coils hummed with high-power efficiency. Other noisy generators pumped aeration and support systems, keeping the biological contamination viable after all these years.

A blaster shot ricocheted off the floor near Thul's foot, and he realized that he was partially visible. So he got up and ran again, ducking past the edge of a huge recirculation fan that blasted sterile air in all directions, stirring the enclosed atmosphere. Its noise would cover any movement he made.

The guards were shouting now, and he heard Nolaa Tarkona also screeching orders. *She* was his target, Thul knew . . . if he could get one clean shot. He held the blaster, always ready, in his hand. Just one clean shot, and he could remove the leader of the Diversity Alliance. No one else had Nolaa's charisma, her power. No one else could hold the disparate alien bands together, with or without the terrible plague.

Taking a deep breath to marshal his courage, Bornan Thul dashed toward her voice. That was the most important thing—to stop Nolaa Tarkona.

As soon as he emerged from between two large cylinders filled with burbling solution, he suddenly came upon the tentacle-faced form of Rullak, the Quarren. The amphibious creature's mouth feelers quivered, and he thrust his blaster forward. "Shall I kill you now, or let Nolaa Tarkona do the job?"

Thul didn't pause, though. He charged forward, smashing into the Quarren, who was too startled at this reaction to fire. Rullak struggled and knocked the blaster pistol out of Thul's hand. Thul let the weapon drop, shouldered the Quarren aside, and fled as Rullak gave a phlegmy howl of anger.

Thul ducked between two more cylinders. Finally, on the far side, he could see Nolaa Tarkona, fuming as she listened to the scuffle. Grim, he paused to decide how best to attack her.

Then Rullak began firing at him.

The angered amphibian shot indiscriminately. Blasts ricocheted off the ceiling, striking the plague cylinders and spheres all around them. The transparisteel containers cracked. Some of the smaller cylinders shattered entirely.

Deadly microbial solutions sprayed into the air.

Bornan Thul ducked, but the canister to his left split open with the flash of a blaster bolt. Plague solution sprayed toward him. He rolled and missed most of it, but still the droplets spattered over his body.

Rullak seemed to be laughing as he shot, but Nolaa Tarkona's bellow was horrible to hear. "Stop firing, you idiot!" As the blaster fire continued, she raised her voice so loud it must have scraped her vocal cords raw. "Stop! There are other kinds of plague here! Plagues that could kill all of us!"

Finally the blasts ceased, and Thul pushed himself forward, panting. His breath rasped hot in his lungs. He saw Nolaa Tarkona ahead of him, and he could think only of staggering toward her. He didn't care about the other guards anymore, didn't care about Rullak or the Gamorreans or anyone else trapped in the chamber with him. He only wanted Nolaa.

But as he approached her, he realized that he no longer had his blaster.

Nolaa's rose-quartz eyes blazed; her head-tail thrashed. When her lips opened in a terrible, deadly smile of pointed teeth, Thul knew he was defeated. He took deep, hitching breaths, and felt dizzy. His lungs seemed to be choked with something that kept him from drawing in enough air. His head throbbed. With each step he knew with utter certainty that he had been exposed to the plague.

He turned, grasping one of the intact transparisteel cylinders for support, an irony not lost on him.

He gripped the bars on its outer casing and turned to look back at the observation window where he had just left his son and Zekk.

To his dismay, Bornan Thul saw Raynar's face looking back at him, stricken with absolute despair.

IG-88 marched toward the central chamber with pounding metal footsteps that hammered the floor-plates like a mallet striking a bell. Lowie followed him closely, guiding the assassin droid whenever it hesitated at an intersection.

IG-88 ripped aside one more sealed blockade before they reached the central chamber, arriving just in time to hear the sound of blaster fire, a vigorous battle. The huge droid picked up speed, and Lowie groaned uneasily as he raced after the metallic hulk.

"Dear me, I do hope it's nothing serious," Em Teedee said.

When they reached the observation windows, Lowie took in the situation at a glance. He saw Zekk, crouching and itching to fight. Raynar pressed his face against the observation window, not caring if he was seen. His face was filled with utter anguish.

Lowie roared as he looked into the chamber, whose door was now sealed again. Nolaa Tarkona stood surrounded by several broken cylinders. Multi-colored plague liquids streamed from the containers, spilling everywhere, splashing, evaporating to suspend billions of disease organisms in the air.

Worst of all, he saw Bornan Thul stagger away from the cylinders, disoriented, already exposed to the deadly plague. Bornan stumbled forward, trying to reach Nolaa . . . but what the human merchant lord would do once he reached his nemesis, Lowie could not guess.

IG-88 had been commanded to assist Bornan Thul, to help him or save him—and seeing the man next to Nolaa Tarkona struggling with the onset of the disease, IG-88 charged implacably toward the wall. The droid knew his programming exactly. He raised his durasteel fists.

Lowie realized what the assassin droid could do. IG-88 would batter his way in, tear down the walls, breach the isolation chamber, and expose them all to the plague-filled air.

Lowie threw himself at the assassin droid, but IG-88 simply batted him away with such a blow that the young Wookiee crashed into the wall. Raynar was too focused on his father's plight to notice.

Zekk shouted, "No! You'll flood all the corridors with the plague!"

But IG-88 paid no heed. He hammered on the wall, and bright polished dents began to appear. He would crack open the chamber in less than a minute.

24

RAYNAR PRESSED HIS face against the transparent barrier that separated him from his dying father. He pounded his fists against it in rage.

As if imitating him, IG-88 continued pounding his powerful fists against the airtight door.

The plague organism was free inside the vault—the plague that his father had hoped to destroy before it could ever be turned loose against human beings. Raynar wished he'd gone inside with his father. He might have been able to do something, use the Force to stop Rullak or Nolaa Tarkona. Or if not, at least he would be inside with his father to comfort him now in his last moments.

Raynar pressed his hands against the transparisteel, harder, *harder*, as if he might reach through it to his father if only he exerted enough force.

At the edge of his awareness Raynar heard Zekk

yell, "No, IG-88! If you open that door you'll kill us." Lowie roared, but the assassin droid knocked the Wookiee aside again.

Inside, Bornan Thul stumbled toward the upper observation window that separated him from Raynar. His skin had a grayish cast now, and Raynar could see how labored his breathing had become. Blotches of green and blue appeared on his skin. He crawled toward the controls of the two-way intercom system in the wall.

Unable to tear his eyes away from his father's agony, Raynar felt an imaginary band of durasteel clamping around his own heart, tighter, *tighter*, until it seemed impossible that it could go on beating.

"Go," his father rasped into the speakers. "It is too late for me."

IG-88 continued to batter at the door to the room. Lowie roared again, to no effect.

"I can't!" Raynar cried in anguish. "Not now. I just found you again."

"Never forget . . . how proud I am of you. My work . . . unfinished, though," Bornan Thul gasped. "I leave it to you . . . to destroy this place—stop Nolaa."

Raynar briefly shifted his attention to the Twi'lek leader of the Diversity Alliance. She stood toward the back of the vault, vainly attempting to stamp some order into the chaos inside the trashed chamber. Rullak writhed on the floor in his death throes, succumbing to one of the deadly plagues his own blaster fire had released.

Raynar knew his father was right. He could not simply give up now because of his grief. Millions of lives were at stake if Nolaa Tarkona put her plan into action. Raynar's mother and uncle would die, and Master Skywalker, Jacen and Jaina, and everyone else he cared about.

His mind railed against the injustice. *It wasn't fair.* His vision grew blurred and distorted, as if he was looking at his father through a current of water. Something hot and wet burned its way down Raynar's cheeks, and his throat constricted so tightly he could hardly breathe.

Suddenly Zekk was beside him yelling something to Bornan Thul. "The assassin droid IG-88 is programmed to protect you—to bring you back alive. You're the only one who can stop him from breaking down that door and releasing the plague right now! Tell him to stay away!"

Suddenly Raynar's vision cleared and he focused on his father, who drew a shuddering breath.

"Stop," Bornan Thul croaked. Though his voice came out as no more than a hoarse whisper, the powerful droid paused to listen. "IG-88, I order you to save the only part of me that can still be saved: my son. I am beyond help." With that, he fell against the wall beneath the transparisteel pane to which Raynar's face was still pressed.

"I love you, Father," was all Raynar had time to

say before IG-88 clanked over to where he stood. His father nodded weakly as the assassin droid grabbed the young man and dragged him away from the chamber of death. A white mist formed across Raynar's vision, and he could see nothing more. All he knew was that IG-88 was leading him by one arm and that Zekk was holding his other. Lowie loped ahead, his lightsaber drawn to guard against any other enemies.

Zekk droned a steady litany of instructions to IG-88, explaining where their ship was and which direction they needed to go. Occasionally Zekk let go of him, and Raynar could hear some sort of safety interlock whoosh shut behind them. For all Raynar could tell, they might have hurried along like that for hours, but it must have been only minutes.

When the droid released his arm, Raynar nearly collapsed. Zekk turned to IG-88. "It's not far to our ship now."

Em Teedee chirped, "Many thanks, IG-88. You are a credit to all droids."

As Raynar swayed to his feet again, the big assassin droid spun about and then marched back the way he had come, unable to escape his primary programming.

Zekk called to Raynar. "We have to get out of here before any more of those explosives blow and bring this place down around us."

Feeling leaden, Raynar followed Zekk and Lowie,

not knowing what else he could do. He looked back the way they had come.

The assassin droid vanished into the shadowy corridors, heading back toward the plague chamber to see if he could do any last thing for Bornan Thul.

25

AS SOON AS she set foot on the Imperial weapons asteroid, Raaba had her blaster out and ready, unsure of what she might encounter. She raced down the corridors. Her instincts were good, and she had found a space to dock on the edge of the primary biological weapons complex.

She understood security systems well and had an uncanny knack for finding her way to the heart of any important facility. It was one of the skills that had made her so valuable to Nolaa Tarkona. This time it might just save her leader's life—or at least, Raaba hoped so as she searched through one tunnel after another.

Hold on, Raaba thought. *I'm coming*. Too many lives had been lost already this day.

Coming upon a sealed doorway with a safety interlock and a flashing hazard symbol, Raaba used her blaster to fry the controls. Then she wrenched the door open using the manual override and her own Wookiee strength.

Good, Raaba thought. Directly before her, she saw Nolaa Tarkona emerging from a vault-locked chamber whose bent and battered door stood wide open. Nolaa's rose-quartz eyes held a strange look, somewhere between overwhelming grief and wild triumph.

"Raabakyysh! I *knew* I could count on you."

Raaba loosed a happy roar to see her leader alive, but her cry of joy turned to a questioning growl when she looked past Nolaa Tarkona to see the body of Rullak sprawled on the floor in the chamber, blotched with disease.

"Rullak is dead through his own fault—and the *human's*," Nolaa said, spitting out the word with obvious contempt. She swayed on her feet, looking very unwell. "Bornan Thul is dead, too. Their foolishness nearly put an end to my plan. Most of my guards were killed, and all my generals are lost to me now. But we have no time to mourn them. You must get me back to the fleet."

Raaba paused in confusion. How had Rullak died? And Bornan Thul?

But then a pair of blaster bolts zinged past her and ricocheted off the vault door, nearly striking Nolaa Tarkona. The emergency distracted Raaba from worrying about any additional questions. Raaba did not think—she acted. She spun and fired on her assailant.

It was the assassin droid IG-88.

Nolaa Tarkona had her own blaster out now and fired, but Raaba could not let the great leader put herself in danger. Stepping forward, Raaba let loose a volley with her blaster and backed down the hallway, pushing the Twi'lek woman behind her and shielding her with her own body.

IG-88 fired again. In desperation, Raaba shot back, but she knew she couldn't hold off an assassin droid forever. They had been very lucky to escape injury for this long. With stubborn determination, Raaba pushed her leader back toward the questionable cover of a corner at intersecting corridors. A blaster bolt grazed Raaba's knee, singeing fur, and she dove after Nolaa Tarkona.

Then a strange thing happened. As soon as Raaba and Nolaa Tarkona disappeared into the adjoining tunnel, the blaster fire ceased abruptly. Stunned and suspicious, Raaba peeked back around the corner, only to find that the droid had apparently lost all interest in them. Instead, IG-88 clanked slowly, almost mournfully, through the vault door and into the steaming, sparking plague chamber.

Although Raaba did not understand why the droid had given up his attack, she wasted no time questioning their good fortune. Instead she grasped Nolaa Tarkona's arm and propelled the Twi'lek leader down the long corridors toward the place where the *Rising Star* waited.

As they ran, Raaba explained that the New

Republic fleet had arrived to drive back the Diversity Alliance armada. Without slowing, Nolaa Tarkona attempted to switch on her mobile comm unit. When there was no answer, Raaba snatched the comlink from her belt and handed it to her. They were almost to the *Rising Star* now.

A burst of static and then a squawk of surprise and delight came over the comlink. "You're alive! Esteemed Tarkona, is it truly you?"

"Yes," she said. "Raaba and I will be with you shortly, but we need your help to escape from this accursed asteroid."

"Anything, Esteemed Tarkona," the voice on the comlink replied.

"Drive the human fleet away from here," Nolaa said. Apparently out of breath, she coughed a few times and gasped. "We'll join you soon. And then I will personally lead you to victory."

26

HAN SOLO WAS taken by surprise when the Diversity Alliance armada did an abrupt about-face from its cautious retreat and surged toward the New Republic fleet. Like a pack of nek battle dogs, the battered survivors of the little armada pressed their attack, pushing back the ships under Han's command.

Chewie roared beside him, and Han gripped his controls. "I see it, I see it!" He swerved to avoid an oncoming strike cruiser, adding more power to his front shields, then did his famous corkscrew maneuver to elude the turbolasers. One of the New Republic snub fighters behind him wasn't so lucky, and spiraled out of control with a damaged S-foil.

"Boy, those guys just got inspired!" Han said. "I wonder what they're trying to defend."

Chewie roared. Han agreed. "Right. Or *who*."

He toggled the *Falcon*'s comm system to the coded military frequency. "All right, blue and green groups—attack formation delta. Remember your training."

Han knew that sooner or later he would turn the plague-storage asteroid into cinders, but first he had to make sure his kids were safe. At the moment, though, all resources were engaged in fending off the Diversity Alliance.

As the New Republic fleet harried the scattered Diversity Alliance warships, Jaina watched from the cockpit of the *Rock Dragon*, still desperately trying to return to the Imperial weapons depot to help her stranded friends.

She flew near the *Millennium Falcon*, protected in part by her father's shields and his talent with the laser turrets—but she knew that she and Jacen could shoot as well as Chewbacca, and she wanted to do her part in the fight on her way back down to the asteroid.

Diversity Alliance ships orbited the weapons depot, reluctant to retreat into hyperspace: somewhere down there on that rock, their leader Nolaa Tarkona still had business to complete. Jaina spotted the blown-out atmosphere containment dome she had wrecked during her escape earlier.

Right now, she wished she knew what was happening to Zekk, or Lowie, or the others they had left behind. She needed to be sure her friends were away from the depot before the New Republic fleet blasted the asteroid to incandescent dust.

The space battle was sheer chaos. The Diversity Alliance ships fought vigorously, taking outrageous chances, careening toward New Republic cruisers and then flitting back. Nolaa's space navy had performed no drills, made no concerted effort—they just shot at their enemies in a free-for-all that caused little damage but much confusion. The Diversity Alliance fleet hit their own vessels as often as they struck the New Republic ships.

Jaina soared around in the *Rock Dragon*, seeking an opening where she could cripple one of the ships. New Republic vessels already outnumbered the enemy fleet, but Nolaa's soldiers fought anyway, recklessly.

Then hyperspace shimmered, the folds of the universe blinked—and even more ships appeared. Another battle fleet.

"Blaster bolts!" Jacen exclaimed at her shoulder. "Who's coming now?"

Jaina had a sudden dread that Nolaa Tarkona had access to additional warships hidden in reserve, another portion of her fleet armed with stolen weapons.

Tenel Ka recognized the ships first. "That is the Bornaryn fleet."

The massive form of the flagship *Tradewyn* took

the head of a phalanx as the merchant convoy, surrounded by numerous security vessels and fast fighters, plunged into the fray.

The comm system crackled with Aryn Dro Thul's iron-hard voice. "This is the Bornaryn fleet offering our assistance to the New Republic. I understand my husband and my son are down there."

Jaina recognized another voice as Tyko Thul's. "If you Diversity Alliance troops know what's good for you, you'll give up right now."

The New Republic ships drew together, and the Bornaryn vessels closed in like the other half of a jagged jaw, squeezing the rampant alien ships. Turbolaser fire crisscrossed space, and Jaina added her own shots, but she didn't cause any serious damage.

One of the Diversity Alliance ships, a small but heavily armored strike cruiser, erupted in space, leaving yellow afterimages on Jaina's eyes. The rest of the enemy fleet began to move away from the depot, driven out of the system. As part of the New Republic fleet peeled off in pursuit, Jaina swerved the *Rock Dragon* back toward the asteroid.

"That's a good start at least," Jaina said, watching the warships with satisfaction. Now they could at last go back to retrieve their friends.

Dodging turbolaser fire from the battle in space overhead, Jaina found a free airlock on the asteroid and docked the *Rock Dragon* again. Before Jaina had even finished powering down the cruiser's engines, Tenel Ka had opened the airlock and begun scouting out a route to the plague chambers.

Grabbing a mobile comlink, Jacen flicked it on. "Em Teedee, can you hear me? We need to know where you are so we can help you."

A Wookiee roar blasted from the tiny speaker. "Yes, Master Jacen, you are quite audible—but, Master Lowbacca urges you to reconsider. Several plagues have already been unleashed. It's far too dangerous here! Do not attempt to open any safety interlocks. He says to set whatever explosives you have left and save yourselves. We will make every effort to find our own way out." The little droid gave an electronic equivalent of a gulp. "Of course, we could be doomed."

Deep in the asteroid tunnels, Zekk kept running with Lowie and Raynar. "The *Lightning Rod*'s up here somewhere," he said. "Once we're away, we can get the New Republic fleet to open fire and blow this asteroid into powder."

Raynar sniffed, overwhelmed by grief at the death of his father. "There's nothing here worth preserving," he said. "Let's destroy it all so it can't harm anyone else."

Zekk's green eyes looked at the young man with hard understanding. They rushed down the corridor through half-opened pressure doors and barricades that had been torn from their hinges by the assassin droid. They raced along tunnels past domed landing bays and access areas.

Zekk knew the *Lightning Rod* was just down one of those corridors. He could almost smell the old cargo freighter's lubricant fumes and exhaust. He wanted nothing more than to be off this weapons depot.

Running ahead, though, Lowie skidded to a halt and let out a roar, grabbing for his lightsaber. Zekk felt the cold tingle of Jedi senses an instant before another cluster of Diversity Alliance soldiers emerged from the branching tunnels. They had been lying in wait, ready to ambush the companions as they returned to their ship.

These alien fighters were not interested in taking prisoners. The soldiers stepped out, drew their weapons, and with a mingled roar from various species, they opened fire.

Zekk and Raynar threw themselves against the walls. Lowie held his ground, powering up his lightsaber and slashing to deflect blaster bolts. But he, too, had to press for shelter against the curve of the wall.

The nine Diversity Alliance soldiers continued shooting. Blaster bolts ricocheted like a sideways-slanting rain of sparkling flames. Zekk yanked out the blaster pistol he had taken from the munitions chamber and fired. His first shot struck a clumsy

Gamorrean just above the knee. The creature squealed and fell on his side, out of commission.

The others scrambled out of the way, but were more interested in shooting than in taking cover. After all, they were faced with only three young companions, and just one of them had a long-range weapon.

Zekk shot again and again, but his opponents managed to keep to shelter. Lowie strode recklessly forward with his lightsaber, and Zekk followed behind him. This was their last chance, and if they couldn't make it back to the *Lightning Rod*, he was going to go down fighting.

After all this time of trying to find himself, searching for a way to remove the shadow of guilt from his past, Zekk understood that he *had* to get his friends out of this situation, even if it meant sacrificing himself so they could get to the ship. Lowie was a good enough pilot. He could take Raynar out of here, back to safety.

Zekk had been with the Shadow Academy, and he had fought against Luke Skywalker's Jedi Knights on Yavin 4. He had gone to his birth world of Ennth in hope of rejoining his people, but he'd found no home there either. Then he had become a bounty hunter, searching for lucrative targets, but not understanding *why* he needed to seek them. He had not bothered to ponder the consequences if Bornan Thul were caught.

No matter what his skills, no matter how good he

was at his job as a bounty hunter, Zekk could never be *just* a mercenary. He had to think through his actions, and he had to choose what was right. Luckily, Zekk had learned his lesson in time, so that he could fight on the right side—and now he had to carry that fight to its finish.

He stood next to Lowie, prepared to fire. Diversity Alliance soldiers pushed forward until the volley of blaster bolts grew so thick that Lowie could not deflect them all. A long bolt singed the ginger fur on his arm.

Then, just when they were at their most vulnerable point in the middle of the corridor, Boba Fett emerged from a side passage.

The grim man in battered Mandalorian armor stepped out boldly. He held a blaster pistol in each gauntleted hand. The Diversity Alliance soldiers cheered, welcoming Nolaa Tarkona's crack bounty hunter. They stopped firing, happy to let Boba Fett finish their job for them.

Fett trained both blaster pistols at Zekk, and Zekk was more afraid of those guns than of all the other weapons held by the alien guards. He recalled how the masked man had reluctantly assisted him, and also how he had tricked Fett into helping Bornan Thul get away. He swallowed hard, prepared to die.

Suddenly the bounty hunter whirled about with such speed that Zekk could barely follow his actions. Boba Fett fired both of the pistols continuously, strafing from one Diversity Alliance guard to another. He ruthlessly mowed them down as they stood paralyzed with shock.

Without wasting time on questions, Zekk reacted as well, opening fire and taking out the aliens Boba Fett hadn't already shot down.

In the suddenly silent, smoke-filled corridor, Boba Fett stood motionless, victorious. Rock dust and sifting debris drifted down from the ceiling. The smell of melted metal burned Zekk's nostrils. He couldn't move.

Lowie held up his lightsaber, not knowing how to react. Raynar had stepped up behind Zekk and Lowie, directly into the line of fire—but no Diversity Alliance fighter remained alive.

Zekk's astonishment gave way to scorn. He looked at the black slit in the helmet of the bounty hunter. "So you're a turncoat? Just like that, you're on our side?"

Lowie also grumbled his disbelief. Raynar exclaimed, "I thought you were working for Nolaa Tarkona. She had you out looking for my father."

Fett turned to him. "Nolaa Tarkona wanted the location of this depot. I gave it to her. My work for her is finished, paid in full."

Zekk stared in astonishment, remembering how Boba Fett had told him that all obligations to an employer ended once the bounty had been delivered. "So what made you choose our side? A twinge of moral responsibility?" He raised his eyebrows.

Fett's impenetrable helmet gave the slightest shake. "A bounty hunter does not take sides."

"Then why are you here?" Raynar asked. A flush colored his cheeks.

"Tyko Thul hired me. He offered a large reward if I could bring you and your father safely away from this asteroid."

Raynar hung his head. Zekk could barely speak himself. "Too late, Boba Fett. Bornan Thul is dead from the plague."

Fett seemed unaffected. "Then I will complete the rest of my assignment, and see that Raynar gets out safely. I will cover your retreat. I trust you can make it to your ship without assistance?"

Zekk regarded the masked man with distrust. "It doesn't trouble you that your very next bounty is to assist the enemy of your former employer?"

Boba Fett straightened, as if the answer to the question should be obvious. "I don't judge right or wrong. I just do my job."

Zekk squared his shoulders and suddenly knew he was stronger than Boba Fett. His mind was clearer. His heart was cleaner. "Then I guess I don't want to be a bounty hunter after all," he said, and tossed his long black hair over his shoulders. "I don't let a paycheck decide between right and wrong for me."

Leaving Boba Fett behind, he walked with Lowie and Raynar down the last remaining tunnel to the *Lightning Rod* and their escape from the asteroid.

27

RAABA'S STOMACH LURCHED as she threw the *Rising Star*'s engines into full reverse and pulled away from where she had been docked against the asteroid.

Yes, it looked as if they might escape after all. But something was terribly wrong with her leader.

Nolaa Tarkona coughed again, and her pale face streamed with oily perspiration. Her single head-tail writhed and contorted in convulsions of pain. Watching the Twi'lek woman, Raaba hovered just above the rocky surface.

Nolaa's breathing was labored, but her eyes burned with unquenchable fervor. "Hurry," she said, "we must get back to the armada. Our time of triumph is at hand. Don't hesitate now."

But Raaba could not deny the evidence before her eyes: Nolaa had been exposed to the Emperor's plagues. One of the diseases had killed the human

Bornan Thul, and another had killed Rullak—and now it was apparent that one was also working its poison on Nolaa Tarkona herself.

Raaba shook her head to clear it and growled a question: how many plagues had been let loose in the Emperor's biological weapons chamber?

The Twi'lek woman looked surprised. "Three, four, perhaps a dozen. What does it matter? Many of the canisters were destroyed." Nolaa reached inside her cloak and pulled out a fistful of vials labeled HUMAN, FAST-ACTING. "Don't you see?" she said. "We have what we came for. The means to destroy our enemies for all time!"

Raaba felt her chocolate-colored fur stand on end. She sucked in a deep breath, but coughed instead. Only then did Raaba understand what she had done.

Yes, she had rescued her leader from the plague chamber—but at what cost? The Twi'lek leader was sick, perhaps dying from one of the plagues she had encountered. Certainly, she'd been exposed to both the human and the Quarren specific organisms. Even if Nolaa's intention was to kill every human in the galaxy, how could she not recognize that she also endangered every Quarren and every Twi'lek, at the very least . . . and who knew how many other species would die if they returned infected to the Diversity Alliance armada?

Raaba shivered involuntarily. She gasped for breath again, but the air seemed heavy and hard to breathe. By going into the plague chamber to rescue her leader, Raaba herself might have been exposed to a virulent plague that could also be fatal to Wookiees. Perhaps she was doomed as well.

With her clawed hands shaking, Nolaa Tarkona attempted to work the copilot's controls and take the *Rising Star* on a heading toward the armada. Raaba knew that the time for a decision was now.

Jaina, Jacen, and Tenel Ka finished setting their last explosives in record time and threw themselves into the cockpit of the *Rock Dragon*.

Em Teedee had just transmitted a message from Lowie, Zekk, and Raynar in the *Lightning Rod* to inform the other young Jedi Knights that they were on their way, escaping from the asteroid. He also passed along the news about the death of Bornan Thul.

But they had no time to grieve now. Not in the middle of a battle, with the fate of the plague storehouse at stake.

Like a team long accustomed to working together, they flicked switches, sealed airlocks, and programmed courses with deft hands guided by the Force. "Fifteen seconds," Tenel Ka stated in a firm voice, referring to the amount of time left on the five detonators they had found and been able to set without going any farther into the weapons complex.

"Fifteen seconds? No sweat," Jacen muttered.

"Almost got it." Jaina slapped the repulsorlifts to full. "Ten, nine . . ."

Tenel Ka hit the switch to release the *Rock Dragon*'s airtight seal on the depot docking hatch.

"Eight, seven, six . . ."

"Hang on. This ride's going to be anything but smooth," Jaina shouted.

"Five, four, three . . ."

The *Rock Dragon*'s engines whined as the Hapan cruiser began to pull away. "Let's just get away from this place," Jacen said.

"Two . . . one."

The *Rock Dragon* lifted fractionally from the pad on which it had rested, then rose higher.

"Zero."

Although the *Rock Dragon* was no longer touching the ground, the asteroid rocked around them. One of the secondary domes exploded in a hail of transparisteel fragments that momentarily clouded the front viewscreen with a crystalline spray. Something struck the *Rock Dragon* hard.

"Get those shields up," Jaina barked at her brother, and he scrambled for the controls. None of the companions had had a chance to fasten their crash webbing, and the blow sent them reeling out of their seats.

Struggling with the panels, Jaina yelled, "Help me! We need to get farther away." Tenel Ka reached out with her mind for Jaina's, felt Jacen's mind join the two of theirs. Together the three minds visualized the asteroid beneath them and placed their combined pressure firmly against it like a springboard and *pushed*. Suddenly the ship spun clear of the asteroid in open space, halfway to the New Republic fleet.

Jacen said, "Uh-oh," as a familiar ship swung into their field of vision in their front viewports: the *Rising Star*. Raaba's ship.

With the Bornaryn fleet holding the Diversity Alliance ships at bay, Han Solo's choice was clear. "Chewie, let's make sure no one else ever gets hold of the deadly stuff down there."

A voice crackled over the comm speakers. "New Republic fleet, this is Zekk in the *Lightning Rod*. Once the *Rock Dragon* is clear, feel free to use the asteroid for target practice."

Han strode to the comm panel. "We copy, Zekk. You're cleared to come aboard one of the escort frigates. Red and silver leaders, bring your squadrons after the *Falcon*. You're with me. We're going in."

Raaba pulled the *Rising Star* into a backward arc to avoid hitting the *Rock Dragon*. "Just shoot them," Nolaa ordered, "then take me to the fleet!" She subsided into a fit of coughing.

Raaba barked a rebuke at her leader. Didn't she know how many people had died already this day? Neither of them could be certain how many plagues they'd each been exposed to in that chamber on the asteroid. If the two of them returned to the fleet now, they might risk killing every loyal member of the Diversity Alliance—and how could killing all the humans help them now?

"Such sentiments are for fools," Nolaa gasped, shuddering as much now with anger as with the chills that racked her body. "In every revolution some must sacrifice themselves to overthrow the tyrants and save the rest."

Just then a voice came over the comm speaker. It was Jacen. "Raaba, is that you? If you need our help, we can take you aboard."

Nolaa Tarkona muted the speakers. "Yes, it's perfect!" she said. "Accept their offer. That is how we can begin to spread the plague among the humans—with those Jedi as our first victims."

A rumble of outrage was building deep within Raaba like the boiling of a geyser. Even after all that Raaba had done, these humans—Lowie's *friends*—were worried about her. They were willing to help.

But Nolaa Tarkona had been right, in a way: in every revolution there must be sacrifices, and Raaba owed her allegiance to the Diversity Alliance. Her leader was dying, and she could not abandon her.

Nolaa toggled the comm speaker back on. Again Jacen's voice spoke. "Hey, Raaba, are you there? Are you all right? Do you need our help?"

Below, New Republic ships bombarded the asteroid with a stream of turbolaser fire and proton torpedoes. Pressurized domes exploded just as Raaba wished she could explode to release the pressure building in her.

"Yes, we are coming, we accept," Nolaa Tarkona hissed.

Shaking her head with a low growl in her throat, Raaba came to a decision. Her long Wookiee fingers flew over the controls of the star skimmer, setting a course and sending them sailing out and away from the asteroid. She increased their speed toward the Diversity Alliance armada. Faster, faster. She allowed herself to transmit only one message, not by voice but by a brief encoded burst that she flashed toward the *Rock Dragon* before starlines stretched out around them.

Together, Raaba and her leader Nolaa Tarkona plunged into hyperspace.

Behind them, unable to resist the concentrated barrage of firepower from the New Republic fleet, the Emperor's weapons depot erupted in a chain reaction of fire and dust, sparkling as it crumbled into nothingness.

Boba Fett sat in *Slave IV*, rising up out of the plane of the asteroid belt and watching the continuing battle below with some amusement. Tyko Thul had paid him for his efforts, and Fett was once again between bounties.

The passion and devotion some people gave to their causes, their sacrifices, never ceased to amaze him. It seemed a terrible waste of energy, and not profitable.

But then, it wasn't his business to understand.

Avoiding all contact with other ships, Fett cruised away, setting a new course. It wouldn't be long before he had another bounty assignment. . . .

28

OVER THE NEXT few hours the Bornaryn ships and the New Republic fleet rounded up the last remnants of the Diversity Alliance armada. But despite the excitement, the time passed as slowly as a century for Raynar.

It would have been a kindness, he thought, if the shock of his father's death had thrown him into a numbing fog that blurred the hours while he waited for the space battle to end, while he waited to go aboard the *Tradewyn* and speak with his mother, to explain to her what his father had done and why.

Instead, Raynar experienced every excruciating moment as if it were an eternity. How could he break the news to his mother that, after months of searching, after hopes that had been repeatedly renewed, Raynar had been unable to save his father?

In the docking bay of the cavernous Calamarian cruiser, Raynar refused even to get out of the

Lightning Rod. He could think of seeing no one but his mother, could think of nothing but her pain— and his own.

Zekk came and went, bringing Raynar reports of the final skirmishes with the Diversity Alliance armada. Raynar heard, yet did not hear, Zekk speaking. Even the news that Nolaa Tarkona had escaped meant nothing to him. His mind absorbed little of the information, as his spirit curled into a tight ball of grief.

Raynar was only vaguely aware that Lowie had not left the *Lightning Rod* either and sat somewhere close by, keeping watch but saying nothing. Later, Jacen, Jaina, and Tenel Ka also came in to see him, one by one.

To his great relief, the young Jedi Knights did not try to cheer him up, did not try to talk with him. Each of them simply entered and laid a hand on his back or shoulder, and then quietly withdrew again. But with each touch of a friend's hand, Raynar felt his pain ease. Peace flowed into him through the Force, and though his sorrow was not diminished, he found that he could face it now, accept it.

By the time Zekk returned with the news that the space skirmish was over and it was safe to take him over to the *Tradewyn*, Raynar was ready to see his mother.

Aryn Dro Thul and Uncle Tyko met the *Lightning Rod* in one of the *Tradewyn*'s docking bays just seconds after pressure and atmosphere were restored to the enormous chamber.

Aryn Dro Thul's midnight-blue gown clung to her as dignity clings to a queen. One look at her told Raynar that she already knew of her husband's death. She wore the multicolored sash of the House of Thul tied in mourning about her left arm, rather than in its usual place at her waist, and she carried an air of regal sorrow about her.

Tyko Thul's moon-round face was damp with tears, and he too wore his sash on his left arm.

Raynar walked slowly down the *Lightning Rod*'s ramp. Then, as if in a choreographed dance, he and his mother and his uncle drew together in a tight circle and embraced.

"You were right about your father," Tyko said in a voice taut with emotion. "He was a good man."

"I'm so proud of him for what he did," Aryn added. "And you." She produced a Thul sash from a fold in her gown and held it out to Raynar. He took the colorful strip of cloth and gravely tied it around the left arm of his Jedi robe, in tribute to his father.

Hearing a noise behind him, Raynar turned to find Zekk standing beside the *Lightning Rod*. "I guess I'll just be going now," the dark-haired boy said. "I think you're in good hands here, Raynar."

His mother nodded. "We'll take him back to the Jedi academy when he's ready. We have a Ceremony of the Waters to celebrate in honor of his father first. Thank you for your help, Zekk—for everything you've done."

"From all of us," Tyko Thul added.

"Will I see you back on Yavin 4?" Raynar asked. "When I get there?"

Zekk's emerald eyes opened wide, as if surprised at the question. "I don't know," he said simply. "I've got some thinking to do."

During the next week, Coruscant was abustle with activity, more so than Jaina could ever remember. Delegations were requested and brought in from every species on every planet that had been allied with the Diversity Alliance. Kur, newly appointed head of Ryloth's government, sent two representatives for his people: one Twi'lek man and one Twi'lek woman.

Jaina's mother spent all but a few hours each day in meetings with the new delegates, both individually and in groups. During her few precious free hours, Leia slept.

The young Jedi Knights spent nearly as many hours as Leia did welcoming delegates to the capital world and giving further reports to the New Republic Senate on what they had learned of the Diversity Alliance. Lusa and Sirra, now back from Ryloth, gave their accounts, as did Master Skywalker and the other members of the investigation team. All of them spent hours interviewing various former members of the Diversity Alliance and finding out their reasons for joining, what they had hoped to accomplish.

Em Teedee was constantly pressed into service to provide translations during these interviews, since, as he often pointed out, he was fluent in over sixteen forms of communication.

By the end of the week, a Cooperative Council of Independent Planetary Governments had been formed with representatives from every species on every world. Their charter included an agreement, signed by every member, to work together for the good of all species and the detriment of none.

Aryn Dro Thul placed the Bornaryn Trading Fleet at the disposal of the new council and its representatives, while Tyko Thul volunteered the resources of his droid manufacturing facilities on Mechis III. The Hapan government offered financial assistance to the Cooperative Council.

There was work for everyone, and when Leia asked Lowie's sister Sirra to become a liaison to strife-torn planets, and to look into and report on the violation of any species' rights, Lowie could not have been more proud if his own sister had been named Chief of State.

Eventually, after weeks of political upheaval, the young Jedi Knights returned to Yavin 4.

29

BACK ON THE jungle moon, Lowie sat comfortably ensconced at the top of a Massassi tree, staring patiently into the starry night sky and thinking about the final transmission burst Raaba had sent from the *Rising Star*.

There had been no voice message, no hologram—only a cryptic line of code in old-fashioned clicks and bursts of static that she knew he would understand. The words, conveyed in Basic, had been simple: "If I survive, I'll find you."

Lowie leaned back and watched a shooting star streak across the sky.

And waited.

Raynar's hand shook slightly and he sought out Master Skywalker's eyes. Even now he was unsure of himself, was not certain he dared . . . was not certain he was *worthy*.

The Jedi Master's eyes were kind and serious. He nodded. "Go ahead, Raynar."

Fumbling slightly because his hands were slick with sweat, Raynar moved his thumb into position and pressed the switch. With a *whoosh-hum*, an energy blade the color of polished pewter sprang from the hilt of his newly constructed lightsaber.

"The workmanship is excellent," Master Skywalker observed. "And I've seen how well you do with the stun-sticks. Would you like me to ask Tenel Ka to practice with you?"

Raynar blanched. "*Now*?"

The Jedi Master chuckled. "Maybe I'd better have you practice with Jacen for a while first. But not yet. Right now, I've got a surprise for you. We have a new permanent student here at the Jedi academy. I thought maybe you could show her around for a while." With that, he stepped back and opened the door to his chambers.

"Lusa!" Raynar exclaimed as the centaur girl appeared in the doorway. "I thought you wanted to work for the Cooperative Council."

Lusa tossed back her long cinnamon mane and gave an eloquent shrug of her bare shoulders. "I might someday, but I have a lot to learn first. I've asked Master Skywalker to teach me more about my powers with the Force."

Raynar found himself with nothing to say. His mouth hung open.

"I think you can put your lightsaber away for

now," Master Skywalker said. "There'll be plenty of time for that later."

Raynar snapped out of his surprise-induced immobility and turned off his lightsaber. "I . . ." Raynar blinked at Lusa and tried to collect his thoughts.

"Would you like to go for a walk?" the centaur girl asked. "I know of a very pretty waterfall."

On a small planet without a name, far out in a barely charted sector of the Outer Rim, Raaba built a burial cairn for Nolaa Tarkona.

She worked alone—she was the only being on this entire world—to find large rocks on the crumbling ridge where she had made their base camp. Using her strong Wookiee fingers, she pried up stones and piled them higher where she had buried the Twi'lek leader.

Nolaa Tarkona had died of the plague the day before.

Raaba had flown here, navigating by instinct rather than any star chart, and she had set down her star skimmer near a cluster of habitable caves on this silent planet. Nolaa had grown rapidly worse, day by day, as the slow-acting disease ravaged her body, destroyed her immune systems. She had thrashed and raved, insisting that Raaba take her back to Coruscant so that she could receive medical treatment in the capital of the New Republic.

But Raaba had refused. She could not risk

bringing the sick Twi'lek woman anyplace where she might infect others, where she might spread the evil plague developed by twisted Imperial scientists. The disease had proved fatal to Twi'leks, and might well be able to cross many species boundaries. Raaba could not take that chance. And so she had tended her leader all by herself.

The chocolate-furred Wookiee had suffered ill effects of her own: a fever, pounding headaches, muscle cramps. Some of her fur had fallen out in patches. Raaba had been sure she would follow Nolaa Tarkona in a lingering death. But her strong constitution had ultimately defeated the plague. She recovered just about the time that Nolaa had died, but even now, she knew she might still carry the disease organism; she might still infect others.

The breeze picked up, whistling along the knife edges of the barren rock. The air smelled like hot dust. Tall brown ferns protruded from cracks in the ridge, rattling their dry leaves together. The sun shimmered thick and orange near the horizon. Raaba piled another heavy stone on the cairn. She would finish her work here soon.

Her star skimmer might also be tainted with the organism; her own systems might still bear the plague. Raaba had to quarantine herself here, at least for a while. After seeing Nolaa's long and suffering death, Raaba wanted no part in spreading such a scourge throughout the galaxy.

She would wait here, for as long as it took.

A group of large rodents with hard shells on their backs scuttled out of their warrens in the cliffside. They stood in groups like miniature soldiers, watching the Wookiee woman's strange activities. Raaba glanced at them, then turned back to her labor.

She piled boulder after boulder atop the place where she had interred the leader of the Diversity Alliance. Finally, she had an impressive monument, a marker to commemorate all the dreams and dedication Nolaa Tarkona had stood for. Her need for equality and reparations had been valid, but her tactics had taken her beyond the reach of reason.

"Rest in peace, Nolaa Tarkona," she said, looking across the burial mound to the distant horizon.

The world was empty, but peaceful and quiet. A good place to think, a good place to heal. Someday she would come back to the galaxy; someday she would find Lowbacca.

But only when she was ready.

"Yes, I'm sure," Zekk said, looking directly into Master Luke Skywalker's eyes. "I wasn't ready before, but now I am. It took a while for me to understand that I don't have to use the dark side if I don't want to. I need you to teach me the right way. Teach me to use the light side of the Force, so I can become a *true* Jedi Knight."

"Do you still have your lightsaber?" Luke asked.

Zekk was surprised. "No, I got rid of that when I gave up being a Jedi, after the Shadow Academy was destroyed. I'll . . . I'll have to build a new one."

"We'll do it the right way this time." Luke Skywalker gave a thoughtful nod. "It's been a while since we got any new trainees here at the academy—and now we're getting two in one day. I have a feeling we needed some new blood here," he said with a faraway look. "Yes, I think it's high time."

The Jedi Master clasped Zekk's hand. "I know how hard this decision was for you. But a well-considered decision is far better than one made in haste." He raised his eyebrows and flashed a mischievous smile at his new trainee. "Would you like to tell my niece, or shall I?"

Zekk grinned. "I'll tell her myself."

All the attendees of the Jedi academy, along with Han and Leia, Anakin, old Peckhum, dozens of New Republic engineers, and a multitude of dignitaries had gathered to celebrate the newly completed reconstruction of the Great Temple. After a ceremony involving several speeches, awards, and commendations in the grand audience chamber, the entire assembly moved outdoors for a celebratory festival.

During the festivities, the young Jedi Knights, both old and new, withdrew to their favorite place by the wide river that flowed past the Great Temple. They waded into the water and spent hours talking and splashing and enjoying the feeling of wholeness that came from being together again.

Em Teedee delighted in his new microrepulsorjets, zipping in and out among his friends or bobbing along on the surface of the river. Lowie actually engaged the little droid in a couple of water games. Lusa and Raynar stayed near the shore, sharing memories of the losses they had experienced and the lessons they had learned. Tenel Ka and Jacen challenged each other to swimming races, while Jaina and Zekk floated lazily and discussed what materials might be most appropriate for the lightsaber the young man would soon build for himself.

After hours spent in pleasant pursuits, the friends gathered on the shore and talked until the sky began to grow dark. The topics were light, and the silences comfortable. They spoke of the *Rock Dragon*, the *Lightning Rod*, Lowie's T-23, Jedi tales and legends that Tionne had told them, the rebuilt temple, and favorite planets they had been to.

In the wake of one long silence, Jaina said, "I wonder what's next for us. Do you suppose all Jedi trainees go through the sorts of adventures we've had before they become full Jedi Knights?"

"After all we've been through together," Jacen replied, "I'm not sure anything in the future could surprise me."

"Ah," Tenel Ka said, turning to him. "Aha." Then she kissed Jacen firmly on the mouth.

"So . . . were you surprised, friend Jacen?" she asked, with a twinkle in her granite-gray eyes.

Lowie gave a bark of laughter at Jacen's astonished expression.

Zekk chuckled and put an arm around Jaina. "I don't know what the future will bring, either. But I'm looking forward to it—and I'm pretty sure it won't be boring."

Almost as one, the other young Jedi Knights replied, "This is a fact."

The adventure has only just begun.

Prepare yourself for an all-new trilogy of novels starring Jacen, Jaina, and the . . .

Han Solo's past is about to catch up with him. When he and the twins take the *Millennium Falcon* to Ord Mantell for a high-speed race, they meet a battle-hungry young woman wielding a lightsaber. Her name is Anja Gallandro, and she knows more about Han's history than he likes.

But Anja Gallandro guards an even more devastating secret—a secret that could mean disaster for the entire Solo family. And her plan is about to unfold . . .

Three new novels by
KEVIN J. ANDERSON and REBECCA MOESTA

RETURN TO ORD MANTELL
RETURN TO CLOUD CITY
RETURN TO KESSEL

Coming soon.

ABOUT THE AUTHORS

KEVIN J. ANDERSON and his wife, **REBECCA MOESTA**, have been involved in many STAR WARS projects. Together, they are writing all fourteen volumes of the YOUNG JEDI KNIGHTS saga for young adults, as well as creating the JUNIOR JEDI KNIGHTS series for younger readers. Rebecca Moesta also wrote the second trilogy of JUNIOR JEDI KNIGHTS adventures (*Anakin's Quest*, *Vader's Fortress*, and *Kenobi's Blade*).

Kevin J. Anderson is the author of the STAR WARS: JEDI ACADEMY TRILOGY, the novel *Darksaber*, and numerous comic series for Dark Horse. He has written many other novels, including three based on *The X-Files* television show. He has edited three STAR WARS anthologies: *Tales from the Mos Eisley Cantina,* in which Rebecca Moesta has a story; *Tales from Jabba's Palace*; and *Tales of the Bounty Hunters.*

For more information about the authors, visit their web site at
http://www.wordfire.com
or write to AnderZone,
the official Kevin J. Anderson Fan Club, at
P.O. Box 767
Monument, CO 80132-0767